CHAIN *of* DECEIT

DAVID MCINTOSH

Chain of Deceit
Book 1
4th Edition

Copyright ©1994 (original edition) by D.A. McIntosh (David McIntosh)

4th edition Copyright ©2021

Contact via novelwriter2019@gmail.com

Cover, photography and internal design © D.A.McIntosh

Manufactured and published in the United States of America.

ISBN: 978-0-9987139-3-9 (paperback)
ISBN: 978-0-9987139-4-6 (Digital)

Previous editions are out of print.

Contents

FOREWORD

T he story you are about to read has its beginning during
World War II when a ship, loaded with supplies for the war
effort in Europe, is waiting for the US Navy to grant permission to leave the New York Harbor. There is concern that any further delay will prevent them from joining the convoy that is so necessary to escort them safely across the Atlantic. (At this time, the seas
are controlled by German-built U-boats and Japanese submarines,
some of which are specially designed to transport gold, mercury, and
other badly needed supplies between the two countries.) Just prior
to departure from the harbor, the ship is loaded with a secret cargo
and a squad of soldiers. Will the ship still have enough time to join
the convoy and complete a safe crossing of the Atlantic? Or is there
another mission about to begin?

More than fifty years later, a large cache of World War II war
material turns up in a warehouse in New Orleans. Davin Pierce, a
retired US Army master sergeant working as an insurance investigator in Palm Beach, Florida, is tasked with finding out why. Gold,
treason, murder, and deception at the highest levels take Davin and
his team on a race to prevent the death and destruction of the United
States of America.

The components of an atomic bomb to be used to bomb Berlin
have been loaded on board and are to be delivered to a US submarine in the North Atlantic, but the unexpected arrival of a German
U-boat changes everyone's plans. The captain's plan is to sink his
ship to cover up the fact that his cargo is still in a warehouse in the
United States and all the crates on board are empty. The captain's

plan is about to start early. His black market ring stays in existence for over fifty years before finally being discovered. Over the years, several of the members have moved up in the ranks of the United States government. Now they are plotting a different mission and are in position to make this their biggest, most successful, and most daring plan.

Chapter 1

THE MISSION

New York Harbor
January 5, 1943,
1100 Hours, Eastern Standard Time

T he loading of the cargo on the *MaryJean* was almost finished, and the crew was ready for a little rest. In less than
two days, the *MaryJean* was supposed to join a convoy that
was assembling in the North Atlantic. She was loaded and ready,
but the Navy had not cleared her to sail and the Navy controlled all
movement on the oceans right now. The crew was told to finish loading and then wait. Waiting much longer would cause them to miss
their escort, and possibly the entire convoy.

The war in Europe was going strong, and convoys loaded with
men and material were leaving the States as fast as they could load
the ships. This was the beginning of the *MaryJean*'s seventh crossing
with her crew of fifteen merchantmen. They were tired and fed up
with the constant danger and unknown of the North Atlantic. The
sudden storms were bad enough, but with a war going on, they had
to cope with another unknown enemy, man.

The crew, at least most of them, had sailed the North Atlantic
for many years before they took over the *MaryJean*. The last ship
they had served on was torpedoed out from under them. That time
they were lucky, luckier than six of their shipmates who had died in

the sinking. Now, along with some new crewmen, they had crossed the dangerous North Atlantic three times with few close calls. The last one, though, had cost them their captain. Captain Howard E. Millstone died trying to save his chief engineer during an attack off the coast of England. Both had died on the bridge of the *MaryJean* during the attack. The ship had sustained heavy damage, but not enough to sink or put her out of commission for very long.

Captain Elmer Bronsly was sitting on the bridge, looking over the charts, contemplating his upcoming thirteenth trip across the North Atlantic Ocean, during a war. He had just taken command of the *MaryJean*. The last ship he served on had sunk with the captain and most of the crew. He managed to survive with three others for two weeks in a small lifeboat before being rescued. For his heroic duties helping save his men, he was promoted to captain and given the *MaryJean* as his first ship.

At six foot, two inches and 195 pounds, this seemingly giant of a sailor would seem to be "unspookable," but something bothered him nonetheless. He wasn't superstitious, but with a war on, you had to be as careful as possible or your end would come sooner than you expected it would.

Born in New York to Scandinavian parents, Bronsly grew up around the docks. His father, a ship captain, had long since retired to Davy Jones's Locker. He had lost track of his mother when he started to work the shipyards.

Sweat was beading up on his forehead as he studied the charts. This was his last trip; he had had enough and wanted out. At least for now that was what he wanted. Bronsly thought about the deals he had made, and he was a little scared. He had done some things in his life that were not spoken about in public, but what he was about to do might change his whole life and the lives of many people that he didn't even know. Yes, he was scared, but a deal was a deal, and this was one deal that had only two options: complete it as planned or die.

He stood and walked out to the bridge overlooking the dock, stroking his full black beard. It had some gray coming in, but that was expected.

Bronsly didn't like the war any more than the next guy did, but what he hated more were passengers on his ship.

"Damn, who put these passengers on my ship?" he yelled as he read the ship's amended manifest, not really expecting an answer. His ship was a freighter, not a cruise liner. But he had a full house this trip, eight passengers in all.

One passenger concerned him more than the rest, an officer of the Eighth Army Air Corps, assigned the only other private cabin on board besides his own. It seemed strange to Bronsly that a member of the Air Corps couldn't get a plane to fly over to England. He had seen this young lieutenant come on board carrying a briefcase, one that was handcuffed to his wrist. *Why?* Bronsly thought to himself.

New York Harbor
January 6, 1943
0600 Hours

The wind was howling through the ship's rigging as the morning sun broke the night's darkness. They had loaded all night, and most of the passengers were on board and asleep belowdecks. Captain Bronsly was on the bridge early, anticipating his orders to set sail. If he was able to pull off this trip, he was assured of a safe, profitable retirement, but he had to live to collect.

The sun was creeping over the rigging. A heavy ground fog had settled in during the night, giving the ship a ghostly look in the early morning. The dampness of the night coated the boat and was now dripping slowly into the bay. All was quiet; very little moved on or around the dock now, but soon it would be alive with workers and ships' crews. Dawn meant the *MaryJean* would soon be leaving.

The *MaryJean* was to meet up with the destroyer escort USS *Robert E. Lee* outside the harbor, which would escort it, with four other freighters, to the convoy rendezvous point off the coast of Maine tomorrow morning. Timing on this trip was critical; all ships had to make it across. The Germans were on the run, and with new supplies, the Allies and US troops could have the winning hand.

"Johnson, have all the passengers arrived yet?" Bronsly asked the chief as he entered the bridge with two cups of coffee.

"No, sir, still missing two," Johnson replied. Ducking through the hatchway, he crossed the bridge and handed a cup to Bronsly.

"Thanks. Don't they know we have no choice but to sail within an hour of receiving orders, with or without them?"

"I guess they do, sir," Johnson said quietly, then turned to the navigation station to work out the course to meet the destroyer.

Johnson was young, but he'd been in the merchant since he was seventeen. In eight years, he had learned a lot and would be looking for his own ship in a few more years.

"Johnson, how was shore leave?" Bronsly asked as he walked over to the navigation station to see how Johnson was doing.

"You know, sir, so many women, so little time."

"No, I really don't know. I'm not the ladies' man that you are. How many this time?"

"Well, I don't like to brag, but if you must know, sir, only two."

"Two! A big strong, blond-haired, blue-eyed guy like you, only with two women in seven days. I'm surprised. We were at sea for two months, and you only saw two women!" Bronsly exclaimed.

"No, sir. What I meant was two per night," Johnson said with a chuckle, but he was just joking with the captain; he only had one girl, and she was in New York. They planned on marrying right after the war; he was true to her.

Captain Bronsly had moved back to the door on the bridge that gave a good view of the dock when he saw two trucks, a car, and a couple of military jeeps filled with armed soldiers pull up to the loading dock. As he watched, one of the men, dressed in a white naval officer's uniform, bolted from the car and raced up the gangplank, barely stopping to talk to one of the crew. The crewman pointed up toward the bridge. The officer then turned and bolted up the ladder toward the bridge.

"What now, Johnson?"

"I don't know, sir, but he looks rather in a bit of a hurry, wouldn't you say?" Johnson replied as he walked out on the flybridge to join the captain.

"Yeah, we don't need this," Bronsly said. Then he thought to himself, *This just isn't going to work, boys. It ain't gonna work this time, boys.*

"Capt'n Bronsly?" asked the man in uniform, gasping for air as he stopped in front of Captain Bronsly.

"Yes...," Bronsly answered, very slow and drawn out.

"Good. I am glad you haven't left yet."

"Why, am I going somewhere?" He turned to Johnson and asked again, "Are we going somewhere, Johnson? No? Okay." And without waiting for a reply, he looked back at the uniformed officer. "Now, what can the Merchant Marines do for the Navy, as if we aren't doing enough now?"

He started, "Well, sir, it's ah...your ship, well, it's the only—"

But he was cut short by Bronsly, who held up his hand to silence the young naval officer.

"What the hell are you men doing down there?" Bronsly demanded to know, pointing toward the truck on the dock.

"That's what I am trying to tell you, Captain Bronsly. Your ship is the only one left in the harbor. That is, the only one left that's heading out to meet up with the convoy and go to England. And we, sir...well, we—the Navy, that is—have some cargo and—"

Again he was interrupted by Bronsly.

"You have some what? Who the hell authorized this? We are already loaded and ready to leave!" Bronsly barked at the officer.

"I'm sorry, sir, but I've seen your manifest, and I know you have the room, and I've been authorized by the War Department to place on your ship three crates and ah...a squad of Marines to guard them."

"Squad of Marines? What the hell are in those crates, Lieutenant...ah...who did you say you were?"

"Lieutenant Jacobs, sir," the young sailor said, holding out his hand, then pulling it back slowly, realizing he would not receive Bronsly's in return. "And Major Peterson will be in charge of the squad while at sea. He will ensure the safety of the crates and the delivery to the proper people in England."

"I am already full of passengers. I don't have enough bunks for a squad of Marines or even a single Marine, Lieutenant...what did you say your name was?"

"Jacobs, sir, Lieutenant Jacobs!" he barked as his temper and courage started to rise. "And don't you worry about the Marines. You just make sure that this damn ship makes it to England, Captain."

Without a word to Jacobs, Bronsly turned and stuck his head in the hatchway and yelled.

"Johnson, call down and have some of the crew assist in loading those crates into hole number 3 before they break something or someone down there! Get Andy to secure the bulkheads in and out of number 3, and make damn sure we have enough food on board to feed, ah, Lieutenant, how many men?" he said as he turned back to Jacobs for an answer.

"Nine...ah..."

"NINE! Johnson, move it!" Bronsly ordered, cutting off Jacobs, who quietly continued to himself, "Altogether...seven enlisted and two officers."

The radio operator then came running out of the radio room and handed Captain Bronsly a handwritten message, ignoring Jacobs. Bronsly paused to read the message. He turned to Johnson abruptly, looking rather upset, paused a moment, removed and looked at his gold Hamilton pocket watch, then looked up to Johnson.

"Get to it, Johnson. We now have clearance. We sail inside an hour." Then Bronsly yelled, "GET WITH IT, MAN! WE HAVEN'T ALL DAY!"

"Captain Bronsly, Major Peterson will get his men on board immediately, and I hope you have a safe voyage," Lieutenant Jacobs said quietly as he turned to leave.

"Jacobs, what in holy hell is in them damn crates that require armed guards on my ship?"

"I don't know, Captain Bronsly. I...ah...I know whatever it is could change the course of the war, so you make *damn* sure this ship makes it to England, or you go down with her!" Jacobs yelled when he stopped climbing down the ladder and looked back up at Bronsly.

His expression was one of grave concern and distrust; he didn't know if Bronsly could be trusted, but he had no choice in ships, none at all.

"I don't give a damn about your cheap threats, Jacobs. This ship will get to whatever destination the good Lord has in mind, whether it be England or the bottom of the sea!" Bronsly yelled. Taking a deep breath, he continued, "And don't threaten me! I might just sink her myself if provoked. So go and tell your high and mighties that if that cargo is so damn valuable, then they should send it on one of your damn battleships!"

Jacobs ignored Bronsly and departed the *MaryJean* just as the second crate was being lowered into the number 3 hole.

"Lotsa luck, boys. You're gonna need it!" Jacobs yelled as he looked back up at the ship from the dock.

The cargo was loaded and the squad was on board with barely enough time to get settled when the anchor was pulled up and the mooring lines were cast off. The *MaryJean* was setting sail.

New York Harbor Entrance
January 6, 1943
0730 Hours, EST

Alongside the *MaryJean* were two tugs to assist in the safe passage out of the harbor. Captain Bronsly was a little uneasy about his new cargo and the Marines. He had not planned on this; he had plans of his own, and up to now, everything had been going well.

They cleared the harbor without a hitch and steamed on to meet the destroyer escort and the other four freighters. The weather reports didn't look any worse than the ones for the trip before. She was old, but strong, built in Connecticut in 1926. She had been a beautiful ship in her day, designed to be fast and strong, but now her paint was faded and chipped and her engines tired. Making only about seventeen knots max, she could carry twenty-five thousand tons of cargo although only a little over 440 feet in length. She was only one of the one hundred ships sailing in this convoy and only one of thousands that would sail to England with badly needed supplies between 1941 and 1944.

North Atlantic Ocean
Off the Coast of Maine
January 8, 1943,
0930 Hours, EST

They met up with the convoy on their second day out, and so far, thought Bronsly, everything was sailing smoothly, except for the weather reports they were receiving, which were never very good. The North Atlantic was very unpredictable, especially in the winter. The seas could be calm for days and then, all of a sudden, there would be hurricane-force winds and a sea running with forty-foot swells, enough to completely engulf a ship of the *MaryJean*'s size.

Captain Bronsly expected that nothing unexpected would happen until they got closer to England other than the normal bad weather. This time of year, the North Atlantic was the mother of a lot of storms.

Most U-boats captains didn't like the North Atlantic very much, but once they were within four or five days of land, they would strike in force. The U-boat traveled in packs of four to ten boats, known as wolf packs, preying on the convoys, hoping for a chance to strike. It was unusual for a lone U-boat to strike when over 250 miles from land, but it wasn't completely unheard of.

North Atlantic
Convoy Number 339
January 16, 1943

The first eight days of this crossing had been relatively uneventful. Four days out, they had run into an ice storm that caused minor damage to the forward loading boom, but so far, all 101 ships were still in the convoy and safe. The *MaryJean* was stationed near the back and center of the convoy because she carried munitions and arms. This location was supposed to be fairly safe.

Captain Bronsly was on the bridge, watching the approach of another storm on the horizon. He watched and listened to the radio for the weather reports from the ships ahead.

January 18, 1943
1900 Hours

The night was cold, very cold, and the storm had been raging for about fourteen hours. It had intensified each hour, first bringing rain, and then hail. The crew was doing everything possible to keep the ship afloat and in the convoy, but due to the severity of the storm, Captain Bronsly ordered the engine room to slow to one-third, slowing the ship to four knots, knowing full well that this might cause them to fall behind the convoy. But this was a chance he had to take; this storm was starting to kill his ship.

The moon was full tonight, but nobody saw it because of the storm. The convoy wasn't a convoy anymore; instead, it had become a scattering of single ships, each trying to save itself. The storm had already claimed a couple of smaller ships and was looking to take a few more.

Captain Bronsly wasn't sure how far the convoy was separated, and he really didn't care. At the moment, he had enough trouble trying to keep his ship alive.

The storm raged on, gaining strength with each passing moment. It took all the willpower a man had to just hang on and survive. Some of the smaller ships completely disappeared in the swells, never to surface again. A couple of older freighters near the fringe of the convoy broke up under the constant pounding of waves; all on board were lost, as there was no way to rescue the survivors, if there had been any. Minutes became hours, and hours became a lifetime for some, an eternity for others.

Somewhere in the North Atlantic
January 19, 1943
0500 Hours

"Full speed ahead!" Bronsly ordered as the morning broke and he could see that the storm had lost most of its strength.

The sun was starting to edge over the horizon, giving the morning a deep, dark forbidding gray hue beneath the heavy cloud cover.

Bronsly was still on the bridge, scanning the horizon for any sign of the convoy, but with the little bit of light and haze, he could not see more than a few miles.

The U-boat was his biggest problem now. No escort, no convoy, no protection. Extra lookouts were put on duty, and the *MaryJean* proceeded at max speed, trying to sight the convoy.

"Johnson, every available man up here, now!" Bronsly yelled in the speaker tube. Looking over at the chart table, he shook his head in disbelief. "Johnson, where are you?"

"Hey, Skipper, here's the best I could get. Pretty heavy cloud cover out there," Johnson said as he entered the bridge minutes later, handing Bronsly a chart. "By the way, all the men are up on deck and scanning."

"Thanks. Where have you been?"

"Up in the crow's nest, sir. Trying to get a fix on our location."

"Any luck?"

"No, sir. I've marked an approximate location on that chart," Johnson said, walking over to the chart table.

Bronsly sat down on the flybridge and studied the chart. After a long twenty minutes, Bronsly finally leaned back in his chair.

"Hmmm, Johnson, you think we are somewhere about here?" he said, pointing to a spot on the chart about fifty miles from their projected course.

"Yes, sir, that far off!" Johnson exclaimed. He had walked out onto the flybridge and was looking over the captain's shoulder.

"Yeah, but without any way of getting a good fix, it's tough to really say where we are. That's just an educated guess, Johnson, isn't it?" Receiving a nod from Johnson, he continued, "So for now, just keep us heading east at max speed, and maybe we will be able to find the convoy." Bronsly leaned back in his chair and pulled out a fresh cigar. Eyeing the Cuban cigar as if it were an expensive piece of jewelry, he slowly clipped off the ends and lighted it, drawing deeply to receive the maximum pleasure from each piece of tobacco. He smiled for the first time since they left New York.

Belowdecks, Major Peterson and his men were trying to recover from a night of sickness. All but one of his men were green from the pitching of the ship during the storm and now, with the seas calmed, were trying to get themselves back into some kind of order, and possibly a little sleep.

"Engine Room, can you get us some more steam?" yelled Bronsly in the speaker tube and moved the ship's engine room controls to full again.

"Negative, Captain. If we push any more, we're gonna blow her," came the response. "We're making twelve knots now, sir."

"Damage Control, storm damage and a casualty report immediately."

"Aye, aye…sir."

Damn, left back here with the wolf packs just looking for some easy prey, thought Bronsly as he stared at the new dawn.

He was lucky in one way; this was a big ocean, and his ship was not very big. Maybe, just maybe, he could slip through. The seas were almost calm now as the sun climbed high in the sky. Occasionally a ray of light breaking through the thick cloud cover gave the crew a bit of hope. The lookouts would have a good chance of spotting a periscope in the calm seas, but of course, by the time they spotted the periscope, it might already be too late.

Captain Bronsly remained on the bridge until he got the answers he needed from Damage Control. He didn't like the situation they were in. They were steaming as fast as they could; they were miles behind the convoy and didn't have much of a chance of catching up.

"Capt'n," said Chief Engineer Burrack as he entered the bridge.

"Yeah, Chief, what ya got?"

"Sir, we lost de main loadin' boom, two boots is agone, da hatch on number 1 done caved in, we've taken on some water in number 4." After a long pause and a deep breath, Burrack continued, "An da starboard anchor chain is gone, anchor and everything. Lucky for us it didn't hit da hull and gorge us, or we'd be on the bottom, too, fer sure. Minor damage to de otter loading booms, and the cargo in number 1 shifted. Two o'de boys is a headin' down there now to shift it back. Otherwise, we will not be stable, and to top off all dat, da… ah, da radio mast isa gone, ripped right off the boot."

"Damn, what about casualties?"

"We have a rash of seasickness wit' da passengers and some cuts and bruises, nothin' serious. A lot of scared people on this boot, sir, and I donna blame em. Dat was one mean-as-hell storm, the worst I've seen."

"Thanks, Chief. Keep me posted on repairs. You got someone who can get us some communications?"

"Aye, sir, and he's already runnin' some wire to the radio room," he said as he headed out of the hatch.

"You got the helm, Johnson. I need to get some coffee." Bronsly headed for the lounge.

As he entered the lounge, he was greeted by two of the passengers sitting around a table, attempting to play cards.

"Morning, Captain," said Mr. Krieger, a gray-haired man at the table in the corner, holding tightly to a glass and looking very green and scared. "How's it going up on the bridge?"

There was an almost-empty bottle of brandy in front of Mr. Krieger.

"Morning, Mr. Krieger. The storm has subsided, as you can well see. The sea is calm and we are still afloat. What more can I say?"

"Damn, are we still with the convoy, Captain?" asked the other man at the table, a younger fellow, dressed in an expensive silk suit, also looking a little green. He, too, was holding tightly to a glass with what also looked like brandy in it. "I have to be in London by next Friday, or else I'll lose my job."

"Don't worry about your job in London, Mr. Connelly. Let's hope it's not frozen in the North Atlantic," Bronsly said.

"We will get to England, won't we, Captain?" asked Mr. Connelly.

"I sure do hope so, son, I hope so." Captain Bronsly smiled a little and enjoyed his cigar.

"You don't sound too encouraging, Capt'n. What's wrong up there?" Krieger insisted.

"If you must know, we've been separated from the convoy and are not exactly sure where they are."

"Don't you have a wireless to contact them?" Krieger asked, his voice trembling a little.

"Normally yes, but that damn storm took care of that. Now, if you'll excuse me, I would like a little peace and quiet for a few minutes." Bronsly turned and strode to his table across the room.

Captain Bronsly sat down and tried to look comfortable. He knew they had little chance of catching up with the convoy, but he didn't want to catch the convoy. The rendezvous was in two days and far south of the convoy's proposed course. Opportunity had presented itself with that storm; separating from the convoy early might cause some other problems, but he would handle them as they came. They were steaming at full speed, the old engines were doing their best, but still they were able to only get twelve knots out of them.

"Hey, Johnny, how 'bout my usual? And do you have any of that cake left over from dinner?" asked Bronsly of the steward, who had just entered the lounge from the galley. Johnny had been with Bronsly for the past four years and was one of the only other survivors from his last ship. He was a middle-aged black man, not highly educated, but a man couldn't ask for a better friend, and Bronsly had few friends.

"Capt'n, that dinner you talkin' bout is all over the deck in the galley. You be lucky to get that coffee," Johnny replied as he turned to go back into the galley.

"See if you can throw somethin' together."

"Do the best I can, Capt'n," he responded, his voice trailing off as he entered the galley.

The captain's usual was a cup of black coffee and a shot of Irish whiskey on the side. He had been drinking coffee most of his life, but it was only since the war started that he added the Irish whiskey. Bronsly never drank enough to get drunk, only to calm his shattered nerves. Captain Bronsly had been at sea for twenty-four years and had never lost a ship for any reason. At thirty-eight, he was planning an early retirement. If all went well over the next few days, he and his partners could retire to a nice little business and live happily ever after. But he was worried that the storm had thrown them too far off course, and not knowing exactly where they were complicated it even more. They had to be at that rendezvous point to deliver the crates the Marines were guarding.

During the first war, his father had run munitions and weapons for the Allies, dodging blockades and patrol boats constantly, and never once lost an entire ship, just various parts of some. Bronsly knew he wasn't going to be as lucky as his father. All he wanted to do was survive the attack, when it came, and he didn't want to spend it in a concentration camp either.

The conversation at the other table was not of interest to Bronsly. All he wanted was a little peace and quiet for thirty minutes so he could return to the bridge with a clear mind.

Meanwhile, belowdecks, the squad of Marines was just changing guard on the secret cargo in the number 3 hole. Major Fredrick Peterson had inspected his men for the third time since they set sail and, as usual, found nothing wrong with them. He didn't know what was in those crates; all he knew was that it was his job to see they made it safely to their destination.

Major Peterson was a lot like Captain Bronsly; they were both quiet men, unmarried, with hopes of finding the right girl and raising a couple of kids back in the States somewhere safe. He also worried about the position of this small ship and wondered why he was here and if he would ever see land again. He was to ensure that the three crates were delivered to the proper destination, two to be loaded on the USS *Wolverine*, an American submarine, and the third to another ship, identified only by the flying of a white flag with a red bar on the bow.

Peterson had contacted Bronsly several months ago to encourage him to join in their operation. It didn't take much convincing for Bronsly. He could see the potential of their operation and the little caper he had already planned himself, working alone. Bronsly could easily work this operation into his own plans.

Major Peterson headed forward to check on the rest of his squad, which was supposed to be getting some sleep now. They had been working a twenty-four-hour rotation shift guarding those crates, six hours on, six off. But after a night of rough seas, these men really needed their sleep; most of them had turned green and couldn't even protect themselves. Now that they were able to sleep, Peterson felt better about this mission. After seeing to his men, he started to the galley to get some coffee and hoped to catch Captain Bronsly for an update of conditions.

Chapter 2

THE MISTAKE

German U-boat, U-49
January 19, 1943
0515 Hours

They were just returning from a deep-penetration mission on the East Coast of the United States when they spotted a ship on the horizon. It looked like a freighter, but due to the dim light of morning and distance, the commander wasn't sure. They had been cruising on the surface after the storm to recharge their batteries and to get some fresh air in the boat. The long cruise and North Atlantic storms had taken its toll on the crew. They needed a rest and were headed home to get it, with one mission left before heading for home. They were to meet a freighter at 06:00 the next morning, retrieve a crate, and deliver it to the island of Crete as quickly as possible.

Oberleutnant Wilhelm Gunter Zehetbauer and his crew had been at sea too long to pass up a sure victory like the one they looked at now. They had four torpedoes left and decided to go for the kill. Zehetbauer gave the order to dive and started his slow, calculating maneuvers to bring them within firing range of the ship.

At eight thousand yards, Zehetbauer came up to periscope depth and began his plan of attack.

"Steer zero-six-zero, steady," Zehetbauer ordered his crew.

He waited and watched the unsuspecting target.

"Range?"

"Eighteen hundred meters," Sonar replied.

He closed the distance slowly. This would be his final kill before making port, and he did not want to miss.

"Steady, reduce to one-third," Zehetbauer ordered.

At 06:30, they were within 1,200 meters range. He planned on firing, then diving, circling 180 degrees, and surfacing to finish off the ship with the deck gun. Their boat had already accounted for six confirmed kills on this mission. Zehetbauer was not proud of killing, but in war it was kill or be killed.

At periscope depth, ever so slowly Zehetbauer maneuvered his U-boat into firing position.

"Three degrees right rudder, hold," Zehetbauer ordered, then stood and gazed around the control room. It was small and very cramped, but what it lacked in size, it made up for in the efficient way she was laid out.

It would take one minute and twenty seconds till detonation, and as they counted, they would be diving.

"Two degrees right rudder, HOLD!" Zehetbauer ordered, adjusting for the target movement.

"Aye!" replied Von Hofner, the U-boat's executive officer.

"Two degrees up bubble."

"Aye."

"Load tubes 1 and 2."

"Ready 1 and 2," Von Hofner responded as he checked the indicator lights on torpedo tube control panel.

"On my mark…"

All was silent as Zehetbauer calculated his last two torpedo shots. He could not take a chance on missing. He was ready.

"Mark…FIRE 1!"

"ONE AWAY!" Von Hofner yelled.

"FIRE 2!"

"Captain, number 2 did not activate!" Von Hofner responded as the number 2 torpedo left the tube and sank to the bottom of the ocean, breaking its wire guidance system immediately.

"DIVE, DIVE! LEVEL ONE HUNDRED METERS!" Zehetbauer yelled, ignoring the response.

Crewmen not immediately needed to run the boat rushed forward to the torpedo room to give the boat the weight in the bow needed to dive fast.

"Heading zero-eight-five degrees!"

"Level one hundred meters, sir!" shouted the helmsman.

"Flank speed!"

One minute and twenty-eight seconds went by and nothing, no explosions. Surely, they did not have two duds. One minute and forty seconds went by, and still nothing. What had gone wrong? They had fired eight torpedoes over the last month; four were duds, not counting these.

"Up periscope!" Zehetbauer ordered. Crouching down as the scope came up, he folded down the two levers and peered though the eyepiece.

"Damn!" Zehetbauer exclaimed as he looked though the scope. He had fired on the ship he was supposed to meet with tomorrow. This time the ship was close enough to accurately identify. He was lucky the torpedoes were duds. He could surface and make the pickup today instead. Why not? They were both in the open ocean and no one else was around.

As he watched, he ordered preparation to surface the U-boat. Just then, the ship in his scope exploded—first, a massive explosion in the bow, then a second in the stern. He couldn't believe it. Had his torpedo run slow and finally struck its target? Impossible! Another U-boat? Possibly.

"Surface!" Zehetbauer ordered, still not believing what he had just seen. Still, he needed to retrieve that cargo.

MaryJean Lounge
0659 Hours

It was precisely 6:59 a.m. when the first explosion occurred. Captain Bronsly had just gotten up from his table to head back to the bridge. The force of the explosion tilted the deck he was standing on, throwing him to the deck. Mr. Connelly, who was sitting at a table near the bar, was thrown out of his chair, his head hitting the bulkhead, causing severe bleeding from his left temple. Mr. Krieger, sitting across from Mr. Connelly, was tossed like a limp rag into the bar, breaking his neck and killing him instantly.

The ship pitched violently, the stern rising sixty feet out of the water. Bronsly knew instantly that a U-boat had struck a crippling blow to his ship. Conscious and only able to get up with difficulty, he stumbled and fell, unable to keep his balance on the angled deck. Finally, gaining his balance, he ran toward the bridge. A second explosion occurred within seconds of the first, this time the sound coming from the bow. The ship again was thrown high into the air. Bronsly was knocked off balance again, landing in the corner of the ladder and the hatch leading to the bridge. He heard a loud snap as he landed. Putting pressure on his right arm caused severe pain. Swelling was already visible around his wrist and hand. It was broken. With great difficulty, he struggled to pull himself up the ladder to the bridge. Slowly, and with great pain, he reached the bridge deck. Scanning the ship from the bridge, he realized that she was doomed. She looked more like a burning junkyard than a ship. He didn't know the exact point of impact, but he knew she was dying.

Major Peterson had been halfway up the ladder when the torpedo hit. He lay on the deck, looking back up the ladder where he had been.

Dazed, but with the urgency of the moment, he forced himself up and ran to the nearest hatch to get out on deck.

"Damn! What the hell happened?" Peterson yelled to the first seaman he saw.

"I don't know, sir."

"Damn," he said again as he looked forward. Turning, he started to run but slipped, fell, and cut his left eye on the handrail.

He slipped several more times in the rushing water that was pushing him back, but he continued to fight his way toward the stateroom, where his men had been sleeping not less than an hour before. They were in the converted crew's quarters located just forward of the bridge and between the number 1 and 2 holes. After what seemed like hours of fighting the inrushing water, Peterson finally made it to the stateroom. He didn't like what he found.

"Damn it! What is going on here?" he cried out as he looked into a large hole, with seawater rushing in, where the stateroom had been. He turned and ran, slipping every few steps. Securing the bulkhead, he was able to keep the rest of the ship from flooding.

Rushing to the number 3 hole to see if the remainder of his men were all right, this time he found four very scared Marines crouched around the three crates they were supposed to be guarding.

"Are you men okay?" Peterson yelled.

"Yes, sir," answered Lieutenant Russell. "What the hell is going on, sir?"

"I do believe we have been torpedoed, Russell. Those crates aren't going anywhere. Get these men up on deck to man that deck gun. Now, let's move it, man!"

"Are you okay, sir?" Russell asked, finally getting a good look at the major's face.

"Hell, no! I am not okay, but we haven't the time to discuss it. Get these men on deck, now!" Peterson yelled.

Without hesitation, Russell rounded his men up and headed for the deck.

"Major, where are you going, sir?" asked Russell.

"I'm going to the bridge to see what the hell is going on."

The dying ship started to list to port at a thirty-degree angle, taking on water faster than the pumps could handle. The ship was almost dead in the water; fires were raging fore and aft, and the crew was attempting to save the ship but was not gaining on it at all.

Below, all hell had broken loose; the second explosion, just forward of the bridge in the number 1 hole, had ripped open an eighteen- to twenty-foot hole to the ocean. Two crewmen had been in the hole, securing loose cargo, and never knew what hit them. This particular hold had held six Army jeeps and one Sherman tank, and it flooded in a matter of minutes.

"Engine Room, can we get any steam up? Can we maneuver?" screamed Bronsly in the speaker tube.

Silence was his answer, so he yelled again and again.

"Aye, Capt'n, Engine Room. MANEUVER! HELL, we can barely move! We've lost the number 2 boiler, and number 1 is badly damaged," the voice responded finally.

"Gimme all ya can or we're dead!" yelled Bronsly.

The crippled ship shuddered and inched forward, although not fast enough for Bronsly. Slowly at first, then faster and faster, she was moving—two knots, three, four, steady at four, holding, four knots. *Well, better than nothing,* Bronsly thought.

"Hard right rudder, all the speed you can give me, NOW!" yelled Bronsly.

"Bridge, Damage Control. Number 1 hold is flooded, but the bulkheads are holding, don't know how. Flooding fore and aft, fires under control, no report on engine room."

"Do you think she'll stay afloat?" screamed Bronsly.

"As long as those bulkheads hold and we don't get another fish up our ass."

"Damn," Bronsly said, shaking his head in disbelief. *I need more time,* he thought to himself.

The ship listed badly to port but managed a hard right rudder and headed straight away from where the torpedoes came from, trying to put some distance between them and the U-boat.

"What's the plan, Capt'n?" asked the chief boatswain, Johnson.

"I figure that U-boat capt'n will surface and finish us off with his deck gun to save his precious torpedoes, and when he does, I hope we are in a position to end his career."

"How's that, sir?"

"We can either ram him or hope to blow him out of the water with that peashooter on the bow. I hope to ram, son, so be ready."

"But won't that sink us? We're severely damaged now, sir, and ramming him might crush those bulkheads," said Johnson.

"That's just the chance we have to take, son. Right now it's him or us, and he has the best cards. Get some men on that gun."

The gun Bronsly referred to was a three-inch deck Howitzer on the bow. It was not sitting quite flat on the deck anymore, but it was undamaged and could still be fired.

One Hundred Meters below the North Atlantic
Bearing 025 degrees
0615 Hours

Oberleutnant Zehetbauer had graduated in the top of his class in everything he had ever done. His ability to second-guess his opponent in sports and strategies had amazed his instructors. He rarely made a mistake. He had positioned his sub 140 degrees from where he had fired his torpedoes. His attack was perfect, but his torpedoes malfunctioned. Yet the freighter was now exploding and burning before his eyes. Why?

Zehetbauer leaned over the scope as the U-boat ascended to the surface. As it broke, he ordered the scope down and prepared to go up the ladder to the bridge. All was silent within the U-boat. They had heard the explosions, but there was no indication of a ship sinking. Where did the explosions come from? Was it part of the cover? She was still alive. Did another U-boat wander into the area and torpedo his target? The next few minutes could be very dangerous for the crew of the U-49.

He climbed up the ladder behind his lookouts. Once on the bridge, he looked in the direction of the *MaryJean*, only to discover she had turned toward his small U-boat in preparation to ram. He jumped back down the hatch with the two lookouts close behind, the last one securing the hatch just as he ordered his U-boat to dive.

"Dive, dive, dive!" yelled Zehetbauer. "Full speed down and ahead!"

MaryJean, North Atlantic
Heading 040 degrees, Four Knots
0615 Hours

Four ragged Marines ran forward to assist in the handling of the deck gun. When they arrived, the boat crew gladly turned it over to the more experienced Marines. They then returned to fighting the fires and trying to save the ship.

"U-boat, starboard bow!" yelled the lookout, pointing to the U-boat periscope breaking the surface less than two hundred yards off.

"Three degrees starboard, and give me all the speed ya got!" Bronsly yelled into the speaker tube.

"Prepare to ram!" yelled Bronsly.

Even with his greatly reduced speed, the U-boat captain didn't have much time to make a decision.

After few very tense moments went by, he then realized that the sub was well within range of that gun.

"Fire that damn gun! Fire, fire!"

The Marines on the gun had taken no time to aim properly, so their first shot was high and long. They reloaded and fired again, this time hitting the control tower, but with little damage. The U-boat was just about gone when they fired their last shot, the shell exploding close to the control tower.

The U-boat had been making a last-ditch effort to avoid being rammed by Bronsly. The Marines on the gun were firing wildly as the U-boat's periscope disappeared below the surface.

U-49
0625 Hours

At 120 meters, Zehetbauer leveled off his U-boat and began to assess the damage. He had lost the use of his control tower from the first hit and its subsequent flooding, and he was not sure but might have taken a second hit in the tower. Maybe it was just some debris falling against the side, which he would check on once he was safely out of range of that crazy freighter captain. Three of his crew were dead, including his navigator and helmsman. His ship survived for now and would fight another day. He was glad to be alive and safe, cruising away from the maniac above.

Zehetbauer left the control room for his small cabin. Once inside, he opened a small safe and retrieved an envelope marked TOP SECRET. As he read again his instructions, a look of disgust came over his face.

"Damn, how could I be so foolish?" he cursed. Reading out loud, he continued, "Proceed to coordinates indicated below and surface at 0600 hours on the twentieth of January. The freighter *MaryJean* will arrive and transfer one crate to your boat. Deliver this crate to Crete as fast as possible."

The MaryJean, *that was the freighter we had fired on, but our torpedoes were duds. I made a tactical error and fired on the wrong ship. But who torpedoed the* MaryJean? he thought. "Who?"

MaryJean
Exact Location Unknown
1045 Hours

It took the better part of the morning to extinguish the fires and secure the remaining hatches. The total damage was extensive and crippling. Loss of life had not yet been accounted for, but preliminary reports showed at least three died in the explosions and possibly two or three fighting the fires.

"This is your captain speaking. Would all passengers and crew that are not required to maintain this ship afloat please report to the ship's lounge immediately?" he said over the ship's intercom system. "This includes you, Major Peterson!"

About three hours had gone by since the attempted ramming of the U-boat, and there had been no sign of it since then. Bronsly had resumed course at even a slower speed than before.

With all the remaining survivors in the lounge or accounted for, Major Peterson sent three of the five surviving Marines to guard the crates. He then joined Bronsly in the lounge. Lieutenant Russell and Sergeant Edwards accompanied him. With the chief boatswain on the bridge and two men in the engine room, all the known surviving passengers and crew were here: nine of fifteen crew, six out of eight passengers, and six Marines, including Peterson.

As he walked about the lounge, Captain Bronsly proceeded to inform everyone of the severity of their situation.

"As you know, we are severely damaged, but we're not out of the ball game yet. With only about one-third power and no hope of restoring the rest, we are…" There was a short pause. "At present speed and course, we are six days from land. If this old tub will hold together and the engine doesn't quit, then we should come out all right, but if that engine quits, well, it's obvious, we will become one very large nonmoving sittin' duck and I'll have only one way to go. And that is for everyone to abandon ship and we will sink her ourselves. We cannot let the Krauts get this ship and the cargo we carry."

"Captain, is there anything that we can do to help?" asked Lieutenant Jorgenson. A green lieutenant, just out of flight school, raised on a farm in Ohio, Jorgenson was used to seeing blood and misery. He grew up poor, fighting his way through school and into flight school with some help from Congressman Adams, his father's neighbor and best friend. Now, here he was on a sinking ship in the middle of the North Atlantic, without seeing his first mission over Germany. He wasn't going to die easy, and he planned on going down fighting. He didn't want to die in the ocean; if he had to die, he wanted it to be in an airplane over Europe.

"No, not right…well, maybe there is. We have to do something with the bodies of those that died, if there is anythin' left of them. Would you take charge of that, son, along with Chief Smith?" said Bronsly.

"Sir, where should we put the bodies?" asked Jorgenson.

"Once you have accounted for everyone, put the remains in one of the staterooms. Before you start on that, Smith, see that all your men are back to their posts and are secured, and keep someone on that gun."

"Aye, sir," said Smith, quietly giving orders to his crew.

All went well for the next few hours. The lookouts had not seen any sign of the U-boat and hoped never to see it again. Captain Bronsly was on the bridge with Johnson. Suddenly, Jorgenson and Smith came running onto the bridge as white as ghosts, sweating heavily and almost slipping because of the angle of the deck.

"Whoa, slow down! We're not goin' anywhere fast. Why should you?" Bronsly said, catching Smith before he fell.

"Capt'n, we have to talk to you right now, sir. Privately, please, sir," said Smith.

"Okay, just calm down. You look as though you've both seen a ghost or somethin'. Hasn't the mornin' been exciting enough for ya? Come on, let's go to my cabin. I need a break, anyway. Johnson, you got the helm. Call me if anything comes up. I mean *anything*."

The three of them headed out and down the side of the ship to the captain's quarters, located directly behind the bridge.

"Okay, Smith, what is so damn important?" asked Bronsly as he walked over to the locker and extracted a bottle of Irish whiskey and three glasses.

"Sir, you better sit down," Smith said.

"Come on, spit it out. We haven't all day," Bronsly said, pouring three glasses of Irish whiskey.

"Well, sir, it's one of the passengers, a Mr. Trinisnoski, or something like that. Well, sir, he's dead," said Smith.

"So what's so special about that? I expect he died in the explosion or fire or something related." He handed each a glass of whiskey. "You look as though you need this."

"He was shot, sir," said Jorgenson.

"Shot! Are you sure?"

"Sir, I've seen bullet wounds before, and this looks like a large caliber," said Smith.

"Damn, where's the body?"

"It's in number 4 hold, sir, beside the crates marked Medical Supplies," said Smith.

"Sir, there is something else," offered Jorgenson.

"Well, what is it?"

"We found this beside the body," he said, handing the captain a .38-caliber pistol and an envelope. "I think you need to read this."

Bronsly started to open the envelope when the bridge called.

"Capt'n, this is the bridge. I think you better get up here, fast."

"Okay, Johnson, I'll be right up." Pausing to look at the envelope, he removed the contents and read quickly. "It's in German, to a...ah...a Herr Gunthur Von Richie, signed by a guy...by someone who can't write. I can't make it out. Maybe ah...Von Hof...something. Hell, we gotta get back to the bridge. We'll handle this later. Let's get up to the bridge now."

On the horizon, another winter storm started to brew, tossing the ship and the men like toothpicks.

They staggered onto the bridge to find Chief Johnson lying on the deck, barely breathing.

"Johnson, Johnson, do you hear me?" asked Bronsly, trying to revive him. Johnson moved slowly.

"Okay, I'm up. What happened?" Johnson said, rubbing the back of his head.

"That's what I would like to know," said Bronsly.

Helping him to his feet and into a chair, Bronsly watched Johnson hold his head as he related what happened.

"I had the ship on course and was leaning over to check the charts when I heard the door open. But before I was able to turn around and see who came in, the lights went out, and the next I knew, you were here."

"Okay, Johnson, do you think you can still navigate this ship?"

"Yes, sir. Can I sit down for a few minutes to get the cobwebs out?" asked Johnson.

"Sure. Get some water for him, will ya, Jorgenson?" Bronsly said. "You called me back up here, Johnson. What was the problem?"

"Oh, I almost forgot. Andy called from the engine room. He went down to help clean up the mess, and well, when he got there, he couldn't find anyone around. The engine was running and the boiler had a full head of steam, but no one around," Johnson said, still rubbing his head.

"Bridge…Bridge, this is Andy," came a call from below.

"Yeah, Andy. Bronsly, what's the problem."

"Capt'n, I've found MacArthur and Arnold, and, sir, they've been shot. They're dead, sir."

"Oh my god. Stay where you are, son. We'll be right there."

Turning off the intercom, Bronsly looked at Johnson and started to say something but stopped.

"Damn, what is going on here?" Bronsly finally said.

"Is that radio operator still sending the Mayday?" asked Bronsly of Smith.

"As far as I know, sir. Should I check?" He turned to go to the radio room.

"Yeah, and see if he has anything on that storm up ahead. It looks pretty bad," said Bronsly.

Smith left, heading for the radio room down the corridor. He found the door locked; he knocked and got no answer. He tried again, with no response. On the third try, he gave up and forced the door open. There in his chair was the radio operator, leaning over his equipment, like he was asleep.

"Hey, fellow, wake up!" Smith said as he touched the operator on the shoulder. The operator leaned farther over and the chair rolled backward, dropping the operator on the deck. Smith reached down and rolled him over to discover a wound in the chest, but very little blood. He had died instantly and his heart did not pump much blood out.

Smith turned and looked at the radios, which he now saw were smashed, with wires pulled out of their sockets. Whoever had done this knew just what to do.

Meanwhile, on the bridge, Johnson had recovered and was briefing the captain on the weather and a possible route change.

"Sir, if we head a little south-southeast, we may just miss that one. It looks pretty clear down that way," said Johnson.

"That sounds pretty good, Johnson. Let's try it."

The sea was getting rougher, and Bronsly had to make some major decisions that affected the life of his ship. He had no idea how long this old tub was going to hold out in rough seas. They'd been lucky so far in holding her together, but for how much longer?

"Capt'n, the radios have been destroyed and the radio operator is dead, murdered, sir," Smith reported after returning to the bridge.

"Damn, who is this maniac? And why is he killing everyone?" yelled Bronsly as he paced the length of the bridge several times.

Hours went by with everything quiet. Bronsly was trying to calculate his next move. He needed to keep the *MaryJean* alive till after delivering his secret cargo, then he didn't care; she could sink and be forgotten about forever. Things were getting out of hand. His plan was to sabotage the ship, but someone else was doing it for him. Who?

Suddenly, a large ball of fire bellowed up from the engine room. The engine went silent and stopped pushing a large puff of black smoke out of the stack. Almost immediately, black smoke started to pour out of every crack in the aft of the *MaryJean*, and the heat from the fire could be felt a hundred feet away.

"Damn! Sound general quarters and the alarms, get the passengers to the lounge, and have them stand by!" yelled Bronsly. "Get someone on that fire before we blow to hell!"

"Engine room, ANDY, answer me! ANDY! DAMN, answer me!" yelled Bronsly in the intercom.

Silence, total silence.

There was no response from the engine room, and there never would be. There was no one left in the engine room. The number 2 boiler exploded, making sure there was no one left.

"Smith, go to…no, wait." Reaching into his pocket, Bronsly pulled out a set of keys, walked over to a cabinet, unlocked it, and removed two holsters complete with brand-new Army Colt .45 pistols. He handed these and extra clips with ammo to Jorgenson and Smith. Bronsly reached in again and retrieved two more for Johnson and himself.

"Here, do you know how to use this?" asked Bronsly.

"Yes, sir," each said together.

"Johnson, do you?"

"Yes, sir, but do you think it is necessary?"

"Yeah, I think so, son, I think so. Get that major up here as quick as you can. We need his help."

The fire aft was raging out of control. It looked like the *MaryJean* was dying; the battle to save her was lost.

Major Peterson and his men were working as fast as they could arming some explosives of their own and placing them in strategic spots on the cargo they were guarding in the number 3 hold.

"Sergeant, how much longer over there?" Peterson yelled over the roar of the fires, rushing water, and confusion.

"Not much longer, sir. How much time on the fuse?" he questioned.

"Make it about an hour. That should give us enough time to get off. Just don't turn it on yet. We will come back to activate them just before we abandon ship."

"Done!" Russell yelled.

"Okay, let's get up on deck and help with the fires. Russell, you come with me. Edwards, take the men to help with the ship. Let's go!"

Edwards departed with his men while Russell and Peterson turned to the crates to check the job they just completed. They wanted to be sure the explosives were not armed yet.

"Okay, let's go, Russell," Peterson said, turning and heading down the corridor to the engine room.

On the Bridge
January 19, 1943
1700 Hours

"Bridge, Damage Control!" blared on the intercom.

"Go ahead, Damage."

"Sir, the fires are under control, but the number 1 boiler is out of commission, and, sir, the engine crew is dead. I haven't found Andy. Sir, it isn't a pretty sight down here."

"Thank you. Secure the area. And do you think we can get that boiler patched up enough to move this tub? Who is with you, Kellenman?"

"It's just Seaman Packard and me, sir, and I don't know if we can get this thing working, but we'll try, sir."

"Okay, do the best you can. In the meantime, I'll send a couple of men down with some weapons to stand guard while you try to get that repaired."

"Aye, sir," came the reply.

"Smith, you and Jorgenson take these M1 carbines down to the engine room and return as soon as you can," Bronsly ordered as he handed each a new Army-issue M1 carbine.

"Roger that, sir!" shouted Jorgenson.

"Wait, before you go below, were you able to account for everyone, Smith?" asked Bronsly. "Who's missing?"

"Well, sir, we can't account for three of the crew and two passengers," said Jorgenson. "Major Peterson can't account for some of his men, but I'll get him up here."

"Which crew members, Smith, and where were they last seen?"

"Morris and Hancock were last seen going toward number 1 hole just before the first hit. I believe they were going to check on the cargo. After the storm, some of it came loose. The new kid, Compton, was on deck this morning, just before the torpedo hit. We haven't located any of them," Smith reported sadly.

"Jorgenson, what about the passengers? You got a head count?"

"Yes, sir. Counting myself, there are only six accounted for. Three are in the lounge, awaitin' orders. Two bodies located—one, Mr. Trinisnoski, you know, was shot, and Mr. Bennett was found dead in his stateroom, apparently from drowning. His stateroom was flooded. The pumps were able to bring the water down enough for us to check. We left his body there. Missing still are Mr. Jones and Mr. Alford."

As they left, the captain turned, sat in his chair, rested his head in his palms, and wept. About ten minutes passed before he was able to compose himself again. Things were not going as planned; he had lost control of the situation. Bronsly just sat there watching the storm ahead and Johnson read the charts. It wasn't supposed to happen like this.

Major Peterson and Lieutenant Russell entered the bridge about an hour later, looking like they were half-dead. Peterson moved over to the chart table and sat down on it. He looked exhausted.

"What the holy hell happened to you?" asked Bronsly.

"Capt'n, I don't know what is going on here, but I have had my own problems down below. I've lost four very good men in the first explosion, and someone is trying to kill the rest of us. Trying, I guess, to steal those crates. We sustained no further injuries, but it hasn't been easy."

"Johnson, how long before that storm hits us?" Bronsly asked, holding up his hand to silence Peterson.

"Just about sunset, sir. The current seems to be taking us south," was his reply.

"Major, we are not out of this yet. Someone has killed one of my crew and a passenger, for reasons beyond me, and now we have another storm to contend with."

"Killed? How? Why?"

"Killed? Yes! How? Shot! Why? Hell, I don't know why, or who, for that matter. What I do know is I need your help to catch this killer and help me save this ship, if we can. This last explosion, I suspect, was no accident. It looks like sabotage and murder, Major."

"Okay, Captain, what do you want us to do?"

"What is the present depth?" asked Bronsly of Johnson.

"Let's see, it's about six hundred fathoms and rising fast. We have just crossed over the continental shelf. I was able to get a half-ass fix a few minutes ago, so I have a fair idea where we are."

Bronsly related his thoughts to Major Peterson, and then Peterson went to find his men. All was quiet for the next hour or so, but Bronsly was starting to worry about Jorgenson and Smith. They'd been gone too long. *Where the hell are they?* Just a few minutes later, they came stumbling into the bridge, hot and sweaty.

"Where the hell have you two been?" Bronsly demanded.

"Well, sir, after we gave the rifles to the men in the engine room, we started to poke around to see if we could flush out our killer. We almost had him in hole number 4. We saw a shadow and approached slowly from two sides, boxing him in, but he saw us and threw this at us," said Smith, handing Bronsly a German stick grenade.

"Holy shit! Get that outa here before it goes off."

"It's a dud, sir. There's no primer. We checked it out," said Jorgenson. "But not until he was long gone."

"Did you get a look at him?"

"No, sir."

"Well, for now, why don't you two go down and load as much of the stores into the lifeboats as possible and then report back here. Are all the passengers in the lounge?"

"Yes, sir. They haven't moved since the engine room exploded," said Smith.

"Okay, keep them there. At least we know they aren't killing anyone and they aren't being killed. Take these two pistols down there so they won't feel unprotected, and don't say a thing about the other murders." He handed them two more new Army Colt .45s.

"Aye, sir," Smith replied as they departed.

"Sir, what's the game plan?" asked Johnson.

"I don't have a plan, my dear boy. I do believe we have only one choice, and it has already been made for us."

"Yes, I think you're right, sir, but I still will pray for a friendly ship on the horizon by morning."

"That's when we go, if we're alive."

It was nearing sunset and all had been quiet for hours, very quiet. Jorgenson and Smith had long returned from loading the stores; they had put two men on guard of the boats, just for safety's sake. Now they were on the bridge with Johnson and the captain, just waiting for the sweet sound of the engine to roar back to life.

The night was quiet, too quiet for Bronsly. The storm had moved off to the north as they drifted south by southeast. He had checked with the engine room numerous times through the night, getting the same response each time: "The engine and boilers are not ever going to move this ship, no matter what is done. It's hopeless."

"Engine Room, this is the capt'n!" Bronsly yelled into the intercom. "Engine Room, answer me."

"Engine Room, aye," came the answer after a long wait.

"What's the verdict down there?"

"Sir, she's dead. Let's bury the remains."

"Okay, it's 03:30, and you've been on that pile of junk for twelve hours. Secure the area and come to the lounge, all of you. Let's bury her."

"Aye, aye, sir. See you in fifteen minutes," he replied.

"Jorgenson, call down to Major Peterson and get his ass up to the lounge also. Tell him to bring his men," Bronsly ordered. "Okay, boys, it's time to go. The sun will be up soon, and so will the U-boats."

By 04:00, everyone—all that were alive, anyway—was in the lounge, except one lookout and three Marines on guard duty. Everyone looked very tired and wished this were over and they were at home, where it was warm and comfortable.

"What I've got to say may come as a surprise to some and not to others. We are a sitting duck right now. We can't maneuver, run, or hide. Our engines are totally out of the ball game. There is no way we can make land safely on board this vessel. And to top it off, we are taking on water faster than we can pump it out. Without the main engines, the batteries will be dead inside of a day, and when that happens, our pumps will quit and there will be no way to stop the inflow of seawater. That is, if the Germans don't find us first. One shot by them and we're gone, anyway. The only chance of survival is to abandon ship, take to the smaller boats, and sail toward England. Each boat is equipped with a sail and rudder for steering. They have been stocked with all the stores we have available, so at sunup we go. Are there any questions?"

A hand went up in the back of the lounge. It was a passenger.

"Yes, what is it?"

"Captain Bronsly, will there be someone in the boat that can operate it?" asked Mr. Phillips. "I've never been to sea before this trip."

"Yes, we will split what's left of the crew between the boats and attempt to stay together until we are rescued. No other questions? Okay, if you have something of value that you have to take, we will go down with a guard now to get it, and then return back here. We leave in one hour. If you aren't here, you go down with the ship."

One hour later, all the crew and passengers were in the lifeboats and in the water. The seacocks had been opened and the ship was sinking.

"Captain, I set the charges to detonate in sixty minutes. They should have blown by now," Peterson said, loud enough for all the survivors in the three lifeboats to hear.

The three little boats were about a mile from the ship, watching for her to sink, yet nothing was happening. The charges didn't blow, and she was still adrift, heading south-southeast with the current.

"Damn, why doesn't she go down?" cursed Bronsly. Then he thought to himself, *I hope she stays afloat long enough to get that secret cargo off. We are cutting this real close.*

"Do you want to try to go back and see why, sir?" asked Smith.

"No, there is nothing we can do except get ourselves killed. That ship just doesn't want to give in, or there is someone helping her. Besides, the current is too fast here. We could never get back there."

By the next morning, the *MaryJean* had either sunk or was over the horizon, because she was nowhere to be seen anywhere around the lifeboats. A total of five passengers left the ship along with seven crew, including Captain Bronsly and Major Peterson with four of his men. Peterson had left ten pounds of TNT on the crates to destroy the contents and left quickly because water was already knee-deep in the number 3 hole.

They were only five days out when they abandoned ship and were in the shipping lanes. Their only hope was that when they were finally spotted, it would be the Allies, not the Germans. And so their three little boats drifted for what seemed to be forever.

Chapter 3

THE DISCOVERY

Singer Island, Palm Beach, Florida
Office of Davin Pierce, Insurance Investigator
April 17, 1996
0900 Hours

"A s I said, Mr. Pierce, we drifted for days and finally lost sight of the *MaryJean*, never to see her again, and I hadn't thought much about her until you called yesterday," said Colonel Jorgenson, US Army retired. He sat in the large overstuffed chair across from Davin Pierce, looking confused and tired.

He had been through a lot in the past fifty years, and it showed. Early in his career, he had almost cashed in on the *MaryJean* somewhere in the North Atlantic, then he had been seriously wounded in both World War II and Korea, and finally he suffered through Vietnam at the end of his career. He had survived all of it and came out highly decorated and considered a war hero. Colonel Jorgenson had also played a key role in another little war back in 1943, one that had come closer to ending his life than anything else afterward. But of course, he had no knowledge of that, until now.

They were in Davin Pierce's North Palm Beach office overlooking the Atlantic Ocean and the beautiful white sands of Singer Island Beach. It was hot outside, and the beach was full of bikini-clad girls of all ages. Davin knew when he took this office that the beach would be a major distraction, but today they all could be running naked and he wouldn't have noticed—well, maybe a little. The story that Jorgenson had just told him had held his interest to the end. His version had holes, but they could be filled, in time. He could not have known or could not have been everywhere on that ship, but what he said did help answer some of Davin's own questions.

Davin Pierce, age thirty-seven, six foot one, brown hair, hazel eyes, 170 pounds, was an independent insurance claims investigator specializing in large equipment, such as ships, airplanes, and tanks. He made a nice living and, on occasion, saved the insurance companies a few bucks. The only problem with this case was, there was no claim to pay, as it was considered a wartime loss and the government had written off the cargo and ship years ago. Davin was running this one as a favor to an old friend, Ted McDonald, with Lloyds of London, who had held the policy on the *MaryJean* but had never paid. Davin owed him one and figured this one wouldn't take long to resolve, because most of the players were dead and the tracks were long since covered by time. Ted's interest was mostly curiosity, nothing more, or at least that was what he said.

"Colonel Jorgenson, you never said what you were doing on the *MaryJean*."

"No, sir, I guess I didn't. I was a scared young lieutenant back then, assigned to the Eighth Army Air Corps as a pilot. I had just finished flight school and was being sent over to fly B-17s out of England. I had with me some important documents for General… ah, I can't remember his name. Well, it doesn't matter."

"Go on, you had some documents and…?" asked Davin as he swung his chair to look out the window facing the beach.

"I was told that the papers were from the Air Defense Department and I was to report to a Captain Rogers with the British Secret Service when I arrived. He was to take the case and I was to go on to my unit," Jorgenson continued. "When all the explosions started, all I wanted to do was to save my ass. Everything seemed so unbelievable at the time I really didn't know what was going on."

"Well, I guess there was a lot of confusion when the fireworks started," Davin said.

"Well, things were happening very fast for a while there, and I guess you could say I was a little bit scared and a whole lot confused." Jorgenson started relating the final minutes of the *MaryJean* but paused first to think about it.

"Go on, Colonel, what happened next?" Davin coaxed.

"I never saw the sub that torpedoed us. I was on deck when the first torpedo hit, and it hit, as I said before, in the rear of the ship on the right side, as if you were looking forward. And then the second one hit, but, well, maybe I was a little dazed, but it looked like it hit on the...well, on the opposite side of the ship. At least it seemed that way," said Jorgenson, slowly leaning way back in his chair, thinking out loud about what had happened. He had an excellent memory of the events; age had not affected his mind.

"That's an interesting assumption. What makes you think the explosions were on different sides of the ship, Colonel?" Davin asked, probing a little deeper. This was a new thought, one that might never be proved, unless they found the ship.

"I'm not sure. I guess you might call it a pilot's sense of touch, or rather feel of the airplane. You know, ah...like when you are flying and something just doesn't feel right? You do understand, don't you?" Jorgenson tried to explain.

"Let me get this straight. You are saying that there may have been two U-boats?"

"Yes, no...hell, I don't know for sure. What I am sure of is that we had two major explosions within a few seconds of each other and on different sides of the ship. Now, if that means there were two U-boats shooting at us, then that's what it means."

"That's interesting. Do, or did, any of the other survivors share this same opinion?"

"I don't know. We were separated when questioned and really didn't talk about it on the way to England."

"Okay, I think I understand. Let's continue with what happened after you arrived in England," Davin said as he stood up and walked over to the wet bar. Looking in the ice bucket, he discovered it was empty. He returned to his desk and pushed the intercom button as he held up a finger for Jorgenson to stop for a moment.

"Stephanie, would you bring us some ice, please?" he said in the intercom.

"Sure thing, Davin. I'll be right in," came the reply.

"Thank you," Davin said, and then to Jorgenson he said, "Sorry. You were going to say?"

"Oh, sure. Well, when I finally arrived at my destination, Captain Rogers of the British Secret Service took the briefcase, and that was the last that I saw of my charge. I was then taken to another building and questioned by several men from the Navy, US and British, about the attack and our leaving the ship."

"So you don't know what was in the case or if it ever got to its destination?"

"As far as I was concerned, I did my part. Captain Rogers was my contact in England, but as far as the case, no, I don't know what happened to it from there. You still haven't answered my question as to why the sudden interest in an old boat."

A light tap sounded on the door, and it quietly opened. Stephanie entered and crossed over to the wet bar with a bucket of ice. "Let's go back to your rescue. How long was it before you were picked up?"

"I'll never forget that. After drifting seven days, we spotted a sub on the horizon. The problem was, it was a damn U-boat. They were running on the surface, I guess, charging their batteries. When they saw us, they turned toward us." Short pause. "Then they opened fire. Damnedest thing I ever saw too. They fired at us, but they were either the worst gun handlers or were experts, because each shot was close enough to get us wet but not enough to do any damage," Jorgenson said.

Davin noticed he had broken out in a cold sweat. He just sat in his chair, watching the colonel, closely.

"They fired four rounds, one for each cardinal point on the compass, missing completely. Then they turned and dived below the surface. I still have nightmares about that one."

"That's strange. Maybe they just wanted to scare you."

"Yeah, maybe, and they did a damn good job too."

"Strange. Well, a lot of strange things happened during the war, I guess. Could you tell if the U-boat was the same as the one that sunk the *MaryJean*?"

"Hell, if it were a Me109 or 206, I could tell the difference, but ships, subs, they all look alike to me. Remember, I'm a flyboy, not a squid, or rather a sailor."

"What, then?"

"Well, around the ninth day, we saw another ship on the horizon steaming straight for us, almost as if we had a homing device on board. We didn't even have a radio or transmitter of any type—at least, as far as I know, we didn't. Well, it looked like they really knew exactly where we were. They came at us at full speed and picked us up late in the afternoon. And it was just in time too. We were just about out of food and water. After they fed us and got us some dry, clean clothes, we were questioned briefly and told to relax until we would arrive in England in about four days. They were kind of quiet about the whole thing, and well, I didn't care. I just wanted to get on dry land and live without fear for a long time."

"After you arrived in England, what happened next?"

"We were all taken to this large house outside of London and questioned about the whole thing, sorta like you are doing now, kinda relaxed and all. There was no pressure. They just wanted to know the facts. I sensed that they were not telling us everything they knew about what happened. I asked how they seemed to know exactly where we were and what they knew of a sub—eh, a U-boat rather—like the one that we described to them. Remember that we had been drifting for nine or ten days and we didn't know exactly where we were. The sky had not been clear for days, and ah, without the stars, we couldn't navigate ourselves to anywhere. We just attempted to head east the best we could. And thinking back now, there was something very strange about the U-boat that fired at us."

"Strange. What do you mean? Was it the shape, size, markings? What do you remember?"

"Well, being an OLE Army man, I didn't and still don't know much about boats of any type. But what I do know, and this is true of any type of vehicle, is that every country will paint or mark with letters or numbers somehow, somewhere in a visible spot, the vehicle's identification for the simple fact that it is very hard to explain to your government that you just destroyed one of your own. And this U-boat did not have any markings anywhere I could see, and she was painted black, jet-black, everywhere. That's what I remember now, Mr. Pierce."

"Before I forget, Colonel, what happened about the murders on the *MaryJean* and that note to Von Richie?"

"Nothing that I know of. They seemed to let that slide, too, considered them as an act of war, and that was how they filed them too. The note, well, I'm not real sure what happened to it. Bronsly had put it in his pocket to read later and probably forgot about it. I never saw it again. Now, will you tell me what this is all about?"

"Well, Colonel, there are two reasons we needed to hear your story. To start with, about half of the serial-numbered cargo from the *MaryJean* has turned up in a warehouse in New Orleans. We don't know how long it's been there or how it even got there, but according to the manifest, what we found is supposed to be at the bottom of the North Atlantic with the *MaryJean*."

"Do you think someone may have found the wreck and salvaged her?"

"No, that couldn't be possible for this stuff. It has no trace of ever being in or around salt water."

"This is all very interesting, but other than the fact that I was on that ship, what has all this to do with me?"

"Well, sir, I was called in by the insurance company that covered the *MaryJean* to investigate why that cargo is in New Orleans, how it got there, and above all, determine where the rest is. And part of my search is to question all the remaining survivors. You were the easiest, since you live here in Palm Beach."

"Have you located any of the other survivors, Mr. Pierce?"

"Yes and no. Of the five passengers and seven crew including Bronsly, only four of you are still alive that we have accounted for so far. Three from the military that were on board were listed as MIAs, one unaccounted for as yet. We are still trying to track down any others that may be alive, but so far only four."

"May I ask who is still alive?"

"Sure. Besides you, there is Smith, the young boatswain you worked with; Mr. Connely; and Richard Johnson. Major Peterson and two of his men were listed MIA after the war. The rest of his men are known dead, and the one unaccounted for."

"You said there were two reasons you called me in here. Would you care to tell me the second reason?"

"You don't miss much, do you? Well, sir, what you saw and heard on the *MaryJean* wasn't as it seemed back in '43. It turns out that some of the supposed dead were in fact alive and were part of what appears to be a mutiny that went haywire. We know of one, for sure, and indications are that at least three others were involved in the takeover."

"But, Mr. Pierce, I saw the bodies, and they were dead!"

"And so there were, but what about the ones you didn't see? The ones that were supposed to have been killed when the torpedoes hit and all the confusion."

"Okay, those we couldn't account for because they were blown up, and the bodies, well, I…ah, I don't know what happened to the damn bodies. They were gone, man, blown to hell or…ah, maybe, hell, I don't know."

"Calm down, Colonel. We aren't accusing you of anything. You were just a puppet in their plan and did what they told you to do. Let me fill you in on what we know, and maybe, just maybe, with your help we can uncover the rest of the mystery."

"Sorry, I got carried away there. So what do you know about the *MaryJean* that I don't?"

"Well, to start from, we can start where you left off, and maybe we can solve this in the next few weeks," Davin said as he got up and walked over to the little wet bar again to fix another drink. Turning back to the colonel, he continued, "Refill that drink, Colonel?"

"Yes, scotch again, if I may. Thank you."

"Ah, yeah. Where was I? Yes, well…maybe we can fill in some of the holes." Handing the colonel a glass of brandy, Davin continued, "For starters, the weapons were not just stumbled upon but found as a result of a long, drawn-out investigation by the FBI. They had been working this case of gunrunning, and to make a long story short, everything came to a head at this warehouse on the docks in New Orleans. About two weeks ago and after a little firefight and the dust settled, the FBI entered the warehouse to find three dead men and a boatload of World War II weapons."

"Very interesting, Mr. Pierce, but what has all that got to do with me? I was just a passenger trying to save his own ass from the sharks."

"Just a minute and maybe you will see. Two of the gunrunners escaped. How, no one knows for sure, but they did. Well, after all that, the FBI ran the prints from the three dead through the files to see if they had any priors and to get a positive ID."

"Well," said Jorgenson, sipping his scotch slowly, "who were they?"

"They were John A. Ericson, age thirty-six; Kelly Hancock, age seventy-three; Dan Anderson, known as Andy, age seventy-four; and Jerry Bronsly, age thirty-four, son of Captain Elmer Bronsly of the *MaryJean*," Davin stated matter-of-factly. "Hancock was the ship's quartermaster, and Anderson the engineering mate on the *MaryJean* in '43, and both were listed as killed in action in January 1943, when the *MaryJean* disappeared. No bodies were recovered."

"I don't see what you're driving at. Please continue."

"Well, if Hancock was supposed to be dead and Bronsly reported him as so, doesn't it make you wonder what Bronsly was up to back in '43?"

"Yeah, but maybe he only thought Hancock was dead but he really survived and somehow made it off the ship and caught up with Bronsly later."

"We thought of that, but Bronsly never changed his statement or record of Hancock's death. As far as the world knew, Hancock was dead at sea, never to be seen again. If he did that to one of his crew, maybe there were others."

"Possibly, but what would he gain?"

"Well, what would you do if you had stolen a shipload of government weapons bound for a war zone?" Davin continued before the colonel could answer. "The only way to hide his treason would be to sink his ship, send her to the bottom forever."

"You mean he was going to sink his own ship?" The colonel gasped.

"Yes, I believe he was going to sink her, but he had to make it look as though she was torpedoed and sinking to convince you and the rest of the passengers that they had really been attacked. But then he didn't expect to be torpedoed, and everything went haywire. The killings on board, well, we can't explain that yet." Davin started on some real-time evaluation. "But Bronsly probably had something to do with them."

"Damn, Mr. Pierce, that would explain the explosions on different sides of the ship," Jorgenson commented.

"Things didn't go well for Bronsly from the beginning. He had a squad of Marines and three mystery crates, but the ship had to disappear and the Germans just did it a little sooner than planned. The cargo was not on the ship and the ship was sunk, so Bronsly was happy and no one was the wiser, till now."

"It seems you have solved the mystery, Mr. Pierce. So what now?" asked Jorgenson.

"It would seem so, but it's all speculation, and of course, there is the matter of the murders, the crates, and I have to prove it, if I can."

"I don't envy you. How are you going to prove it?"

"I don't know, but what the hell? It's a great day to get out and see the world. I've been stuck in this office for too long as it is."

"Great, but do you have any idea what was in the crates?"

"No, not yet, and maybe never will."

The colonel just sat there looking more confused than he was when he came in. Running an old hand through his gray hair, he contemplated the conversation.

"Is there any record of the crates being on her?" he finally asked.

"So far we haven't located any, but you know, with a war, things could have been destroyed or lost over the years," Davin said. He finished his drink and headed back to the bar for another. He stopped to look out the window facing the beach as a nicely tanned girl in a small white bikini strolled by; his thoughts were distracted as he watched this vision of beauty walk out of sight. Deciding he really didn't need another, he put his glass in the sink and returned to his desk.

"Mr. Pierce. Are you okay, Mr. Pierce?"

"Sorry. I knew I shouldn't have taken this office. I'm too easily distracted by the views."

"I can understand that. She has great assets."

"Yeah, great. Now where were we, Colonel? Oh, yeah, the cargo. It looks like Bronsly had planned on sinking the ship until this new cargo arrived. Then he probably had to rethink his plans, but he had already committed himself by falsifying records and not loading the weapons and munitions as he was supposed to. We don't really know what was on that ship. What we do know is the cargo that was supposed to be on board, or at least part of it, is sitting in a guarded warehouse in New Orleans."

"Okay, how can I be of help?" asked Jorgenson, handing his glass to Davin for a refill. "Please."

"Well, with what you have told me of what you heard and saw on the *MaryJean*, I think we can move on. If you remember anything else, please give me a call as soon as possible. We are talking to the others and getting statements from them to compare and try to put it together."

Finishing his third scotch, the colonel said as he stood to leave, "If there is anything further that I can do, please let me know. As you know, I still have friends in high places and can pull some strings if you need some. I would like to see what the outcome of this is. I don't like being a stooge, even if it was fifty years ago."

"Thank you, sir. We will be in touch," Davin said, shaking the colonel's hand and escorting him to his office door.

After the colonel left, Davin Pierce leaned back in his over-stuffed chair and looked out the picture window again. He didn't see the black Ford sedan parked across the street. He was too engrossed recalling the conversation and statement made by Colonel Jorgenson. The only distraction he had was that white bikini about forty yards down the beach. She was just lying there, getting darker. She was out there every day, and Davin wondered about her and how she could afford to be on the beach every day.

Pentagon Building, Arlington, Virginia
April 17, 1996
1135 Hours

Meanwhile, in an office deep within the confines of one of the most secure buildings in the country, two men were talking about a letter they had just received, marked URGENT.

"Okay, Jack, what do we do now?" asked the man behind the desk. This was his office, and he was concerned about the contents of the letter. He knew that whoever wrote the letter would be dead if ever he was located. "You know, if he decides to turn state's evidence, we all go down. You had better be concerned!"

"Right now we can't do anything without attracting attention to you and the others. Let me handle it for the next week, then if I don't come up with anything, well, then…I guess it's your turn," the man named Jack said confidently.

"This says they will reveal to the newspapers and FBI the location of that damn freighter and who she got there," the man behind the desk stated.

"So what? That boat has nothing on her to link you or any of your buddies to her."

"Do you have any idea who may be threatening to expose the operation?" Jack asked.

"Yes, I do, but I hope it's not true. It could only be one group of people."

"Can you give me a lead and we will stop them before it's too late?" Jack asked, probing to get a solid answer from him, as he had been skirting around a solid answer since he had arrived.

"Look, Jack, if I tell you what I know, then you must keep it to yourself. If word gets out, then a definite link will be drawn and we all go down."

"Well, spill it. We've been friends long enough to trust each other, Admiral," Jack said, leaning forward in his chair in anticipation.

"You have only been in the operation for, what, eight years now, correct?" the admiral stated. After getting a positive response from Jack, he continued. "The entire operation started many years ago with the freighter *MaryJean*, a Gato-class submarine, and some friends we would rather not talk about. Well, to make a long story short, that sub has been in service for the operation since the war, and very profitably, if I might add. Well, she disappeared about three months ago, without a trace or communication to our island."

"Okay, then, maybe this is a letter from them, kinda like they want out and didn't really know how to say it."

"That's who I think it is from, but maybe not."

"Any idea where they may have gone?" Jack asked.

"No, and I think the Navy needs to do the search. The FBI does not have the equipment, and this sub could be almost anywhere in the world," the admiral said.

"Okay, sir, it's your ball game. Just let me know when it's my turn to play," Jack said and then got up to leave.

Palm Beach, Florida
April 17, 1996
1215 Hours

"Davin, Davin," Stephanie said loudly as she entered the office, getting no response from him. Finally, as she got close enough, he acknowledged her presence. "Davin, it's about time. I've been trying to get your attention for ten minutes."

"Oh, sorry, Stephanie. I've been thinking about this case, and well, you know me, I kinda got lost in my thoughts. What's up?"

"Oh, nothing much, except it's twelve o'clock and I would like to get some lunch. Do you want anything?"

"Yeah, I would. I'd like to take you to lunch and get outa here for a while."

"Great, let's go."

"Have you heard from Eric or Dan today?" asked Davin as they headed out to the car lot.

"No. Neither one has called in."

"I wonder how they are doing with Smith and Connely. And did Jane get anything on the last known location of the *MaryJean*?"

"Yes, she did, and she'll be in the office tomorrow with a complete report, with projected courses and possible destinations," Stephanie said as she got in Davin's new BMW 635csi, which she loved. The car was white with black leather interior and handled like a dream on wheels. "Where are we going, Davin? I'm starving."

"Oh, I don't know. How about the yacht club? I need to check on my boat while we're there."

"Sounds good to me. I haven't been there for a while."

The drive over was short, and Davin noticed that a black Ford had pulled away from the beach just as he turned south on A1A heading for the bridge. But he didn't give it much thought. Conversation between him and Stephanie was light, mostly about the *MaryJean* and what his next move might be. As he pulled into the parking lot of the club, the black Ford slowed but continued on down the street and turned up a side street.

Lunch was good and the drinks were cold, but Davin couldn't get his mind off the *MaryJean* to really enjoy the company.

"Davin, this case has really got you bugged, hasn't it?" asked Stephanie.

"Yes and no—well, just a bit, maybe. Why would a man sell out his country, especially during a war?"

"Well, things were different then, and maybe he had a good reason. Maybe Bronsly was following orders too. I don't know. What I do know is that your steak is going to get cold if you don't start eating soon. And besides, I have a lot of typing this afternoon, and I need to get back soon."

"Hey, who's the boss here, you or me?"

"You are, of course. Most of the time, anyway. But I still have a lot of work that you gave me to get done, so eat up."

"Okay, okay. By the way, I want you to go with me when I interview Johnson in Miami, okay?"

"Sure, sounds good to me," said Stephanie. After she thought for a moment, she asked, "Is this work or play?"

"Work. I need you to transcribe the interview. My recorder is broken again."

"Will we have time to stop at the beach for a little R&R, or is this strictly business?"

"Let's take care of the interview first, and then we'll see about the R&R, if there is time, okay?"

Palm Beach Marina, Dock Side
1330 Hours

Finishing lunch, Stephanie and Davin walked out to the dock and started out to where he kept his boat.

"Hey, you ole bilge rat, how the hell are you?" called a heavyset middle-aged man from the cockpit of a forty-foot Scarab powerboat.

"Bilge rat—is that any kind of talk in front of a lady?" Davin replied.

"Sorry 'bout that, lady. Kinda lost my manners lately. So how ya been, Davin?" he asked as he broke out in a smile.

"Not bad, Josh, not bad at all. This tub yours?"

"Yeah, how do ya like her?"

"Drug business must be good," Davin said with a little laugh.

"Not bad, but don't say it too loud. You never know who's listening. Come on board. I'll open us some vintage wine. But first, you have to introduce me to this vision of loveliness."

"Why, thanks," Stephanie responded.

"Sorry, this is Stephanie Parker, my secretary. And this, my dear, is Joshua Randel, Josh to his friends, a real company man. Hasn't done a real day's work since I've known him. Ha ha! And when did you start drinking vintage wine? No, wait, let me guess. It's a new bottle of Chateau la Screwtop, ah, 1992, January, maybe."

"Nice to meet you, Josh."

"The pleasure is all mine, Stephanie. Come on down. What's your pleasure?" Josh asked as he reached up to help her on board. "Well, the wine is a little young, vintage February '93 from a little vineyard in Southern California, but it isn't bad. Kinda fruity with a bite."

"Josh, I'll pass on the wine, ah…I need to run down to the Seagull to check her out and pick up a few things. I'll be right back. Just have a cold beer ready when I get back."

"What's her name, Josh?" Stephanie asked as she settled onto the lounge in the stern of the boat.

"RAVIN' MAD. What'll you have?"

"Interesting name. Is that any indication as to the state of mind of the owner? Oh, a screwdriver, please."

"Haven't got time. Davin will be here too soon, maybe later. Now, what are you drinking?" Josh said quickly. "And yes, named her myself."

"Vodka and OJ, you dirty old man!" She laughed.

"Not yet, not old enough. Be right back with your drink," he said and disappeared belowdecks.

Conversation continued till Davin finally returned about twenty minutes later.

"We almost had enough time, Josh," Stephanie said quietly.

"Almost enough time for what?" Davin asked as he stepped down on the deck, looking hot and confused.

"Oh, nothing, nothing at all," she said.

"Catch, *ole* boy!" Josh yelled, tossing Davin an ice-cold beer.

"I need to talk business. Can we take her out a ways?" Davin asked as he tossed a leather pistol case on the lounge chair beside Stephanie.

"Sure. Finish that beer and toss off the bowline. We can be outside the inlet and three miles out inside of ten minutes."

"Wait a minute, I didn't come dressed to go boating, boys," Stephanie protested mildly.

"No PROBLEM!" Josh and Davin said in unison, first looking at each other then back to Stephanie, smiling.

"Huh?"

"Stephanie, go below and look in the locker on the left at the bottom of the ladder. You'll find some appropriate boat wear, and something for your boss too. Just pitch his up here."

"Well, okay," she said and disappeared below.

Shortly after she left, a pair of men's bathing trunks came flying up on deck. A multicolored tank top followed a second later.

Minutes later, they had cleared the inlet and were making their way east, slowly, waiting until Stephanie was back up on deck.

"How's this, boys?" she said, standing in the hatchway in a small but tasteful light-blue string bikini.

"Like wow, you can come with me anytime, anytime at all," Josh said. "Now please sit your body in that lounge and hang on."

"Not bad, Davin," she said, looking at him standing beside the hatchway in the suit she had passed up. "Not bad at all. Yummy!" she said quietly, licking her lips.

"WARP ONE, SCOTTY!" Josh yelled to no one in particular.

She sat just in time. Josh pushed the throttles of the Scarab to the wall, and the large boat almost jumped out of the water when the twin four-hundred-cubic-inch engines caught and propelled them from five knots to sixty-five in a matter of seconds. They skimmed across the almost-flat ocean for about fifteen minutes before Josh started to pull the throttles back.

"Is this okay, Davin?" Josh asked.

"Great!" Davin commented, seeing no other boat for miles around.

Josh had shut down the big engines and disappeared below, returning with fresh drinks for all. After passing around the drinks, he pulled off his shirt and sat on the sideboard of the boat, letting it drift with the current. Josh was heavy, but there was not much fat on his well-tanned body.

"Here's to good drinks and good friends," Josh toasted, looking at Stephanie. "You had better hang on to that girl, or I might grab her up."

"Stephanie, Josh and I will be below. You stay up here and keep an eye out for other boats. If any get too close, let us know, fast," Davin said as he and Josh headed below.

"Loosen up, *ole* boy, and tell me your problems," Josh insisted lightly.

Stephanie took the cue and got comfortable on the sundeck to catch some sun. As soon as they had closed the hatch, she removed her top to take advantage of the sun.

"Josh, I need the help of the company."

"You were a company man. You know the rules." He paused and shook his head. "Hell, I don't know…damn, I could get into a lot of trouble if caught. What the hell, what are friends for, anyway? Tell me what's going down and I'll see what I can do. No promises," Josh said as he reached over to turn on the air conditioner.

"Great." Davin told him the story without leaving much out.

"Pretty wild, huh? Well, what can I do?" Josh asked.

"First, remember Jack Malone, FBI?" Davin reminded him.

"Yeah."

"Well, I've got a bad feeling about this, and Jack is working the weapons side. Well, I am really looking in all the corners for whatever I can find. If you could just poke around and see what you can find out about the *MaryJean*, her crew, her cargo, you know, all the routine stuff. That's all," Davin said as he finished his beer.

"That's all, he says, that's all! Okay. I'll see what we have on her."

"Thanks. I need another beer."

"Help yourself. Can we go back up on deck now?" Josh said as he opened the hatch to see Stephanie lying on her stomach on the sundeck. "Damn, she's a beauty. Why don't you leave her with me for a while?"

"Not a chance. You would have a better chance of getting ice water in hell."

"Ah, come on, this tub needs a 'double-breasted bow sitter,' and she is perfect."

"Figure the odds, *ole* chap. In your line of business, hell, I wouldn't trust some of your friends with a nickel, much less a jewel like her."

"Steph, we're coming up now, and we will be leaving soon!" Josh yelled.

She sat up with her back to the boys and put her top back on and then turned to slide back into the cockpit.

"I need a drink, thanks," she said as Davin handed her a fresh screwdriver.

It was close to 3:00 p.m. when they arrived back at the dock. Josh had given her a cover for the bikini as they were heading back so she wouldn't have to change back into street clothes.

"I'll call you soon, Davin, and, Stephanie, please stop by when you can."

"Thanks for the bikini, Josh. I love it."

"It looks better on you than me, anyway. Enjoy."

"Bye, for now," Stephanie said as they stepped onto the dock.

They started back to the office and didn't see the black Ford fall into the traffic about six cars back and didn't see the car follow them all the way back to the office and park across the street again.

"We're not going back to the office like this, are we?" Stephanie asked, indicating that all she had on was a cover-up over a very small bikini.

"Sure, why not?"

"At least you were able to slip on your pants, but look at me."

"I am, I am."

"Give me a break. Drop me off at my apartment."

"We'll only be at the office for a few minutes. You can use the shower there and put on your dress. But of course, you don't need to do that. The office will look great with you in that bikini."

"Okay, okay, to the office."

Davin unlocked the door to his office and entered. As he stepped in, he saw an envelope on the floor that had been slid under the door while they were gone. He picked it up as Stephanie walked to her desk to start to check for messages.

"I'll be in my office, Stephanie. Please filter my calls. I really need some time to think," Davin said as he headed for his desk, carrying the envelope with him. As he crossed the room, he opened the envelope and sat down before unfolding the paper inside.

He read it.

> *Mr. Pierce,*
> *For your own health, stay away from the* MaryJean.
>
> *—a friend*

Chapter 4

THE FBI

"Jack, what's the latest on that weapons bust?" Chief Hicks asked as he approached Jack Malone's desk.

Jack was busy scanning a computer printout and did not see his chief walk up. Jack had been a member of the FBI for eighteen years. He had distinguished himself numerous times for bravery and his ability to follow through on a case. He had an almost-perfect record of cases assigned and cases solved. Maybe he was lucky, only getting assigned cases that were solvable. Some of the other agents were not as lucky. Jack Malone was a widower with one son and one daughter. Debbie was in college, age twenty-two, and a senior and on the honor roll for the third year. She had the world ahead of her and knew how to handle it, majoring in computer engineering and planning on going on to get a master's degree in engineering from Georgia Tech. Jack was proud of her and would do anything to protect and support her. She was his life's blood. His son, David, age twenty-four, was a recent graduate from George Washington University, majoring in criminal justice. The CIA upon graduation last year hired him.

"Oh, hi, Chief," Jack responded, finally looking up from the computer. "Not much more on that. I have a few feelers out, but nobody's talking."

"Lloyds of London is now involved. It seems as though some of those weapons turned up on a manifest of a ship that sank in 1943. And now they have hired a private adjuster named Pierce to look into the matter."

"Pierce. That wouldn't be Davin Pierce, down in Palm Beach?"

"Yeah. Heard of him?"

"You might say that. He used to work for the company, until he had a disagreement with a few head honchos. Punched out and moved to Florida. He's good, Chief," Jack commented. Then he thought to himself, *I know he's involved and only hope he will take that note I sent to stay away seriously. Otherwise, he may get real hurt, and I don't want to see that.*

"Jack, I'd put a tail on him. I don't need a civilian sticking his nose in FBI matters. I don't care if he worked for the company or not. You may want to contact him and see what he has learned."

"Right, sir. I'll call as soon as I get finished with this report," Jack said. Then thinking, *Maybe getting with Davin may be the best way to prevent him from getting hurt. I'll call him and arrange a meeting. Maybe they will join forces. He has some connections that may prove to be useful in the future. This black market ring is pretty large and very dangerous.*

"You do that, Jack. Keep me posted," the chief said, turned, and left Jack's office.

Davin Pierce's Office
Singer Island
1545 Hours

Davin got up and poured himself a Coke and turned to look out the window, again contemplating the note. This time he saw the black Ford across the street just sitting there. He wondered if it was the same one that followed them out to lunch and then returned here to leave this note, or maybe it was just a coincidence. He didn't believe that, so to test his theory, he decided to go for a ride. Before leaving his office, he retrieved a Colt Commander from the leather case he had retrieved from the boat, checked the clip, and stuck it in his belt.

"Stephanie, I'll be back in a little bit."

"Okay, but first, where are you going?"

"For a ride. I need some air. Call me on the car phone if anything comes up that I need to know about." Davin left through the front office door without waiting for a reply.

"I'll be on the beach, Davin. I'll call you tonight." Her words faded as he disappeared down the walk.

Minutes later, in his car, Davin fastened his seat belt and headed out of the garage parking area. He headed south on A1A toward Blue Heron Boulevard and across the bridge that would take him over to I-95. The black Ford was following about five cars back. Davin could not make out who was driving at this distance.

Minutes later, he was on the ramp to I-95, with only a cream-colored Camaro and the black Ford sedan behind him. I-95 had its usual amount of traffic for the afternoon, so he had to accelerate hard to merge into the traffic. Both cars behind him did the same. Once on the highway, cruising at seventy-five miles per hour, which was the usual speed on this section of I-95, he watched his rearview mirror to see what the black Ford was doing.

"Well, damn," Davin said out loud after seeing the Ford leave the highway. "I guess I was wrong about that."

Davin continued north, occasionally glancing at his rearview mirror, but not seeing any sign of the black Ford. As he proceeded north, the traffic had started to thin out, leaving only two cars close behind him: a green Volvo, about forty yards back and a light-blue Chevy that was pulling up to pass him. Davin planned on turning around on the next exit and heading back to his office. Just as the Chevy pulled up beside him, he caught, out of the corner of his eye, a shotgun leveled at him out the window. The gunner had a ski mask over his head. Without thinking about it, Davin jammed on his brakes just as the shotgun fired, missing him and his car completely.

The Chevy slammed on its brakes and spun around to come back at Davin just as he floored the accelerator of the BMW, shooting him forward to over one hundred miles per hour. The Volvo had spun off the road and stopped safely in the ditch. As Davin sped pass the Chevy, another shot was fired and again missed him. The driver of the Chevy spun his car around again, forcing oncoming cars to brake and drive off the highway to avoid a head-on collision with the Chevy. He accelerated in pursuit of Davin. Several cars slammed into the car ahead of them, not stopping in time or were not able to avoid an accident. Within seconds, there was a nine-car accident on I-95.

Damn, who are these guys? thought Davin, reaching for his gun as he weaved though traffic.

The Chevy was not closing fast, but he was closing.

What in holy hell has he got in that thing? wondered Davin as he realized the traffic wasn't moving as he approached PGA Boulevard. His seeing a lot of flashing red and blue lights indicated there might be an accident up ahead, and at 125 miles per hour, he had to make a decision real quick. Looking up in his mirror, he saw a car had come back on the highway and was closing in on the Chevy.

What now? thought Davin, seeing that it was the black Ford. It pulled up behind the Chevy and started to shoot at them. The Chevy's gunner immediately turned and returned fire at the Ford.

Suddenly, the black Ford slowed and pulled over to the side and stopped, with smoke pouring out from the engine compartment.

Without much of a hesitation, the Chevy's gunner turned and resumed firing at Davin's BMW. The range was about fifty yards, so the gunner was not scoring any hits, but the distance between the two vehicles was closing rapidly.

"I've had enough of this!" Davin yelled as he slammed on his brakes and skidded to a stop on the side of the road. He jumped out of his car, ran about twenty feet back down the road, and jumped into a culvert. He took careful aim at the Chevy as it closed in on him.

He waited, and waited. The Chevy pressed on, firing at Davin as it got closer, coming on like the charge of the Light Brigade. He waited still. *Don't fire until you see the whites of their eyes.* Davin wasn't waiting that long. He must be crazy, going up against a shotgun with a pistol.

He fired three shots rapidly at the oncoming car. Then he rolled to the left and fired three more of the heavy .45-caliber rounds into the oncoming car.

Steam and water exploded from the front of the Chevy as two bullets smashed into the radiator.

A split second later, the entire windshield disappeared, throwing glass into the faces of the driver and his gunman, but they pressed on. The gunman was firing wildly in Davin's general direction, but with no success.

Davin's fourth shot hit the left front tire, blowing it out and causing the Chevy to swerve to the left and flip into the median. It flipped several more times before finally landing on its top. Before Davin could get up, the Chevy exploded in a large orange ball of fire. His last two shots had smashed into the side of the Chevy as it swerved and started to roll.

Looking back down I-95, then over to the burning Chevy, Davin ran back to his car, jumped in, slammed the BMW in gear, and accelerated, spinning the car around and heading the wrong way down I-95 toward the Ford. The traffic was nonexistent in the northbound lane because of the nine-car accident just south of them that was caused by the Chevy.

The Ford was smoking from the engine compartment and idling roughly.

Davin jumped out of the BMW and ran over to the smoking car, stopping just short of the driver's door, with his gun leveled at the window.

"Throw out your gun and get out slowly!" Davin yelled toward the Ford.

There was no response. All was quiet, very quiet, and he didn't like that at all.

"Throw out your gun, *now*" he yelled again, waiting for a response. "I will count to three, then I will open fire. THROW OUT YOUR GUN, NOW!" He ignored the sirens that were approaching from the south.

"Okay, okay, don't shoot," a weak female voice from inside the Ford replied.

A large-caliber revolver dropped out the partially opened tinted window and fell to the ground.

"Damn it!" Davin said to himself for being caught in a situation like this. "Okay, now get out slowly!" he ordered.

"I can't," replied the weak voice in the car.

Holy shit, what now? he thought. The smoke and steam from the engine were now pouring out and making it difficult to see around the Ford.

Taking a chance, Davin moved slowly toward the Ford, never lowering the Colt Commander. He slowly reached out and opened the door.

"Damn!" he exclaimed as he looked at the driver leaning over the steering wheel bleeding from a wound to her left shoulder.

"Hi, honey. Sorry about the car. I think I've ruined this outfit too. Could you be a doll and undo my seat belt? I seem to have my hands full," she said weakly, but with a little smile, holding a blood-soaked handkerchief on the wound.

Without giving it a second thought, Davin put his gun in his belt and helped her out of the car. The jumpsuit was tight and unzipped almost to the waist, so she could get a handkerchief to the wound. After getting her safely out of the car, he laid her down beside the BMW.

"Damn, lady, why didn't you tell me you had been shot?"

"Oh, it's not bad. I'm in better shape than my car," she said. The wound looked worse than it really was; she had lost a lot of blood. "Where are the bad guys?"

Without saying a word, just looking over his shoulder, Davin looked briefly down the road at the burning Chevy.

"Did I get lucky, or is that your handiwork?" she asked.

"I got lucky, but thanks for the help."

"Good, but the report on this one will take days to fill out."

"Let's not worry about reports and get you to a hospital. St. Mary's isn't far from here."

She didn't say anything, just smiled. She needed medical attention, or she would bleed to death.

After picking her up and gently placing her in his car, he placed a blanket around her to keep her warm and to prevent shock. He ran back to her car, grabbed her gun and purse, and got in the BMW.

Two police cars pulled up just as Davin climbed back into his car. One officer stopped in front of the BMW and jumped out, weapon drawn and aimed at Davin.

"Hold it right there, Mister!" the cop yelled.

"Officer, I've got a wounded lady in here. Can we discuss this later? Right now I need to get her to the hospital!" Davin yelled back.

The officer approached carefully, without lowering his weapon, and looked inside the BMW.

"Davin, what are you doing here?" the officer asked, recognizing who was in the car.

"I'll explain later, Rex. Right now she needs medical attention, now! I'll answer all your questions at the hospital," Davin said to his friend Rex Wyman of the Palm Beach Police Department and next-door neighbor.

"Davin, follow me. I'll escort you and the lady to the hospital," Rex said. Then to his companion, he said, "Carol, stay here till the fire department arrives. I'm going to the hospital with Mr. Pierce and friend." He turned and ran back to his patrol car, and the two cars sped off.

Officer Rex Wyman called the hospital and his station to report the incident and request assistance. About two miles from where he left the Ford, two more patrol cars intercepted them and helped clear traffic to the hospital.

Within twenty minutes, they were in the emergency room, with the blonde being cared for and Davin talking to the officer about what had happened.

"Mr. Pierce, I'm Lieutenant Brown, North Palm Beach Police, and this is Agent Price of the FBI. May we talk to you in private?" Lieutenant Brown asked as he entered the waiting room, holding out his badge. "Thank you, Officer. I'll take over from here."

"See you later, Davin." Officer Wyman turned and left. Lieutenant Brown looked concerned, and the FBI guy, well, Davin couldn't make out what his problem was.

"Mr. Pierce, do you know who she is?" asked Agent George Price.

"No, we hadn't really met, and there wasn't much time for introductions in her present condition," Davin said sarcastically.

"Well, sir, she's Agent Connie Young from my office. What I would like to know, right now, is what the hell happened?"

"Calm down a sec, Price. I didn't shoot her, and I don't know what's going on either. But I do know how she got shot, and that I'll tell you."

"Okay, I'm all ears, Mr. Pierce," Price said as he looked closely at Davin Pierce.

"Just a minute. I have a few questions I need answers for, Mr. Price. First, what is the FBI doing following me? And second, who were those guys with the shotgun?" Davin demanded a little too loud, getting the attention of the nurse across the room.

"I think we can answer all your questions, Mr. Pierce, when Connie is awake, but first, tell us what you know of the shooting, so Lieutenant Brown can get on with his job. You and I can cover the fine points with Connie," Agent Price said in a more controlled manner, taking a seat in the corner. The emergency room was starting to get crowded with injured people, most likely from the accident caused by the Chevy.

"Okay," Davin said with a little more civil tone, sitting down across from Price and Brown.

"Thank you. Now, what happened?" asked Lieutenant Brown quietly.

Davin related his story about the Chevy and the Ford, her car, and the I-95 shoot-out. He asked about the accident victims and tried to cover everything about the last two hours. There were three dead and twenty-eight injured in the accident, which finally ended with eighteen cars and four trucks involved and causing a massive traffic jam.

Just as he was finishing, the doctor came out of the treatment room and walked over to the three in the corner talking.

All three stood up as the doctor came over, with a question on their tongues, the same question.

"Well," asked Davin first, "how is she, Doc?"

"She'll be all right. The wound wasn't as bad as it looked. Shotgun wounds are always nasty. She will sleep for about an hour or so, and then with a change of bandage, she can go home to rest if she wants to. I'll call you when she wakes up."

"Thanks, Doc," Price said.

Lieutenant Brown finished with his questions and asked if Davin would come down to the station later to sign a statement.

"Thanks, Lieutenant Brown. I'll stop in tomorrow morning, if that's okay."

"Fine, see you then. Good day, Price," Brown said as he turned and left.

"Price, why don't we step next door for a cup of coffee or something? I'll tell the doc where we are so he can reach us," Davin said.

"Sounds good to me. Let's go," Price said.

There was a little coffee shop on the corner about a block from the hospital. After about an hour or so of their talking and drinking coffee, the waitress came over to tell them the hospital had called and their friend had awakened. Price paid the tab, and they headed back to the hospital.

Washington DC
Office of Admiral Jacobs
1700 Hours

"Okay, okay, General. We have dispatched the *Nimitz* carrier group to the South Atlantic. They have a battalion of Marines and two companies of SEALs on board," Admiral Jacobs commented to General Walter Faint, Commanding Officer of the 101st Airborne Division. He and Jacobs were discussing the situation in Nigeria.

This was a problem that had the United States worried; the country was in a state of war and had threatened the US and the Soviet Union with a major terrorist act if either interfered with their affairs. "The tension in the White House over Nigeria is mounting. The president feels this could be another Vietnam or Iraq, if they push it too far," Faint said between sips of his coffee.

"But a Nam that can grow into a worldwide conflict, if we are not careful. One that will make Nam and Korea look like a picnic," Jacobs stated.

"Yeah, well, the 101st is ready, but I hope we will not be called," Faint was saying. "That little party in Iraq in '91 and again in '92, and in Libya in '94 and '95, took its toll on men and equipment. They need a break! Damn, it almost seems that the good old US of A is becoming the world's policeman."

"You know, you are right, General. But maybe that is the way it should be. The Soviets are now our friends, and well, they couldn't last in a war against us. That was proven in Iraq. So they may as well join us and become world cops too."

"Sounds good to me."

St. Mary's Hospital
1830 Hours

When Davin Pierce and Agent George Price got back to the hospital, they were directed to the recovery room, where they found Connie sitting up in bed, drinking some orange juice and talking quietly with a nurse.

"Hi, George, and Tall-Dark-and-Handsome. Where have you been all my life?" she said as the two walked in.

"Hell, I guess you're ready to get out and maybe answer some questions?" Agent Price asked as he and Davin entered the room.

"Not right now or here. They said if I promised not to rough up this wound, I could get out of here, but I have a major problem, guys," Connie said, looking sadly down at the hospital nightgown she had on. "That was a new jumpsuit too. Damn."

"I'll run over to your apartment and get you something to wear," George volunteered.

"No, the nurse called my sister and she is already on her way to the mall to pick up an outfit I had on layaway. She should be here any minute. It's just that I just paid one hundred bucks for that outfit and now it's ruined."

"Well, is there anything we can do for you?" asked George.

"Yeah, there is, come to think of it, George. That old Ford you signed out to me is in bad need of replacement. I think I got it killed today. Can I pick out my own car now? I won't spend too much, okay, George? Please...," Connie said in the sexiest voice she could, turning her head slightly and smiling.

"Oh, okay, but not before I see it and give the final okay. Deal?"

"Deal. Now, get out of here while I get dressed," Connie said as her sister came through the door. "Hi, Julie."

"Connie, are you all right?" Julie asked excitedly.

"I'll be fine. It's just a small scratch. Give me a hug."

"Are you sure you are going to be okay?" Julie insisted.

"The doctor is sure enough to let me out of here, so yeah, I will be okay. Now, don't worry."

"Hey, big sisters worry."

About fifteen minutes later, Connie was wheeled out of the recovery room and was heading out the door with George Price, Davin Pierce, and Julie pushing the wheelchair.

Connie talked quietly with her sister for a moment, and then she turned toward Davin.

"Davin, I can call you Davin, can't I?" Connie asked and got a nod and a smile from Davin. "I will answer your questions if you drive me home. Julie has to go back to work."

"I'll drive you home, but you don't have to answer questions if you aren't up to it."

"Great." She paused and turned toward her sister. "Julie, I'll call you later. Thanks for running out here so fast."

"Hey, Connie, what are big sisters for, anyway? You just take care of yourself, and please stay away from loaded guns, okay?"

"Okay, love ya."

"Bye! Now, call me soon," Julie said as she walked toward her car. Davin followed to retrieve his car.

Minutes later, Davin and George helped Connie into the BMW and strapped her in. Davin turned toward George, and with a puzzled look on his face, he stared off into the distance for a moment.

"What is it, Davin?"

"Oh, nothing, I just had a bad thought about today."

"Have you got your gun?" asked George.

"Yeah. Why?"

"Well, someone tried to use you for target practice once. They might try again. Do you want me to assign some protection for a few days?"

"Not right now, George, but give me your number just in case."

"Here's my card, and Connie can reach me through a few unlisted numbers if needed."

"Thanks, George. We'll be talking again soon," Davin said as he got into the car.

George waved as the car pulled away. As Davin turned the corner, George waved again, but this time to another car sitting in the parking lot nearby. Immediately, the car moved out of the parking lot, following Davin and Connie at a safe distance. George was not going to take any chances this time.

"Davin, I don't really want to be alone this afternoon. Can we go over to your place and talk?" Connie asked as they pulled out of the parking lot.

"Sure. Sounds fine to me," Davin said as he turned north on US-1.

Forty minutes later, Davin and Connie pulled into his driveway. Davin lived in North Palm Beach, an exclusive area of expensive homes, quiet streets, and neighbors that left him alone. His house was relatively modest, with a private drive, lots of trees, and very secluded, located on about a half-acre of land on a deep canal where he wished he could park his boat. But until he finished rebuilding his dock, the boat had to stay at the marina.

"Come on inside, Connie." He stopped for a moment. "Do you need some help?"

"Thank you. No, I can manage, Davin," Connie said as she got out of the car and made her way to the door of the house. "I've been dying to see the inside of your home. For days, all I've seen is the outside."

After they went inside, a light-blue Porsche with a young man and woman inside pulled up and stopped across the street. Davin saw them but didn't pay them much attention. Once Davin and Connie were out of sight, the driver turned on his surveillance equipment. "Apple 1, this is Blue Bird. Target is in nest," the woman in the Porsche radioed the report to the FBI office in Palm Beach.

"Be advised that his visitor is not part of the plan," the radio cracked.

"Roger," the woman responded. Then to her driver, she said, "What do we do now?"

"Leave and try again later," he answered.

"Okay," she said. She picked up the microphone and said, "Apple 1, this is Blue Bird. Mission abort. We are leaving the area. Out."

"Roger," was all that was said. The blue Porsche started its engine and drove away.

"Care for a drink?" asked Davin politely, ignoring her comment.

"Sure, some white wine would be nice, but the doc said no booze for a few days. Too many drugs pumped in me by the doc. So maybe a little OJ or a Coke," Connie said as she looked around the living room and out to the pool beyond the sliding glass doors. "This is very nice. Kinda big for one person."

"It only seems big until Phoenix shows up."

"Phoenix, strange name," Connie said. Then she thought, *I don't remember seeing another person. Maybe she's out of town. The fax didn't say anything about a wife or live-in girlfriend.*

Davin headed into the kitchen as Connie walked into the family room and started checking out every inch of the room.

"Is she here?" Connie asked, hoping not to get a positive answer.

"What?" Davin responded.

"Is Phoenix here?"

"Yeah, somewhere. She usually can be found on my bed. Can't seem to keep her out of there."

"Your bed, huh?" Connie replied, then thought to herself, *A sex kitten. What kind of bimbo is this girl?*

"Make yourself comfortable, Connie."

"Maybe I shouldn't be here."

"Why not? I don't mind. Phoenix will just love you."

"Are you sure Phoenix won't mind?"

"Why should she?"

Connie said, "Most girlfriends—"

"Girlfriend?" Davin interrupted, starting to laugh. "Phoenix is not my girlfriend. She's my cat."

"A cat! You've got a cat? Where is she?" Connie asked as she sat down on the sofa.

"She's an it. I don't know where she is right now, but be assured, once she makes an appearance, look out."

"What kind of cat is Phoenix?"

"Hell, I don't know. Kinda a mixture of everything, I suppose. I take it you like cats, too?"

"Yeah, I guess you could say that."

"Here, I don't have any OJ, and you said you would prefer wine, so here is a little near-wine—white grape juice, lightly chilled, clear golden color, excellent fragrance, vintage unknown. I hope you like it," Davin said, handing her a tall glass.

"I'm sure I will." Then after taking a sip, she added, "Yes, very good choice, Davin. Light, full-bodied, excellent choice." Connie gave a small laugh. "I shouldn't laugh. It hurts when I laugh. May we sit on the patio by the pool?" she asked as she got up and walked out through the sliding glass doors. She kicked off her shoes as she stepped onto the patio. "This is great. Do you have many parties out here?"

"Sure, and yes, a few."

Connie sat with her back to the sun, facing Davin, who sat in a lounge chair near the pool's edge. It was a beautiful day for April. No rain, a few clouds, and a temperature of about eighty-eight degrees. A light breeze made it very pleasant.

"What time is it?" Connie asked.

"It's almost seven," Davin replied. "Okay, Connie what is going on? Why were you following me? And why is the Palm Beach FBI involved?"

"The Washington office heard you were hired to investigate the appearance of weapons from the *MaryJean*. We, the Palm Beach office, were asked to watch you and find out what you already know. George told me this morning that he received a call from Jack Malone and we are now to assist you in the investigation of the *MaryJean* weapons case. It seems that you are a close friend of his, and he felt that you might need some government pull to open doors or whatever. George said to give you all the help that I could," Connie said in her sexy little voice, a voice that would melt butter—it was so smooth.

"Do you know Jack?"

"Jack and I met about a year ago on a little assignment in New Mexico. We have been good friends ever since," Connie said as she started to unbutton her blouse to allow the sun to warm her.

Connie undid the ribbon in her golden blond hair, and as it came undone, she bent over at the waist to shake out the tangles, then stood straight up again quickly with a little bounce.

"Davin, why don't you get out of those hot clothes and relax?" Connie suggested.

Connie lay down on the chaise lounge next to Davin. Davin got up and headed in the house. *This is unbelievable,* he thought as he started in.

"Where are you going?" Connie asked.

"To get more near-wine for you, and I seem to have emptied my glass," Davin said nervously. *Boy, what a day this has turned out to be!* he thought.

"Hurry back and get comfortable. I don't bite, nibble a little maybe," she teased.

Once inside, Davin called Stephanie at her home for any messages he might have received before she left the office. He also asked her to call Jack Malone in Washington to have him run a check on a Connie Young of the Palm Beach office. He needed the information on Connie today, so he was to call him back as soon as possible and leave a message on his machine. He would be in the office in the morning and really didn't want to be disturbed tonight.

Palm Beach Marina
Josh Randal's Boat
2100 Hours

Josh went below to answer his cellular phone, which had just begun its annoying little ring.

"Yo, you got me, speak your mind, you're running out of time. Beep. This is not a recording!" Josh said into the phone and then paused, getting a very concerned look on his face. "Oh, right, boss… okay, will do." Another pause while he listened. "Okay, by noon tomorrow. No way! But Pierce is a friend!" He paused to listen. "Yes, I know where he started…yeah. You know, he is not going to stop just because you say so…right, sir. Life does go on and on and on. Good night," Josh said then hung up by tossing the phone on the sofa. "Damn him!"

Twenty minutes later, Josh was cruising out the inlet toward open sea. He needed time to think before he called his friend Davin. The power of his boat soon became evident when he cleared the channel and pushed the throttles forward to the stops.

As he sped along, he thought, *How the hell did the chief know Pierce was working the* MaryJean *case? I just found out this morning. And why did the chief want me to stop him? Something ain't cool in paradise!*

Davin's House
Palm Beach
2100 Hours

Davin went into his bedroom, stripped down, and stepped into the shower to rinse off the dirt from the I-95 shoot-out. Moments later, he had slipped into his bathing suit and left the room. Entering the kitchen, he refilled his glass and put some wine in an ice bucket and started out to the patio. About halfway to the patio, he stopped and looked out at the vision of loveliness on the lounge. This was a dream come true: wine, woman—what a woman, too—and soft music. Soft music, that was what was missing. Davin turned to the stereo and put on some easy listening music, a station that played music more and commercials less. Once he was satisfied with the music and his composure, he went back outside.

He found Connie sound asleep in the lounge chair, with Phoenix curled up at her feet, so he sat and drank his wine, admiring this beautiful lady and wondering what was going on that would cause someone to try to kill him.

Connie slept almost two hours by the pool. Davin had covered her with a light blanket so she wouldn't burn.

It was 9:15 p.m., and they were talking quietly on the sofa when the phone rang. Davin reluctantly got up and picked up the phone on the table beside the sofa, hoping it was Stephanie.

Click. Then a dial tone was all he heard. Looking at the receiver, he slowly returned it to the cradle.

Two minutes later, the phone rang again. Reluctantly he got up, and after the fourth ring, he picked up the receiver. "Hello!"

"The true story about the *MaryJean* can be known, but the price is high," the voice said.

"Who is this? What do you mean the true story?" Davin insisted.

"Can't talk now. I'll call again," came the reply, and then a dial tone.

Looking strangely at the receiver, Davin shook his head in disbelief. What did he mean the true story? Did he have something that could put the puzzle together? And if so, what did he want in return? And was it worth it?

"What is it, babe?" Connie asked, noticing his expression.

"I didn't tell you earlier, but I received a note telling me to stay away from the *MaryJean*. And now this call offering to sell me information about the *MaryJean*."

"Do you have any idea who it is?"

"No," he answered but was cut short by the phone ringing again.

"Hello!" he yelled into the receiver as he answered it on the first ring.

"Hi, Davin, Stephanie here," came the answer on the other end. "What's wrong? You sound frazzled."

"Oh, hi, sorry. Nothing's wrong. What did you find out?" Davin said as he calmed down a little. "I'm fine, just tired," he added, lying to spare her.

"Okay, well, I got ahold of Jack and he said that Connie is one trustworthy agent. She saved his life in New Mexico when the sting went bad. She has also been on several other operations where she really was an asset. He said that her method of operation may not be by the book, but she gets the job done. Oh, he also said to treat her right, or else."

"Thanks! See you tomorrow," Davin said quietly then hung up the phone.

"I sure hope we aren't bothered with that phone all night," Connie said with a hint of hope in her voice. "Can we get something to eat, Davin?" she asked half-heartedly.

"Sure. What would you like?"

"Pizza, with lots of cheese and pepperoni."

"Okay, I'll call for one."

Davin called the nearest pizza shop and ordered one medium pizza, which would arrive in about thirty minutes. But long before the pizza arrived, Connie fell asleep again on the sofa. This time it looked like she was out for the night.

The night was short, and dawn broke in her normal spectacular way. It was a little cool when Connie and he left the house; he was going to drop her off at her apartment on his way to his office. She lived on Singer Island, about a mile north of his office, so it wasn't much out of his way. Connie answered most of his questions on the way to her apartment and agreed to rest today, except for a few phone calls to research the crew and passengers of the *MaryJean*. She would use whatever systems were available to get everything possible.

After dropping Connie off, he proceeded to his office to pick up Stephanie.

He didn't see the Porsche across the street from his house when they left. He did, however, see a tan Corvette pull up and park across from his office. A tanned young redhead climbed out and headed for the white sand. It was kind of early, but some people liked to start early on those tans.

Being single in the Palm Beaches has its advantages, Connie and Stephanie for example, he thought. *But it also has its disadvantages.* But he couldn't think of any right now.

Chapter 5

DEEP COVER

"Okay, Jack, calm down, calm down. What's wrong now?"

"To start with, ole buddy, I think our plan to scare off Davin Pierce just took a shit," Jack said into the phone.

"What do you mean our plan? You're in charge of protection, and what you are protecting is your own ass and this whole operation. If you can't stop him and anyone else who gets in the way, then maybe we need to replace you," the voice responded with a bit of feeling and change in tone.

"Don't threaten me, Senator. You got to where you are now with this operation. Now, don't pull any crap. If it falls, we all fall!" Jack yelled into the phone.

"Okay, Jack, don't get so worked up. I understand what you are saying. What is he doing now?" the senator asked quietly.

"Sleeping, I guess. I haven't received my morning report yet. But don't you worry, Senator. Davin Pierce won't get close enough to hurt the operation."

"You better hope he doesn't!" the senator said quietly and then hung up.

Jack just sat there thinking for a few moments before he hung up his phone. Davin was a friend and he did not want to see him killed, but if he got too close, he would be. Jack had sacrificed a lot to complete this assignment, and now he was being put in a position that could get a friend killed. It had taken years to get this deep in the organization, and to blow it now could mean many more people would die needlessly. Too many people had died already. He wanted the members of the organization to pay for their crimes, and the only way was to follow through on his assignment as planned. Besides, the only way out of the organization was to die. There was no quitting and walking away, not in this organization. He was trapped.

Jack had joined the organization early in his career as a FBI agent. When a young field agent, he accidentally had come across information that led him to the head of what he thought was a small gunrunning operation. During a raid on a warehouse and the suspected operation, Jack found himself surrounded by bad agents and ex-military that had helped organize the raid. They wanted Jack in a position to recruit him into the organization. Jack was given one and only one deal: join or die. But before dying, he would get the unique opportunity to watch his wife, son, and daughter die. That was eight years ago; his wife had died three years ago, and his kids were now grown, with lives of their own. But back then he had no choice. To save his family, he agreed to cooperate, but he never really went over to the organization. Working both sides of the fence as a deep operative, Jack had saved his family and was collecting information for the FBI that would see the end of this large corrupt organization of crime. Now he was working to destroy the organization from within.

Only two people knew of his involvement, the director of the FBI, John Sampson, and the director of the CIA, Samuel Harrison. As long as nobody was getting killed, Jack was to stay deep and collect as much evidence as possible. No drugs were involved, at least not yet, just a simple black market ring selling to all the third world countries.

Jack was put in a hard position; he had to keep Davin alive without blowing his own cover. Jack was in charge of protection for the organization, and he might be ordered to have Davin killed if he got too close. He had almost enough information to close down the operation, but the list of members was not complete and he needed more time.

Palm Beach
April 18, 1996
0900 Hours

Josh Randel crossed Davin's mind. Now here was a man who played with fire and someday would get burned. Being a member of the company gave him a lot of chances to die, and without warning. Davin would stop by to see him again today, after getting back from Miami. Josh was a man of many resources and, when asked, could produce the information desired, and usually when you needed it.

"Good morning, Davin. Did you stay up too late again last night?" she said, handing him his coffee.

"Good morning, Stephanie. Are you ready to go? Got your bikini?"

"Yes. It's in my purse. It doesn't take up much room. Oh, Mr. Goode called. He wants to hear from you this week, or he will tow that garbage scow of yours out and sink it for a new reef."

"Call him back and tell him that garbage scow is just a little run-down, and as soon as I get the chance, I'll get my dock fixed so I can move it to my place. And tell that scumbag that if he had any... well, never mind. I'll call him after this meeting. Or better yet have him meet me, or better yet have him meet *us* for lunch on Thursday."

"Roger, boss. And by the way, Jane's in your office. Thanks for the invite."

"Hell, I probably owe you a million lunches. It's about time I started to pay you back," he said, turning to enter his office.

"How 'bout dinner sometime? That'll get rid of quite a few lunches."

"Okay, okay, soon," Davin said, looking strangely at a piece of mail before tossing it on his desk. He'd read it later.

"Hi, Jane. What you got for me?"

"Not a whole lot, really, but look at this," Jane said as she rolled out a chart of the North Atlantic. Jane was a tomboyish five foot, four inch, average-looking girl who never used makeup, preferring a natural look. Her long hair was pulled back into a ponytail so she could easily put on her motorcycle helmet, which was sitting on the edge of Davin's desk. She had a way of getting things done and didn't worry about how she did it. She stood over Davin's desk, studying a map of the North Atlantic Ocean and its surrounding countries.

"Her last known position was here," Jane said as she leaned over the desk and pointed to an X she had put on the chart. "Well, taking in all the variables we could think of puts her inside of this area here without any power," she said, pointing to a circle around the X. She could have gone anywhere if she had any power at all."

"Okay, now, if she had power, where is the nearest safe harbor back in '43?"

"Anywhere along this coast," Jane said, pointing to the coast of Spain, Portugal, and the coast of Northern Africa as a long shot.

"These are known safe dockage. A military base is here now, and these are resorts," she added, pointing again to the coast near South Spain.

"Anything else?"

"Yes. The *MaryJean*'s manifest indicated war materials and medical supplies, and of course, those mystery crates with guards. In checking the list that I found and the capacity of her class of ship, all indicates to me that she was way overloaded from the start. Almost as if she had two manifests, maybe."

"Very interesting. Follow up on that and get back to me as soon as you can confirm that. Check on flights for two to each area. We might have to do a little personal research."

"Great! See you in a couple of days," she said as she rolled up the charts.

His thoughts wandered between Connie and the *MaryJean*. The information she had on the weapons raid was interesting. It seemed that not all the cargo had been accounted for, which raised the question, Where is the rest? On the bottom of the ocean, sold to rebels, in another warehouse, where? Wherever it was, it was now his job to find it or at least find out what happened to it.

Starting for the door, Davin stopped and went back to his desk. He picked up the envelope he had tossed on his desk and put it in his pocket.

Ponce De Leon Hospital, Emergency Room
Tampa, Florida
April 18, 1996
2100 Hours

"Doc, is he going to be all right?" asked the pretty young redheaded girl as she approached the nurse's station hurriedly. She was directing her question to Dr. Thomas Eden as he reviewed a chart at the nurse's station.

"Who? Is who going to be all right?" Dr. Eden asked in return with a puzzled look.

"Sorry, Doc. Is Donald Peterson going to be okay? I got here as fast as I could. Is he all right? Please say he is," the young redhead asked again.

"Miss…ah…" Waiting for a name, he received none. "Miss, we don't have a Donald Peterson, just a John Doe, which may be your Donald. If that is he, then yes, he will be okay. Would you please follow me? Maybe you can identify him for us. He's resting down the hall." Dr. Eden came out from behind the nurse's station and led the redhead down the hall.

"Thank you, sir. Thank you," she said quietly.

"I didn't get your name, miss?" Dr. Eden asked politely.

"Oh, sorry. I'm Joanne Morris. Donald is my boyfriend," Ms. Morris said as the walked down the hall.

"I must warn you, Donald doesn't look very good right now. He is in a pretty bad shape. I must say that whoever did this to him should be locked up for a long time."

"Wait, are you saying he was beaten? I thought he was in an auto accident," Ms. Morris asked.

"He was, but not before someone worked him over real good. The beating almost killed him. The auto accident was staged, or maybe he was trying to get away from his attackers and ran off the road. We don't know for sure," Dr. Eden replied.

They stopped at the door to intensive care. "Are you sure you are up to this?" Dr. Eden asked. "He is not a pretty sight." She nodded in response. "Okay, put this on," he said, handing her a mask and white surgical robe.

Upon entering the small cubicle that housed the battered body of Donald Peterson, Ms. Morris took one look and fainted dead away. Dr. Eden was quick enough to catch her and called a nurse to assist in carrying her out to the waiting room.

Once in the waiting room, she slowly recovered and began to cry uncontrollably.

"Nurse, bring me a mild sedative," Dr. Eden ordered.

It took twenty minutes to calm her down, and then she began to talk slowly.

"Doctor, will he really be all right?" she asked.

"Yes, though it will take time. Is that Donald in there?" he asked quietly.

"Yes, I think so. But he is so…so…" Her voice trailed off to nothing. "Who would want to hurt Donny? Who?"

"That is something the police will want to know," Dr. Eden said, trying to calm her. "Nurse, bring her a cup of coffee, black."

I-95 Southbound to Miami
April 19, 1996
0830 Hours

The drive to Miami was uneventful, and the interview with Johnson didn't turn up any more clues. His story was almost identical to the colonel's. The sub that had surfaced to finish them off with the deck gun was marked, and he could remember that one as if it were yesterday. The U-boat had a large U-49 painted on an all-black surface.

The interview was done by noon, and after a little lunch, they drove on down to Miami Beach for some sun and relaxation.

Stephanie hadn't lied about the bikini. There was more material in a handkerchief. It was smaller than the one Josh gave her. The bottom was a French thong, and the top string covered enough to make it interesting. She filled out the suit better than he had imagined. Davin really didn't know Stephanie as well as he should, and seeing her in that tiny string bikini convinced him that they really should spend more time together. The only problem was his golden rule of not dating his employees.

As they relaxed, Davin remembered the envelope and removed it from his tote bag. He looked at it and then tore it open. The envelope had no return address and was postmarked West End, Bahamas, dated April 4. Inside he found an old piece of paper, one that looked like it was torn out of a ledger or a book of sorts.

Davin carefully unfolded the page and stared at it with a shocked look.

"Holy mother of pearl," he murmured.

"What is it?" Stephanie asked, looking at Davin inquisitively.

"I'm not sure, but this, if real, could change the whole scene of the *MaryJean* mystery."

"Well, are you going to enlighten me, or do I have to beat it out of you?"

"Oh, no, just a minute, though, while I read this," Davin said in amazement as he read.

After what seemed like hours but really was only a few minutes, Davin looked up from the page and then over to Stephanie. "Okay, what is it, Davin?" she asked again.

"According to this, which as I said earlier, if it's for real, well, this could possibly be a page from the captain's log off the *MaryJean*. And if so, it could prove that the *MaryJean* didn't sink when everyone thinks she did," he said, handing her the page.

"How?" Stephanie asked.

"Look at the date and signature."

"January 24, 1943. I can't make out the signature. What's wrong with it?"

"Well, the *MaryJean* was supposed to have sunk on January 19, 1943, according to the report Bronsly turned in. This page from the log says the twentieth, which means someone may have been still alive on the ship for another day after she was abandoned. Someone stupid enough to continue log entries, or Bronsly screwed up the dates. Wait…here's a note…" He paused to read. "It says here that this is a sample of the information that is for sale. The buying of the information may save a life, mine. Details will arrive soon, signed, 'a friend.' What do you make of that?"

"I don't know. Sounds pretty scary to me!"

"I think we had better get back, let's say in a half hour, and then home."

"Okay by me."

Chapter 6

IN SEARCH OF THE PAST

The Sailboat Ghostfinder II
Off the Coast of Nigeria, Africa
April 18, 1996
0900 Hours, Greenwich Mean Time (GMT)

"Hey, Sam, we're getting a strong signal here. Bring her around for another pass," Roger McKinney called out from below. It was his turn in the hole.

"Roger, Roger!" came the reply from the helm.

"What ya got, honey?" asked Penny Collins as she bounced down the ladder to the "hole," as it was referred to. The hole was actually the control station for some highly sophisticated electronic underwater scanning equipment that was designed to locate shipwrecks of all types and at depths of up to three thousand feet.

Penny wore her normal summer-morning string bikini bottom and a pair of Ray-Bans as she leaned over the console that Roger was working. She was here, like the rest, to locate and identify sunken ships.

"Look at this, love," Roger said, pointing to the screen on the console. "What do you make of that? You're the metal expert."

"Not real big, but all in one piece," Penny commented as she typed a command on the computer. "Computer says it is mostly steel."

Roger turned slightly and started entering commands on another terminal to his left. "Sam, drop the hook anywhere along here!" Roger yelled to the helm.

"Ken, drop the hook!" Sam yelled to the bow. Samantha Frederick, Sam for short, sat at the helm with nothing on but a smile, a pair of Ray-Bans, and suntan lotion. She loved the sun, the sea, and sailing.

She and Ken had met while studying electrical engineering and computers at the University of Miami and hadn't been separated since.

"Anchor away!" Ken yelled and ran to assist Sam in securing the mainsail. They were working on a grant to search out and map shipwrecks for the Navy Department.

That was the cover story, anyway. In reality, they were running some sophisticated listening devices targeted for the Nigerian rebellion that had Washington sitting on pins and needles. As of today, they hadn't intercepted anything of importance, just low-level chatter and some troop movements, which just backed up some earlier reports. Their mission was to monitor and report any Soviet activity within the country and then get out as fast as they could.

As part of the cover story, they recently had discovered a new wreck, a German destroyer that looked like it took a torpedo in the engine room that put her on the bottom at 150 feet. They had not been able to identify her as yet, because they were not connected to the German archives in Munich.

For the past six months, the four of them had been sailing around the Atlantic, searching the shipping lanes, known battle areas, and anywhere a suspected wreck might be, building a foundation for the cover-up. The equipment on board was real and did do what it was supposed to do, find wrecks. It was designed by Ken and Roger and built under contract with the US Navy, called project *Ghostfinder*. The idea had been to build and test for two years by looking for and identifying shipwrecks in the Atlantic. Using this as a cover story, they should have free access to most of the waters of the world, or so they thought. This mission cover was highly publicized, and each time they entered a port for supplies, they made sure the local newspapers were aware of their arrival and departure and, of course, their next destination.

The equipment was designed to locate by means of metal detection, sonar, and various other electronic devices on board. Once a wreck or suspected wreck site was found, other probes would be lowered in the depths to test for iron deposits and water temperature and take samples to analyze. A video camera would be lowered to scan the wreck and photograph. Tests would determine age, radioactivity, if any, and size. Computer scans would determine the type of ship, and finally, if it was determined to be safe, they would dive on the wreck and get still photos and more videos, and possibly some artifact to help identify her. The electronic process took, for the most part, a full day, and it was usually determined to dive on the wreck on the second day.

"Hey, Rog, what'd you find for us today?" Ken asked as he and Sam looked down the hatch at Roger and Penny scanning the CRTs. "Something on the James Bond equipment, perhaps?"

"Nothing on the spook stuff, Ken, but we have ourselves a pretty intact wreck close by. Lower the camera and probe pack. I believe we have a hot one off the starboard side at about twenty yards and eighty feet down," Roger said, never looking up from the console.

"Roger, Rog," Ken said as he turned to set up the motorized probe and camera package. "Give me a hand, Sam."

"That must be her over there," Sam said, pointing to a dark spot about twenty yards out. "It's clear enough that we should be able to get some great videos."

"That does look like our target. Hold this…thanks…okay…ready," Ken said as they assembled the underwater probes and lowered them over the side. "Roger, you have the con."

"Got it!" Roger yelled as he started to guide the motorized camera and probe pack toward the wreck.

"Hey, guys, come and see this!" Penny yelled up the hatch.

"Damn, she's beautiful," Sam commented.

"Get the book on subs, Penny," Roger asked.

"One step ahead of you…ah…here it is…ah. She's a Gato-class attack sub. Ah…let's see…vintage 1940. It says here that they were built for operation in the Pacific against the Japanese. What the hell is she doing here?"

"Run the probe around her slowly, Rog," Ken requested.

"All slow to one-third, steady as she goes. I'm sure glad it's clear water. Wow! Look at the size of that cuda, must be six feet. Oh, well, does that book say anything about paint schemes? This boat seems to be painted all black, or is that just slime from sitting on the bottom so long?"

"Roger, you talk too much. That's gotta be slime. The Navy had only gray paint and no imagination. She looks pretty good. No damage so far. What's that? Oh, okay," Penny rattled on and saw a ray take off from the bottom beside the boat as the probe made its way down the port side.

"No markings," Roger commented.

"That's interesting," Sam thought out loud.

"Any adverse readings from the probe?" Ken questioned as he glanced over Roger's shoulder.

"Nothing yet!"

"Anyone hungry?" Sam asked as she walked over to the galley.

"Yeah. What are we gonna fix, Sam?" Ken asked.

"Since we still have some fresh veggies, how 'bout a salad and soup?"

"Sounds good. Need any help?" Ken offered.

"Sure. Let Penny and Roger run the probe and test."

Several hours went by after lunch as the probe continued to search and analyze the sub below them. Later analysis revealed that she was totally intact, and all indications showed that she was not flooded. A low amount of radiation was detected near the engine room. This was decided to be from the batteries, which, strangely enough, showed a low amount of radiation, indicating that they still had some life left, but not much and not for much longer.

Lagos, Nigeria, Africa
April 18, 1996
1030 Hours, GMT

General Hector Samula of the Nigerian Army, and head of the Secret Police, was sitting at the head of the large mahogany table, surrounded by his most trusted officers.

The look on Samula's face was not convincing. It seemed his little war was going poorly. The guerillas were not winning, and his hope to become the next president was slowly slipping down the drain.

Samula had been trained by the Soviets and worked his way up through the ranks, stepping on many of his peers and fellow countrymen in the process. But for all the toes he stepped on, he acquired several very loyal, close friends. Or more to the truth, other survivors, ones that felt that the only way to live was to join the efforts of Samula. Most of those friends sat around the table in front of him. Some, of course, were not here because of an unfortunate sudden accident, which most often had resulted in death. Others that were not here were on a vital mission leading his own guerilla forces to overthrow his government.

"Where are the federal troops, Mohammed?" Samula queried of his chief intelligence officer, Mohammed Achemi.

"Sir, most of what is left of the Third Battalion are held up in the hills outside the capital, waiting orders. The Second Battalion is a nonentity. They were destroyed, and what was left has been merged with the First, which is located at the port," Mohammed stated, showing very little concern.

"And the guerillas?" Samula continued.

"Our last reports show them moving in the vicinity of the capital. Sources indicate that they will be attempting to take the city in the next couple of days. We will know exactly when by morning, sir," Mohammed said and looked down the table to the only non-Nigerian member there.

"I see our money wasn't wasted by sending you to the United States to study at Harvard. Very good, Mohammed. Now, Mr.

Corning, do you have any comments?" Samula asked as he looked at the fifth man at the table. The other four members all turned to face Mr. Corning also.

"General, as you know, my country will support you in this overthrow. But we cannot condone terrorist acts against any country. And if you expect money and material, then you must forget about any terrorist plans that you may have. Understand, General—or should I say, Mr. President?—that my country will react quickly and in force if provoked," Mr. Corning replied.

"Mr. Corning, we appreciate everything your people are doing. We will curtail our terrorist activities outside our borders, but we do not have control of our neighboring countries…yet, anyway. We will work with you as best as possible, as always. Now, let's get the hell out of here," Samula said, changing his tone quickly from a quiet, soft, understanding voice to a harsh, demanding one. Then he stood, turned, and left the room. The meeting was over.

Ghostfinder II
Coast of Nigeria
April 18, 1996
1300 Hours, GMT

"Well, I think we've got all we can get from up here," Roger stated as he spun around in his chair. He started to make the computer link to various databases he had access to via commercial satellite links.

After several hours on the keyboard, running through all available records of missing subs, he stopped, put his hands on his lap, and quietly turned around to face his friends.

"Okay, Roger, tell us all you know. Is thirty seconds enough? Ha ha!" Ken spouted, and laughter rang out by all.

"Ha ha, almost, little man, almost. Well, let me tell you a story, a story so fantastic that I don't know that I believe it either," Roger began. "It seems that a long time ago, we had this submarine designed and built to exacting specifications, and when done, she was launched and then reported missing on her first and only voyage. The Navy didn't have a lot of time to search for her, and well, there was a war on, you know, and she was finally written off as MIA, like many other ships, planes, and people were."

"Is this the missing sub?" Penny interrupted.

"Let me finish. It gets better," he insisted. "Well, it is the government's way to cover mistakes, unanswered questions, and poor planning. In the case of the ships, it is easy to just say—after the required waiting period, of course—that she's lost and presumed missing and then eventually officially listed as MIA, or *missing in action* to you laymen. Now, according to the records I was able to obtain through our satellite link to the Navy's big computer and also to Lloyds of London, it would seem that our little friend out there is a real 'fer sure' MIA. From what I can piece together, her name is the *Wolverine*, the SS 701, last seen leaving New London, Connecticut, on January 2, 1943. There were several radio messages from her around March '43. But nothing or nobody has seen her since then."

"That's great!" Penny piped up.

"Wait a minute. That is just a theory. She could also be the *Shark* SS-707, which was lost on December 18, 1943, with her last reported position at about two hundred miles from here. Both are fleet-type submarines, known as Gato class, approximately 310 feet in length, and both were built around the same time. Their basic arsenal consisted of one three-inch deck gun mounted just forward of the sail. They also had a .50-caliber machine gun on the sail and two 20-millimeter Oerlikons. Belowdecks, they had ten twenty-one-inch torpedo tubes, six forward and four stern. Let's see what else I can tell you. Oh, yeah, a crew of sixty-five to seventy-four. They were powered by General Motors Diesels and electric motors, mounted in two separate engine rooms, and could cruise at twenty-one knots. Impressive for World War II technology."

"Yeah, impressive. But for sure, we have a real MIA and a boat that the Navy has been searching for since '43. Okay, in either case, the *Shark* or *Wolverine*, that boat is in too good a shape to have sat on the bottom for fifty years. Something ain't cool in the White House, if you expect me to believe that boat has been down for forty-plus years with little or no growth on her. Give me a break." Ken questioned Rogers's remarks.

"I agree, Ken, 100 percent. That boat has not been here for fifty years. My guess is that she hasn't been here for more than six months max. Come over here. I need to show you some of the results of the probe and the video. You ain't gonna believe it. Hell, I ran the tests and I don't. But they are, honest. Lookee here," Roger said as he handed Ken and the girls the test results and walked over to get a beer from the cooler.

"The Navy will be very interested in this, believe you me. When is the next chance that we can get a direct secure link to Washington?" Sam asked as she scanned the pages of computer printouts and photos.

"Somewhere around midnight from here, the satellite will be in the right orbit to give us about twenty minutes, unless we try Ma Bell's satellite—we can hit hers anytime from here," Ken replied. "Our phone bill is gonna be a monster after that bout with the computer link."

"Let's wait for Tweedy Bird and talk secure. Ma Bell's too easy to bust into, and I don't think the Navy wants everyone in the world to know about this boat. Especially since she is completely intact," Roger suggested between sips on his beer.

"Roger, let's leave the James Bond stuff on autoscan and record mode tonight. I'd like to spend time on the sub problem," Ken suggested.

"Sounds good to me. Maybe we can link up to the main computer in London again and get more info on her."

"No, that might alert the wrong people. I just want to run some tests on the hull and surrounding waters and try to find out how long she's been here."

"Right!"

"What time is it now?" Penny asked.

"Let's see. Mickey's big hand is...," Roger started.

"Ah, come on," Penny interrupted and started after Roger with a pillow to hit him with.

"Okay, okay, it's eight fifteen!" Roger yelled, running around the cabin and then up on deck, with Penny right behind.

Racing around the deck once, Roger dived overboard, leaving Penny on deck.

"Hey, big boy, I wasn't gonna hurt you."

"Water's great. Come on in!"

"Naw. Why don't you come on out?" she said as sexy as she could without breaking into a laugh. She removed the only bit of clothing she had on, the string bikini bottoms. Swinging them on her finger, she slowly walked forward to the bow.

The sun was on its way down, and light was fading fast. Roger swam over to the ladder and climbed on board, with hope of finding Penny shortly.

Penny lowered herself down the bow hatch to their stateroom, leaving her bikini bottoms beside the hatch, and lay on the bunk, waiting for Roger to return. Within a few minutes, Roger appeared over the hatch. Seeing her waiting on the bunk got his attention real quick.

Washington, DC
Central Intelligence Agency (CIA)
April 18, 1996
0935 Hours, Eastern Standard Time (EST)

"What's the latest from our man in Nigeria?" asked the gray-haired agent in Room 103. He had been with the company for fifteen years and had worked hard to get to where he was, chief of overseas operations, Europe and Africa zones. Fred Murphy was thirty-eight years old and had a family of three children, a wife of twelve years, and two dogs.

"Fred, our agent has not reported in today, but as of his last report, it looks like the government will fall, although not without a fight. Seems like those people don't know the meaning of *defeat*," Agent David Malone reported. Malone was young, full of desire and very new to the company, and the son of Jack Malone of the FBI. David did not know of his father's connection with the organization.

"Okay, David, keep me posted as to his progress," Fred asked.

"Right, sir," David said as he stood and left the office. Turning left, he headed for his own little office at the end of the long hall, Room 188. His phone was ringing as he approached; quickening his pace, he reached his office before the phone stopped ringing.

"Hello, Dave Malone."

"Hi, David. How are you?" the voice asked.

"Just fine, Dad. How's it with you and the FBI?" David asked as he recognized his father's voice. "What's up?"

"Not much, just that I'm going to be tied up on this new case and out of town for a couple of days. Would you stop by and check on the house and feed the fish?" Jack asked quietly.

"Sure, no problem, Dad. Anything else?"

"Oh, no, not right now. Got to run. I'll call in a couple of days."

"Okay, talk to you later. Bye!" David said.

"Bye, son. Love ya!" Jack said and hung up.

David slowly hung up his phone and sat behind his desk. Something seemed wrong, but he could not put his finger on it. His father seemed very stressed. Maybe it was the case he was working on; FBI work can be very stressful.

Ghostfinder II
April 19, 1996
0730 Hours, GMT

Morning came too early for all. The sunrise was the best they had seen in days, breaking over the blue Atlantic in a rainbow of colors that would make Kodak proud.

"What'd the Navy have to say about our little friend?" Roger asked as he stumbled into the galley.

"Oh, not much, just that we are to stay off her and not to attempt entering or anything else without assistance from them. Other than that, they said to wait for complete instructions at noon today, our time," Ken replied as he sat eating his breakfast. "They seemed real interested. There's some scrambled eggs and bacon over there for you."

"Did you sleep well?" Sam teased.

"Sleep, *sleep*, slept like a baby," Roger said as he helped himself to breakfast.

"Then we must have had some choppy seas last night," Ken said, continuing the teasing.

"I thought it was pretty calm," Roger returned.

"Calm! Why do you think I fixed scrambled eggs?" Ken retorted, laughing.

"That bad, huh?" Roger shook his head as if in disgrace.

"Yeah," Sam and Ken replied together.

"Sorry."

"No problem. How's Penny?" Sam asked.

"Still asleep."

"Can't imagine why!" Sam replied.

"Oh, by the way, the Nigerians got a little active last night, and we got some pretty good stuff," Sam commented as Roger ate.

"How so?"

"It seems the Libyans are moving some pretty heavy equipment into Nigeria to help combat the rebels. You know, tanks and a couple thousand troops."

"They said that over the air?" Roger asked, surprised. "The Libyans aren't that dumb."

"It wasn't the Libyans. It was the rebels reporting back to their command. Kinda nice intercepting their spy's traffic, huh?"

"More like luck. That equipment is better than I gave it credit," Roger commented.

After breakfast, Penny finally made an appearance. She looked refreshed and ready for almost anything.

"What's the good word?" Penny asked as she dished up some breakfast.

"Well," Ken stated, "today we dive. Are you two up to it?"

"What about the Navy?" Roger asked quietly.

"What about them? It's gonna take at least two days for the Navy to get here, and by then we should have some pretty good pictures and a complete layout of the boat—exterior, anyway."

"Okay, sounds good to me. The water temp is eighty-six degrees. I don't think we'll need wet suits. It's seven fifteen now. Shall we say, a nine o'clock splash?" Roger offered.

Palm Beach, Florida
April 19, 1996
0900 Hours, EST

On the way back to the office, Stephanie and Davin stopped at the Marina to check in with Josh, hoping he had some information for him. Josh was a quiet, efficient man, one who didn't take any crap from anyone. He would do as he was told and only rock the boat when necessary. He knew how to get around the brass to accomplish a mission and come out smelling like roses. He hadn't been like that all the time. There was a time that he was the perfect yes-man. Age and experience finally set in on old Josh.

Parking the car, they could see his boat, but no sign of Josh on board. He might be down below or in the lounge. His car was two spaces over, so they knew he was in the neighborhood. Getting out, they started down the dock for his boat.

"Yo, Josh, permission to come aboard?" Davin yelled as they approached the boat.

No reply came from the boat. Noticing the hatch was open, Davin jumped on board and looked below.

"Stephanie, don't come on board!" Davin shouted as he looked below, seeing Josh lying on the deck in a pool of blood.

"What is it?"

"Call the police and paramedics, go! Now!" Davin said quietly as he pulled his Colt Commander from its holster, releasing the safety. Slowly he turned and started down the hatchway to the deck below.

Stephanie turned and quickly ran back up the dock toward the lounge.

Davin reached the deck and scanned the interior of the boat. Reaching down, he checked Josh for any signs of life and found a very weak pulse. He turned and slowly opened the lockers, looking in every possible hiding place on board, and found no one.

Turning once again to Josh, he quickly but efficiently did a scan of Josh to see where and how he was injured.

Locating some towels, Davin was at least able to slow the bleeding. He started to scan around for any clues Josh might have left as to who wanted to kill him. He was a good agent and would have left some kind of clue somehow.

After a couple of minutes, Davin found what he was looking for. Crumpled up in Josh's right hand was a small piece of blue paper, from the note pad on his navigation console. Davin took the paper and read.

305-777-6731 bilge rat

As he sat on the sofa, looking at the note, he didn't hear the footsteps on the deck above till it was almost too late.

"Cast off that line," he heard from above, realizing someone was preparing to take out this boat.

Slowly he stood and glanced quickly up the hatch, wondering how he could get up on deck before being stopped. Then he heard the sirens from the approaching police.

"Freeze! This is the police. We have you surrounded!"

Two shots fired from the boat was the reply the officer received.

Several more shots were fired, and the engine on Josh's boat came to life. One of the boatmen jumped down the hatch to avoid being shot, only to discover Davin standing there with his Colt leveled at him.

"Ah, shit!" was his reply, and he sat down on the ladder.

"You okay, Rick?" the guy on deck yelled as he started to maneuver the boat away from the dock. Keeping his head low to avoid being shot and seeing where he was heading was not easy.

"No. As a matter of fact, there's a guy down here with a very large gun pointing at my head!" the kid yelled back.

"Shit!"

"You up on deck, your buddy is going to die if you don't shut down the engines right now!" Davin yelled to the guy at the helm.

"Who the hell are you?" was all the kid could say.

"Does that really matter? Right now I've got the gun and your friend is about to eat a bullet. Shut down the engines NOW!" Davin yelled again. Then, to the kid at the end of Davin's Colt Commander, he said, "You better convince him real fast, kid."

"Johnny, this guy is nuts. He just pulled back the hammer. He means to use this thing. Shut 'em down! We can't win."

"This is the police. Drop your guns and come out with your hands behind your head!" the police on the dock yelled.

"Okay, okay, we give up. Don't shoot, don't shoot!" yelled the guy on deck. "Rick, throw me your gun!" he yelled below and shut down the big engines.

Davin picked up Rick's revolver and carefully emptied it, then tossed it up on deck.

"Here are our guns. Don't shoot!" he yelled and tossed both weapons on the dock.

"Now, stand up and put your hands behind your head!" the officer yelled. "Where's your partner?"

"Right here, Officer!" Davin's hostage yelled as he exited the hatchway.

"Officer," Stephanie said as she finally got his attention, "Davin Pierce was on that boat when those two guys started to steal it. Is he all right?"

"Lady, I don't know anythin' about Pierce. We just got a call about a murder and ended up in a shoot-out ourselves."

"I called in the murder, and my boss, Davin Pierce, found the body on that boat!"

"Holy shit! Maybe he shot the other guy," the officer said with half a smile on his face.

"Okay, okay, I should have known you were involved somehow," Daryl O'Quinn said as he approached the boat. "Is Josh the victim?"

"Hi, O'Quinn. Yes, he is, but he isn't dead yet. Where is that paramedic team?" Davin said as he greeted his old friend and West Palm Beach Police captain.

"They're coming. What's your scenario?" Captain O'Quinn asked.

"What brings you down to a shooting, O'Quinn?" Davin asked.

"I was two blocks away, heading uptown, when the call came in. Figured I'd check it out, being the closest to the marina."

"Well, for what it's worth, I don't think it was those kids. They were just looking for a free ride and got in over their heads. It looks like a poorly done pro hit. Josh got lucky and the bullet didn't kill him," Davin stated.

The distant sound of sirens could be heard approaching. The medics arrived and proceeded to go to work on Josh on the boat. Two officers had secured the boat to the dock and were standing guard, trying to keep the crowds away.

"What have you and Josh got going that would get him shot?" Captain O'Quinn asked.

"That, O'Quinn, I can't answer right now, but you will be the first to know when I find out," Davin answered.

"You two used to work together, didn't you?" Captain O'Quinn asked quietly, trying to gather some inside info on what was really going on.

"Yeah, years ago in another life, Josh and I had some pretty wild times together. But that was then, and well, times have changed. Josh does help me on some of my insurance work, nothing like before."

"Don't bullshit me, Davin. If something that you and he were working on got him shot, I need to be involved. I don't need you to go and get killed either, you hear? We've been friends too long, and well, just be careful." He paused, then asked, "Look, stop by the station and give Lieutenant Gonzalez a complete report in the morning, okay?"

"Sure, no problem. Right now I think I might just follow the ambulance to the hospital, just to make sure Josh is going to be all right. Do you plan on posting a guard on him?" Davin asked as he and Stephanie turned to follow the medics.

"Sure, Davin. An officer will be waiting by the time he is out of the operating room. See you later," O'Quinn said and then turned his attention to the lab techs that just arrived.

Chapter 7

BILGE RAT

Three hours later, Stephanie and Davin arrived at their office, only to find it had been redecorated. Nothing had been left alone. All the files had been emptied on the floor, the desk and furniture turned over, and it was real clear that someone was looking for something and wasn't at all pleased when they could not find it.

Once again, Stephanie called the police, and once again they waited for them to arrive so they could give their statements. This time, however, there were no shootings or blood to clean up.

The telephone rang, breaking the silence in the room.

"Do I dare?" Davin asked,

"Nothing ventured, nothing gained," Stephanie replied.

"Hello?"

"Shut up and listen. I'll only say this once. I have something very important to sell. If you are interested in the captain's logbook from the *MaryJean*, then for $100,000 you may have it. Call this number tonight at midnight for the details: 813-456-3333. Ga'day." *Click.*

"That was strange. He said if I want to buy the captain's logbook from the *MaryJean*, I must call this number at midnight."

"That book would put a lot of puzzle pieces together, wouldn't it?"

"Yeah, it would, I think."

Soon the police came and went.

"This has been one hell of a day, hasn't it?" Stephanie casually said as they headed back to the car.

"Sure has, and I don't think it's over yet. I don't think it would be wise to go to your apartment, or my house, for that matter. We may find more trouble there. Let's get a couple a rooms at the Hilton for the night and then, in the morning, see what's going on with the cops."

"Sounds fine," Stephanie said as they reached the parking garage level.

"Hold it," Davin said quietly as they turned the corner then quickly stepped back into the shadows. "There is someone over by my car. Do you have the gun I gave you?"

Stephanie replied with a nod and slowly removed a small Llama 9mm automatic from her purse.

"Good. You stay here and cover me. I'll go over to check this out."

"Right!"

Davin pulled out the Colt Commander, checked the clip for a full load, chambered a round, and put the safety on. *For a couple of minutes, anyway,* he thought. Once out of earshot, he removed the safety and walked toward his car.

"Hi. Can I help you?" Davin asked as he approached his car.

"Naw. Just locked my keys in the..."

Realizing he was talking to the owner of the car, he reached into his jacket and removed a large pistol but was not fast enough. Davin moved up to the man with his Colt planted firmly under his chin. With his left hand, he took the pistol from him and threw it across the parking lot.

"What the hell are you doing to my car?"

"Nothing, man, nothing."

"Right. Get down and spread 'em. MOVE!" he said, commanding the man to lie on his stomach with his arms and legs spread apart.

As soon as he was down, Davin reached down and removed the guy's wallet.

"Holy shit! What the hell are you guys up to? Stephanie, get over here quickly. Look at this. He's a company man, damn CIA. Look here, this is a super-sophisticated long-range tracking device he was putting on my car. Get up!" After the agent got to his feet, Davin threw his wallet at him and demanded, "Look, Agent Bumble Butt, you go back to your little office and tell them that you screwed up and didn't complete the job. If I catch another one of you trying to follow us, I won't be as easy to get along with. Now, get outa my sight."

"Let's get outa here," Davin said as he and Stephanie drove off. "Look, first thing we do is change cars. He may have gotten a bug on this one before we arrived. To the airport."

Two hours and another car later, Stephanie and Davin were sitting down for a quiet dinner at the Hilton Oceanside.

"We need to call this number that Josh left us and find out what almost got him killed. I hope it will tell us, anyway, and let's see, at midnight, we need to call about the logbook. Sounds like a busy night."

It was 9:00 p.m. before they finished dinner and were able to call the first number. Much to their dismay, all they got was a busy signal. On the second try, they got a busy signal. They waited ten more minutes and tried again, and this time the line rang—one ring, two, three rings, stop. Tone. A computer link tone was all they heard, but they didn't have a computer to connect with it.

"Damn! Where can we get a terminal tonight?"

"The hotel should have one." And she dialed the front desk to ask.

"The hotel has a terminal in the accounting office they said we could use. Come on."

Once in the accounting office, they dialed the number and again got a busy signal. Three more tries and three more busy signals. Finally, after trying four more times, they got through and were connected.

"Welcome to Hammond House. Please enter your access code."

"Bilge Rat."

"Hello, Bilge Rat. If you are reading this message, then I must be dead, or otherwise temporarily out of the picture. Oh, well, I knew I would cash in sooner or later. I hope nothing has happened to that pretty little lady of yours. If something has, I'll come back and get you, Bilge Rat. Old friend, someone in high places has ordered me not to assist you in the MaryJean caper. But I don't follow orders too good, anyway. Maybe my own guys put me out of commission. Oh, well, just a thought. Let's move on to the good stuff before someone discovers this unauthorized connection. You are now connected with the CIA's mainframe computer, which is satellite-linked with the big house in Washington. Access is limited, but I was able to build a path for you to obtain some info that will keep you alive. By the way, I have also built in a bomb to destroy this program upon completion. If you tell your terminal to print text now, all text will be printed for you. Pretty good, huh? You do have a printer, don't you? If not, end the program now and call again. If you do, then enter the words 'right on,' then hit Enter at the prompt. If you don't have a printer, then type 'next time,' then hit Enter at the prompt."

Davin and Connie looked carefully at the text and then proceeded with the proper command.

"Right on."

The computer responded immediately.

"Great! Now, only the important stuff will print on your printer, and the rest will just dry up and blow away. Here goes…"

The printer in the accounting office started to print at very high speed, and the screen ran the text along with it.

"In 1943 a man named Jacobs, a young ensign at that time, had high hopes of becoming an admiral but didn't have the power to make it. He was smart, third in his class at the academy, but no real connection to help him grow at the rate he wanted to. So with the help of some friends, he became very powerful, mostly in the black market arena, and is now in charge of the special operations branch of Naval Intelligence. He buys and sells politicians as he needs them. His connection to the MaryJean was that he controlled the loading of all war materials out of New York Harbor. The story goes that he pulled some pretty shady deals while there and was able to buy his rank, so to speak. We haven't been able to get

anything to stick on Jacobs but are watching him real close. The file on him is very thick, but most is only hearsay. Nothing solid, but with the MaryJean, *we may have a bit of thickening.*

"*Captain Bronsly has been under the watchful eye of the company for many years. His connection with the black market is well-known in most parts of the world, and he has even acted, unofficially, as a purchasing agent for military weapons for numerous third world countries. The FBI recently killed Bronsly in a raid of a warehouse in New Orleans. He was connected with the sale of military weapons to a group of Iranian terrorists, and the warehouse was full of weapons and other contraband, some of which was supposed to have been on the* MaryJean *when she sank. Bronsly disappeared after being rescued in 1943, only to turn up sporadically around the world selling weapons and working the black market. He has been to trial three times for racketeering and twice for murder. The charges were dropped during the trial, or just before, so he was never convicted. It was rumored that he held several high-ranking government people in his pocket, but nothing was ever proved.*"

The report went on and on for many pages, listing each crew member and his known and suspected part in the black market. Of all the crew that was listed as dead, five of them turned up alive years later; two were now serving time in Leavenworth, and two were killed in a shoot-out in a New Orleans warehouse a few weeks ago. The fifth one, Chief Engineer Norman Burrack, was last seen in Miami, Florida, in 1963. He hasn't been seen or heard from since. The report mentioned that the ring had many members; some suspects were listed, but the rest were unknown as yet. Some names he recognized; most he didn't know.

"Damn, Josh sure did his homework, but this doesn't tell me who may have tried to kill him, unless the company is in the habit of killing their own," Davin said as he reread part of the report.

"Look at the last line. Maybe that will tell us something," Stephanie said, pointing to the last entry.

"*Bilge Rat, beware of people you give trust to. Some of them are not worth the trust their positions demand. Beware, my friend. Lotsa luck.*"

"That could mean almost anyone in the government. Who the hell can you trust, anyway?"

"Look at the time. It's almost midnight!"

"This just finished. Tear off that printout and let's get outa here. We'll make that other call from down the street. I don't want to be traced to this hotel."

"Good idea. I need to get some rest. This has been one hell of a day."

"Right, let's go," Davin said as he and Stephanie left the office and went through the lobby to the car. Once in the car, they drove south several blocks to locate a telephone booth.

CIA Headquarters
Washington, DC
April 19, 1996
2330 Hours, EST

"What? Josh Randel shot? By who? When?" Chief Russell Black yelled. Black was the senior chief of internal affairs, mainland. Fifty-one years old, he'd been an agent for ten years, then moved up the ladder to senior chief. He had seen good agents come and go. Luckily, most retired before they were killed. Josh Randel was a good friend and a good agent. His latest assignment was undercover drug agent, assisting the local Drug Enforcement Agency (DEA). He was supposed to be a passive adviser, not to interfere with the operation, just give advice and assist where necessary.

"Sir, Randel was shot by a .357 magnum at close range. He is expected to live but is presently unconscious and in the ICU at St. Mary's in West Palm Beach. We have a guard on him for protection. The doctors expect he will lose the use of one lung, and part of his liver was damaged, but the bullet luckily went right through him. Recovery time, three, maybe four weeks, then months of therapy," Helen Reed said as she sat across from Black. Reed was his personal secretary and confidante, twenty-nine, single, and very attractive. He always wondered why she had not married, but that was her choice.

"Who found him?"

"Davin Pierce, sir, at about 11:00 this morning, on his boat," she responded.

"Pierce! I ordered Randel to stay out of Pierce's business. I only hope he followed orders!" Black said.

"Yes, sir. I'll keep you posted on Randel's condition," Reed said as she stood to leave.

"Thank you, Helen."

Singer Island Bar and Grill, Florida
April 19, 1996, Midnight

Stopping four blocks away at a well-lit shopping center, Davin made the call at precisely midnight, or at least as close as possible.

Three rings and then the phone was answered.

"Hello, hello," Davin said.

"Listen carefully, Mr. Pierce. For the sum of $100,000, I will deliver to you the complete accounting of the last trip the *MaryJean* ever made. The captain's ship's log, the only surviving document from her. Also in the deal will be the complete manifest collection for the last ten trips she made. All these complete and guaranteed for the small fee of $50,000. A bargain at any price. A deal that should not be passed up. It will not be offered again. Call now and receive absolutely free a copy of *War and Peace*, signed by none other than Ronald Reagan. Call now and receive all this: 813-456-9879. I say again, 813-456-9879." *Click.*

"Damn, sounds like an ad for Ginsu Knives or something on that line. Let's try this again," Davin said as he started to dial the new number.

"Hello, Mr. Pierce," a voice responded on the first ring. It sounded a little muffled, like someone talking though a handkerchief.

"Yes."

"Good. So you wish to make a deal. For your prompt response, I will make the delivery easy for you."

"Okay, how do I get it?"

"In the morning you are to go to Palm Beach International Airport to the Continental counter. There will be a package for you. The waybill number is 'JAX 6783-4521-08.' Inside the package, you will find a briefcase with photocopies of the first part of the ship's log. These, of course, will not help you, because she was built in 1926. They are provided to you to prove that I have the log and to show good faith. You are to fill the briefcase with the money, small unmarked old bills, nothing larger than a fifty, US currency. No funny money or the deal's off. Now, have you got something to write on and with?"

"Yeah, go ahead."

"Okay. Book yourself—no, better yet, book your girl Stephanie on the 5:15 Delta flight from Palm Beach to San Francisco, with stops in Atlanta, St. Louis, Denver, and Los Angeles. She will have a layover in each city for two hours and in Denver till the 7:05 in the morning. She is to check the briefcase through to each stop and retrieve it at each baggage claim when she arrives, then recheck the case before each flight. Once in San Francisco, she is to check in to the Sheraton Airport for the night. She is to call room service for breakfast, then check out and return home. Is that understood, Mr. Pierce?"

"Yes, but what if the airlines lose the case?"

"They won't lose the case. Remember that she is to pick up and recheck the case at each airport. If, for some reason, the case doesn't show up at the baggage claim, she is to report it to the airline, as with any lost baggage. Now, do you understand what is required? If she arrives in San Francisco and all has gone well, room service will deliver a package containing the log to her room. One other thing, Mr. Pierce. She is not to open the case at any time during the trip, and she is to remain on Delta Airlines for the whole trip. Continental on the return trip would be acceptable. Do you understand?"

"Yes."

"Have a nice day." *Click.*

"Holy shit!"

"What's going on?" Stephanie asked.

"You're taking a little trip tomorrow. I'll explain on the way back to the hotel. Let's go."

On the way back, they talked over the plan of action, and they decided that Stephanie would fly back to Washington and catch up with Davin and Connie. Connie—they had completely forgotten about her. Hopefully, she was all right. Davin pulled over to the next telephone to call her. After the fourth ring, a weak voice answered.

"Hello," Connie said as she tried to wake up.

"Connie, Davin. Are you okay?" Davin asked.

"Sure. Why shouldn't I be? What time is it, anyway?" she asked.

"No reason, just checking. It's twelve thirty. Sorry. See ya in the morning about 10:00 a.m., okay? Good night."

"Okay, thanks for checkin', I think. Good night." *Click.* Silence.

"She's okay?"

"Yeah. Let's get outa here and get some sleep," Davin said as he climbed back into the car and drove back to the hotel.

The Pentagon, Arlington, Virginia
Office of Special Operations and Research
April 19, 1996
1900 Hours, EST

Admiral Henry Barker had found it very hard to believe the information he had received. Thanks to the sophisticated equipment on both ends of the satellite, he was able to view short videotape of the submarine just located off the coast of Nigeria.

"Ensign, are we still in contact with the *Ghostfinder?* By the way, what time is it over there?" Admiral Barker asked.

"Yes, sir, for about twenty more minutes. And it's just after midnight, sir," the young ensign replied.

"Great. Send them this reply: Congratulations on a great find. A destroyer is on its way to assist. Do not attempt entry for any reason. Repeat. Further instructions at noon, your time. Make no further contact. Hostilities growing. Your safety and cover may be in jeopardy. Sign my name to it."

"Aye, aye, sir," the ensign said and turned sharply to depart.

"Wait, before you go, one other thing. After you get that message off, get me the latest on the activities in Nigeria."

"Yes, sir."

"Thank you."

Sitting quietly for what seemed to be hours, Admiral Barker finally turned to the phone and started to dial.

"Hello. Admiral Barker here. Is Jacobs in?" he queried. After a short pause, he said, "Thank you."

Sailboat Ghostfinder II
April 20, 1996
0900 Hours, GMT

The water was clear and warm. Visibility was estimated at over one hundred feet. As Sam and Ken hit the water and got their bearings, they could easily see the submarine's shape off in the distance. Sam normally didn't like to swim with a bathing suit, but when she dived, she always wore some kind of protection. Today she had on her hot-pink dive skins, a type of second skin made of Lycra that gave protection from scrapes and various underwater hazards. Sam carried a Nikonos VII underwater camera with a thirty-five-millimeter lens and twin strobes. Ken also had on his dive skins, black, of course, and carried a Nikonos VII also, but with a fifteen-millimeter wide-angle lens, a lens that would capture most of the boat in fine detail.

They approached the *Wolverine* slowly from the port side, scanning the length of the boat as they closed in. She was sitting on the bottom at eighty-five feet, which meant they could stay down for only twenty-five minutes without having to make a decompression stop on the way back up. They planned on staying at about sixty feet to look over the superstructure and photograph as much as possible. This would allow an easy forty minutes of bottom time and no decompression stop.

Sam and Ken arrived at the control tower of the boat and started a slow inspection of the tower, then moved forward to the escape hatch located in the forward torpedo room. Although she was almost completely void of barnacles, a heavy coat of green slime had formed on the hull, the first stage of sea growth. An abundance of fish around the boat was feeding on the growth that had started, which made the dive very enjoyable.

Forty-five minutes after entering the water, Ken and Sam were climbing up the ladder on the *Ghostfinder*, allowing for a slow ascent and a safety stop. They ended the dive right on schedule.

"Wow! What a sight! You gotta see her!" Sam exclaimed as she climbed up the ladder.

"Yeah, that is some find, Rog. She is in perfect shape, no holes, and a few air and oil leaks. Looks like she is fer sure dry inside."

"Great! Let's get the photos developed and see what ya got. Then Penny and I will go down for a little visit."

"We really don't need the dive skins. Not much to scrape against and no jellies in the water," Sam commented as she struggled out of hers. "Ken, I'll take care of the gear if you want to process the film."

"Okay," Ken answered and then started down the hatch after depositing his gear in the cockpit.

Sam and Penny took care of the gear, then removed their bikinis and lay down on the bow to catch some sun as the guys went below to process the film.

On the horizon, a small dot appeared and grew at a tremendous rate, heading straight for the *Ghostfinder*. The sound of the jet reached them seconds before the fighter.

Penny and Sam sat up abruptly and saw with fear and disbelief as the MiG-23 passed over them at about a hundred feet. It sped past them, turned, and headed back.

"WHAT THE HELL WAS THAT?" Ken yelled from below. He and Roger sprang through the hatch just as the MiG made a second pass.

"Damn, where did he come from?" Roger yelled.

"How should we know?" Sam said as she and Penny wrapped a towel around their nude bodies. "Maybe he is just out for a joyride."

"Not a chance, not a chance. MiG-23s don't go for joyrides. He's looking for something, and I hope we aren't it," Roger stated.

"Operation Tourist. Now, MOVE!" Ken yelled as the MiG started another turn.

Quickly they grabbed for the binoculars and cameras that were in the cockpit and started to take pictures and wave at the fighter as it made a third pass.

"As soon as he is outa sight, we move. How far are we from shore?" Ken asked.

"'Bout twenty miles, maybe twenty-five. I'd have to check," Roger replied.

"Damn, this gig may be up before it starts. If they somehow intercepted our transmission last night, they will know we aren't what the papers say we are," Ken said matter-of-factly.

"Yeah, but how? That equipment is line-of-sight microwave. They couldn't have intercepted it. Maybe he is just on a routine patrol, maybe," Sam said.

"True, but they know something, and I don't like it," Roger replied seriously.

"Okay, we move as soon as he gets outa sight. We don't want them to find our sunken treasure," Ken said and turned to pick up the binoculars. He viewed the MiG-23 as it turned and headed away from them.

"I hope he got some good pictures. I know I did," Penny stated as she turned to pick up her towel.

"We can't outrun them, but maybe we can outsmart them. You two had better put some clothes nearby in case we get some visitors," Roger remarked.

"Do you think they were just cruising, or were they looking for something?" Sam asked.

"Babe, we have about two, maybe three hours before they get here, so we have to convince them that the cover story is for real and we are, in fact, lookin' for shipwrecks. So get ready for the performance of your life," Ken replied.

"Can we get a message off to the Navy?" Penny asked as she looked out to the horizon where the MiG had disappeared.

"Yeah, but if they intercepted our transmission last night, that might have spurred their interest. Another one might get us in deeper than I'd like to be, but then again, if we are boarded, we're dead," Ken said.

"Right, ole chap. How 'bout a burst transmission?" Roger suggested.

"Yeah, maybe. We do have that option in an emergency, and this could be considered one. Rog, you get the equipment ready. We transmit in fifteen minutes. The Navy's Micro SatCom should be near the proper position now."

"Aye, aye, Ken. Should I dig out some artillery?" Roger asked.

"Not yet. First, the message and see what they say, then we pray."

"What do you want us to do?" Sam asked.

"Keep an eye on the horizon for ships or anything that moves. In the meantime, let's get that anchor up and some sheets in the wind and move off about a mile and drop the hook again," Ken said as he headed forward to pull up the hook.

Sam and Penny slipped out of their towels and into action to prepare the ship for the move. Twenty minutes later, the anchor was up and they were sailing to the northwest at seven knots.

"The Navy said they had a cruiser on its way here, estimated time of arrival 18:00 today," Roger said as he and Ken climbed up on deck again.

"This is what it's all about, boys and girls, so let's prepare for our visitors," Ken said. "Take a heading of three-one-zero degrees and we'll drop anchor in about thirty minutes, all right?"

Chapter 8

JUST A JOB, MAN!

Palm Beach, Florida
St. Mary's Hospital
April 19, 1996
1730 Hours, EST

"Hello, ICU. May I help you?" the intensive care unit head nurse said into the phone. "Yes, sir. Mr. Randel is still here, and no, we don't know how long he'll be here. His condition, well, yes, he's still on the critical list. That's all I can say, sir, unless you are a relative. I'm sorry, sir." After a short pause, Nurse Davis continued, "Goodbye, sir." And then she hung up the phone.

"Thank you, Ms. Davis," Captain O'Quinn said as he leaned over the desk. "If he calls again, tell him that his condition has not improved, but nothing more."

"Do you think he will call back?" Nurse Davis asked.

"No. I really believe he will come down and try to finish the job. But don't worry, miss, I have enough officers on duty in here to stop him if he tries. Besides, from here on out, if anyone asks, direct them to the ICU in the next hall," O'Quinn said as he scanned the area.

"But we don't have another ICU in the next hall," Ms. Davis said, looking a little puzzled.

"We know that and you know that, but as far as anyone else is concerned, he is in a special ICU area so he can be protected and out of the public-use areas."

"Right, so are you placing someone there to act as a patient and have guards on both areas?" Davis asked.

"Kind of like that, miss. I've got to check on my men, so just be calm and we will try our best not to create any new patients for you," O'Quinn said with a little laugh.

"You do that," Nurse Davis replied and then turned to her control panel that monitored the vital signs of the three patients she had under her care.

Time passes slowly in an intensive care unit. The nurses monitor the vital signs panel, and as long as buzzers do not sound or lights flash, all is well. Tonight was no exception. Nurse Davis had been on duty for seven hours of a nine-hour shift. She was tired, and the added stress of the police being in the area was taking its toll on her. Glancing at the clock on the wall, she saw that it was 9:48 p.m., another hour before her shift ended.

"Nurse..." A soft voice broke into her trance. "Nurse."

"Oh, sorry. You're not supposed to be here unless you are a relative, sir," Nurse Davis said to the tall gentleman dressed in a hospital smock and blue slacks. But even in her tired state, she had noticed he wasn't wearing a hospital identification tag.

"I'm Dr. Doug Harris, here to check on a patient of mine, Mr. Josh Randel. I understand he has been shot," Dr. Harris said without hesitation.

"Dr. Harris, before you can see Mr. Randel, you need to check in with the resident doctor. You can find him in his office on the fourth floor, Room 412," Nurse Davis said politely.

"No, you don't understand. I must see him now. You see, Mr. Randel has a rare condition that only he and I know about."

"And what might that be, Dr. Harris?" Nurse Davis asked, showing a little annoyance for this doctor.

"I cannot discuss that with you," Dr. Harris said as he reached over the countertop and sprayed a small vial of liquid into Nurse Davis's face, instantly causing her to fall asleep at her desk. Quickly looking around the desktop, Dr. Harris saw that Randel was in room 101. Dr. Harris looked down the hall toward 101. Not seeing anyone, he started to walk toward the open door.

"Sir, can I help you?" Officer Pike asked as he stood. Pike was sitting at the end of the hall just out of sight from the nurse's station.

"No!" was the reply from Dr. Harris as he pulled a silenced Glock 17 pistol from his belt, firing two shots, striking Officer Pike in the left shoulder and chest. Pike fell back and landed in the chair he had just been resting in. Pike never had a chance to draw his own weapon. No noise was heard by anyone in the area; the chair was large and overstuffed, which silenced Pike's fall.

Dr. Harris moved slowly down the hall, weapon ready for action to stop anyone who would try to keep him from completing his mission. Only ten feet to go, then into room 101, and the end of Josh Randel.

As Harris approached the door, he stopped, listened, and then slowly stepped into the doorway. His weapon level, he fired four shots into the occupant on the only bed in the room. Within an instant, he turned and was out of the room.

"FREEZE!" yelled O'Quinn from the end of the hall near his downed officer.

"UP YOURS! YOU'RE TOO LATE!" Harris yelled back, turned, and fired four rounds in the direction of O'Quinn's voice, hitting nothing but the wall. His Glock 17 held fifteen rounds; with six fired, firing four more left him with five to go before he had to reload, which was simple for the Glock, as with most automatic pistols.

O'Quinn never did like the Glock; he felt that due to its light weight, in a firefight a shooter could not maintain a tight shot pattern. This was only true for novice shooters, and this guy was not a novice.

O'Quinn returned fire from his own sidearm, a Beretta 9-millimeter automatic. Dr. Harris was still in the open when O'Quinn fired two rounds, hitting Harris with both shots. Harris spun around and tried to run, only to discover that all his strength was flowing out of his two wounds. Dropping his Glock 17, he turned, stumbled, and fell. O'Quinn, two detectives, and three uniformed officers rushed over to the fallen Harris, weapons drawn and pointing at Harris.

"Bradshaw, get a doctor up here, now!" O'Quinn yelled to one of the uniformed officers.

Kneeling down beside the downed killer, O'Quinn started to ask a question but decided it wouldn't matter. This guy was a pro, and he wouldn't talk, not even to save his own hide.

"Good shooting, cop. Where did you learn to be so good?" Harris asked between coughs.

"Army, son. Twenty-two years as a combat infantryman." After a short pause, O'Quinn asked finally, "Why are you trying to kill Randel?"

"It's a job, man. I did it for the money. What else is there?" Harris commented and grimaced with pain.

"You know, you failed in your mission," O'Quinn said, looking into the deep-blue eyes of the killer.

"No…way…man. Four solid hits into that guy. I don't miss either…"

"Oh, but you do. You should check a target before you shoot. Randel is not in 101. He's not even on this floor."

"Okay, let me get to him, Captain," the resident doctor said as he came over to where Harris lay. "Your officer will be all right. That vest saved his life, but his arm is a mess. They are sewing him up right now."

"If this guy lives, book him on attempted murder," O'Quinn said to his sergeant. "And whatever else you can think of." He turned and left the ICU.

Ghostfinder II
Off the Coast of Nigeria
Same Day
1530 Hours, GMT

It didn't take long for the Nigerian Navy to launch a boat to check out the *Ghostfinder*. A small dot appeared on the horizon, coming from the east and growing rapidly.

"It won't be long now, guys. Let's just do as we were trained and maybe they will just go away," Ken stated as the patrol boat closed in on the anchored sailboat.

"What time is it?" Penny asked, as if hoping the destroyer was going to get here first.

"Penny, my dear, the time is 15:45. That destroyer is still almost two hours away. By the time they arrive, we will be very dead or on our way to prison as spies."

"They wouldn't kill us, would they?" Sam asked.

"Sure would, with all that equipment down below. We wouldn't have much of a chance explaining that we are only looking for gold and sunken ships."

"This is my first operation, Ken. Give me a break. We're not at war with them."

"No, but tell them that," Ken said as the patrol boat closed to one hundred yards. The boat slowed and turned to circle the sailboat, its deck guns pointed at the sailboat as it circled. The circle was slowly reduced in size until the patrol boat was within fifty feet of the *Ghostfinder*.

Ken, Sam, Penny, and Roger stood on deck, watching and waiting for the patrol boat to make its move.

"Ahoy, *Ghostfinder*. Prepare to take boarding party!" the captain of the patrol boat yelled over the bullhorn as he maneuvered his vessel closer to the sailboat. She was a modified Wellcraft Scarab complete with a .50-caliber machine gun on the bow and heavily armed sailors in the cockpit. A very fast attack patrol craft would be putting it mildly.

"If we're boarded, it's all over!" Roger said.

"Only if they go below," Ken said with relief.

"Sam, Penny, move to the other side of the boat, and when I tell you, get overboard fast. I secured two scuba rigs on the anchor line, just in case," Ken said quietly as the boarding party approached in the rubber dinghy.

"What ya got in mind?" Roger asked with a little hesitation.

"I don't know yet."

"Swell!"

"Welcome aboard, Captain. How can we be of service?" Ken said, greeting the boarding party.

"Cut the crap. You are in Nigerian territorial waters, and powerful satellite radio transmissions have been identified as coming from your location. Since you seem to be the only ship in the area, it is highly possible they emitted from your vessel. I'm here to inform you that you and your crew are under arrest for spying and will be escorted to Port Harcourt for trial and execution."

"You can't do that!" Roger yelled.

"Wanta bet?" the captain insisted.

"Captain, we are in international waters on a pleasure craft. Does this look like a military vessel? Really, now. You haven't got much evidence to prove anything you have said. So why don't you take your pretty little Scarab and leave us alone to enjoy your waters in peace?" Ken came on strong, hedging that his firmness would get this guy off his boat.

"You, my friend, are going to die. And if you press your luck, it might happen right here and now!"

"We're not afraid of you and your little speedboat. Killing us will only bring your country into war with the United States, and I don't think you want to do that, now, do you?"

"What makes you think the US government gives a damn about you, anyway? Unless you are spies, as I have said, and they want to cover up their childish mistake of sending you here?"

"Your English is pretty good, Captain. Where did you attend school?" Ken asked calmly, changing the subject to stall for time, as his eye caught the rapidly growing shape approaching from the west.

"University of Miami, class of '88. Why?"

"Why? Well, I thought you looked familiar. Sam and I graduated from Miami in '88 also. Small world."

"Very interesting, but that doesn't change a thing, sport. You are still under arrest, but this means we have a little in common and I will feel a little pain when I watch you die."

"If you're gonna kill us, why wait?" Roger asked as the captain started to walk around the deck, picking up on Ken's lead.

"Just a minute. We are in international waters and you have no right to come on our boat, pointing guns and saying we are spies," Ken demanded of the captain, now seeing the shape of the incoming aircraft to be that of an Sikorsky S-76 attack helicopter.

"I have all the right in the world, young man. My country is in a state of war, the rebels have been getting intelligence and arms from someone, and right now this is the only vessel in the vicinity of covert radio signals intercepted by our intelligence office. So you see, we have the proof, and I'll bet that if I look hard enough, I will find a transmitter of the type that could be used in a spying operation. Proof or not, we plan on making an example of you in front of the world, anyway."

Ken and Roger just looked at each other, then over to the girls. The Navy chopper approached at an angle that prevented the patrol boat from seeing it, directly out of the sun.

"Nothing to say? Well, I guess I wasn't wrong." Then turning to his men, he yelled, "Search the boat!"

"Maybe we can work this out somehow," Penny suggested as she started to remove her top, keeping the captain's attention long enough for the helo to get in real close before being noticed.

"I've always hated killing ladies, especially ladies as lovely as you two, but spying is illegal and I must do my duty."

The roar of the patrol boat's engine and the concentration on the sailboat allowed the US Navy helicopter to approach within a few hundred feet before being seen or heard by anyone. By then it was too late.

"Damn!" the captain yelled and pointed toward the helicopter, directing his men to open fire.

The crew of the patrol boat turned their machine guns on the helicopter and opened fired with everything they had, not giving the helicopter a chance to even ask them to surrender.

Immediately pulling up to avoid the heavy fire, Commander Wilson banked hard to the right to take up a good firing position so he wouldn't hit the sailboat. At the same time, he unleashed a string of fire from his minigun, commonly known as point defense, to try to convince the boat to stop firing. The gunner on the boat got a few lucky hits on the helo as three rounds penetrated the cockpit. Convinced the gunner on the boat would not stop, Wilson continued to fire his point defense and prepared missiles for firing.

"Pull the pins on 1 and 2…firing 1!" he yelled as he received the armed readout on his console.

The pilot of the helicopter, being an old Vietnam war veteran, did not take to being shot at as a welcome greeting of his liking.

"One away, ready 2!" Commander Vernon Wilson of the US Navy helicopter yelled into his microphone.

"Ah, 2's ready," he replied.

"Secure 2, prepare to drop boarding party to the sailboat, keep your M-60 on the boat," Wilson ordered, seeing that the missile did its job effectively.

The single missile fired by the helicopter hit its target and, with a great ball of fire, destroyed the small patrol boat. The whole confrontation took less than fifteen seconds from the time the first round was fired.

With this distraction, Ken and Roger jumped their captors, and within seconds, the captain and his guards were the prisoners. One of the boarding parties was knocked overboard and lost his weapon. Throwing him a life preserver was the only act of compassion that could be acknowledged.

"I do believe we have visitors, mein kapitän. May I inform you that you are now our prisoner of war and will be remanded to the US Navy for disposition? That war you have in your country has just now become international, and the taking of American prisoners is an act of war in the eyes of our government," Ken said as he held the captured Uzi at the stomach of the captain.

The helicopter maneuvered over to the other side of the sailboat and dropped a raft and two sailors. Minutes later, they were on the *Ghostfinder*.

"Lieutenant Griffins, and this is Seaman Fletcher, from the USS *George Washington*. The ship will be here shortly. We thought you might be in trouble."

"Thank you, Lieutenant. Your timing was near perfect. I'm Ken, this is Roger, Sam, and Penny," he said, pointing to his friends. "And this is Captain…ah, you know, I didn't get your name, sir."

"Captain Andrew Raphael Conitrizona, at your service, and my, well, what's left of my crew," he said, indicating the two men he boarded with.

"Let's lock them up on the bow until the ship gets here," Lieutenant Griffins said, handing Seaman Fletcher another pair of handcuffs.

"Aye, aye, sir," he said as he and Roger escorted their prisoners to the bow.

"When you get those guys secured, keep an eye on them. I don't trust them for a minute."

"Can I interest you in a beer?" Ken offered.

"I'm still on duty, but what the hell. One won't hurt, and let's get one to Fletcher. It's gonna be hot up there."

USS George Washington
Eighteen Miles from Nigeria
April 20, 1996
1915 Hours, GMT

It wasn't long before the USS *George Washington* arrived and the prisoners were taken on board for questioning.

Ken and Sam went over to meet with the commander and explain to him what they had found. In turn, the commander explained the importance of the find, as much as he knew, anyway.

Commander Russell Grey was in his early fifties but still had coal-black hair with just a trace of gray at the temples. He was a serious man who had raced his vessel to this war zone to save a sailboat and didn't know why. He wanted answers, and he wanted them now. All he knew was that the sailboat was on a secret mission for the Navy and they were in trouble.

"That is all real interesting, Commander, but it still doesn't explain why the Navy is so interested in an old boat such as this," Ken insisted.

"Son, they didn't tell me why but only said to get here fast, save your ass, and secure the area. Which means that you and your boat have to leave, and well, as you can see, it's not the safest port in town. We will escort you to an area that is out of range of their jets, and then you are on your own," Commander Russell Grey stated.

"Okay, I agree. We don't want to be fish bait, but we were sent out here by the Navy to do their dirty work and almost lost our lives for it. And I resent being left in the dark about a damn sub that we found for them."

"I can't help you there. I don't know why all the secrecy either. I'm just following orders, and my orders are clear. Secure the area and await further orders. Now we have to get moving. It isn't going to be long before they send out a search party for that patrol boat. And when they get here, they aren't gonna be too friendly finding us here."

"Okay, Commander. The Navy wins this one, but may I request of the Navy that we be allowed to look at the final report on the *Wolverine*?" Ken asked very diplomatically.

"You'll have to take that up with Admiral Jacobs. Now, can we get outa here, before we get any more visitors?"

"I'm all for that. Let's go, Ken," Sam insisted.

Minutes later, Ken and Sam were back on board the *Ghostfinder* and making preparation to set sail.

"Anchor on board, raise the main, let's get as much up as possible!" Ken yelled. "Let's show the Navy what the *Ghostfinder* is made of."

"Roger, bring her around and let's grab some air!" Sam yelled as the craft responded to the breeze and came around. She accelerated faster than the crew had expected and immediately jumped to sixteen knots and heeled over to the challenge. The *Ghostfinder* was designed to race but then modified with a winged keel and all the electronics to perform the mission they were on. On a good day, she would cruise at around eighteen knots and was designed to do twenty plus—unheard of for a sailing vessel, but she was unique and not to be taken lightly.

The *Washington* turned and stayed about fifty yards to the port side of the *Ghostfinder*. All on board were on alert for any activity from the coast and would be that way for the next two days.

Two days later and six hundred hundred miles from the coast, the USS *George Washington* and her crew waved farewell to the crew of the *Ghostfinder II*. They turned to return to the *Wolverine* site. As the *Washington* turned, Sam and Penny removed the tops of their bikinis and waved to the ship, getting a roaring response from the crew.

"Damn, I'm glad to get that off," Sam said as she massaged her breast in an attempt to revive the circulation.

"Me too," Penny replied.

"Do you need any help?" Roger asked.

"No, not right now, but I will need some lotion later."

"Just call me, I'll be there."

The crew of the *Washington* waved goodbye as they turned the ship around and headed back to the site of the sunken submarine. They were to meet with the British cruiser HMS *Montgomery*, and the two were to remain on-site until advised to leave.

The return trip was uneventful; the *Montgomery* met them on schedule, and both proceeded back to the Nigerian coast in calm waters.

Nigerian Capital, Lagos
Office of General Hector Samula
April 20, 1996
2130 Hours, GMT

"Damn it, Corning!" General Samula yelled across his office at the little man sitting in the chair in front of the two-hundred-year-old mahogany desk.

"General, calm down. Maybe that destroyer is just a coincidence," Corning said calmly.

"Corning, we sent a fighter out an hour ago to see where our patrol boat was, and do you know what they saw? Do you know what they saw, Mr. Corning?" Samula repeated himself, and then not waiting to get an answer, he answered it himself. "I'll tell you what they saw, Mr. Corning. They saw one of your country's destroyers, a large armed ship and a small sailboat, sitting within a mile of where our patrol boat should have been. No patrol boat in sight, Mr. Corning!" General Samula yelled at Corning.

"General, I'm only one man. I can't control everybody! My connections are not on every damn boat in the Navy. I'll contact my superior in the States and have them move that boat out of your area. Okay, General? Is that what you want? Remember, we are the good guys supplying you with the weapons to run this war, so don't threaten the hand that feeds you, General," Corning stated calmly.

"They have seventy-two hours to leave, or we will blow them out of the water!" the general ordered. "Or better yet, Mr. Corning, we need a new ship. Just have them surrender to us and I'll release the crew and keep the ship."

"Get serious, General. We are not going to submit to extortion. Did the ship see your fighter?" Corning asked.

"No. He was too high and used his camera for surveillance. Time is running out, Corning. You have seventy-two hours. No more!" Samula insisted. He had enough problems with a civil war going on. True, he started it, but he did not need any interference from any country parking a warship off his coast, especially one from the United States.

Washington, DC
Admiral Jacobs's Office
April 21, 1996
1200 Hours, EST

"Sir, this just came in secure, coded addressee," Mrs. Hicks, the admiral's secretary, said as she entered his office. She was working through lunch because her daughter was flying in today and she wanted to leave early. She also brought the admiral a fresh cup of coffee and his usual lunch, a Caesar salad and a slice of apple pie from the cafeteria.

"Thank you, Mrs. Hicks," he said as he took the message. "Oh, by the way, when is your daughter due in?"

"Two, sir," she replied.

"You had better be going, then. I'll only be an hour or so behind you," he offered. He wanted some privacy to decode the message. He knew it was from his man in Nigeria, Corning.

"Thank you, sir. See you tomorrow," she said as she turned to leave.

"No, Mrs. Hicks, take the next few days off to be with your daughter. I'll be okay. Mrs. Drake in General Prado's office can cover for you. The general is in California for the next two weeks."

"Why, thank you, sir. I guess I'll see you in a few days, then." Mrs. Hicks left the office smiling.

After she left, Admiral Jacobs stood and walked over to the door, locked it carefully, and then crossed to a picture of a lake in the Alpine Forest. He removed it from the wall, exposing a wall safe. Five minutes later, he'd decoded the message, sat back, and read in disbelief.

> *Tigerlily:*
>
> *We have a major problem. The conflict here is not going well. Samula wants arms, not interference, and it seems we are interfering. Unknown to you yet, there is a US sailboat that is possibly on a covert mission that has just been rescued by the USS* George Washington. *Samula wants that boat out of his face and says he will sink her and that sailboat in less than seventy-two hours if they don't leave. An international incident is not what we need right now. Get them to move out of the area now.*
>
> *Please advise on next weapons shipment and why that ship is there.*
>
> *—Cannonball*

"Damn. First, that phone call from Barker, now this. That damn sailboat has stirred up a mess, finding the *Wolverine*. Why is it there, anyway?" Admiral Jacobs said to himself quietly.

USS George Washington
April 22, 1996
2300 Hours, GMT

"Helm, estimated time of arrival?" Commander Grey asked as they turned to head back to where the *Wolverine* was resting.

"That's 06:00, on the twenty-fourth, at present course and speed," was the reply.

"Good. Keep me posted on any changes. I'm going for some coffee."

"Aye, aye, sir."

Commander Grey headed back to the galley for some coffee and a little bite to eat. It had been a long time since chow.

"Lieutenant Commander Sheppard, come join me in the galley," Commander Grey said as he ran into him in the passageway. Sheppard was heading away from the galley.

"Sure, sir. What's up?" answered Lieutenant Commander Sheppard. He was young, blond, blue-eyed, about five foot eight. He'd played football for Navy at the academy, left guard, and also enjoyed classical music in his spare time; he was soft-spoken yet could command when needed.

"Oh, not much. Just need to get your opinion on what's going on."

"Okay," he said as he turned toward the galley, following the commander.

They were the only ones in the galley, and this pleased the commander. He needed to talk and didn't want to be disturbed. They got some coffee and a couple of stale Danish from the tray in the corner.

"Over here," Grey said, indicating a couple of seats near the port hatchway.

"Okay, sir. What gives?"

"Well, if you'll be quiet, I'll tell you. First off, I think we are asking for trouble by going back into that area without more support. Second, this damn sub has something about her that isn't right. I don't know what it is, but it's gonna get us killed."

"That's pretty harsh, sir. But to be honest, I feel the same way. The Navy isn't telling all they know, and when they do that, someone usually gets hurt. And the Nigerians are out for blood. That rebellion is starting to become international. They have no way of knowing we had anything to do with the patrol boat, but we will be in the area."

"Yeah, I don't trust those radicals any more than I can throw this damn boat," Grey commented. "What is your best guess as to their next move?"

"Hard to say, sir. You know, when you have a radical, almost certifiably crazy, in charge of a country, almost anything can happen, especially now that the people he is trying to control have gotten ahold of some high-tech weapons and are shooting back. You can't relate all the trouble to the rags they wear. A lot of them don't wear the rag. It's the heat that gets to most of them. This area is unbearable most of the time."

"Okay, let's just cruise the area about twenty miles out and wait till the Navy tells us what to do. Maybe drop a couple of divers on the wreck to get some photos of our own. And let's keep that chopper in the air at all times that we are anchored. No, let's keep one in the air at all times and the other on standby, armed and ready."

"No problem, sir. I don't want to be caught off guard, like that patrol boat."

"How are the prisoners?"

"Very comfortable. They say our brig is a palace compared to the ones they use. Ha ha!"

"Who's on midwatch?" Grey asked.

"Ensign Chuck Harrelson, the kid from Boston."

"Good man, knew his dad. He'll make a good sailor. Has it in his blood. Okay, I'm off to the rack. Wake me at sunrise."

"Aye, sir," Sheppard said as he and the commander got up to leave. The commander headed off for his cabin, and Sheppard to the bridge to check in before he went to his cabin.

USS George Washington, Bridge
Twenty-One Miles Northwest of the Wolverine Site
April 24, 1996
0600 Hours, GMT

"Commander, ship on the horizon, bearing 230 degrees," reported the deck officer as the commander entered the bridge.

"Can you ID her yet?"

"Negative, sir."

"Course and speed?"

"Stationary, sir, anchored!"

"Identify as soon as possible. Launch the helo for recon. Try to establish radio contact."

"Trying, sir. No contact yet, sir."

"Use all frequencies."

"Aye, aye, sir. All frequencies in use," he responded. "Helo away, sir."

"Estimated time of intercept, air and sea?"

"Helo, twenty minutes. Ship…two hours forty, sir."

"Thank you. Can we get some coffee up here? Hand me those glasses, son," Grey asked, indicating the pair of binoculars on the chart table.

He scanned the horizon, hoping that he could get a better view of the ship that lay ahead. Time passed slowly, too slow.

"We have contact, sir. They are asking our helo to identify or be shot down. He is doing so, now…wait…our helo is returning. They said to proceed with caution. One of their ships has been sunk, and they are looking for survivors. Commander Wilson of the helo advised them of the distress call we received and that we rushed here to assist."

"I hope they buy that, or we may be the next thing on the bottom."

"We'll know real soon if they don't," Lieutenant Commander Sheppard remarked.

"Can we make contact with the vessel ourselves?" Grey asked.

"Not yet, sir. They are using an FM transmission on low power, for some reason. They should be able to hear us, but we get nothing but static here."

"Keep trying, but continue with the relay through the helo until you make positive contact."

"Aye, aye, sir."

"I don't like this. Slow to two-thirds, Helmsman. Maintain present heading," Grey ordered.

Two hours passed, and the *George Washington* was a hundred yards from the ancient cruiser that flew the flag of the Nigerian government. The vessel was about three hundred feet long, probably built before the Second World War. She was, according to the computer on the *Washington*, an old Russian-built battle cruiser, similar to US destroyer-class ships, about fifty feet shorter than the *Washington* and not as well armed, but still very deadly.

"This is Commander Russell Grey of the USS *George Washington*. We have been running at near max speed in response to a distress call at these coordinates for three days. Can we be of assistance?"

"Commander Grey, this is Captain Vlademir Karamazov. We appreciate your effort to help a ship in distress, but as you see, we are here and have found only wreckage and no survivors. We have no problem with your staying in our waters to rest your men," was the reply from the Russian cruiser captain.

"Captain Vlademir Karamazov, we will move the *Washington* over to shallower water for some repairs and stay out of your search area. If you need assistance, please advise. We are here to help if needed," Grey sent back to the cruiser.

"Thank you again, Commander," Captain Karamazov said and broke off transmission.

"Helmsman, heading 110 degrees, one quarter power. Proceed with caution. Let me know when we have recovered the helo."

"Aye, sir," came the response, and the *Washington* started to turn and proceed to its destination over the *Wolverine*.

"Have all the lookouts stay alert and have two extra men on watch to do nothing but keep an eye on our friend," Grey ordered.

"Have the boys in the radio room monitor all the messages from the ship continuously. Tape all transmissions. I want to known what he is up to at all times."

"A Russian ship in these waters, even an old one, bothers me," Grey said to no one in particular.

"Radio, come up here. We need to get a message off to ComNav right now," Grey ordered through the intercom.

Grey paced the bridge, contemplating his next move. He had never in his military career been in such a situation as this. Sure, he had been in a combat area; two tours off the coast and one on the mainland of Vietnam gave him a lot of firsthand experience. But here, he didn't know if he had an enemy or friend on the Russian cruiser, and now he was sitting anchored eighteen miles from a country that was having itself a civil war, one that could very well be fed by his nearby neighbor.

One thing was for sure: he was very uncomfortable with the whole situation. And some orders from ComNav would surely help relieve some tension.

"Commander, Seaman O'Donnell, radio room. You sent for me, sir," the seaman finally said as he stood in the doorway, waiting patiently for the commander to see him.

"Huh? Oh, sorry, son. Got wrapped up in my thoughts. Come in. I need to send an encrypted message to ComNav using burst trans and will be getting a reply in the same manner. Just a minute and I'll write it out," Grey said and then turned to the small table in the back of the bridge to write out the message.

Chapter 9

WHO CAN YOU TRUST?

Norfolk Naval Yard, Virginia
April 24, 1996
0630 Hours, EST

"JD, how long have you been in the Navy?" Lieutenant Commander Robert Batuman asked his commander while standing on the bridge of the newest Ohio-class nuclear-powered submarine in the US Navy, the USS *Seasnake*.

"Seventeen years, Batman. Started out in Naval Security Group at Skaggs Island a long, long time ago," JD Henderson replied as he watched the movement of a freighter leaving the docks on the commercial side of Norfolk Harbor.

They were returning from four weeks at sea, running the *Seasnake* through her initial sea trails.

"Didn't you have the *Seadragon* for a few years?"

"Yeah, real fine boat. My first command on a nuke boat after signing into the program. What's that freighter doing?" JD questioned, pointing toward the outbound ship.

They were now paying particular attention to a freighter that was maneuvering out of the civilian side of the harbor. They wanted to allow enough room between the two vessels to prevent any mishaps.

"Keep a good eye on that tramp freighter!" Batman yelled to the lookouts.

"Steer two degrees port for one minute, then back on course," JD ordered to the helmsman.

Batman was really Lieutenant Commander Robert Batuman, but as a boy, he'd been nicknamed Batman because it was easier to pronounce than Batuman. He knew submarines inside and out and wouldn't trade his job with anyone's.

"Batman, port bow!" the senior lookout yelled, pointing toward the freighter. She had changed course and was heading straight for the *Seasnake*. The channel being small had forced both ships to pass within a couple hundred yards, but her abrupt change in course and speed was decreasing that distance. The black smoke billowing out of her stack indicated that she had increased her speed to near max.

"Helm, FLANK SPEED NOW!" JD ordered in an attempt to outrun the charging freighter. "Secure the hatches!"

"What the hell are they trying to do?" Batman asked.

"I don't..." JD started to say but didn't finish, because when the freighter steamed to within one hundred yards of them, she exploded with a force that caused the *Seasnake* to roll completely over on her side. The sail was completely engulfed in water, first when she rolled over on her side and then when the tons of water crashed down on her like a tidal wave after the initial explosion. After what seemed like an eternity but was really only a few seconds, the *Seasnake* slowly righted herself. She sat dead in the water. No life could be seen on deck, and the freighter was now in a million small pieces scattered all over the harbor.

The *Seasnake* was taking in water through the hatches on the stern, which had not been secured in time. Water rushed in the stricken sub faster than could be stopped. The hatches were normally open on the stern deck to allow fresh air to circulate through the boat while on the surface, in calm water. But today those hatches that allowed life-giving air to enter were now allowing thousands of gallons of water to rush in, sending the boat and its crew to the bottom of the harbor.

Ships were damaged at over a thousand yards away; windows had broken, and debris landed as far away as the administration building, located a mile inland.

JD awoke on the deck of his boat, only to find his head and shoulder hurt like hell. Looking around, dazed but catching up, he located Batman lying under a piece of metal that had belonged to the freighter. Upon further inspection, he found one of his lookouts, his neck broken and still strapped onto the tower; the other man was nowhere to be found. Henderson noted that his boat was not moving forward and there was no vibration coming from within the boat, indicating the engines had been shut down.

Realizing his submarine was sinking and there was nothing he could do to stop it, JD quickly moved to free Batman. Cut and bruised, but otherwise not seriously injured, Batman scanned the boat for damage. Men started to exit the hatch on the sail behind Henderson; first out was Ensign Keyes, pulling an injured sailor up with him.

"Keyes, what's happening down there?" Henderson yelled.

"She's sinking, sir! The hull was breached, and she's taking in water. The pumps are down. We cannot control the water. I ordered abandon ship, sir!" Keyes yelled as he continued to pull sailors up the hatch. Henderson and Batman assisted as best as they could. Opening the compartments that held the life rafts, they started to inflate two. Minutes later, twenty-three survivors floated near the stricken boat as the first of many rescue boats arrived.

The *Seasnake* slowly sank below the waves as more survivors were being pulled into the rafts. JD Henderson and Batman were the last to leave, but not before securing the hatch. Water was up to their ankles on the sail when they swam off toward the lifeboats.

Reaching the closest lifeboat, they turned to see the periscope dip below the waves and vanish.

Sirens could be heard in the distance, and a fireboat was heading directly for the *Seasnake*.

Twenty minutes later, the body of the missing lookout was found floating facedown forty yards from the life rafts.

The initial report to the papers indicated that a freighter had caught fire and exploded close by the *Seasnake*, causing severe damage, which resulted in her sinking. Divers were immediately sent down to the wreck to see if there were any more survivors trapped on board. Rescue efforts were nonstop and massive.

Eighteen hours later, divers had saved fifteen more men who had been trapped in the forward torpedo room. No other survivors were found. A total of thirty-eight survived the sinking, and fifty-four men lost their lives.

The initial findings indicated that the commander of the *Seasnake* had done everything he could do under the circumstances. Damage to other ships was minimal, and injury onshore and the surrounding area was also minimal.

Palm Beach, Florida
Davin Pierce's Office
April 24, 1996
1030 Hours, EST

"Hello," Stephanie answered the ringing telephone.

"Hi, it's Davin," he said.

"Davin, where the hell are you?" Stephanie cut in. "I've been worried sick. No calls, no messages."

"Sorry, but I did try to call and your answering machine must not be working and the one in the office has been broken for months, you know that," Davin responded, defending himself.

"Look, I got back from San Francisco late last night with the logbook. Now, what do you want me to do with it? Where you calling from? There is a lot of noise."

"The airport. I'm catching a plane in a few minutes. Look, just hang on to the logbook for now. Better yet, take it to the bank and lock it in a safe-deposit box. When I get there, we will study it thoroughly. I'll be in Washington for the next few days. Just take it easy and keep the office open most of the day. Has Jane called in?"

"Yes. She said she has some interesting information about the *MaryJean*. Nothing more from the guys," Stephanie said.

"Okay, I'll call Jane next."

"No. She is in Vermont for a few days. Says she is tracking down a lead."

"Okay, I'll call her in a few days. Anything else?" Davin asked.

"Yes, be careful."

"Thanks. See you in a few days. Bye," Davin said, hanging up the receiver.

NAVSECGRU HQD
Nebraska Avenue, Washington, DC
April 24, 1996
1300 Hours, EST

Admiral Harold (Hal) Jacobs, deputy director of Naval Intelligence and commander of Naval Security Group Headquarters Detachment (NAVSECGRU HQD), a member of Admiral Henry Barker's staff, sat quietly at his desk, rereading the message he had just received. Admiral Hal Jacobs was very interested in the contents of the message, more than Barker anticipated when he sent it over to him. Admiral Jacobs didn't have to research his computer to recall the ship mentioned. He knew her by the nightmares and fear that swelled inside him from the lowest corners of his body and soul. Barker had casually mentioned in a phone conversation earlier that a ship had been found, but would not discuss the details. Then Corning in Nigeria sent that message about a US ship and British ship in Nigerian waters with a small sailboat.

The message had been sanitized before he received it, but he knew where it came from, not the exact individual, but he knew of that special covert operation of Barker's. It had to be them. Their cover story was to search for sunken ships, and they just got lucky, or maybe unlucky. Time would tell.

An old World War II submarine, in what looked like almost-new condition, was located in about eighty feet of very clear water. The message stated that the sub looked as though it had just been recently parked and left, as though the crew decided to go to town for dinner and would be back soon. The only markings on the sub were located on the stern in small letters. They were "SS-701 *Wolverine*." Everything was starting to make sense now; Barker's covert operation had turned up the old boat, and the *Washington* was sent to protect her and the boat. Did Barker know what a hornet's nest he was getting into with that boat? Probably not.

Commander James D. Henderson and Lieutenant Commander Robert Batuman (Batman) were in Admiral Jacobs's office, sitting silently as Jacobs read the message to them. He had requested through CINC to use them on a special assignment since they had just lost their boat, and Jacobs knew Henderson had a security background. And he needed someone with his experience in security and on submarines. Batman was just an added benefit to the package.

Jacobs needed to buy time and also to get as close as possible to the salvage operation that he knew was going to take place real soon on the *Wolverine*. The latest message confirmed that the old boat was in fact the USS *Wolverine*, which was reported missing in World War II, but he knew she had only been missing for the last four months.

After reading the message to the men in his office, Admiral Jacobs leaned back in his chair and started to chew on his Cuban cigar, trying to think of what to say first. Finally, he started to speak.

"Henderson, you and Batman are without a boat for the moment, and I am very sorry about the loss. I hope you have recovered from your injuries. I need some help and asked CINC to loan you two to me for a special job. I know this doesn't fall in your normal duties, but this is no ordinary sub chase. What I am about to tell you is classified top secret and must not be discussed with anyone outside this office. Understand?" He waited for a reply and continued after receiving a nod from both. "Admiral Barker doesn't know about this operation and will be briefed as soon as we have some answers. That's where you two come in. I need some answers, and I need them fast. First, I need to know why this sub is where she is. She is over a thousand miles from where she was reported as being lost. I want to know how she got there and what happened to her crew. This is no ordinary sub investigation, boys. She was officially reported missing early in '43 with all the crew lost. That was the official story. In reality, she remained active on various covert missions till the end of World War II, and then disappeared. Just dropped out of sight, permanently, without a trace or any further contact, till now. And now she turns up off the coast of Africa. Why is she there?" stated Jacobs, lying about when she was lost.

"Sir, we will do our best to find out. How much latitude do we have?" asked JD.

"JD, you two do whatever is necessary to uncover the reason and story behind this."

JD and Batman looked sharply at each other for a moment, trying to read each other's thoughts, and then turned their focus back to Jacobs.

"I want some answers in two weeks, boys, and a full account in thirty days, even if you have to raise that damn sub yourselves. Understand?" Then Jacobs added, "By the way, we have a destroyer and a research vessel on station, but they are scheduled to leave within the next sixty hours. So if you need answers from them, get them early. Just find out about that damn ghost ship." Jacobs knew most of the story about the *Wolverine* but hoped the *Wolverine* would never be salvaged.

"Yes, sir," they sounded off in unison, standing up and saluting the admiral. They turned to leave when the admiral started to say something more, and then stopped.

"What is it, sir?" asked Batman.

"I don't mean to be hard on you, fellows, but...well, I guess I shouldn't say anything," he said, stopping for a moment to clear his thoughts. "*Damn*, you'll find out soon, anyway. My older brother was commander of the *Wolverine*." Without a word, the two quietly acknowledged the statement, turned toward the door, and exited.

Washington, DC
April 24, 1996
2015 Hours, EST

Davin and Connie were supposed to arrive at Washington National Airport at 6:05 p.m. on the flight from Palm Beach, Florida, but it finally landed at 8:15 p.m. The flight had its normal delays and late departure from Atlanta, which was the busiest airport in the South.

Jack Malone was patiently waiting for them in the airport lounge. He was on his third drink, but he was a patient man and knew that some days everything didn't go the way it was planned, especially when you were talking about the airlines.

"Jack, *ole* buddy, how have you been?" Davin said as he approached Jack, who was sitting on a barstool near the window.

"Davin, Connie, it's about time you two got here," Jack said as he stood up and hugged Connie and took ahold of Davin's out-stretched hand.

"Damn, you look good, for an old fart," Davin said with a smile.

"I'm doing okay. How about you? I hear my girl here has been waltzing with a loaded shotgun." Then, looking at Connie, he said, "You okay, kid? You gave us quite a scare."

"Oh, I'm fine. Just a little scratch," she said, pausing to catch her breath. "Let's get outa here. I'm sick and tired of airports for one day."

"How about bags? You got any more?"

"No, Jack, ole buddy, we travel light, so let's get before they charge us rental on this floor space."

The drive over to the hotel was short. They were out of the airport and heading up George Washington Parkway within a couple of minutes. Everyone was quiet till they were in the hotel suite and had wine and a snack on its way up via room service. Room service was a luxury that Davin normally avoided because of the prices. *What the hell, it's not too often that old friends can get together like this,* he thought.

Once the drinks arrived and they were all comfortable, the conversation led its merry way through the adventures of Connie and Jack. First, in New Mexico running a Sting operation, then off to Miami and a major drug bust, then to Seattle to uncover the case of the missing top secret documents at a defense plant, only to find that the security manager had them stored illegally in a safe in his office.

Conversation continued until they noticed that Connie had fallen asleep on the sofa. It was around twelve thirty when Davin got up and carried her into her room and put her under the spread. Upon returning, Jack and Davin talked for about an hour more.

Then Davin got up and threw Jack a pillow and blanket, so he might sleep on the now-empty sofa, and Davin headed off to his adjoining room for some sleep.

They never did talk about the case that brought them together; they had figured tomorrow, or rather, in the morning, they would start out the new day with a new case, together like the three musketeers. Davin was tired, but sleep just didn't want to come; he lay there and could only think of this old ship that might, at least from the clues at hand, have never sunk. But where was she now?

Naval Hall of Records
April 15, 1996
0745 Hours, EST

JD and Batman arrived at the vault for classified war records in the Navy Department's Hall of Records at 07:45. They knew they would be there for a long time, trying to uncover what they could after forty-plus years of storage.

"Good morning, sir," said Ensign MR Duval.

"Good morning, Ensign Duval," said Batman. "I understand you are to help us locate the information on this UI sub.

"Yes, sir, and I think we have a lot of work ahead of us. These files haven't been touched in over fifty years, and when they were, they were not put in any acceptable order," Ensign Duval replied.

"We three are going to be spending a lot of time together until we solve this, so let's cut the bull with rank and all, okay? I go by JD, and this is Batman. And you are?"

"Ensign Duval, sir. But my friends call me Micky or Michelle," she said, getting the required laugh from JD and Batman.

"Okay, guys, let's get going. This is going to take long enough as it is," JD stated. "Micky, what's your background with submarines?"

"Mostly as a hobby. They haven't allowed women to serve on subs yet. But I've studied everything there is to know about them and have even been on several World War II boats, US, German, and Japanese. I spent two weeks last summer on the *Eagleray* during a training exercise. I was the helmsman and navigator for the mission and then the exec for the last three days."

"Great. You will fit right in," JD said.

"Holy cow, where do we begin?" stated Batman, looking into the vault containing all the classified naval records from World War II. "In this room of unorganized, dusty records, files, and whatever, we are supposed to locate something about a submarine that disappeared in 1943. You have got to be kidding, pal. It looks like a tornado blew through here. This is gonna take forever, guys."

"Stop your complaining, Batman. It could be worse," said JD.

"How?"

"Well, first off, we could be stuck here with each other, but instead we have some lovely company to keep you in line, so let's get started. I am up for retirement in three years, and I don't want to spend all of them in this vault."

The search started in three different areas of the room, with no particular direction planned, mainly because the files were in no apparent order. They soon discovered that someone long ago had attempted to organize the files but either gave up or died trying. Because what they found was that the year 1941 was filed alphabetically, A to Z, and 1942 was done numerically, starting with 0001 to 42-9872, according to the one and only card file they had found. However, the 1942 files were not in the order listed on the card file. It was going to take a long while to find anything.

"Hey, Micky, how is your knowledge on submarines?" asked JD.

"Pretty good. Why?"

"Well, I know Batman knows about subs. He's served on them with me for the past three years. I just needed to know if you have a working knowledge of this type of boat."

Talking quieted down for a while as they rummaged through the stacks and stacks of old files and records of ships, movements, convoys, and everything else imaginable, and some things that were unimaginable, in a war.

Hours went by as they searched all categories of documents from top secret on down. Most should have been declassified years ago or should have been destroyed years ago.

"Micky, did we try launch dates or dates the hulls were laid?" asked Batman.

"No, not yet, but let's try that."

"You know, someday, someone will organize this mess and maybe put what's left on computer, so we could find something," said JD.

"Figure the odds, *ole* boy. By the time they do that, this stuff would have decayed from age," Batman responded.

"You know, if someone really wanted to write a history of naval warfare and the Second World War, they should be locked up in here for a year or two," JD said sadly.

Hours turned into days and days into a week, and the sum total of their efforts was zero.

Lagos, Nigeria
April 25, 1996
0800 Hours, GMT

General Samula sat quietly in his office overlooking the port. His gaze out the large picture window held his complete attention. He thought about his country, his hands held in the shape of a triangle, elbows on the arms of his chair as he thought.

"Good morning, Mr. Corning. It is customary, even in a backward, primitive country such as mine, to knock before entering a room. But do come in and sit down, Mr. Corning. Please sit down," General Samula said without turning from his gaze. Seeing Mr. Corning's reflection in the plate glass was his only clue that the man had entered the office.

"Thank you. I didn't know you were here," Mr. Corning said. "Your secretary is not at her desk, and I figured I would just sit and wait until you arrived."

"Yes, I know. I normally do not arrive this early in the morning, but times are changing and I must be ready for anything. Especially when my most trusted countrymen decide, well…ah…when they decide that the cause we are fighting for is not the right one and turn against me," Samula said with a tone of sorrow in his voice.

"Sir, I informed my contact in Washington about the warships off your coast, and he said he would order it out of the area within the time you set," Corning responded, ignoring Samula's comment about his countrymen.

"Mr. Corning, one of my patrol boats has failed to report in and has not been seen since it went to investigate that damn sailboat. I feel it has come to foul play by your warships!" Samula stated as he turned to face Corning. "I dispatched a heavy battle cruiser to patrol the area and to keep any unwanted ships out of the area the patrol boat was last reported heading."

"Don't do anything that you will regret, General. If my government has a destroyer or whatever in your waters, they will move as soon as ordered to. But if you fire on them, well, they will return fire and, believe me, sir, there will be hell to pay if any American lives are lost."

"You are in no position to threaten, Corning, only to listen."

"Okay, I'll listen, but don't get too pushy, General. The American people will not tolerate any American lives being lost in your little war. Just look at what happened in Iraq in '92."

"Yes, the United States is the most powerful nation in the world. And you have the world trembling in their shoes. Saddam was a wimp, using one of your own terms. He had the military power but did not know how to use it. We, on the other hand, have a powerful army and are not afraid to use everything at our disposal. You heard about the ship explosion at Norfolk Naval Yard, Mr. Corning."

"Yes. That was you, wasn't it, General?" Receiving a nod, he continued, "Look, General, we will not tolerate terrorist acts against any country, especially mine!" Corning yelled and stood, looking directly at the general, who had a smile of satisfaction on his face.

"Mr. Corning, we did it once to show that we can. Now, you tell your government that I will detonate the other twenty bombs if they don't cooperate. But first, you will do me a big favor, Mr. Corning." General Samula returned Corning's stare.

"What do you want now, General?" Corning asked, getting a bit aggravated with the general.

"You, Mr. Corning, are going to supply me with the detailed plans for that nuclear device we have. We may need it to defend our borders," General Samula said coldly.

"That is not possible, General. I have and will provide to you all the conventional weapons of destruction you desire, but I will not provide any information or assistance with that bomb," Corning said and then turned to leave. "Good day, General!"

"Mr. Corning!" General Samula said quietly. "Stop right where you are and listen to me!"

Corning stopped and turned around to face the general again, only to find the general with a small but lethal .380 automatic pistol, the barrel leveled at Mr. Corning's chest.

"As I started to say, you will provide the complete assembly instructions and detonation device for that bomb by noon tomorrow, or you will have a very unfortunate accident. Do you understand, Mr. Corning?" Samula asked, not once changing the quiet but deadly tone of his voice.

"General, you may as well pull that trigger now. I will not provide you a means to destroy the world now or ever. I don't know how you got the damn thing, but I do know, as long as I'm alive, I will do whatever I can to prevent you from assembling that bomb."

"Mr. Corning, my dear friend, you are a dead man now, if not by me, then by your own country. You haven't been a very patriotic man. Killing you here will only save your government the expense of a trial and execution for treason. I will just be saving your government a lot of money. So live longer, Mr. Corning, and give me what I need."

"No! Never!" were the last words that Mr. Corning spoke. The .380 penetrated his heart, which caused death instantly, leaving very little blood. General Samula had had the forethought to place a large piece of old carpet on the floor, so all he had to do was roll up the carpet and dispose of the body and carpet together.

Twin Bridges Hotel
Washington, DC
April 25, 1996
0815 Hours, EST

Davin awoke with a jolt. The smell of bacon and eggs was overpowering, almost as if they were being cooked right next door.

"Morning, Jack. That smells great. Is Connie up yet?"

"Dig in, Davin, and yeah, she's up and in the shower."

Davin started to fill up his plate and then heard Connie come in the room.

"Good morning, boys. Did you sleep well? Any coffee over there, Davin?" Connie asked as she walked across the room.

"Yeah. Black, right?" Davin answered and asked in the same statement.

"Great!" Connie smiled, taking the cup from Davin and sipping slowly.

"First, some coffee and food, then down to business. We have a lot of ground to cover and not much time to do it," Jack said between bites.

"Whoa, let's back up a minute. What's this about time?" Davin asked once he had realized what was said.

Jack didn't say anything for a long time, slowly chewing his food. Davin looked at him seriously for a moment or two, wondering what he meant. Finally, he realized he wasn't going to volunteer anything, not easily, anyway.

"Well," Jack started just as Davin opened his mouth to ask again.

"Well, what, Jack? No secrets here. We go too far back to hold anything back. Now, what do you mean 'not much time'?"

"Yeah, Jack, what do you mean?" Connie inserted.

"Okay, okay, no ganging up. That's not fair, and you know it."

"Well?" Davin asked again.

"I was going to tell you everything right after you had finished your breakfast, but if you insist."

"We do!" Connie and Davin said in unison.

"You know about Bronsly being identified in the warehouse. Well, the two old guys with him were also from the *MaryJean*. They were listed as missing and assumed dead, because no bodies were found. Well, it seems as though the Navy is interested in this little caper now. An admiral by the name of Jacobs heard we had found the weapons, and I went over to talk with him yesterday. And you will never guess what I found out."

"Jack, if the Navy is getting their fingers in this, then there may be more to it than what we see so far. But go on," Davin said, pouring himself another cup of coffee and offering some more to Connie and Jack also.

"This admiral is now deputy director of Naval Intelligence over on Nebraska Avenue, but back in '43, he was a little lieutenant working the convoys and cargoes out of New York Harbor. He remembers the *MaryJean* quite well. He says she arrived in New York with a manifest showing that she was half-full of munitions and weapons. And she was to pick up some medical supplies and vehicles only, which she did. But then, just before she was to sail, he was instructed by his higher to load three additional crates of unknown contents and a squad of Marines to guard them."

"That's interesting, Jack. Did he say if he ever found out what was in those crates?" Connie asked.

"No, he didn't. The *MaryJean* also took on her passengers there. Jacobs said that within an hour of loading the crates and Marines, she set sail and that was the last he heard or saw of the ship, till now."

"That's all very interesting, Jack. Did he say anything else that might help us?" Davin asked after thinking the information that Josh had provided confirmed this. But he wasn't ready to let anyone know except for himself and Stephanie. The less they knew, the safer they were.

"Yeah, he did, and this is where the Navy comes in, guys. He, meaning Jacobs, wants answers, and he wants them as soon as possible. In other words, within the next thirty days, he wants an accounting of the *MaryJean* incident. This guy is only a rear admiral, but he does have power and resources, which he has given us permission to use. So there you have it in a nutshell. Now, it's your turn. Bring me up-to-date."

Davin filled him in on what he had on the *MaryJean* and about the shooting on I-95 and attempted to piece it all together. Their assumptions fit their proof, or at least Stephanie was picking up some of it. Davin told them about the log and what it cost him to buy it, hoping Stephanie was all right.

It was ten o'clock in the morning before they arrived at the Naval Archives Vault in the Navy Department. They were escorted into an area located deep within the confines of the building. Once they finally arrived, they were directed to twelve filing cabinets in the corner of the room. The cabinets were old and dusty but otherwise in good shape. Jack and Davin started looking through the files for anything on the *MaryJean*, knowing that the odds of finding anything were a million to one. Connie went to another part of the vault to research convoy procedures and time schedules.

After about two hours of rummaging through those files, Jack came up with a folder on the *MaryJean*, but it turned out to be the construction plans and the order to build. The plans would be handy if they found her.

A couple of hours later, they found that one of the cabinets contained records, or rather copies, of the manifests for each ship of each convoy, also listing the crews and date and time of sinking, if applicable. In this case, the *MaryJean* was listed as sinking on the twentieth of January 1943. The list included an accounting of the dead or missing in action. The last known location was shown. There was something missing, but Davin didn't know what; he just knew something was missing from this file.

"Think we got enough, Davin?" Jack asked as he stood and stretched.

"Yeah. Let's get outa here and find Connie," Davin answered as he also stood and tried to get some of his muscles working again.

It was nearing 1:30, and they hadn't heard from Connie for quite a while. The receptionist told them that she was over in the area marked "Classified War Records, World War II." "It's down the hall to the end. Take a left and then down the stairs to the next floor and turn right, and it's the eighth or ninth door on the left." After the second turn, they got lost and ended up in the janitor's closet. Connie finally found them wandering up and down the hall. She wasn't alone.

"Hi, guys. Where've you been?" she asked, as she walked down the hall toward them.

"There you are. We've been looking all over for you."

"I bet. Hey, I'd like you to meet Commander JD Henderson and Lieutenant Commander Robert Batuman, also known as Batman. They've been helping me locate what we need."

"Pleasure to meet you, and thanks for helping our girl," Davin said as he and JD shook hands.

"No problem. We needed a little break from our own research," JD said. "If there is anything else we can help you with, let us know, or let Micky know. She will know where we are."

"Wish we could stay and chat, but we need to scoot off. Hope to run into you again," Jack said as they started off.

During the drive back to the hotel, they talked about the *MaryJean* and decided that this trail was quickly running into a dead end.

"Let's get something to eat before we make any decisions, okay? I'm starving," Jack said finally.

"You're driving. Take us to food," Connie replied. "I need food too. Let's eat."

Lunch was just what the doctor ordered. They were a little more relaxed and could think of what their next move should be.

"Okay, what next, guys? It's getting close to three o'clock in the afternoon, and we still don't know enough to point us in the right direction," Connie said and then finished off her ice tea.

"Well, look, we know the *MJ* was torpedoed by a German U-boat and then abandoned. Then she disappeared, apparently with some crew still on board, right?" Davin stated, looking to be corrected.

"Right. Some of the supposed dead crew," Jack added.

"Okay, with the engines also dead supposedly, and a few not-so-dead men on board, let's speculate a little. What if—now, follow closely—what if the *MaryJean* had an operational engine, okay? What would you do if you were part of a conspiracy to steal government arms and sink a ship to cover that up and then had everything go off-center? And now you are supposed to be dead on this ship in the North Atlantic, and the captain is still trying to follow through with the scenario, so he abandons ship, leaving you and a couple others with a partially dead ship. And remember the charges that were supposed to have detonated but didn't, and the ship disappeared over the horizon before morning. Kinda quick, wouldn't you say, for a ship without power? Now, what do you do? Attempt to sail her to shallower waters to scuttle her? Or do you abandon ship once out of sight of the others, or just crank up and head somewhere?" Davin speculated and then took a long drink from his beer.

"According to Jorgenson and the others, there were no more lifeboats, right?" Connie questioned.

"Correct. There were no lifeboats, so we can assume the crew left on board planned on sailing her somewhere they knew they would be safe and then sink her. But where?" Jack responded.

"I need to call my office and see if my people have come up with anything more," Davin said and then finished off his beer.

"Let's get back to the hotel and map out what we need to do," Jack added as he stood up, took out some cash, and left an adequate amount on the table with the check.

It took thirty minutes to get back to the hotel because of midafternoon traffic. They could have walked it in ten, but they didn't want to leave the car parked on the street too long. If things are left alone too long in the city, they seem to grow legs and walk away. The hotel parking lot was only somewhat safer.

"I think a trip to Munich to visit the German Naval Archives is in order. We may as well find out about that sub that torpedoed the *MJ*. Maybe they can tell us something the survivors don't know, mainly how many torpedoes they fired and from where," Davin said after they got back to the hotel and were heading up in the elevator.

"What is that going to prove, Davin?" asked Connie.

"Well, for one, it's going to tell us who is blowing smoke, and also, it could confirm that Bronsly had intended to sink her himself. And that, my friend, could really help fill in some blanks. And besides, we need all the help we can get."

"Okay, I'll make some reservations. When shall we leave?" Connie asked as they exited the elevator and started down the hall to their suite.

"Well, Connie, dear, I would like to leave tomorrow, and you and Jack need to follow up on the crew list and see if there are possibly any other living crew members that are supposed to be dead. Sorry, babe, but I'm going alone."

"That's okay, Davin. I'll still see if I can get you a good flight, but when this is all over, you and I are going to take a little R&R somewhere. Deal?"

"Deal," Davin said, assuring her that he was sincere.

They had reached the suite and entered to find that the maid either decided to get even for all the mess they had made or someone was looking for something and didn't care about the mess he left. The room was totally trashed. Somebody really had gone out of his way to do this.

"Holy shit!" Jack said quietly as he reached for his gun. Connie and Davin did the same.

"You check that room, Davin. I'll check this one," Jack said, heading for Connie's room. Connie stayed near the door and kept both of them in eyesight.

Davin's room proved to be just as messy as the main room. There was nobody hiding in there and no sign of forced entry.

"Davin, come in here," Jack called from Connie's room. "Connie, call the police. I think we have a problem."

Jack, on the other hand, had found someone in Connie's room, but he wasn't talking. Lying in a pool of blood beside the bed was the body of a man who looked around twenty-five, with brown hair, a beard, long and unkempt, wearing blue jeans, a dark brown T-shirt, and tennis shoes.

Jack searched the body for identification and found a wallet with a driver's license, a couple of dollars, and a few old family pictures. The driver's license said he was John Alan Dobbs of 131 South Bradley Avenue, Allentown, Pennsylvania. He was twenty-six years old and very dead.

Chapter 10

MORE GHOSTS

Admiral Jacobs's Office
April 25, 1996
1830 Hours EST

"Admiral Barker, this is Jacobs. Got a problem, sir," Jacobs said into the phone. He was starting to sweat a little. The air conditioner was not working up to par, or was it the pressure of what he was involved in?

"What's the problem, Jacobs?" Barker asked. He never did like Jacobs, always felt that he was a glory hound, attempting to cut corners, maybe just to make himself look good.

"Can't go into it over the phone. Can we meet in the vault in a couple of minutes, sir?" Jacobs asked, sweating.

Twenty minutes later, the two admirals were comfortably sitting in the secure conference room in the vault. In the vault, they could talk freely without worry of any intrusion or anyone without proper security clearance overhearing what was said. It was a completely private and secure area where many strategic and tactical conferences had been held during the past twenty-five years.

"Well, Hal, what did you drag me down here for? Let's make this quick. My wife said if I get home late tonight, she will feed my dinner to the dog," Barker said with a laugh.

"At least she doesn't think you are seeing some bimbo," Jacobs commented.

"I hope not. Now, what's on your mind?"

"Henry, we have some problems to handle before morning," Jacobs started, then stood and started to pace around the room.

"What's wrong, Hal? You look scared as hell. Is Millie on your back again about the child support?" Barker asked, hoping it was that simple.

"No. I only wish that were the problem. Sir, I think I may have started another Vietnam!" Jacobs said but could not make eye contact with Barker.

"What! Sit down and tell me what makes you think you've started a war." Barker sounded confused but wanted to get to the answers as quickly as possible.

"I have some inside information that the Nigerian coup is just the beginning of a major conflict, involving all of its surrounding countries, the Soviet Union, and us," Jacobs began.

"Details, Hal. Lay it out on the table," Henry Barker insisted.

Twenty-five minutes later, Jacobs had told most everything he knew, only leaving out his connections with the underworld and his black market dealings. He said that reliable sources indicated that US weapons had been sold to the Nigerian government, but amounts and by exactly who was not specified. The last transmission from his operative in Nigeria was a plea for assistance and information that the recent explosion of a ship at Norfolk might have been a terrorist strike against the US by Nigeria. This was not confirmed as yet because contact with his operative had been lost.

"Okay, Hal, you've made your point. We can't do anything except put the forces on alert. But first, we need to talk to the president. As soon as we leave here, I'll call the president and then we head over there, together."

"Yeah," was all that Jacobs could say.

Lagos, Nigeria
General Samula's Office
April 25, 1996
1945 Hours, GMT

"Dr. Frankel, you have the information I require?" General Samula asked as a well-dressed young gentleman entered the office through the side door.

"Yes, General. Has Mr. Corning left?" was the reply. Dr. Frankel was young and greedy. He knew what power was and wanted more, recently gaining another level of power on both sides of the war in Nigeria. Dr. Frankel worked as senior British ambassador to Nigeria, a position he gained through years of hard work and a doctoral degree in psychology from Harvard. He was short, a little overweight, but a member of the ten best-dressed males in the country, in a list that always started with General Samula.

"Mr. Corning will not be of service to anyone. He has departed, shall we say, permanently."

"Okay, sir. Now, I will give you what you need in exchange for, let's say, oh, the two million in gold that we had agreed on earlier."

"Delivery of the gold to a Swiss account has been ordered. Here is the number and the name of the bank," General Samula said, handing Frankel a small passbook and an envelope.

"Thank you, sir. Ah, yes, the airline tickets to Zurich. Thank you again, sir. You are too kind. Now, the information you require will be found at the embassy. When the raid starts, only a small skeleton crew will be there. Most have left for safer havens. Please try not to kill them. They have families and will surrender at the least bit of aggression. Make it look good. Here, General," he said, handing the general a single sheet of paper containing the combination to the safe that held the detonator and complete detailed plans for a nuclear bomb. Neither were any good for the bomb the general had, but Dr. Frankel liked living on the edge.

"I must leave now, sir. We have a lot to do before you invade our embassy. Good day," Frankel said as he stood and started for the door.

"Doctor, if what you just sold me is not what I seek, then your life is not worth the dirt you stand on. Understand, Doctor?" General Samula said as Frankel reached for the door handle.

"Sir, in good faith, I sell you what you request, so don't treat me like a common criminal. You have what you desire. Now, good day, sir." Frankel turned and left. He did not return to the embassy but instead went directly to the airport and took the first flight out of the country. He knew that his life would end if he went anywhere near the embassy.

Washington, DC
Twin Bridges Hotel
Suite of Davin Pierce
April 25, 1996
2030 Hours, EST

"The police are on their way. What have we got?" Connie asked as she came in the room. "Why my room?"

"Any idea what he was doing here?" Davin asked.

"It's possible someone broke in here to kill you and stumbled on him, mistaking him for you. Well, hell, I don't know, but it's a possibility," Jack said after searching the body for any more clues and finding none.

"Connie, I think we had better get another suite. This one is going to be a little crowded real soon," Davin suggested.

"Sure. I'll call down and get the manager up here and try to explain the situation. Be right back," she said just as there was a knock on the door. Stopping, she turned to answer the door.

"You make the call, Connie. I'll get the door," Davin said as he walked over to answer the second knock.

"Come on in, guys," Davin said to the two blue-suited officers and one obvious detective. "The corpse is in there, getting cold."

"Lieutenant Jamerson, Metro Police," Jamerson said, showing Davin his badge as he entered. "Check it out, Gary." He directed one of the officers to the bedroom. The other one remained at the door to control comings and goings.

"Lieutenant, this is Jack Malone, FBI, and Connie Young, also FBI, and I'm Davin Pierce. If you would care to have a seat, we will tell you what we know, if, ah…" He stopped as the officer named Gary came back in the room after looking at the body.

"Lieutenant, I think he's our man. The description matches," Officer Gary announced.

"Thanks, Gary. Call the coroner's office and get the lab boys up here," the lieutenant ordered.

"Could you enlighten us, Lieutenant? The description matches. Matches what? Who?" Jack asked, looking very confused.

"Whose room is this?" Jamerson asked abruptly.

"It's mine, Lieutenant. Why?" Davin answered.

"Well, that man in there, or rather, body, is, well, was being hunted for by every officer in my precinct. He gunned down two of my men in cold blood two days ago. Reason, hell, I don't think he had a reason except maybe the coke or crack that he was high on. Gary Baxter was one of the officers that witnessed the shooting. I have three more witnesses. Two are on the critical list, and the other one is resting with two holes in his shoulder. Does that answer your questions? Now, I have a few, but first, let's get out of this room and seal it off. Gary, you stay with Harry until the rest of the troops arrive," the lieutenant ordered.

Just then the manager showed up, looking very puzzled.

"What can I do for you, Mr. Pierce?" the manager asked as he walked up. "What's with all the police? I truly hope we don't have a problem."

"There has been a little accident in our room. Is there another suite available for the remainder of our stay?"

"Sure, but why?" the manager questioned, looking very puzzled. He took them to a suite about four doors down the hall and let them in.

"Will this do, sir?" he asked as they walked in. "Now, will someone please tell me what is going on?"

Jamerson explained to the manager that there had been a murder in the other suite and that he would require that no one be allowed to enter without his permission until they had finished the investigation. This seemed to not sit well with him, but there was not much he could do, so he left, advising them that he would take care of the room change, and asked that should there be anything they would require, to just call him.

"Okay, which one of you iced him?" Jamerson asked straight out.

"Wrong, Jamerson. We didn't do it, even though he deserved it, from what you said" Jack came back quickly and then went on to tell Jamerson about finding the body and the suite as it was.

"Okay, if you didn't, then who did?" Lieutenant Jamerson questioned.

"We don't know, Lieutenant. We have told you all we know, which isn't much, but that's it. There isn't any more," Davin said.

"Well, is there anything else I should know?" Jamerson asked, then paused and looked closely at them. "No. Well, then as soon as we can, we will release your stuff from the other suite. Until then…" He paused. "Good night." Jamerson turned and left.

For the next hour, they just sat around and talked about what had happened.

It was getting late, and none of them had eaten since lunch, so after making Davin's reservations for Germany, they headed out for some late dinner. There was a little Chinese place just down the street that had an excellent wine list.

Naval Hall of Records
April 26, 1996
0800 Hours, EST

After their first day of working in the vault, it was decided that the wearing of a work uniform was desirable as opposed to the standard dress uniform they all were accustomed to. The old paper and dust in the vault would mess up a dress blue uniform inside twenty minutes, and the cleaning bills in Washington could break Fort Knox.

"Hey, guys, I think I've found something!" exclaimed Micky.

"Let's see what you have, Micky," said JD, taking the document. "By Joe, I think she's got it. Listen to this, Batman. Marked TOP

SECRET: EYES ONLY OF NAVAL SPECIAL OPERATIONS SECTION. 'August 5, 1941, special modification to Gato-class submarine, SS701, SS673, and SS706. These had some major improvements to enhance their speed and long-range capabilities. Detailed improvements were classified under another cover. (See OPERATION ATLANTIC WOLF PHASE I, DTD, June 23, 1941).' Wait a minute, it goes on to say that all three subs were to be assigned special duty and had the new experimental Mark 18 torpedoes. Batman, look up those torpedoes!" JD stopped to read on quietly as Micky continued to look through the file she found.

"Listen to this. Projected completion of SS 701 *Wolverine* is April 1942, with sea trials and recertification by May of '42. Boy, that was quick!" exclaimed JD.

"Hey, remember, JD, there was a war going on," said Micky with a girlish little laugh.

"Okay, right, now that you mention it, there was a little war going on," retorted JD.

"What else does it say?" asked Micky, looking over JD's shoulder and accidentally leaning very close, pressing her breast into JD's back.

"Oh, not much, just that completion and sea trials were on schedule and the two sister ships were only two weeks behind her. Now, that is some fast work on a boat," JD said, smiling, as he felt Mickey's firm breast resting on his back. "Well, back to work. This isn't going very fast."

Time went on without any more clues, but they were getting there, slowly.

"JD, Micky, listen to this: 'TOP SECRET, NAVAL SPECIAL OPERATIONS SECTION, DTD, April 14, 1941, Mark 18 torpedoes...' Wait a second, guys. This is unreal! It says here the new Mark 18 torpedo is a special design to run without a wake, deeper, farther, and faster than the old 14s. And are designed to allow the sub commander to set the depth of the entire run up to one hundred feet, and the fish will run deep and quiet until within one hundred feet of target. Then will alter its own depth at a rate of thirty feet a second until detonation. It says here that they used a magnetic proximity fuse, which allowed the torpedo to detonate under the hull, inflicting greater damage. That is unbelievable for the forties. A torpedo like that gave the target no warning at all!" Batman exclaimed, then paused to read more. "The warhead had three times as much explosive power as the 14s, so with a guaranteed hit, only one fish per ship or sub, they could take out more of the enemy than any other sub."

"That is interesting. What else does it say? What about range and speed?" asked JD.

"Just a minute, JD," Batman said, pausing. "Here it is. They had a range of about 30,000 yards, weighed in at 3,765 pounds, and had a max speed of forty-eight knots. Top speed cut the range to around 19,500 yards."

"They sound like an improved version of the G7e German torpedo that had the battery problem, don't they, Batman? I wonder how we were able to solve that problem."

"But what about the boat itself? Didn't it say she could carry more fish and stay out longer?" asked Micky.

"Yeah, that's right. That must mean she carried fewer crew and more provisions and fuel," said Batman.

"Hey, lookee here, crew lists. These are lists for all naval ships in the Pacific. Wait...wait. Oh, here, I think, yeah, here it is. The Atlantic fleet information. Let's see here, they're dated 1939, 1940... ah...1941. I'm getting there...1942. Okay, let's see here, carriers... destroyers...corvettes...ah, here we go...submarines. Be patient, guys. Okay, here it is SS701 *Wolverine*. Commander Robert Ernest Jacobs." Puzzled, Micky looked over to JD and asked, "Do you think this Jacobs is any relation to Admiral Jacobs?"

"As a matter of fact, yes. Robert is the admiral's older brother," said JD matter-of-factly after a long pause. "Don't lose that list. We will need it later. Micky, are you okay?"

Micky looked sadly down at the list, then back to Batman and JD. Without another word, she laid the list in the stack of information they were accumulating and continued to search through the file in front of her.

Dulles International Airport
April 26, 1996
0830 Hours, EST

Connie and Jack dropped Davin off at Dulles for his flight to Munich, Germany. If everything went as it was supposed to, then he should arrive in Munich in about ten hours. His flight left on time, at 10:15 a.m., not bad for a scheduled 10:10 departure. Davin always loved flying, especially in first class, and these new, wide-body jets were very comfortable. The stews were usually very receptive in first class too. So why did he feel so crowded and restless?

Arrival at an international airport such as Munich is an experience in itself. The flight landed fifteen minutes early, but that did not help one little bit at customs. One hour, twenty minutes after landing, Davin was standing in front of the rental car agency behind four other tired travelers. At least the agent could speak English and each transaction only took a few minutes. Finally, after two hours, he was on the Autobahn, heading for downtown Munich. Davin arrived at the Urland Hotel near Olympia Park via the local cab service, which was far better than any in the States. Davin had stayed at this hotel several times before. It was old, and the rooms were either too hot or too cold, but there was elegance in the way it was built, with the high ceilings and not-so-modern accessories. Besides, the owners and he had become good friends over the years.

A day of air travel could really tire a person out, so Davin figured that a little dinner and bed were in order. He knew of a restaurant around the corner, another old place. That had been around forever, but the food was great and the wine was beyond compare. And then to bed, with plans of an early start tomorrow. And that was exactly what he did.

Lagos, Nigeria
General Samula's Office
April 26, 1996
0900 Hours, GMT

"General, the British and American Embassies have fallen into our control. Also, our troops are ready to move into Ghana," Amid reported. He was a colonel in the republic's Army, aide to General Samula.

"Was the information we require at the British Embassy?"

"Yes, sir, and it is being studied by our scientist in preparation for assembly," Amid said to the general as he scanned around the office.

"Good, Colonel Amid. Now, is the aircraft ready for its mission?" General Samula searched for answers.

"Yes, sir. Four Boeing 727 and one 747 aircraft are fueled and waiting for their cargo. The aircraft have been modified to carry the bomb, and the pilots are ready to fly as soon as the bomb is ready."

"Very good, Amid, very good. One final question before you go. Dr. Frankel, how was his departure? Successful, I hope," Samula queried.

"Sir, Dr. Frankel met with an unfortunate accident while crossing the street at the airport. I'm saddened to say. A passing bus killed him. We have sent flowers to his wife in London. She will miss him."

General Samula sat down in an overstuffed chair across his desk and picked up a recent copy of *Newsweek*. Noticing the front cover, he commented, "Did we send this picture of me to *Newsweek*?"

"No, sir. One of their photographers must have used a telephoto lens to get that. No photos of you have been released that I know of," Amid answered, looking at the article over the general's shoulder.

"If a photographer can do this, then so can a rifleman. Increase my bodyguard force, and get my doubles up here for screening."

"Yes, sir," Amid said and then departed the office immediately.

Reading the article about himself in *Newsweek* proved to him that he had a leak in his organization. The article stated that Nigeria had nuclear and chemical warfare capabilities and was not afraid to use them. Almost his exact words were repeated in print. How was this possible? A leak in his organization? He would find it, if he had to kill everyone to do so.

Munich, Germany
April 26, 1996
1300 Hours, GMT

Munich is a large beautiful city with a lot to offer the typical tourist or the inquisitive researcher. Davin fell into a category somewhere between those two. His mission was to find out about the U-boat that sank the *MaryJean* and also to see and interview anyone that served on the boat at that time.

It didn't take long to find out which U-boat attacked the *MaryJean*. The Germans were very careful about records and maintained accurate historical data.

Oberleutnant Wilhelm Gunter Zehetbauer commanded the U-49, aged thirty-one at time of taking command. He died with crew on January 20, 1943, when torpedoed by an unknown attacker while making repairs to damages to his boat that were caused by an attack of an American freighter. The report indicated that two torpedoes were fired from approximately 1,200 yards; one torpedo malfunctioned and sank to the bottom after leaving the boat. The other ran true and hit the stern at the engine room or just behind it. Zehetbauer circled and surfaced to finish off the freighter with his deck gun. He was almost out of torpedoes, but when he broke to the surface, he discovered the damaged ship was heading directly at him on a collision course. He immediately went into a crash dive, narrowly escaping being rammed by the freighter. Staying deep, Zehetbauer decided to leave the area instead of trying to fight it out. He surfaced twenty miles away and started repairs. While he was doing so, the sub was torpedoed and sunk, with only three survivors; these men were responsible for the report. The coordinates of the wreck were given, and when Davin checked the charts, it showed that she went down in twelve hundred feet of water.

The survivors were Hans G. Bauer, the ship's chief machinist mate; Josef Von Hofner, who was the executive officer; and Eric Kellenburg, who was a gunner's mate and lookout on that morning.

Davin didn't know if these guys were alive or not, but he was sure the people here would know how to find out. This report told a lot and answered some questions, but answers were still needed for a few more.

The receptionist was an average-looking blond German girl with deep blue eyes. She spoke perfect English, which was great, because Davin's German was barely understandable to anyone. She directed him to an area in the back of the museum and to a person in charge of records.

"Hello. May I help you, sir?" asked the lady behind the desk.

"Yes. I'm researching the U-boat U-49 and was wondering if there is any way I might find out if the three survivors are still alive and, if so, how I might reach them," Davin said as he handed her the list of names.

She turned to a terminal on her desk and typed in the names, then leaned back and waited.

"Please have a seat, sir. This could take a while," she said, indicating the empty chair against the wall.

After what seemed like hours but was only about forty-five minutes, she turned and handed Davin a printed sheet of paper, which he read.

Hans G. Bauer: DECEASED, May 24, 1967, Hamburg
Josef Von Hofner: Last known address of residence on file at Hall of Records in Bremerhaven
Eric Kellenburg: DECEASED, December 2, 1983, Wiesbaden

"Why do you seek these people, sir?" asked Ms. Linderhan.

"Why, well, that is a long story, but to make it short, they could help solve a fifty-year-old mystery, Ms. Linderhan," Davin answered, seeing her name tag pinned to her blouse.

"I don't want to be too pushy, but the war was a strain on a lot of people, and they may not want to be reminded."

"Looking at this list, it would seem that there is only one member of the crew alive, and I hate to pour salt on open wounds, but I do need to get some information that only he can provide. But believe me, I mean no harm to him," Davin replied sincerely.

"If you insist on seeing Von Hofner, I will take you to him tomorrow."

"Do you know him and where I might find him?" Davin asked.

"Yes on both. You see, Josef Von Hofner is my father, and I don't want him hurt anymore by that war!"

"That does make a difference. I would be honored if you would introduce me to your father, Ms. Linderhan."

"It is a long way to Bremerhaven. I suggest we get an early start, but first, you need to convince me that you are sincere about your quest," she stated quite bluntly.

"Okay, how about dinner? And I will explain everything that I know about this mystery. Then you decide."

"I get off work at 1800 hours. Pick me up out front at 1810, and don't be late," she said in a sweet, sexy little voice. "Oh, who will be picking me up, sir?"

"I'm sorry, my name is Davin Pierce, and I'll be there."

"Mr. Pierce, please wear a coat and tie," she insisted.

"No problem, Ms. Linderhan, no problem." Davin smiled.

"Now, get out of here. I need to get some work done before I can leave, Mr. Pierce," she replied.

"Call me Davin, please," he requested as he turned to leave.

"Anything you say, Mr. Pierce," she said to herself as Davin left. Reaching for the telephone on her desk, she started to dial.

Two dead, one alive. I guess I'm off to Bremerhaven. Located on the North Sea, it should be nice up there this time of year. But before I go, a phone call to Jack and Connie would be in order. I haven't talked to them in two days and need some input on what has been happening, Davin thought to himself as he exited the library and looked for a telephone booth.

It took no time at all to make the call back to the States. Cellular phones and satellites have practically eliminated congestion and bad connections; it sounded like they were in adjoining rooms, talking over this line. The only thing he forgot was the time difference, and it was about one o'clock in the morning back in Washington. Connie answered on the third ring, but she didn't sound like he had awakened her from a sound sleep. As he soon found out, he was right. She and Jack had just gotten back to the hotel and were polishing off the remainder of the wine before heading for bed. As it turned out, not much had happened since he left, or at least they were not discussing it over the airwaves.

Next, Davin was to pick up Ms. Linderhan, have a quiet dinner, and make plans for their trip to Bremerhaven, in search of the only survivor of the U-boat that was involved in this growing mystery.

Washington, DC
Late Night News
April 26, 1996
2100 Hours, EST

"This just came in: LATE BREAKING NEWS! Earlier today, guerillas, killing three and taking an undisclosed number of hostages, overran the American Embassy in Nigeria. Fifteen members of the building have escaped and are now safe in the neighboring country of Ghana. The 101st and 82nd Airborne Divisions have been put on alert and are preparing to depart for the Ivory Coast at the request of their government. They fear for their safety, having seen two other countries fall to the military forces led by this man." A photograph of General Samula flashed on the screen. "Sources indicate that General Samula was the cause of the ship explosion in Norfolk, Virginia, earlier this week. Connecting this as an act of terrorism and his desire for world domination, General Samula is believed to be the most dangerous man on earth since Saddam Hussein. It is now believed that Samula had Saddam assassinated so he could become the most dangerous man on earth. Kind of like a soap opera, in a way, but they are playing with real guns. Wait, more here. All combat US Army, Navy,

Air Force, and Marine units have now been put on alert. The Soviet military is now on alert also. Please stand by for further updates," the news anchor said and then broke to a commercial.

Admiral Jacobs sat in the living room of his plush Alexandria, Virginia, home and watched. He knew deep down that he and his organization had created Samula. But the man promised not to harm US citizens. Yet he was killing the hand that fed him by attacking US warships, ordering terrorist attacks on US soil, and who knew what else he planned. Jacobs and the organization had put trust first in dealing with Samula, but it seemed that trust was just one-sided.

The phone rang in Admiral Jacobs's kitchen. Attempting to ignore it, he sat and listened as it continued to ring.

"Hello, Admiral Jacobs," he said finally, picking up the receiver but not wanting to speak to anyone right now. It was late, war was on the horizon, and he just wanted some peace and quiet. *Another war in less than four years from the short war in the Persian Gulf and only two from the conflict in Libya. No more wars. We have had enough already,* he thought.

"Jacobs, listen to me. This war may get very messy and a lot of things can get covered up with it. You make sure that things disappear so the organization and its members don't take the fall. You reported to me that they found the boat. That boat must never be opened. It may have information implicating us in the organization. Have it destroyed. No questions or excuses—destroy her and whoever gets in your way. Understand?" the voice said in no uncertain terms.

"Yes, sir. But I have already set things in motion to ensure your safety. You need not worry. If anyone takes the fall, I will."

"Destroy that boat and anything that can connect us to it. This war will help you do so. Just do it." There was silence on the line.

Admiral Jacobs just stared at the phone before he hung up. He knew his days were numbered. Tonight he would destroy all records that he had on the organization. No, wait, maybe he should keep them and use them to bargain with. No, if he did that, he would surely die, by the organization. No one retired from the organization, and you just didn't quit.

Munich, Germany
April 26, 1996
1810 Hours, GMT

Davin picked up Ms. Linderhan at 18:10 in front of the library and was directed to a quiet little restaurant a few miles outside town. During the drive, she didn't speak except to give a new direction to turn. It was 19:15 by the time they arrived at a small castle on a river. It was a beautiful country setting, kind of like a small Camelot, lots of trees, flowers, birds.

They parked and walked across a drawbridge to the main gate of the castle and were greeted by a large bearded gentleman in an era costume, probably from the 1800s.

"Ah, Nanette," a giant of a man said to Ms. Linderhan as he gave her a great big hug. "It's so good to see you again. We have your special table prepared as you asked."

"Thank you, Uncle Max," she replied, placing a kiss on his cheek and handing him the car keys, which she had gracefully retrieved when exiting the car.

"Who is your gentleman friend?" Max asked.

"Oh, sorry. This is Mr. Davin Pierce, from America. He is doing some research on father's U-boat."

"Pleasure to meet you, sir. Maximillun Von Hofner, at your service. If there is anything you need or desire, please don't hesitate to ask," Max proclaimed. Then in German he said to Nanette, "How much does he know?"

"I don't know yet. That is why we are here," Nanette replied in German.

"Let me show you to your table, and the feast shall begin," Max concluded.

"Thank you, sir," Davin replied to Max. And then he said to Nanette, "What was all the German about, if I may be so bold to ask?"

"Just family talk, nothing to concern yourself about."

"Your table, Nanette, as you requested," Max said with bravado and a sense of pride.

"Thank you, again, Uncle Max. May we have a bottle of Mosel '73 to start with?"

"Right away!" Max said as he turned and left them at a round table located within the round corner tower room overlooking the river. The table had been set with an elegant tablecloth, crystal goblets, and fine china. A table fit for a king and his queen.

The wine and dinner arrived precisely on schedule. It was so well orchestrated that the conversation during the meal flowed as smoothly as did the courses. Every bite was superb, and the wine was the best that Davin ever had. Nanette was the most perfect hostess that Davin lost complete track of time.

Eventually, conversation got around to Nanette's father and the war. Max had returned several times to bring more wine and start a fire in the fireplace. The room was deserted except for Davin and Nanette.

"Nanette, my dear, I will be retiring now. Your rooms are ready as you requested. Please enjoy the fire and tell your father I send my regards," Max interrupted one last time.

"Thanks a million, Uncle Max," Nanette said as she jumped up and gave her uncle a hug and kiss. "We will be leaving early."

"Good night, sir," Max said to Davin with a bow, turned, and departed.

Nanette gave Davin a detailed picture of her father, the life he had built for her and her mother. When her mother died ten years ago, he had gone into seclusion on the coast; he loved the ocean and could not stay away from it.

"Now it's your turn, Mr. Pierce. Why is it so important to bring back things that should be forgotten?"

"Well, let me start at the beginning." Davin related the story as he knew it, and as he told it, Nanette sat quietly, sipping her wine, barely blinking an eye.

"That does sound interesting, and if we are to leave early, we had best get some sleep," she said as she took Davin by the hand and stood up. "Let's go."

Within a couple of minutes, they had climbed the narrow steep staircase to the third floor. Davin was admiring the paintings, old statuary, and thinking about Nanette. She was not the most beautiful girl in the world, but she was outgoing and intelligent, obviously coming from wealthy stock, but had a flair to her that was unique.

"Okay, here is your room," she said finally, stopping in front of a large carved wooden door. She reached out, opened the door, and pushed it open wide, exposing a large eighteenth century poster bed with a fire in the fireplace on one wall; paintings on the other walls could have been masterpieces, but Davin was not an expert on paintings. They were large, like the ones seen in museums.

"In you go, Mr. Pierce."

"I wish you would call me Davin."

"Maybe later. Good night," she said. As she turned to leave, Davin didn't let go of her hand.

"Where are you going?" Davin asked.

"My room is right next door. The door will be locked, so don't even try," she teased.

"I only wanted to know what time you wanted to leave," he asked.

"Seven o'clock okay with you?"

"Sure, sure. See you then. Good night," he said as he released her hand.

"Good night, Davin," Nanette replied as she turned and walked the short distance to her room. Before she entered, Nanette stopped, looked at Davin, winked, and blew him a kiss.

Chapter 11

WAR FRONT

Abidjan, Ivory Coast, Africa
US Embassy and Headquarters,
Eighty-Second Airborne Division
April 26, 1996
1945 Hours, GMT

"Sir, this just came in," Staff Sergeant Hughes said, handing General Ernie Sellers a folder marked TOP SECRET. Staff Sergeant Hughes waited until the general signed for the document, retrieved the empty folder and his pen, and then started for the door of the general's temporary office.

"Staff Sergeant Hughes, aren't you supposed to wait for a reply to this message?" General Sellers asked as Hughes reached for the door handle. He had laid the document on a stack of other documents on the corner of his desk.

"Yes, sir, but I assumed you would read it first, draft your reply, then call me back," Staff Sergeant Hughes answered as he stopped at the door.

"You were correct to assume that, but if you assume too much, you will never get that stripe you are waiting for. Please have a seat. I'll have a reply to the president in a moment, and by the way, when you return to this office, I expect you will be wearing the correct stripes on your uniform, Sergeant First Class Hughes. We will do an official pinning on when we get back home. Congratulations." General Sellers insisted he liked all the men and women that worked for him, treating them more like close relatives than soldiers. Sergeant Hughes had been with the general for the past three years and enjoyed working with him. His way of surprising people with promotions, awards, and almost anything was refreshing, his way of saying you were doing well. As easygoing as the general was, when it came to work, he was dead serious. He was honest and worked hard and expected no less from everyone in his command. Was what was expected was 110 percent, and it was what was received.

General Sellers turned, picked up the document, and began to read. The expression on his face went from a smile to dead, cold white. The color drained from his face, a serious, disbelieving look taking over. He turned and sat behind his desk as he read.

"Hughes, take this down, verbatim. 'Top secret, priority code 1, direct to the White House. No info copies. Code word: *Airborne*, repeat, *airborne*. End transmission. Zebra 6.'"

"That's it, sir?" Sergeant First Class Hughes asked as he stood to leave.

"Yes, son. Now get that off immediately. Then call all the battalion commanders for an emergency staff meeting in my conference room in two hours. That will be 2230 hours tonight. Mandatory! And get the 101st commanders here also, and the British and Soviet consulates. Tonight," General Sellers ordered.

"Yes, sir," Hughes said as he rushed out of the office. He had not seen the general this serious since the Persian Gulf last year. Something was up, and it sounded like they were going to see some action real soon. On his way to the command center, he issued orders to several of his crew to start calling the required parties for tonight's meeting.

North Coast of Germany
Twenty Miles Outside Bremerhaven
April 27, 1996
1345 Hours, GMT

Nanette and Davin drove quietly for most of the morning, and then, finally, she broke the silence as they approached the crest of the hill.

"Davin, my father lives in that house over there," she said, pointing to the last house on top of a hill. There were only about six houses in view, if one looked in all directions, that is. Josef wanted to be alone and watch the ocean. And he had found a spot where he could do just that. The nearest house to his was about a mile away, down the hill, in a small valley.

Davin and Nanette stopped the car, walked up to the door, but received no answer to their knock.

"Maybe he's out back," Davin said.

A couple of minutes later, Davin found a gentleman walking up a path toward the house. Nanette had stayed on the front porch, waiting for Davin to return. She had said she wanted to wait in the shade.

Before Davin could say anything, the older gentleman started speaking in German. Davin had no idea what he was saying but knew it wasn't friendly, because of his tone.

"Do you speak English, sir? I don't speak German!" Davin finally said, trying to interrupt politely.

"Yes, and Polish, Russian, and some Italian. So what?" he said sarcastically. "What do you want?" he asked again, but this time in Russian. They continued up the path to the back porch of the house. They had the best view of the ocean from there.

"I'm looking for a Mr. Josef Von Hofner. Would that possibly be you, or do you know where I might find him?"

"Depends on who's lookin' for him," he answered in perfect English.

"Sir, I'm Davin Pierce, of the IRS, Insurance Recovery Services, of Palm Beach, Florida, and I'm looking for Mr. Hofner in connection with his duty on a U-boat during the war," Davin said as they reached the porch and stopped, looking at each other.

"Everything you need to know is in that damn museum in Munchen. Go ask them!" he said, waving his left hand as if he were shooing away a fly.

"Are you Josef Von Hofner?" Davin asked bluntly.

"Yes, or at least I get all his mail," he responded with a little chuckle.

"Huh, oh, okay, Mr. Hofner, can I ask you some questions about the final days of the U-49?" Davin insisted as they climbed the few steps to the porch.

"Sure, if I can remember back that far. Pull up a chair and, ah, call me Josef, Mr. Pierce," he said as he turned to move a chair close by so they could talk. His attitude had changed suddenly. Davin had no idea why and didn't care, as long as it remained this way. "Mr. Pierce, I live alone up here because I just want to be close to the sea and spend my final days quietly and alone. So how did you find me? Now, what couldn't you find out in the museum?"

"Sir, as I started to say, the reason I'm here is to get some answers about what really happened when your U-boat and the freighter *MaryJean* met back in 1943." Short pause to catch his breath, then he continued. "Recently, the police in the United States raided a warehouse suspected of storing weapons for a gun-smuggling ring. They were right about the warehouse and were able to recover a lot of weapons. Among the ones recovered were several hundred crates of weapons that were manifested on the *MaryJean* on her last trip. The records at the museum show that the U-49 attacked a freighter at about 06:30 on the morning of January 20, 1943. It was later identified as the *MaryJean*. Will you tell me in your own words what happened from the time the torpedoes left your U-boat?" Davin asked, ignoring his first question.

"Why?" Josef said as he looked out over his land and the ocean beyond and then spotted a young lady, his daughter, leaning on the white fence that lined the edge of a steep cliff overlooking the ocean. "Did she bring you here, Mr. Pierce?"

"Yes, she did."

"You know, I haven't seen my daughter for about two years, and now here she is. Why did you bring her?" Hofner asked, a small tear forming in his eye.

"Sir, she brought me because she wanted to see you," Davin said, noticing the tear.

"No, she doesn't. If she wanted to see me, she would have come a long time ago. She's just hoping I'll tell you where the gold is so she can get her hands on it."

"She's your daughter. Don't you think she just loves you?"

"She does, but not for me, only for what I have."

"Maybe she has changed...," Davin started.

"She'll get the gold, all right, but only when I think she deserves it, not until," Hofner insisted.

"I didn't mean to restart a family fight, sir. I only need some information about your U-boat."

"You want to know where the gold is, don't you? I'm the only one who knows now. The rest are dead. You know that, don't you? I'll tell, but not now. First, you tell me why I need to talk to you at all," Hofner said as he sat and stared at his daughter.

"Well, okay. Besides the weapons that were supposed to be on the ship that your U-boat reported sinking, her captain and two of the crew who were supposed to be dead were also there. I'm researching everything that had anything to do with that ship and her crew. Okay?"

"Damn!" was all Josef could say, still looking at Nanette.

"How it got there, we don't know for sure," Davin continued.

"Mr. Pierce, the U-49 had been on patrol for three months and was heading home when we received an urgent communication from Berlin confirming a recent plan," Josef started as the two men watched Nanette stroll over to the porch. As she approached, Josef stopped and stood. Walking down the steps, he greeted his daughter. They walked a short distance, stopped, and talked briefly. Moments later, they were embraced in a hug that was long overdue. She kissed him on the cheek, and the two of them walked back to the porch, smiling.

Nanette went inside to fix some coffee, while Josef continued with his version of what had happened to him and the crew of the U-49 fifty years before.

"As I was saying, Mr. Pierce, we received this urgent communication from Berlin. Marked TOP SECRET, it instructed us to rendezvous with an American freighter named the *MaryJean* at a specific location and time. The mission had been in the planning stages for months, and we were not sure if it would happen. I cannot remember exactly the coordinates, but we were supposed to meet at 0600 hours, retrieve a single crate from the ship, and then sink her," Josef said. He stopped while Nanette served coffee.

"Interesting!" Davin stated.

"Mr. Pierce, only the captain and I knew the extent of the mission. The crate we were to get was full of gold, to help us end the war by overthrowing Hitler. But what made the whole thing strange was that the day before we were to rendezvous, we came upon a lone ship. We dived and proceeded to attack this ship. We fired two torpedoes, which should have exploded within two minutes of firing. Neither one exploded! We thought we had missed. With only two torpedoes left, the captain decided to surface and use the deck gun to sink her. Before we surfaced, we heard two very large explosions. Not knowing what to make of this, we decided to surface anyway. The captain was still on the periscope as we broke the surface, watching in amazement the ship we had fired on. She was burning and listing to port. As we broke surface, that ship started to fire on us and turned to ram."

"What did your captain do?" Davin asked.

"Dived, of course. We had been hit, not severely, but we lost several of the crew during the attack." Josef stopped to sip his coffee, then continued. "Well, the captain said we had just fired on the ship we were to rendezvous with. We were confused but happy to be alive. We immediately left the area and headed for the rendezvous site, hoping the freighter would make the trip. We were having bad luck with our torpedoes. We had had several duds, as you would call them, over the past three months," Josef stated.

"You didn't know it was the *MaryJean* until you surfaced?" Davin asked.

"No. It is hard to identify a ship by name through a periscope, Mr. Pierce. But when we surfaced, we got a good close look at the name on the bow."

"What happened next?" Davin pressed on.

"Well, as I said, we dived and headed toward the rendezvous site. En route, we surfaced and made some repairs. The next morning, at 0600 hours, we were waiting, but no *MaryJean*. Around 0630 hours, another submarine approached, flying a white flag on her bow. We did not fire on her or she on us. Both boats just sat and waited, about one hundred meters apart. An American submarine, we identified her as a Gato-class fleet boat." Josef paused again, asking Nanette to go inside and refresh his coffee.

"Did the *MaryJean* ever arrive?" Davin asked.

"Oh, yes, about 07:10 she came over the horizon, smoking and listing badly. She approached slowly. Stopping about two hundred meters away, she signaled for us to approach slowly, which we did. Once we were beside her, a cargo boom with a crate attached appeared, lowering the crate to our deck. Once it was secured, we moved away. The American boat moved over and retrieved two crates in the same manner. As the two boats moved away, we noticed the crew of the *MaryJean* boarding the American submarine. As we moved away, we were loading our two remaining torpedoes. We never fired them. Once that other boat was safely away, the *MaryJean* exploded and sank almost immediately. The American boat submerged, and so did we. That was the last we saw of either one."

"Very interesting. I talked with one of the survivors of the *MaryJean* recently, and he mentioned a letter addressed to a Von Richie. What do you know about that?"

"I wrote that. Richie was one of our contacts in America. He was supposed to help Bronsly sabotage his ship and get the gold to us. I do not know what happened to him. We saw several members of the crew leave with the American submarine. Maybe he was among them. The letter detailed the transfer if Bronsly was able to get the cargo on board. How did your friend know about the letter?" Von Hofner asked.

"He said that he and another crew were searching for injured when they came across Von Richie. Richie fired at them and ran, dropping the letter. Is there anything else you want to add?" Davin asked.

"I guessed you might ask. We were four days away from there, running on the surface, when an American destroyer came over the horizon. They saw us, and we dived for the cover of depth, but they located us and sank the U-49 before we were able to deliver our cargo."

"Where?"

"We were near the Canary Islands when attacked. The report says we went down in very deep water, but she isn't deep or where reported," Josef said.

"She isn't? Then where is she?" Davin's interest was piqued.

"Mr. Pierce, here's the deal. I tell you where the U-49 is and you recover the gold. I want it to be known that we of the U-49 were part of a master plan to eliminate Adolf Hitler. The gold was being given to us to help finance our new government and to rebuild Germany. But we fell prey to an attack that erased all hopes of completing our mission. The gold is in water too deep for salvage technology of 1943. But not with today's equipment. My men died trying to end the war, and the gold was lost. We will split the gold with you. Will you help?" Josef asked.

"Why me?" Davin asked. "You don't know me."

"That is where you are wrong, Mr. Pierce. You see, my daughter and brother Max have done some checking on you. They both feel that you are the right person for the job," Josef concluded.

"You mean that part about you not seeing your daughter for a long time was a lie?"

"Sorry to say, but yes."

Davin was shocked but delighted that they would trust him with the missing gold. It was agreed that once Davin was ready, he would contact Josef and Nanette. Josef would give the location of the U-49 to Nanette and she would meet Davin for the recovery operation. A tentative schedule was decided on for later this year.

Three hours later, Nanette and Davin were headed back to Munich so he could catch an airplane to New York.

Conference Room, American Embassy
Abidjan, Ivory Coast
April 28, 1996
2235 Hours, GMT

"Welcome, gentlemen. I'll get right to the point. It's very late, and we haven't much time to react. It seems that we may have walked into a trap," General Sellers stated to the members of staff and invited guests. He and about fifteen thousand troops had not been in-country very long, some arriving just today as part of the advanced party to set up operations, others arriving over the past couple of days.

The room was silent, but the stares and look of shock on everyone in the room conveyed disbelief.

"I have information from a very reliable source that the Nigerian government, namely one General Samula, has at their disposal nuclear devices and the general plans on using them on us, the combined forces of four nations in this country. The time and day are unknown as yet, but as I see it, one, we can take this as an idle threat and plan accordingly, or two, we can evacuate the area as quickly as possible, that being an option I do not foresee using. The indication is that Mr. Samula plans on detonating a nuclear device on Abidjan within two days. So we must locate and destroy his weapon," General Sellers said, then stopped when he saw the raised hand of Colonel Maxwell. "Yes, Colonel, you have a question?"

"No, sir, not a question as such, but does your informant know where the attack will come from? And if so, why don't we just drop in some special ops types and eliminate the problem?" Colonel Maxwell asked.

"Well, Colonel, we do not have an exact location yet but hope to by morning. The best thing I can tell you is to get your troops dug in real good and be prepared for anything. The delivery system is not known. It could be by plane, missile, or whatever. We hope to have an answer to that real soon," Sellers said. "As you all know, this man has little or no respect for life. He has killed his own countrymen for no reason. If there are no questions, thank you for coming. Good night."

General Sellers departed the briefing as everyone came to attention. Speculation resounded among the commanders as to how and when the attack would come, but nobody knew for sure.

Since being alerted for combat duty on the twenty-fifth of April, General Sellers had deployed three quarters of his division to the Ivory Coast, and General Campbell of the 101st Airborne Division had deployed 90 percent of his division. These were part of the Rapid Deployment Forces, and when called to move, they moved to any part of the world within days, not months. During Operations Desert Shield and Storm, they deployed in three days. Then, as more and more troops were prepared, they were sent to back up the 82nd and 101st. Total deployment of men and equipment took almost six months, but a fighting force was on the ground within three days from the initial alert.

If Samula planned on using a nuclear device on the 82nd and 101st, then now was the time to do so, before a lot of the antiaircraft and antimissile batteries arrived.

New York, Kennedy Airport
April 28, 1996
1645 Hours, EST

New York Kennedy International Airport is one large busy airport, and Davin's flight was on top of the stack, waiting to land. The captain had said they arrived on time but due to the poor weather and the backlog of incoming flights, they would be in the holding pattern for about forty-five minutes. His connecting flight left in forty-five minutes. Would he make the connection?

One hour, twenty-five minutes later, Davin was sitting at the gate for his connection to Washington National, waiting for the plane to arrive. It seemed that they had been late leaving Pittsburgh and also ended up in the stack. Fortunately, they were above the plane he was on.

After the delay in Kennedy Airport, it felt good to be back in Washington with friends. Connie and Jack were at the airport to pick him up, but they were not smiling.

"Hey, guys, why the long faces? I come with good information," Davin said as he picked up his bag, crushed, but still in one piece.

"We'll tell you in the car. Let's go," Jack said matter-of-factly as they headed out the door.

Once they were in the car and heading toward the hotel, the silence was killing Davin.

"Okay, what's up, Jack?" Davin asked finally to break the silence.

"Connie, you tell him," Jack said quietly.

"Davin, we have been going through everything we can find on the *MaryJean* and Bronsly," she stated with a cold fear in her eyes and voice. "Davin, we're not sure yet but are about 90 percent positive that the *MaryJean*'s secret cargo was an atomic bomb!"

"A what!" Davin gasped; his lower jaw dropped and eyes popped.

"Yes, a bomb, Davin. Look, it's late and we are all tired. I'll drop you two at the hotel and pick you up at eight in the morning. Get some sleep. Tomorrow's going to be a busy day," Jack said. "We can talk about it in the morning. It has been waiting fifty years since it disappeared. Another day will not hurt."

Thirty minutes later, Jack dropped Davin and Connie off at the hotel and disappeared into the evening traffic.

Local Restaurant
April 18, 1996
1650 Hours, EST

"Hey, it's getting close to 17:00, and we haven't a clue as to what is going on. Besides, I'm hungry." Micky spoke up from behind a stack of file folders.

"Me too," Batman piped up from across the room.

"Okay, let's get out of here. Anybody want to try that new place, the Chatter Box?" JD asked.

"Fine by me," Micky answered as she stood and stretched.

"Sure, let's go," Batman said as he headed for the door.

By 1845 hours, the three were at their table, with drinks in hand and considering dinner.

"Micky, I hear the lobster here is the best in town and the steaks can only be beaten if you are out in the middle of Texas, driving a herd and picking the one you want as it walks by," said JD.

"Gimme a break, guys. I need at least two drinks before I order any food. How about a bottle of wine?" Micky said, eyeing her strawberry margarita.

"Fine by me. What do you think, JD?" asked Batman.

"Okay, what will it be, German or French? Or maybe a good imported California vintage?" JD asked.

"German, of course. We won the war so we could drink their fine wines, so let's have some German, okay?" Batman stated.

The dinner and German wine were excellent, and the only thing that was not right was what was going to happen tomorrow. Conversation finally worked itself off the findings and on to the plans for tomorrow and beyond.

"You know we have to go to Africa and see this sub, don't you?" said Micky.

"That's right, JD. We better do it soon. You know it's getting pretty sticky over there, like war real soon. Are you a diver, Micky?" Batman asked.

"Yes. Do you think we can get in and out safely? And yeah, I'm pretty good with a Nikonos too," stated Micky.

"Good, we'll need some good photos. I guess tomorrow we make our reservations for Africa. Do you think the admiral will authorize a plane and equipment?" asked Batman. "You know, the 82nd and the 101st are already over in a staging area, ready for a fight. I understand the Navy has turned the Atlantic Task Force south, with its destination the Nigerian coast."

"Yeah, sounds pretty wild over there. That's a party I don't mind missing," Micky stated.

"You heard what he said, didn't you? Anything we need, we get. Tomorrow we need to get ahold of Flight Operations and schedule a plane," JD reminded them.

"What else for tomorrow, JD?" asked Micky.

"Well, let's see, ah…we also need to find us another qualified diver with some sub experience. Let's meet at my office at 0800 hours—no, better yet, at 0700 hours—at the Officers Club for breakfast, to set everything in motion," JD requested.

"Okay, sounds great. Is it time to go yet?" asked Batman.

"Yes, Batman, it's time to go. Did you pay the bill?" JD asked.

"Me? I thought it was your turn to buy," Batman responded, suddenly wide-awake.

"Okay, my treat," JD said, looking for the bill, which had been lying on the edge of the table.

"Thanks for the offer, boss, but it's already been taken care of," Micky responded. "Well, it's been great, but I need to get some sleep, so if I may be excused, I'll see you two at breakfast tomorrow," said Micky.

"Thanks, Micky. Tomorrow, my treat. But before we break up, there are a few things we need to get answered before we head off to the African coast and get sunburned," JD said quietly as Micky got up to leave.

"Well, I agree there is, but I can't think very straight right now, big guy, so spit it out so we all can get some shut-eye," Batman said. "Can we go now? I'm fading fast."

"Okay, okay," JD said as he got up, and the three started to walk out. "Something to think about, What happened to the other two subs? And do you think that we ought to, maybe, run down some of the crews' relatives if they are still around? They may know something about this Atlantic mission."

"Do you think Jacobs knows more than he's telling?" asked Micky as they reached the door.

"Maybe, just maybe," JD answered, looking at Micky.

"Can we finish in the morning? I'm fading fast, and only hope I make it to the car," Batman stated.

"Okay, Batman. By the way, where *did* you park the Batmobile tonight, anyway?" asked JD.

Washington, DC
Twin Bridges Hotel, Room 693
April 29, 1996
0745 Hours, EST

"Davin, Davin, wake up. It's morning," Connie said as she shook Davin from a deep sleep.

"Okay, I'm awake already," Davin responded slowly.

"Look." Connie handed him the morning paper. The front page described the conflicts in Nigeria, the overthrow of the US and British Embassies, and the murder of the hostages in the capital city of Lagos. It went further to say the leader, General Samula, had declared war with any country that would attempt to stop his move across Africa.

"Damn, Connie. What the hell does that nut think he's going to accomplish?" Davin asked.

"I don't know, but we have to get back to work," Connie said as she stood and walked out of the room, returning moments later with a red windbreaker and her purse.

Twenty minutes later, she and Davin were heading out of the hotel.

"Jack asked us to meet him at his office at 0830. He has some new information about that bomb," Connie said as she climbed into the rental car.

Officers Club
April 29, 1996
0730 Hours, EST

Morning came too early for all concerned.

"Good morning. I hope you two slept well," said JD as he reached the table where Micky and Batman were seated.

"Yes, thank you, JD. And how are you this morning?" asked Micky.

"Fine. Well, have you two thought over what we talked about and come to any conclusions or ideas?"

"Not on an empty stomach, boss," declared Batman laughingly.

"Okay, no business till after breakfast. Deal?" JD said in response.

"Deal," was the reply.

Breakfast came and went, then it was on to coffee and plans. They decided that Micky would spend the morning researching transportation to Africa, setting up points of contact with local authorities and the destroyer that was already there. Then she was to find another qualified diver for the trip. JD and Batman would return to the vault and find out what happened to the two sister ships and anything that they could about Operation Atlantic Wolf. Batman would also find someone to trace down relatives of the crew from the *Wolverine* and any living crew or relatives from the sister ships. JD had to stop by Admiral Jacobs's office to brief him as to what they had found up to now and also of the plans for the next two to three weeks. All three were to meet back at the vault when they had completed their assignments.

Lagos, Nigeria
April 29, 1996
1530 Hours, GMT

Amid started, "General, we have a minor problem with our time schedule. Your request to build five bombs is running a little slow. We have all the materials, but—"

But he was cut short by General Samula. "I don't want excuses, I want results!" Samula yelled. "We drop on May 1 or else."

"Yes, sir! I'll pass that on to the engineers immediately!' Amid said hastily and hurried out of the general's office.

General Samula turned and paced his office, lighting one of his favorite Cuban cigars as he paced.

Amid, knowing his life could be shortened by his next move, ran to the garage and jumped into his Alfa Romeo Spider sports car. With a little hesitation, the engine caught. He slammed the little car into gear and sped out of the garage, turning north toward the laboratory, where the country's finest engineers were constructing five atomic bombs, modeled after the one that General Samula had acquired only four months ago from the American submarine.

Amid didn't agree with the war; he thought General Samula was crazy for power. But working as his aide helped him protect his family, and over the past month, he had been able to get his entire family moved to America, where they would be safe from that crazy man. Now it was his turn. He had the information required by the American commander in Abidjan. He just had to live long enough to deliver that information.

Pentagon, Arlington, Virginia
Hall of Records
April 29, 1996
0930 Hours, EST

Batman arrived back at the vault first and proceeded to look for the file on Operation Atlantic Wolf. He was not having any luck at all, as if the file never existed, at least in here, anyway. He looked in Records of Destruction, which only indicated approximately three hundred documents destroyed since the war. None of them had anything to do with submarines or the Atlantic War. After exhausting what seemed like hours with no luck, in files marked SPECIAL OPERATIONS, ATLANTIC/EUROPEAN CAMPAIGN, he was about to give up when behind a stack of folders pushed down almost under the file drawer he saw an envelope with the word *wolf* lightly penciled on it.

Picking up the envelope, Batman walked over to the only table in the vault to read its contents.

"How's it going, Batman?" asked JD as he entered the vault.

"Well, I don't know yet. I just now found this envelope marked WOLF and was just going to sit down to check it out. It may be just what we're looking for. It seems to be pretty full, but with our luck, who knows? It could be someone's lunch," Batman commented to JD as he sat down at the table with the package.

"Don't just sit there, open it up," JD insisted.

Batman carefully opened the envelope, only to find another envelope inside.

"At least it isn't someone's lunch," Batman said with a smile. Upon removing the inner envelope, he read the markings:

TOP SECRET. EYES ONLY, SPECIAL OPERATIONS BRANCH, SUBMARINE WARFARE, OPERATION ATLAN- TIC WOLF, PHASE I, COPY I OF 4.
Dated August 18, 1941.
For SS-701, SS-673, SS-497.
DESTROY AT START OF MISSION.

"Well, are you just going to stare at the envelope or open it, Batman?" asked JD.

"Oh, yeah, okay," he said as he cut open the top of the inner envelope. "Holy shit, JD, there is nothing but shredded paper in this thing. Wait, there is a whole sheet. Here." He handed JD the paper. Batman continued to sift though the envelope.

"All this is is a document receipt for the other three copies. It says that copy 2 was signed for on April 30, 1942, by Lieutenant Commander Jacobs, USN, and then copies 3 and 4 were destroyed on June 4, 1942, along with the original, and all destroyed paper was placed in this envelope," JD said, reading.

"I guess the only way we will find out what was going on is to board the *Wolverine* and hope we can get some solid clues from her," Batman commented.

"Hey, fellas, why the long faces? I've got good news and pizza," said Micky as she entered the vault.

"Pizza? I didn't know it was lunch yet," said Batman.

"It isn't, Batman. This is dinner. It's 1745," said Micky. "Aren't you guys hungry? I'm starved."

"Well, let's eat that thing before it gets cold, and we will fill you in on the latest curve," said JD.

While eating the pizza, JD told Micky about the destroyed file. She filled them in on plans for their trip to the African coast. The admiral had been satisfied up to now, but he still needed more infor- mation, and the sub, if possible.

"Batman, did you get someone to work the relative angle and to run interference for us while we're gone?"

"Yeah. Remember TC Evans, the redheaded captain over in CID?" Batman asked between bites.

"The guy from Alabama that talks funny? Yeah, I remember him. He owes me fifty bucks," JD said.

"Well, he is attached to the local CID and agreed to run down our crew and relatives."

"Great. When did he say he could have some answers?" JD asked.

"No promises, but maybe before we leave, and for sure by Monday."

"Micky, you said you had some good news. What is it? Or are you going to keep us in suspense all night?" asked JD.

"Oh, maybe I will, maybe I won't," said Micky.

"No secrets, young lady. I'd hate to pull rank on you," JD said laughingly.

"You wouldn't, would you?" Micky asked seriously.

"No, just kidding, but it is a thought."

"Okay, you win. I have confirmed a flight for the four of us for day after tomorrow via a Grumman Gulfstream III that needs some flight time. The crew has the time to drop us off and, if necessary, come back and pick us up when needed. Also, before you ask"—she looked at JD, who was about to ask about the fourth person—"we have another diver, fully qualified and ready to go with an okay from you. Her commander will release her to us for this mission."

"Her? Her who? This isn't a pleasure dive in the Bahamas," said JD. "It isn't going to be easy, Micky."

"Calm down. This isn't the sixties or seventies. It's 1996, and women are getting involved in a lot of things. Kelly is a fully certified Navy diver and is attached to the SEAL unit out of Norfolk. She is the best in her specialty," Micky reassured him.

"And what is that, may I ask?" JD asked.

"You may. It's underwater demolition and salvage, submarine salvage," she replied.

"Great. I guess she will fit right in. Sorry if I jumped before looking, Micky," apologized JD.

"And besides, she's a friend of mine," stated Micky.

"When can she be here, Micky?" asked Batman.

"She can be here tonight if JD will call her commander and okay it. And she can stay with me. You'll get to meet her tomorrow morning, if you can wait."

"Hey, let's wrap it up and get out of here. We have a lot to do before flying off to Africa," JD commented to his crew.

It was around 2100 hours when they finally gave up in the vault and headed out for a quick drink. Micky had to pick up Kelly at Washington National around 22:30, so she didn't stay long. JD and Batman closed up and headed out, still with a lot of unanswered questions.

JD had called Commander Godwin of the SEALs in Norfolk before they left the vault and agreed to his conditions of first visit of the *Wolverine* if and when she was returned to Norfolk.

"Let's have one more before we call it a night, JD," Batman said as they relaxed in the hotel lobby bar.

"Barkeep, another round, please," JD requested. He glanced up at the television over the back of the bar to see a naval ship on the screen, burning.

"We repeat, at 10:00 p.m. local time, the destroyer USS *J. F. Kennedy* was attacked by what is believed to be two MiG-23 fighter aircraft off the coast of Liberia. No country has claimed responsibility as of yet. Exact number of dead is unknown, but it is believed that at least twenty-one men from the ship died during the attack. They were attacked unexpectedly and without warning in international waters. The ship is dead in the water at this time. Rescue ships are on their way and expected to arrive shortly. One of the MiGs was severely damaged, and its fate is unknown. More at eleven thirty."

Chapter 12

RESURRECTION

USS Wolverine, Africa
April 29, 1996
0800 Hours, GMT

T he morning was brisk for April, even in Washington, as Commander JD Henderson and Batman waited in the lobby of the passenger terminal at Andrews Air Force Base. Waiting was something he would never get used to. The time was 08:15, Greenwich Mean Time, which meant it was 3:15 a.m. in Washington, too early to be waiting for an airplane. Micky and their new partner, Kelly McKern, had not arrived yet.

Micky and Kelly were approaching from the far side of the lobby when JD and Batman saw them. Kelly McKern was not what JD and Batman expected. She was twenty-nine years old, the only woman to ever pass the entrance exam and complete the course, becoming the first woman SEAL, specializing in underwater demolition.

"Damn, JD. She's one sharp sailor," Batman commented about Kelly McKern.

"Yeah, Micky says she won Miss Physical Fitness America two years in a row. Which means don't mess with her. She can break you in half," JD answered, laughing.

"She is kinda cute in a special kind of way. But I like the more intelligent type," Batman retorted.

"She's got you there too. Top of her class at the academy. Let's go meet our new partner," JD said as he started to walk over to Kelly.

They were supposed to meet with a Navy captain Phillips, who was going to fly them and their equipment over to Nigeria. They had been waiting for a little over an hour when the Gulfstream III finally pulled up outside.

It was, or appeared to look, like any other civilian jet, white, large, and with a blue stripe down the side, which went up the vertical stabilizer and flared out. The aircraft looked new or very well kept. As they watched from inside the lobby, the jet turned and parked. In doing so, the entry doorway slowly opened, exposing the interior and a gentleman in the doorway dressed in a pair of light-tan slacks and a leather flight jacket.

JD headed out to greet the man from the jet just as the engines were winding down.

"Captain Phillips?" JD asked as he approached the jet.

"Yes. Commander Henderson, I presume?" Phillips asked.

"You presume correct, Capt'n," JD offered, and then continued. "When do we leave?"

"Let's go inside, where it's quieter," Phillips said, pointing toward the terminal door.

"Okay," JD agreed as they moved into the lobby.

The two of them walked over to Batman and the ladies, who were waiting patiently with the equipment inside the terminal building. Seeing Captain Phillips, Micky smiled and walked rapidly over to him.

"Max Phillips, are you...?" She paused, smiling, forgetting she and he were in uniform for the moment." Sorry, sir. Captain Phillips, are you flying us over?"

"Sure. What did you expect when you asked for a plane and crew? I wouldn't trust anyone else with such valuable cargo," Max said. "Now, cut out the captain stuff and give me a hug."

"Oh, Max, don't be so corny," Micky said as she turned a little red. "Have you met everyone?"

"No, can't say I have," he responded as he looked over toward Kelly. "Captain Max Phillips, United States Navy Shuttle Service pilot, at your service. That's my copilot, Rhonda Livingstone, a new ensign, but damn good," he said, pointing to Rhonda, who was instructing the ground crew in what was required for fuel and other services for the aircraft.

"Kelly McKern, and Henry Batuman, known by his friends as Batman, and you've met JD," he said, introducing them to Max Phillips.

"Long time no see, Max. What ya been up to? When do you think we can get outa here?" Batman asked.

"Soon. We'll have a short wait so we can take on some fuel and snacks. It's going to be a long flight." Then he turned to Batman. "I've been good. What about you? Still playing with them nukes? Come on, I'll buy," Max said as he pointed toward the soda machine across the lobby.

"Same ole stuff. Just like you, we have our ups and downs," Batman said quietly as they walked over to the soda machine. Minutes later, they started to carry their gear out to the waiting jet. Batman and JD were loading the rest of their gear when they noticed Micky and Max stroll off back toward the terminal building, talking as if they were long-lost lovers.

She caught a glimpse of JD's expression as she was walking with Max. It had been four years since they had set eyes on each other, a couple of phone calls a year and an occasional letter. But their careers had kept them apart until now. They were to be married at one time, but their careers had gotten in the way and they had decided that the only way to solve the problem was to go their own ways.

JD was not real pleased at the way Micky was acting with Max. He didn't know for sure, but maybe he was a little jealous. JD never thought of himself as a jealous man, but seeing Micky and Max together stirred some emotions in him that were very unfamiliar. JD had, over the past few weeks, fallen in love and now didn't know how to handle his emotions.

They departed Washington at around nine fifteen in the morning for the long flight to Africa. It would be late when they arrived, and with any luck, the hotel would have transportation. JD sat quietly for most of the flight, sleeping when he could. Micky, when not on the flight deck, was asleep like the others.

"JD," Micky said about four hours into the flight.

"Yeah, what's up, Micky?"

"Well, it might be my imagination, and this may sound a little bit strong," Micky said as she stared out the window.

"What are you trying to say?" JD coaxed.

"Well, damn. I don't want this to sound stupid, but I saw the look you gave me and Max while we were talking, and I just wanted to clear the air about us. I feel that you care a lot for me," Micky stated, getting a nod from JD. "Well, Max and I are old friends and were, at one time, going to be married. But that is history now."

"Why are you telling me all this?"

"I was hoping that you and I could continue to see each other when this is all over," Micky stated.

"Micky, you're right, I do care for you, and yes, I would like to see you again, on a more personal basis. But right now, I'm your commander, and you know Navy policy. So let's keep, not sink, the ship before it is launched, so to speak."

"Okay, Commander Henderson. But as soon as this is over and I no longer work for you, I expect to be more than an employee. Deal?" Micky said.

"Deal," JD agreed.

Twelve hours and five minutes after takeoff and three brief fuel stops, they were almost there.

"This is your captain speaking. We are making our approach. Please ensure that your seat belts are fastened and all smoking material extinguished, and thank you for flying Air Monkey Business. The local time is 2220 hours. This has been a recording. Click," Max said into the intercom.

The landing was textbook perfect, and soon they were taxiing to who knew where. Unknown to the passengers, Rhonda had flown the entire trip and completed the perfect landing.

"It's showtime back there. There have been some major changes in the program, ladies and gentlemen. The tower has directed us to your next mode of transport, so get your stuff together. We will be stopping in a few minutes," Max said over the intercom, his voice seemingly tense. "It seems that the war has come to us. The tower has just been evacuated and we are on our own, so let's not dawdle back there. There is a helicopter waiting to transport you to your floating hotel." After a short pause, Max ordered, "JD, get that door open, NOW!"

Max and Rhonda were already going through the checklist in preparation for an immediate departure. Looking through the windshield, they could see the fires and explosions on the far side of the airfield. It would only be a few minutes before troops would be heading toward them. Hopefully, that would be all the time they needed to unload and get airborne again.

"Rhonda, I'm going back to unload. When I yell, point her into the wind and go for a max combat departure," Max said as he stood to head for the cabin. A max combat departure was his way of saying to Rhonda to go to maximum throttle, holding the aircraft in position with the brakes. Once the engines reached maximum revolutions, she was to release the brakes but hold the aircraft on the ground until one hundred knots were reached. At which time, she was to pull the aircraft into a vertical climb, gaining as much altitude as possible before the airspeed reduced to stall speed. He planned on unloading and securing the door as quickly as he could after he indicated to her to go.

Within minutes, they were stopped and transferring their gear to a waiting helicopter. The engines were running, so they could not talk to anyone until on board. They yelled some quick goodbyes to Max and Rhonda, then boarded the helo for their floating hotel.

"Lotsa luck, guys. You're gonna need it!" Phillips yelled as he started pulling the door closed. The jet's engines were already spooling up to maximum thrust as the door was pulled closed. Both the jet and helo departed the airport just as the government troops arrived at the other end of the runway. No shots were fired, but an attempt to stop the jet was made by blocking the runway. But due to the emptiness of the aircraft and the combat takeoff procedure, Rhonda was able to use less runway and easily clear the vehicles that blocked part of the runway. Flying without lights, they were able to get to safety before any fighters were airborne.

"JD, what did Max mean we're gonna need luck?" Micky asked after the helo lifted off. With the door closed, which brought the noise levels down, it was easier to communicate. They still had to speak loudly, but at least they could hear. "We're booked in the Sheraton on the beach, and this doesn't look like the right taxi," she continued.

"I know there have been some changes in plans. We're heading for the *Washington*," a freckle-faced young ensign replied once everyone was strapped in and had on a headset. "I'm Ensign Matthew. Welcome aboard. As you can see, there have been some changes to your plans. It seems the country here has become very hostile, and for your safety, you will be our guest on board the ship. While you were enjoying your flight over, old General Samula's Army invaded and captured most of the country. Ghana is no longer a free country. This airport was still safe, up until about twenty minutes ago. We have been watching the troops move in, hoping you would arrive before we had to scoot. When they got to the airport, they found very little resistance and were moving across it as you landed. Not my idea of a fun Saturday night. Captain Grey will brief you on the rest as soon as we get on board. Until then, just sit back and relax. Henry is our pilot tonight, and he is the best."

After a short pause, Matthew continued, "As you know, Nigeria has recently declared war on the world and is presently under military rule by a General Samula. If you look out your port window, you will see the troops moving across the city and not getting much resistance. They have been setting fire to most of the cities as they move through. This guy is bent on total destruction. You know the term *scorched earth*? Well, that is what this nut is doing to every place they go."

"How did you get this helo in without being detected?" JD asked.

"Sir, with a little help from some friends and lots of luck," Matthew said and then got up to check his own gunner's positions.

The *Washington* had been called on station as soon as the submarine had been found. She was escorted by the British destroyer HMS *Montgomery*. They were being flown out to her, where they would be operating until, and well, until whenever.

Once on board the *Washington*, they were escorted to the captain's conference room, a small room just behind the bridge, used for planning and/or whatever the captain wanted.

"Welcome aboard, Commander Henderson. Please come in and have a seat," he said, indicating the seats around the table. Picking up a microphone from its hook beside a hatchway, he requested Lieutenant Commander Sheppard to be sent up there.

"I've just asked for my exec to come up. He is also my chief diver. I'm Captain Russell Gray, and welcome aboard the USS *George Washington*. Just to our port side is the HMS *Montgomery*, our escort. I know it's been a long day for you, and we will keep this as short as possible. Can we get you anything—food, drink, trip to the head, anything?"

"Yes, sir, a quick trip to the head and some real food would be just perfect," Kelly said quickly.

"Sounds good to me," Micky agreed.

"Down the hall and to the right. Lock the door. We're not coed on board."

"Thanks, sir," Kelly said as they departed.

After the girls returned, they found a plate half-full of sandwiches and chips with all the trimmings waiting. Batman and JD had already started to eat and exchange small talk with the captain.

"Okay, help yourselves and I'll get started with this so you can get some sleep. First off, we have been here too long. When we first arrived, we had a Russian-built cruiser waiting for us. She was flying a Nigerian flag and had a Soviet captain. He indicated to us that he was just here on a search and rescue and he didn't want any trouble, it wasn't his war and he didn't want any part of it, and neither did we. We left and returned after he had gone. As far as the sub, we've been down several times, mainly to check her condition, but we have also taken numerous photos of her to help with the identification process. As far as we can see, the sub we have within two hundred feet of us is, in fact, the SS-701, also known as the *Wolverine*, which, as you know, was reported missing in 1943."

"The positive ID is one of the reasons we are here, and we thank you for that, Captain. But I get the feeling there is something else you want to tell us," JD said between bites.

"I'll let Lieutenant Commander Sheppard fill you in on the rest. Jake?" he indicated to his executive officer to take over by calling him by his nickname. Most military services frown on the use of nicknames or other terms to refer to other members of a unit. But on a ship, where quarters are much closer, it is only natural that the members of the crew grow to know and respect one another in a much closer sense. And it is not uncommon for the skipper or captain of the ship to refer to some of his crew by a nickname or even by a given name.

"Hi, thank you, sir. Call me Jake. We are kind of informal around here. Well, I've been down to her six times. My last dive was at ten this morning. The water is crystal clear, with a lot of marine life. In front of you are the photos that Russ told you about. You will notice the minimum amount of any sea growth on her, and upon close inspection of her hatches, they, well, they look as if they would not be any problem to open. She looks like she hasn't been on the bottom for forty-plus years, and we can't explain why. At least not yet!"

"Okay, how's the current around her?" Kelly asked straight out.

"Nonexistent," Jake replied.

"How far away are we from the fresh water run out off the coast?" Batman asked.

"That's a good one, Batman, but sorry, we thought of it too. We took some water samples here and at one-mile intervals until we hit fresh water. We did this over several days to get a comparison, and what we found rules out fresh water this far out. The water temp is between eighty and eighty-five degrees, which makes for some great diving."

"How long do you estimate she's been here?" JD asked.

"No more than six months, JD. She has no visible damage, a little oil seepage and a few air bubbles. But we believe she isn't flooded yet," Jake stated as he passed out some photographs of the boat.

"Great, maybe a little onboard recon is in order," Batman commented as he looked at the photos.

"Yes, but not yet. A couple more dives, then in we go," Jake agreed, smiling.

"Are there any more photos?" JD asked.

"No, that's it for now. Look, you guys need to get some sleep. We have a long day tomorrow," Jake said. "So I wouldn't stay up late."

After studying the photos for about an hour, JD said finally, "We're not gonna solve this here, guys. Let's get some sleep and hit it first thing in the morning, okay?"

"Okay, you're right, JD. Take me to my chambers. I'm fading fast," Batman replied, using his favorite term when he was tired or bored.

"I'd like to study some of those photos before I retire. May I?" Kelly asked. She picked up several, sorted them, and set several back on the table.

"Sure, which ones did you want?" Jake asked.

"Just the ones of the hatches and the stern."

"Batman and I will take the rest," JD commented as he picked up the balance of photos.

"Chief Smyth will show you to your quarters. Get a good night's sleep," Jake said as they departed the conference room.

"What about our gear, Jake?" Kelly asked.

"It's already been stowed, and your personal gear is in your quarters. Good night," Captain Grey said.

Abidjan, Ivory Coast, Africa
Headquarters, Eighty-Second Airborne Division
April, 28, 1996
1215 Hours, GMT

General Sellers was in conference with his intelligence officer and the commander of the Special Forces Group assigned to the Eighty-

Second, Major Howard. They were planning Operation Quickkill, designed to eliminate the nuclear and chemical threat from Nigeria. The operation was to insert a squad of six Special Forces Deep Penetration specialists in Nigeria, armed with light weapons and explosives. Mission 1 was to destroy the atomic weapons factory and all material required to produce a nuclear device. Mission 2 was to destroy the chemical warfare storage facility located fifteen miles outside Lagos.

Deep-penetration units such as the ones used here had been used successfully in Vietnam, Panama, Grenada, and more recently, the Persian Gulf War when five teams were in Baghdad to collect intelligence and to disrupt communications.

A knock on the door interrupted the planning. Major Howard answered the knock after the general acknowledged that if someone was trying to see them, then it must be important. He had left instruction that they not be disturbed unless it was urgent.

"Yes?" Major Howard said to the soldier at the door.

"Sir, we have a prisoner that has vital information. He refuses to talk to anyone expect General Sellers. He said to mention *cactus*," the young Lieutenant said, with a very puzzled look on his face.

"One moment," Major Howard replied, turned, and closed the door. "General, Lieutenant Lewis said they have a prisoner who said to tell you *cactus!*"

"Tell him I'll be right out and to take the prisoner to my office," General Sellers ordered. Then to the group, he said, "Continue with your planning, gentlemen. I should not be very long." Then he started for the door.

"Sir, what's *cactus?*" Major Howard asked.

"Major, if you must know, it's a succulent that grows in the desert and it will either provide life or take it away. Depending on your need to know, you would know which. But you don't, so forget you heard it. It will only get you killed," General Sellers said to Howard. Then without much hesitation, he added, "Lieutenant Bradley, what are you sitting down for? I need you with me. Let's go."

"Yes, sir," the young intelligence officer said as he stood and followed the general out.

USS Washington
April 29, 1996
0530 Hours, GMT

Morning came early, too early, but they needed an early start on the sub. The weather could get real nasty real quick around here this time of year. After they had a breakfast of eggs and bacon with Captain Grey and Lieutenant Commander Sheppard, during which they planned their dive on the *Wolverine*, it was decided to dive at 09:00, with Kelly and Batman photographing the hinges on all the hatches, the sail and its structures, and also the seals around the propeller shaft.

The dive was in eighty feet of water, so they planned their dive for forty minutes, not going below the deck level, which would ensure staying at or above sixty feet. They wanted to avoid decompression dives, as they took too long and were not needed yet. If they needed to stay down longer, they would start with decompression dives.

"Jake, do you have salvage equipment on board?" Batman asked after breakfast.

"Well, yes and no. We have equipment for emergency use, for rescue work, but nothing of the magnitude you might need to salvage anything like a submarine," Jake replied.

"It was just a thought. We need to see what we have down there first. She may not be worth the trouble."

"I don't know about that, Batman," Kelly replied. "I've been working salvage only a few years, but I've been studying salvage and the ocean for more years than I care to say. And what I'm getting at is that, from what I see in those photos, well, that sub hasn't been on the bottom very long. I agree, less than six months."

"That is kinda strong, Kelly. There could be some very logical reasons that she looks the way she does. I don't know what, but that's what we're here for, right?" JD finally spoke up.

"Okay, maybe, but let's not just sit here. Let's go see for ourselves," Kelly commented.

"Lieutenant Commander Sheppard, ah, Jake, would you supply us with a couple of safety divers?" JD asked as he stood up to get ready to dive.

"Sure, I'll go and bring along Jimmy Wilson. He's served on a sub before he came over to us."

"Good. See you on the stern in fifteen minutes," JD said as he and Batman departed.

"Jake, you've been down there. What do you think of her?" Micky asked.

"It's hard to say. She has been missing for fifty-odd years, and no one really knows what or where she's been. The real answers are not up here or around her, but well, you know as well as I do, we may have to enter," Jake stated.

"If we can," Micky added as she got up to get ready. "You coming, Kelly?"

"Sure. See you aft," Kelly replied.

After they left, Jake and Captain Grey sat staring at each other for a few minutes. The silence was finally broken when a young seaman knocked on the door.

"Come in!" Grey yelled.

"Sir, this message just came in," said the seaman as he entered and handed Grey a small envelope.

"Thank you." He paused to take the envelope. "Stand by for a moment, outside. I might need to reply," Captain Grey said to the seaman.

Grey opened the envelope and looked at the message quietly. The message was encrypted and marked SECRET. Then he got up and walked over to the safe to get the decryption tablet. After about ten minutes, he sat back and read what was sent.

"Damn," was all Captain Grey could say.

"What is it, sir?" asked Jake.

Grey handed him the message as he took out a sheet of paper to write down a reply. After writing, he proceeded to encrypt his reply.

"*Damn* is right, sir. Do we tell Henderson and his party?" Jake asked.

"Yes, but not yet. Read the last line," Captain Grey said as he wrote a reply.

"Okay, but this could complicate things."

"I know," Captain Grey said and then called out to the seaman. "Seaman Terry, come back in here."

Seaman Terry entered and took the sealed envelope from Grey and started out the door.

"Terry, see that it is sent right away. Thank you. And info-copy both to the *Montgomery*," Captain Grey ordered.

"We are not prepared for what might happen. Is there any relief in the area?" Jake commented, scratching his head, as if he were trying to dig up a new idea.

"No, there isn't, and this could get real sticky before it's over. You better get ready to dive, or they will be leaving without you. Where is that Russian cruiser?"

"Yes, sir. Besides, there is nothing we can do right now anyway. The cruiser is sixteen miles due east of us and heading south at seven knots."

"Good, keep an eye on him. Let's get aft and see what is going on."

Once they arrived aft, they found Kelly and Micky already in dive skins and with all their equipment on ready to dive. JD and Batman were not quite ready. They were having trouble with one of the regulators.

"What's the matter, JD?" asked Jake as he walked up.

"The regulator is free flowing. Can't seem to get it to stop. Guess I'll use my spare and fix this one tonight," JD said as he reached for the spare regulator.

"We'll be ready in a minute," Jake said as he and Jimmy suited up. "This here is Jimmy Wilson. Jimmy, this is the gang." Jake introduced him to the group.

They all acknowledged the intro and started for the water. Kelly and Micky were the first in, with JD and Batman next. Jake and Jimmy picked up a couple of spearguns as they started for the water. They would only use them as a means of defense, and only then if nothing else would do. This area had a lot of shark activity, although usually they would stay away and not bother the diver. But they would rather be safe than regret it later.

Admiral Jacobs's Office
April 28, 1996
1700 Hours, EST

Admiral Jacobs's secretary was just leaving the admiral's office. She left a fresh pot of coffee and some Danish, as she always did before going home for the evening. The admiral bade her good night and walked slowly to his file cabinet. Unlocking the cabinet, he opened the top drawer and extracted a bottle of fifty-year-old brandy. This had been a standard ritual every night for over ten years, but tonight he did not return the bottle after pouring his standard one drink. Instead, he placed the bottle with a second glass beside the tray of coffee. He then went over to an overstuffed chair, sat down, took out a Cuban cigar, and lit it. Sitting, smoking, and sipping on his brandy, Admiral Jacobs waited for his visitor.

Thirty minutes passed before he heard the knock on the door.

"It's open. Come in!" Admiral Jacobs said without looking up from his cigar.

"Admiral, you're looking fine this evening," the visitor said, extending her hand in the customary handshake.

"Cut the crap. You need something. That's the only reason you're here. Now, what do you want?" Admiral Jacobs said to his female visitor as he stared at his cigar, still not looking up at her.

"I want out, Admiral. I've had enough. I didn't agree to murder!" she said as she poured herself a brandy.

"No one has been killed yet."

"What do you call Josh Randel, a TV game show?" she demanded.

"He's not dead yet, but he will have an unavoidable accident, my dear. He was sticking his nose where it doesn't belong. In a day or two, he would have put names to those deals that would cause total destruction to that end of the operation. He knew about the Miami connection, the drugs and weapons. He had only to put names to the players, and that, my dear, was only a matter of time. He was good, too damn good for his own good. Nobody knows all the players, but we stood to lose forty million dollars if he screwed that deal for us. He had to be stopped. I feel sorry it has to come to his death."

"Hal, I don't like killing, and I will not be any part of it. No killing, or I'm out," Lieutenant Commander Sally Morrison finally agreed, but not without some misgivings. Sally Morrison was in charge of logistics and personnel for the Pentagon; she was thirty-seven years old, tall, brunette, with green eyes and a figure of an eighteen-year-old model. She prided herself in her personal appearance and also in the company she kept. Admiral Jacobs was only one of many that she dated. He was more of a plaything; they enjoyed each other's company, especially in bed.

"Okay, no more killing," Jacobs lied. "Listen, Sally, I need some help. There is an operation going on that right now could cause us more problems. It seems that the *Wolverine* has been found, but not by our side. There is a team of divers looking her over right now, and I've got someone covering them. But there is another group of nosy civilians that are looking for the *MaryJean*. Well, if they should get lucky and discover something that links her with the *Wolverine*, or in some way link us to either, well, I guess I don't have to tell you what might happen then." Admiral Jacobs's tone said he was not overly concerned about either situation.

"What do you want me to do?" Sally asked as she started to feel the effects of the brandy and loosened the top buttons of her blouse.

"Well, to start with, I need one of your girls, ladies rather, to be assigned to a Captain Phillips. He is a pilot that is assisting the team off the coast of Africa on the *Wolverine*." Pausing for a moment, he watched Sally slowly undo the rest of the buttons on her blouse. "Do you need help with those?"

"No, you just sit there and enjoy," Sally commented. "I'll have a girl report tomorrow. Anything else, sweet?"

"Just one thing. Have her report her findings to me daily, or as often as possible. She does not need to know why, except that I'm interested in locating the *MaryJean*. Now, come here and I'll help you out of those."

"You dirty old man," she said with a sexy little laugh.

Chapter 13

THE FIRST DIVE

USS Washington
April 29, 1996
0855 Hours, GMT

As the six divers approached the *Wolverine* from the stern, Kelly and Batman stopped to take a few photos. Once at the sub, Kelly and Batman started to photograph the hatches while JD and Micky explored as much of the sail as possible. They were looking for signs of recent use or anything that would give them a clue as to why this was here. Jake and Jimmy hovered over the *Wolverine*, just watching.

This is really eerie, not much fish, no coral growing on her. You would think she would have some growth if she had been here for fifty years, Micky thought as she approached the submarine.

Not much growth, interesting. Few fish, maybe because there are no places to hide on a sub. She hasn't been here long, JD contemplated as he swam toward the bow of the sub.

After a while, JD and Micky had worked their way to the forward escape trunk located in the forward torpedo room. Close inspection of the hinges showed wear and a shiny bit of metal. Micky saw it first and pointed it out to JD. Looking around, they could see that Kelly and Batman were busy photographing something on the control tower. Micky had brought a camera also, so while JD inspected the fuel filling station, Micky photographed the hatch. They joined JD at the filling station, where he was pointing to the well-worn hinges.

Checking the time and the air they consumed, they realized that this first dive was at an end. Moving back toward the sail, with eyes constantly searching, JD spotted something on the sandy bottom. He tapped Micky on the shoulder and pointed down. They started down toward the object and then froze.

They were within twenty feet of the object in question, about halfway down the side of the sub, when they disturbed a large unhappy mako shark, which was right now circling them very slowly. Micky and JD got together to make themselves look larger. A shark has poor eyesight when looking at objects at a distance, so the bigger you are, the better. After what seemed like a lifetime, the big guy just turned and swam away. Looking up, they saw Jimmy and Jake about thirty feet away, waiting to see what that shark would do.

JD checked his air, then headed on down to the object he had seen on the ocean bottom. He brushed away the sand and picked up an emergency breathing apparatus, known as a Steinke hood, vintage, approximately 1943, marked SS-701. It looked in pretty fair condition. He and Micky headed for the surface with their find.

"Wow, did you guys see that shark?" JD asked as soon as they were on the cutter.

"What shark?" Jake said, teasing.

"No, we didn't see a shark, but that is one hell of a wreck," Batman commented.

"Let's get someone to process that film and meet in the conference room in twenty minutes," JD said as he removed his gear.

"Okay, see you there," Micky said as she unzipped the top of her dive skin to just below her breast, exposing her complete tan and no bikini top under the dive skin. After removing her gear, she headed to her stateroom to change into dry clothes.

Twenty minutes later, they were seated around the conference table. Each had quickly changed into dry clothes, the guys into tan slacks and shirts, and the ladies in shorts and T-shirts. Captain Grey came in to hear what they found. As he entered, he saw the Steinke hood on the table.

"Hell, I haven't seen one of those in at least twenty years. Where'd you find it?" Grey asked.

"It was on the bottom near the escape hatch and being guarded by one big shark," JD said with a little laugh.

"What else did you find?" Grey asked.

"We were just going to discuss that, Captain. Please have a seat and listen in. You may find this interesting," Batman offered, indicating an empty chair.

"Okay, Batman and Kelly, what did you see?" JD asked.

"Well, to start, we didn't, as expected, see much growth on her. Except for the green slime that is the first stage of growth, there was no marine growth on the hull. We inspected the hinges on the tower hatch and found that the hatch had not been used in a long time. We attempted to turn the handle, and it wouldn't move. We checked the forward torpedo tubes and found that two of the outer doors are open, no torpedoes in either one. We went aft to the props. They didn't look too worn. And the seals around the shafts didn't show any leakage. As far as that goes, the hull didn't look as though it was leaking much either."

"Any more, Batman?" Pause. "Micky?"

"Only one thing, JD. I noticed that lack of growth in the general area. This could mean several things, but I don't know what yet. I do think we need to check for any kind of leakage, oil, radiation, etc.," Micky stated.

"Radiation. This is not a nuke boat, it's diesel and electric," Batman said, rebutting.

"I know that, but why take chances? Radiation can be anywhere," Micky defended her position.

"Okay, okay, I agree," JD said. Then he asked, looking at Jake and Captain Grey, "Do you guys happen to have a Geiger counter or something to test for radiation?"

"Sure, we have something that may work," Jake said.

"What did you guys see, besides that invisible shark?" Kelly asked and teased.

"Well, we didn't see any physical damage to the hull. What we did find was this breather near the escape hatch, proving someone got out, at least one," JD declared.

"That is something we didn't see on our dives, but we weren't looking for anything like that," Jake acknowledged.

"How long before the photos will be ready, Captain?"

"About an hour or two, JD. We have to do them by hand. A one-hour photo shop we ain't," Captain Grey answered.

"Okay, let's get ready for another dive, and this time, let's take a radiation reading and examine that escape hatch a little closer," JD suggested to his group as he stood up to leave.

"Hang on a second. Sit back down. Commander Henderson, we have an added problem I need to make you aware of. What I have to say is classified, and even though we are on a ship in the middle of the ocean, I don't want to hear it repeated. Understand?" Captain Grey announced matter-of-factly. Then he turned toward Sheppard and said, "Jake, get a guard on the door before I go on with this."

Jake got up and left the room for a minute. During that time, no one said a word. The only sounds heard were made by the ship, caused by the constant rolling of the ocean. Three minutes later, Jake returned, closed the door, and locked it behind him. He did not sit down but instead leaned against the door and watched.

"Ladies and gentlemen, we have a time limit imposed on our, your work. We received a coded message a short time ago advising us that we seem to be violating the rights of the Nigerian government by being here. They consider this vessel and the *Montgomery* war ships that are here to attack Nigeria. They have advised our government to order us to leave immediately."

"How far do they claim, Captain?" Batman asked with a tone of seriousness.

"That is not the issue in our mind. We are twenty-seven miles off their coast, but of course, they are claiming a hundred," Captain Grey replied.

"Is there any support in the area that could back us up if we don't leave?" JD questioned.

"No, but our government has convinced them that for now all we are doing is making repairs after rushing here in response to a distress call. They gave us three days, and then we must be gone," Grey continued.

"And how did they explain the *Montgomery*?" Batman asked to no one in particular.

"And if we aren't?" Kelly responded quickly.

"Well, it's hard to tell. Their country is poor and run by a maniac by the name of Omar Kelopoti. He is liable to change his mind on a moment's notice and blow us out of the water, or he could just watch and wait. General Samula runs the military and, for the most part, runs the government. He will, for no better reason, just go out and kill a busload of people. Right now, he is in the process of invading the surrounding countries and not taking many prisoners. No matter what he does, I am putting this vessel on yellow alert for the duration of our stay. I am going to brief the crew on the possibility of hostile forces in the area, but that's all."

"Is that it, sir?" Micky finally spoke up, obviously a little scared.

"No, ma'am, not all. When you dive, you will be accompanied by no fewer than six divers. They will be armed with special weapons and also carry charges to blow that sub if the need presents itself. That will be a last-resort move. I don't want to do it unless this becomes life-threatening and we have to get out fast. And we don't want anyone salvaging her. There may be something, even after fifty years, that only we should see."

"Okay, then the plan is to wait for the photos, study them, and then when we dive again, we do a radiation and leak check. And I suggest, if the photos confirm what I think they will, then we open the escape hatch. If what I think is true, then someone exited through there and the chamber is still flooded," JD stated.

"I agree with JD. That hatch was used and not too long ago," Micky added. "I do believe that if that chamber is full, then we may be able to get inside. If not, then there is no way in."

"That sounds pretty risky. No telling what you may find," Jake replied.

"Exactly why we need to get inside. The exterior isn't going to tell us what we need to know. We either need to raise her, which is not possible, or enter her, which is," Micky said, defending her argument again.

"Okay, that settles it. We check it out this dive, and then if it looks good, we open the hatch on the escape trunk," JD stated.

"You know very well that if that chamber's bottom hatch is open, we will flood the boat," Micky piped up.

"Yeah, but if the chamber isn't already flooded, the hatch will have been sealed and locked from the inside, which will prevent any movement of the wheel at all. Correct?" JD said.

"That's right. If the safety is in place, that lever will not move one inch. We may never get in, or maybe we will," Batman added.

"I think someone left her and took the time to close the hatch as he left. Or maybe someone inside closed and secured it. And if that's the case, the chamber is not flooded and we will not get in. It's worth a try," JD decided as he stood up a second time. "Are we finished, Captain?"

"Not yet. There was an attachment to the message addressed to you, Henderson. It's from a Captain TC Evans of CID Norfolk, Virginia. Here it is." Grey handed JD the two-page message.

"Good. TC came through after all. It's a list of the crew for the *Wolverine*. I don't get it. According to this, Lieutenant Commander Jacobs, seven officers, and sixty-two enlisted members were assigned to her. But this list doesn't make sense. It has the name and the date each member died. Most indicate they were dead long before sailing. All except the officers and one...no, three enlisted members. The rest were dead before sailing. That doesn't make any sense. Why would they sail with only a skeleton crew? Unless they didn't want any record of who actually sailed her or they were going on a mission that required them to be invisible to the American public!"

"Wow, that really puts a kink in the system. Make sixty people disappear from society. Why?" Micky asked.

"Not a chance. There was something going on that someone wanted covered up, some kind of covert operation, maybe," Batman said, looking dumbfounded.

"We can go over this later. We are not going to prove anything up here. Let's get ready to dive," JD said to hurry up the group.

"Okay. Jake, you can open the door and dismiss the guard. JD, let's be careful down there."

Two hours later, they were back in the conference room, studying the photos. They had brought along photos of Gato-class boats and construction plans for that type of boat. In comparing the two, they decided that she was in fact a Gato-class boat, but with extensive modifications to the sail, the propeller, and the stern area in general. They didn't have plans for this exact boat, but at least they had something to go by.

At 1430 hours, all ten of them were preparing for another dive. The crew had been told of potential hostile activity in the area, and they were ready.

As soon as they hit the water, a twelve-foot shark came over to investigate. He swam around for a couple of minutes before leaving, apparently deciding he wasn't very hungry.

JD and Micky, along with Jake and two of his divers, proceeded to the aft hatch. Kelly and Batman, with their escorts, stopped at the sail to look over the periscope and start taking readings on the Geiger counter.

JD looked closely at the hatch, with everyone looking at him. He proceeded to turn the hatch lever. It seemed to move freely, indicating the escape trunk was flooded. Then as he neared the end of its pull, he stopped and looked around at his partners. They were giving thumbs-up, indicating that he should continue. If it were possible for a person to sweat underwater, then now was the time.

JD started to pull the lever again and then stopped as he felt a heavy clunk when the bolts released. He swam over to the other side of the hatch to get a better grip to open it. In his doing so, Micky had to back-paddle a little, causing her to float about ten feet away from the hatch. If the chamber weren't flooded, then it would not have unlocked so easily. Everything was going so smoothly. JD and Jake started to lift the hatch slowly, with Jake's divers on either side watching closely as the hatch was raised.

The hatch was opened about four inches when suddenly it flew wide open. A tremendous force blew all of them backward and upward. The force of the explosion rolled across the deck of the submarine until it reached the other five divers on the bow. The wave hit them like a wave breaking on the beach, causing them to drop the Geiger counter. After a quick recovery, they turned and swam as fast as they could toward the escape trunk to see what happened.

Within seconds of reaching the escape trunk, each one had grabbed one of their lifeless friends and attempted to replace their regulators, which the force of the explosion forcefully removed. They immediately started for the surface, realizing that nothing could revive them down there.

Once they were on the surface, a dozen men were diving in to assist in the rescue.

"What the hell happened?" Captain Grey yelled to Batman as he was climbing onto the dive platform.

"I don't know, Captain."

Within minutes of the explosion, everyone was back on the cutter in some form of consciousness. The ship's doctor was leaning over JD when he started to wake up.

"What...what happened?" JD slurred as he started to come around.

"Just hold still, sailor," Dr. Mason said, pushing JD back down to administer a shot. "You'll be okay. Just stay still for a few minutes."

"Will they be all right, Doc?" Batman asked as the doctor got up from JD's side.

"I think so, but I can't be sure until I run some tests," the doctor replied.

Lagos, Nigeria
General Samula's Office
April 29, 1996
1300 Hours, GMT

"Amid, where have you been?" General Samula asked his most trusted aide as he entered the general's office.

"Sir, I personally went to the laboratory to inform the scientist of your plan," Amid answered. "And when I returned, I stopped by the motor pool to inquire of your new car. It will be ready in the morning, and a gift for you, sir. Some of your favorite cashews."

"Thank you, Amid. You are always so considerate," General Samula said, taking the cashews from Amid. "And how is your family? Safely moved out of the city?"

"Yes, sir, they are fine," Amid answered quietly. "Is there anything you require of me today, sir?"

"No, you may take care of your normal duties," the general commented as he opened the bag of cashews.

"Thank you, sir," Amid said, giving a short bow and turning to leave the office. He didn't feel safe, and now that he did not need to be accounted for, he would make his escape to the border and then to the Ivory Coast. His cousin Rafael had already left, taking the message to General Sellers, but even he didn't have all the information needed by the general. He hoped Rafael made the trip without being captured by Samula's troops.

General Samula was preparing for a meeting with his commanders on the destruction of the American and Allied forces that surrounded his country.

"Gentlemen, the countdown starts now!" General Samula declared to the members of his council and his commanders. "At 1200 hours tomorrow, the first of five atomic bombs will be detonated over Abidjan and four other strategic locations known only to me and my pilots. While the Americans eat their lunch, we will strike. Victory is ours!" General Samula exclaimed as he looked around the conference room.

USS Washington
April 29, 1996
1615 Hours, GMT

Micky woke up in sick bay with a splitting headache and, luckily, nothing more. Jake and JD were not as lucky, but luckier than the two other divers were. Jake, besides the headache, had a broken wrist, and JD two broken ribs. Jake's two men had been a little closer to the hatch, and both had minor concussions, several broken ribs, and one had a broken arm and the other a broken wrist.

"How you doing, kid?" Batman asked as he and Kelly entered sick bay, directing his question to Micky.

"I won't be going dancing tonight. What the hell happened, anyway?" Micky asked, trying to shake out the cobwebs.

"We're not really sure. But maybe JD and Jake could shed some light on it. How 'bout it, guys? What happened?" Batman asked, looking over at JD and Jake.

"I'm not really sure. Everything happened real fast. We were lifting the hatch when one of Jake's guys started to push him and me back, and then boom," JD answered.

"Hey, Doc, are Jimmy and George gonna be okay?" Jake asked the doctor when he came into sick bay.

"Sure, but they won't be diving for a while," the doctor answered.

"Are they awake yet?" JD asked.

"Let's see," Doc said as he walked over to the bunks where Jimmy and George were resting.

"No, not yet," he said, pulling the curtain across to close them off. "I'll be back in a few minutes. You just rest." Then he departed the sick bay.

"I don't know what they saw, but I sure as hell want to thank them," JD declared.

Captain Grey came in just as JD finished and walked over to JD and Jake with a look of grave concern on his face.

"I asked earlier but didn't, or rather couldn't, get an answer. So now that you two are alive and awake, would you tell me what happened? But before you do, I have something to tell you."

"What is it, sir?" Jake said.

"Whatever happened down there will cause quite a stir in Washington. When you surfaced and were being pulled on board, one of our crew spotted something bobbing in the water with you. We pulled it in, and I emphasize *it*."

"You have a habit of sensationalizing everything, Russ. Come on, what was *it*?" Jake teased, looking over at JD and Micky.

"*It* was a body, Jake, a very dead, very old body. Doc has been going over the body while you guys have been taking it easy down here. And since Doc is here, maybe he has some info on who he is… was. How about it, Doc?" Captain Grey said and turned as Doc came back into sick bay.

"Okay. Well, from what I could tell, he has been dead anywhere from three to four months. He apparently died of old age, a massive coronary, but he has a lot of water in his lungs. The uniform he's wearing is that of a naval submarine commander, and his dog tags are of a Lieutenant Commander Jacobs. And he was wearing his Steinke hood, with no air left in the cylinder."

"He was the last commander of the *Wolverine*, but how did he get in the escape trunk?" JD asked the room.

"That's one we may never know. I know that we still need to get inside more than ever now," Batman stated.

"Before anyone leaves this room, I want some answers!" Grey yelled.

"Could we get a little quiet? I'm trying to sleep over here!" a voice yelled from across the room.

"Jimmy, you're awake!" Jake yelled back as he attempted to stand, thought better of it, and sat back down on the bed.

Doc walked over and pushed the curtain back and rolled Jimmy's bunk out so he could talk.

"Yeah, I'm awake. What happened? Where am I?" Jimmy said as he started to focus on the room and its surroundings. "Ouch! Damn, why am I all bandaged up, Doc?"

"Hell, easy on the hundred questions and lie still, or those ribs will never heal," Doc said as he stopped the bunk in the middle of sick bay.

"How's George?" Jimmy asked, looking around for his buddy.

"He's fine, just sleeping a little longer."

"Okay. You guys okay?" Jimmy asked when he finally realized who was in the other bunks.

"Yeah, Jimmy, are you up to some questions about what happened?" asked JD.

"There isn't much to tell. We were watching you and Jake open the hatch, and I saw what looked like a trip wire or something and I swam up to stop you from opening any more. But I guess I was a little late, sorry," Jimmy said.

"Booby-trapped! No way. Why booby-trap a sunken ship? And besides, that wasn't a big-enough charge to do any permanent damage," Jake said in defense.

"I agree with Jake. If someone didn't want to destroy the boat, only discourage invaders, then they would use a small charge or maybe no charge at all. Batman, in the morning you and a couple of others check it out. Maybe it wasn't a trap, maybe just a broken pipe or something. Let's not assume till we know, okay?" JD paused. "You and one of Jake's men go in. Kelly will wait until it's considered safe by Batman," JD continued.

Kelly protested. "I object. I think I am being discriminated against. Why can't I go in with Batman?"

"Now, cut that crap, young lady. You are not being kept out because of your sex. You are my salvage expert, and I cannot afford to send for another one right now, understand?" JD said and grinned a bit, feeling a sharp pain in his rib cage.

"Sorry," Kelly apologized.

"Now, wait a minute, JD. I still haven't got the full story about what happened. Will you please enlighten an old sea goat like me, before I keelhaul all o' ya?" Captain Grey insisted. He then sat down on an empty bunk.

"Captain, it's all very simple. Jake and I were opening the escape hatch and had it moving when Jimmy saw something and tried to stop us. But it was a little late—no fault of his—and we had a little expenditure of gas, air, or something in a very short period. See? Simple, huh? Now we need to find out what it was and how our friend got there," JD said and looked around sick bay, expecting comments.

"Is the hatch open fully, now?" Grey asked.

"Yes and no. We were kinda busy and didn't look," Jake replied.

"Okay, what about the radiation check? Did we get any readings?" JD asked.

"Oh, I almost forgot. We had just finished the bow and sail with no readings above normal. But in our haste to help these clowns, we didn't get to the stern. We will continue when we go down again," Kelly said, looking around for approval. "Oh, the Geiger counter is near the bow on the bottom. I kinda dropped it with all the excitement, sorry," she concluded.

After a couple hours of rest, Jake and JD forced themselves out of sick bay and up to the galley to get some food.

Damn, where are those two? I should call security and report two runaways. Naw, they aren't hurt that bad, the doctor thought as he entered sick bay and did not see Jake or JD. *I'll just check Jimmy and George and go up to the galley. Those two clowns are probably up there, anyway.*

He checked Jimmy and George, who were resting quietly, and headed for the galley. Micky was allowed to rest in her room under Kelly's care.

"What the hell are you two doing up here?" Doc yelled as he entered the galley. "You are supposed to be resting. Do I have to strap you in those bunks?"

"We were hungry and you were not around, so we left," Jake said with a little laugh.

"You think it's funny? Well, until I release you two, you will comply with the following prescription, or else. First, no diving. Second, no women. Third, no booze. And finally, no harassing the doctor," Doc insisted with a smile.

"The second and third will be no problem on this tub. Well, number 2 will be tough with Micky and Kelly on board, but we can handle it. The first one, I don't know, Doc. A broken wrist and two broken ribs never stopped me before," Jake commented with a healthy laugh. JD laughed, too, but with some pain.

"Look, check with me tomorrow and we'll see how you are. Right now, how about some coffee? I really could use some," Doc agreed.

"Right on, Doc," JD said as he poured a cup for Dr. Mason.

Chapter 14

CARDINAL OF DECEPTION

Fayetteville, North Carolina
Fayetteville Airport
April 29, 1996
1330 Hours

"Ground Control, this is Cardinal Airlines Charter Flight 603. Request taxi clearance, IFR Abidjan, Ivory Coast," the pilot of a Boeing 747 radioed to the Fayetteville control tower.

"Roger, Cardinal 603. Cleared to taxi to runway 4. Contact clearance on one-one-eight-point-five-five," the tower responded.

"Runway 4, roger."

"Clearance delivery, Cardinal 603 ready to copy clearance," the pilot of 603 requested.

"Six-o-three, clearance as follows. Maintain runway heading, climb to fifteen thousand, squawk zero-seven-eight-two, contact departure on one-three-three-point-zero after departure, contact tower on one-one-eight-point-three when ready. Have a nice flight," Clearance Delivery stated.

Flight 603 repeated the clearance back as transmitted.

Ten minutes later, after Cardinal 603 reached the end of runway 4, they said, "Tower, Cardinal 603 ready for departure runway 4."

"Cardinal 603, Tower, cleared for immediate departure runway 4. Runway heading and contact departure after takeoff. Have a good flight," the tower said as they watched the Boeing 747 roll down the runway, gaining speed and finally breaking ground.

"Good day." Cardinal 603 then switched frequencies. "Departure, Cardinal 603 is with you, climbing to fifteen thousand. Heading zero-four-zero."

"Cardinal 603, maintain zero-four-zero, climb to three-eight-thousand after leaving US-controlled airspace. Squawk code four-five-eight-three and contact Ivory Coast approach on one-three-niner-point-seven-five at two hundred miles out DME," Departure Control said as the jumbo jet climbed through the clouds.

"Roger, Departure. See you next trip," the pilot of Cardinal 603 responded and then looked at his copilot with a smile of confidence.

Admiral Jacobs's Office
April 29, 1996
1900 Hours EST

"What the hell is going on over there?" Admiral Jacobs screamed at his aide.

"They dived on the *Wolverine*, sir. It seems that she is in excellent shape and they decided to go in, and well, ah...," his aide started to explain.

"They? Who decided? Admiral Barker left orders not to penetrate that damn sub!" the admiral yelled as he stalked around his office, puffing on his Cuban cigar. "I don't mean to pick on you, Ensign, but you are here, and well, sorry, but I hope you understand that you are the only one I have to yell at right now."

"Yes, sir. I just report the facts, I understand," Ensign Jones finally said, getting a bit angry about the way the admiral was treating him. *You know, don't kill the messenger for bringing bad news,* Jones thought to himself.

"Yeah, I guess we shouldn't kill the messenger, should we?" Admiral Jacobs said, as if he read Jones's mind. Jacobs knew his alternate career in crime would be short-lived if they entered that sub and were able to retrieve any evidence that linked him, that boat, and the years of running a black market and pirate operation. He didn't need that, but he wanted to know what had happened to his older brother and why the *Wolverine* was where she was. The last official recorded time she was seen was in 1943, but he personally had been drinking coffee in her galley not more than five months ago, off the coast of Marsh Harbor, Bahamas. That was the last time he had talked with his brother and the last time he had seen the *Wolverine*.

Her last mission had been discussed that day Jacobs was on board. It was to deliver a package to their operative in Nigeria, known only to the crew as Mr. Corning, then head for Italy to pick up a load of wine. In the package were the detailed plans for construction of an atomic bomb and the complete assembly of the detonator. Only Jacobs knew that the plans were bogus and, upon assembly, the bomb would not blow a hole in a shoebox and the detonator was really a detonator simulator for display purposes only. As bad as Jacobs was, he still could not sell a nuclear device to a third world country. His only problem was, Could the Nigerian government scientist figure out the detonator and construct and design their own bomb?

Abidjan, Ivory Coast
Headquarters, Eighty-Second Airborne Division
April 30, 1996
0720 Hours GMT

General Sellers was having breakfast in the main dining room of the hotel they were staying in. The US government had acquired several hotel rooms around town to accommodate all the press and military visitors. Sellers was staying at the Hyatt Ocean View, just outside the city limits. He was in the presidential suite but always chose to eat in the main dining room on the second floor, overlooking the ocean. He had a lot to think about. The first of three teams had successfully penetrated deep into Nigeria without being detected. The second team wasn't as lucky. Their aircraft had been spotted, and with much difficulty and the loss of three members, they had made it back to a safe airfield. The third team was due to take off at 0430 hours this morning, but he had not heard if they had succeeded. Time was running out. His intelligence had told him that they were to be the receiver of an atomic bomb today, around noontime. He must be ready to strike if that should be a fact.

"General Sellers, sorry to disturb your breakfast, but this just came to our attention." Captain Patrick interrupted and handed the general a sealed envelope.

"Have a seat, Captain. Would you care for some coffee?" General Sellers offered.

"That would be fine, sir," Patrick answered. He reached for the pot of coffee on the table as he sat down.

Reading for a moment, General Sellers became very quiet, and the expression on his face turned to one of grave sorrow.

"Anything I can do, sir?" Captain Patrick asked as he saw the general's face but continued to sip his coffee.

"No, nothing can be done now. One of our deep operatives was discovered and killed last night as he was trying to leave the country. He had some information we needed, but even more so, his death saddens me greatly. He was a good friend and a damn good agent. He spent six years of hard, dangerous work to get to a position where he could gather information, only to die before completing his mission."

"Sorry, sir. I must be going. Is there a reply to the message?" Captain Patrick asked as he finished his coffee.

"No reply, Captain, thank you," General Sellers said, then crumpled the message, stuffed it in his pants pocket, and picked up his coffee cup, hand shaking slightly, and sipped his coffee.

"Thank you for the coffee, sir. Good day," Patrick said, then stood and departed.

USS Washington
April 30, 1996
0800 Hours, GMT

Batman, Kelly, and three safety divers hit the water early. They needed answers, and time was running out. They only had two days left, maybe. Yesterday, the lookouts had spotted a couple of jets on the horizon flying toward them, and then turning before they got too close. They were identified as possible MiG-23s, but they had stayed just far enough away to keep from being positively identified.

This morning was different. The divers had been in the water about fifteen minutes of a planned fifty-minute dive when the radar operator yelled that he had three bogeys at fifty miles closing fast. At thirty miles, the destroyer would man the weapon systems and wait. The *Montgomery* already raised her anchor and was moving slowly around the *Washington*, on continuous red alert.

"Bogeys, twenty-five miles, five hundred knots, ten thousand feet!" yelled the radar operator to the deck officer, who instantly relayed it to the commander on the bridge.

"BATTLE STATIONS, RED ALERT!" Captain Grey yelled over the intercom.

JD, Micky, and Jake felt helpless on the dive platform. All they could do was watch and wait.

"Bogeys, ten miles, 550 knots, descending, nine thousand... eight thousand five hundred...eight thousand...six miles, six hundred knots..."

"Do not fire unless fired upon," Captain Grey ordered. "Radio the *Montgomery*. Advise them that we will move if we have to, but we have divers in the water."

"Bogeys, nine o'clock high!" the lookout yelled.

"Three miles, five thousand feet, six hundred knots...wait, they are climbing...five thousand five hundred...six thousand... one mile...heading change to zero-niner-five. They're heading back home...zero-one-zero degrees."

"Condition yellow, condition yellow, return to your duty stations," Captain Grey ordered fifteen minutes later, waiting until the attackers had left their radar space.

"What was all that about, Russ?" Jake asked as he entered the bridge with JD.

"I guess they were testing us, and we passed, I hope," Grey commented seriously.

"I hope they don't make a habit of that. I don't think I could handle too many of those," JD commented to Jake.

"You're not alone, big boy. You're not alone," Jake agreed.

He knew waiting is the hardest part of being injured. They had five divers down and no way of contacting them if they needed to. If those MiGs were to attack, the only way for the divers to know would be when this tin can settled on the bottom beside the sub—that is, if there was anything left of her.

Fifty-five minutes later, five heads popped up on the surface beside the ship. Kelly swam over to the dive platform and climbed aboard with Batman close behind. Ten minutes later, all were on board and preparing to dive again.

"What did you find, Batman?" JD asked as soon as Batman had his mask off.

"You'll never believe it, damn, never," was all he said. "It's weird."

"Believe what? And what about the explosion?"

"JD, the explosion was no explosion. It was a rapid release of air that was under pressure. The pressure was in the form of a fire extinguisher that was jammed in the escape chamber. It was a trap. The old guy knew he was dying and set the trap before he died," Batman said as he started to change his regulator to a new tank.

"Okay, what about the escape trunk? And what won't we believe?" Jake asked before JD could.

"Well, I think we could blow the water out of the escape trunk, but there isn't enough high-pressure air left on the sub to do so. If we had a diving bell, then I know we could," Batman said, turning on the air on his new tank, checking the air pressure and quality of air in the cylinder.

"A bell? Hell, why didn't you say so, sport?" Jake said. "Didn't you know this old tub only looks like a destroyer? She was modified several years ago to work as a search and rescue vessel. We are equipped with a very small bell for sub operations and deep recovery operations. Why didn't I think of that earlier? We don't use it very much and kind of forget we even have it. The Navy decided to equip some of her older destroyer-class boats to be used in search-and-recovery operations."

"Where is it?" JD asked and glanced over at the *Montgomery* cruising about six hundred yards off the stern.

"Hey, Chief, prep the bell for a dip in the bay," Jake ordered, signaling the deck chief. Then to JD, he said, "It's in the helo bay."

"Sure thing, Captain. We can have it ready in about an hour," Chief Jeffery Peterson replied.

One hour later, Batman and one other diver were in the small bell and were being lowered into the ocean. Four other divers were already in the water to guide it over the hatch. Micky, Kelly, and JD stood on the dive platform and watched the operation.

Forty minutes later, the *Washington* was repositioned with her stern over the wreck of the bow of the *Wolverine*, and the bell was almost ready to take the plunge. Batman and Seaman Alan Gold were inside the bell, with divers outside guiding it toward the forward escape trunk. As they approached, one diver swam ahead and closed the hatch that had remained open after JD opened it earlier. The operation took about twenty-five minutes, but the bell fit securely on the escape trunk.

Batman and Alan took deep breaths in unison as they looked down at the hatch between them and the boat. Alan increased the pressure in the bell as Batman opened the bottom hatch, exposing the hatch on the *Wolverine*. With the pressure increased in the bell, they should be able to open the *Wolverine*'s hatch without flooding the bell.

"Well, here goes nothing," Batman said, sweat dripping down in his eyes. Reaching down, he spun the handle and opened the hatch. All they could see was water and darkness.

Into the water Alan lowered a hose that was connected to a pump that they hoped would draw out the water. If all worked well, the escape trunk would be empty in about fifteen minutes. Alan turned on the pump, and the water level began to lower. He and Batman stared into the black hole.

Twenty minutes later, the water was gone. Alan turned off the pump.

"Well, good buddy, it's showtime," Batman said as he lowered himself down into the escape trunk.

Looking up at Alan, Batman got the nod indicating that he should open the hatch. Batman crouched down and attempted to turn the handle.

"Damn!" Batman exclaimed as he tried to turn the handle. "Pass down that crowbar." Reaching up, he retrieved the crowbar. "If this doesn't work, you come down and the two of us should get it opened."

"Roger, sir," Alan replied, watching from the bell. "Rusted?"

"Yeah, but we will get it open, or else," Batman said as he propped his feet on the bar. Placing his back against the bulkhead, he pushed. Once, twice, then a loud crack. The handle moved slowly, but it moved.

Moment's later, Batman was shining a flashlight into the forward torpedo room of the *Wolverine*.

"Dark, isn't it?" Alan said with a chuckle.

"Yeah. You ready, Alan?" Batman asked as he slipped on a backpack with a small cylinder of air and put the hood over his head. The hood was equipped with a microphone and headset so they could communicate.

"Yeah, are you?" Alan replied, looking down into the open escape trunk. "How do you hear me?"

"Loud and clear. Here goes," Batman said as he descended into the torpedo room.

"Good luck!" Alan said.

"Yeah, I guess so. Now I'll stay in constant comms with you, so don't leave without me," Batman said.

"You got it, Batman."

He looked up and smiled, then crossed his fingers. Then he looked up again at Alan and started to walk around the torpedo room. Alan closed his hatch as a safety precaution and secured it.

"Batman, do you still read me?" Alan asked over the radio transmitter.

"Roger. Still got you loud and clear. Turn on that recorder and pray," he said as he continued to look around the forward torpedo room and then started toward the control room.

"I'm at the hatch separating the torpedo room from the rest of the boat. The hatch is closed and stiff, but it moves. I am now pushing open the hatch," he said. He pushed the hatch all the way open and looked around with the bright flashlight he had. "Looks like nobody's home. Do you think they would mind if I looked around a little?"

"Naw, go ahead, Batman," Alan said with a smile and chuckle.

On the surface the conversation was being heard by all, as it was being piped into the intercom system.

"I've found a light switch. What do you think? Any power in those old batteries?" he asked, reaching out to turn the switch but stopping short. "I better check for gas first, or I might just blow us up. Ha ha."

Reaching in his pocket, he pulled out a new little device that would measure the amount of air and oxygen in the room. It was primitive, but it was all he had. The dial showed that the area he was in had some oxygen and no gas, or at least none that showed up on this gadget.

"I'm getting an oxygen reading down here. I'm gonna lift my mask and see if I can smell anything. Stand by up there," he said as he slowly lifted the bottom of his mask. "Damn, it stinks in here, not gas, like something that is rotten. Alan, why don't you open that hatch and have them pump some fresh stuff in here? Then you come on down. I'd like some company," Batman said as he scanned the compartment he was standing in.

"What do you think, topside? Do I go in?" Alan asked on the phone to the surface.

"Stand by," was the reply.

"Affirm. Open the hatch and stand by for fresh air." The reply from the surface was positive and reassuring.

Alan reached down and opened the hatch and immediately saw Batman's smiling face looking up at him.

"Come on down," Batman said with a big smile, just like a game show host.

Alan only hesitated for a moment and then scrambled down the ladder.

"We are securely attached, aren't we?" Batman asked once Alan was beside him.

"Now's not a good time to ask," he said, looking around the cramped space of the old boat.

"Well, let's be off!" Batman said cheerfully, as if he were on an afternoon stroll through the park. The oxygen being pumped in almost covered the stink in the boat and was soon getting through the entire boat.

"Wait a minute," Batman said before he and Alan had moved more than ten steps. "Does that bell have a plug for the shore power connection in the chamber?"

"No. Why?"

"Just a thought. Let's go," he said, reaching over to the light switch. "Hey, JD, I know you can hear me. I'm attempting a light switch. Here goes nothing." *Click.* "Oh, well, nothing. Maybe a burnt-out light bulb. We'll try another later."

He and Alan started down the corridor heading toward the control room and sail. That was the place where answers would be and the place to start.

As they moved slowly forward, they continued to scan the interior, looking for leaks, or anything that would tell them why she was here. There was water on the deck, not a lot, but she was leaking somewhere. It was very damp down here, and although it was not hot, each man was sweating as if they wore fur coats on the beach in the middle of summer in Hawaii. And being afraid was something neither one would discuss right now.

As they proceeded, they made comments to topside that the boat did not look bad.

"Hey, JD, we are in the galley and gonna try the lights again. Wish us luck." *Click.* Flickers. *Click. Click.* "Lights weak, and dirty contacts, but the old girl has a little juice in her," he said as he and Alan looked around the small efficient galley. It was a little messy, some rotting food on the counter; checking the refrigerator showed more rotting food and more smell.

"How many men on one of these, Batman?" Alan asked as they proceed toward the control room.

"Normally, sixty-five to seventy-five, plus or minus a few. Let's move on," Batman replied as he shone his light toward the control room.

"Right behind you," Alan assured him.

They turned off the galley light as they exited, turned, and followed his flashlight beam down the narrow hall.

"We are almost to the control room. You know, from what I've seen so far, this boat is not like the other ones we looked at in books. There isn't the crampness of other ones. They seem to have gutted a section that we are passing now and installed something I haven't identified yet, but it's large and boxy. Damn, will you look at that? Alan, see if that light switch works. Now, that is—wow, JD, you have got to see this! Oh, sorry, I guess I better tell you what we are looking at. Well, are you sitting down? Good. We have light. Good. Alan, check out that console…okay, here we are in the control room, and I mean *control room*. It looks like it came right off the Starship *Enterprise*, a little older and larger, but well, that area we passed must be the computer banks for this baby. She looks like she has been fully or almost fully automated," Batman said as he walked around the control room and admired the equipment. "Personal computers, keyboards, this baby hasn't been out of service long."

"Alan, check the air tanks," Batman ordered.

"Gauge says they're empty. Maybe that's why the guy was still in the escape trunk. First, he lets out someone and then is trapped when there is no compressed air to drain the trunk, so he drowns. But before he does, he shoves that fire extinguisher into the handle," Alan concludes.

"You may be right. Did you hear that upstairs?" Batman asked the crew on the *Washington*, not expecting a response. But he got one.

"Sounds possible, Alan," JD responded from above.

"Hey, look at this," Alan said as he leaned over the plotting table and the book on it. "This looks like the ship's logbook. And look at the plot on that board! Interesting."

"JD, this boat has some interesting history. Remember that freighter those civs were looking for? Well, this boat was with her on

January 20, 1943, according to the logbook. I'll bring it up, and if we can get power to the batteries, maybe we can fill the compressed air tanks. We're coming up now. We've been here too long. We'll talk to you all the way back," Batman said as he skimmed through the log.

Twenty minutes later, Alan and Batman were back in the bell and had closed the hatch to the sub at the bottom of the escape trunk. They flooded the trunk and closed but did not secure the exterior hatch, and then their own. But before they did, they checked out the shore power connection box and made plans to construct a connector. Forty minutes later, they were standing on the diving platform with JD, Jake, and Micky.

"Let's go up to the conference room and go through this log-book page by page," JD said as he looked it over.

"Fine," Batman answered. Then to Alan, he asked, "Can you see if we can get a connector made up, quick time?" Then he headed toward the conference room.

"Already in the works, sir," Alan commented.

"Thanks," Batman said.

"Thank you. That was great," Alan said and then turned to move some tanks over to an air fill station.

The next three hours were very tedious, spent by them reading and not believing what was written. The mystery of the *Wolverine*'s disappearance was still not really clear. The log indicated she had delivered some components to Nigeria and taken on supplies and fuel. As she sailed out, she developed engine problems. They sat dead in the water, working on the engines, but were unable to get them restarted. After the third day, the crew started to become ill, and one by one, they died. The captain and one other member were left, so they decided to scuttle the boat. They blew the ballast and sank her to where she now rested. The log got a bit confusing from there on. As the log stated, the captain and remaining crewmember were to get into the escape trunk with Steinke hoods and leave the ship, sealing the hatch when they left. The last entry stated that both he and his only surviving crewmember were very sick and were not sure if they could make it to the surface.

"Does it say who that last crew member was?" Jake asked.

"Let's read on and find out. 'Ah, 2030 hours, January 28, 1996. I've ordered Chief Petty Officer John O'Bryan to abandon ship. We are both very sick. All the rest are dead. Senior Chief Harry James, Engineering Chief David Pierson, Ensign Matt Conners, crew members David Johns, Samuel McKinley, Joe Danials, Phil Wolfe, John Thompson, Steve Williams, Randal Mailer, Eugene Mueller, John Locke, Bryan Ball, Billy Meredith, John Griffin, Max Bennett, and our visiting guest, Frederick Peterson. Goodbye to all of you and thanks for the many years of loyalty. I regret it had to end this way. I feel that the food we picked up at Port Harcourt was poisoned, and now we are paying with our lives. Thank you, General. At least we died without pain. I never did trust him like my brother did. He said it was strictly business. Now I cannot prove it, but maybe whoever finds us can. The following is my confession to crimes against the world and humanity. What we did was wrong, maybe not in the beginning, but it eventually went wrong. We never ran drugs, just a simple little black market ring that helped many people get to a level in life that money could buy. Thanks, little brother, for the good life, while it lasted. Not a bad run, little brother. Thanks to the Navy for keeping this old boat in great shape. Too bad they did not know why. May you live long and prosper, little brother. Must go now. O'Bryan is a little stronger than I am, and he has half a chance to live, but I must help him out of the escape trunk with the raft. This log is officially closed.' Signed, Lieutenant Commander Jacobs, US Navy, semiretired, scratched out and replaced with *deceased*." JD paused for a moment. "There is another note here."

"Read it," Batman insisted.

"It just says, 'Say hi to the president for me,'" JD said. "Wonder what he means by that."

Chapter 15

ENGLISH TEA PARTY

Washington, DC
FBI Building, Jack Malone's Office
April 29, 1996
0915 Hours, EST

"What makes you so sure the *MaryJean* was transporting an atomic bomb to England?" Davin asked from across the office.

"We're not 100 percent positive, but everything we have learned is pointing in that direction," Connie replied seriously as she read through more documents that Jack had produced from his file cabinet.

"Let me get this straight. You believe someone put an atomic bomb on the *MaryJean* in January 1943?" Davin questioned, still not believing the story as Jack told him. "That's almost two years before the Hiroshima drop."

"Yeah, we know," Connie replied as she studied a small note that was attached to the inside of the second classified report she was reading.

Jack had been quiet during this conversation, and that bothered Davin. Jack wasn't usually this quiet, unless he had something heavy on his mind, something that really bothered him. And anything he did say, one could take as being as accurate as a diamond cutter's knife.

"Jack, what does this mean?" Connie asked as she held out the short note.

"Let's see." Jack took the note from Connie. Reading it out loud, he said, "Jack, the transfer has been made. Will contact you later for verification. Signed, HJ."

"What do you make of it?" Connie asked again.

"I really don't know, Connie. I think it has something to do with a case I had a few years ago," Jack replied, with a little perspiration showing on his forehead.

"Jack, what is your opinion, old buddy?" Davin asked, noticing the sweat on his forehead.

"On the note?" Jack said, his voice showing a little nervousness.

"No, the bomb," Davin said again.

"Davin, you know me too well to know that I'm not bullshittin' you when I say that this one has me real scared. If there was a bomb on that tub, where is it now?"

"Could the thing be any good after all these years?" Davin asked, throwing the question out for general comment.

"Fifty-three years, maybe a bit of rust, cobwebs. Hell, Davin, I don't have any idea if the thing is safe or not. As far as we know, it's a time bomb waiting to go off just as a ship with the Queen of England on board crosses over it. But the experts say the case was made of a material that would outlast time itself, so it should be intact. They think it is perfectly safe, but no promises," Jack replied bluntly, still sweating.

"You mentioned cobwebs. Was that just a slip of the tongue, or are you really saying that you think the bomb is not really on the bottom of the ocean?" Davin asked.

Connie cut in, first glancing at Jack, then Davin. "Well, let's look at the facts. First, the weapons found in New Orleans, and second, the growing list of names associated with that boat who seem to have been in strategic positions back then and who are now in even better positions to feed even more arms through a well-established black market weapons system."

Davin didn't notice the expression on Jack's face as Connie was talking about the list of persons involved in the gunrunning operation. Jack knew his name was soon to be added to that list, unless he could prevent it. But how?

"The bomb would explain two of the crates. They would ship the components separately to prevent an accident. The third crate could have been more equipment to assist in the assembly," Jack stated, trying to hide the guilt he had in this affair, playing both sides of the coin. He knew that someday it would end, but he wasn't ready for it now, or was he?

"What tipped you off about this bomb, anyway?" Davin asked.

"My son, David, is with the CIA now, and he is on a case and working with the Nuclear Research Center in Rockville. They ran across an old report by a Dr. Samuel Blum on early atomic research and read that there was an early experimental bomb to be detonated in March of '43. He got curious and started digging deeper. When he discovered that it was to be shipped over to England on the *MaryJean*, well, he knew I was helping you on that old tub, and so he sent over the report. Connie has it in that stack she is digging through."

"Glad to hear David is doing well and is now with the company. Tell him I said hello and wish him luck." After a short pause and taking a deep breath, Davin continued, "Do you have any concrete evidence that the bomb was made and that it was put on the *MaryJean*, other than that report?" Davin asked. "Is this Dr. Blum still alive, so we may talk to him?"

"Nothing concrete, except that report, so far. And sorry to say, the good doctor passed on about five years ago," Jack commented as he stood and walked over to the coffeepot, poured himself a cup, and quietly offered some to Davin. Getting a nod, Jack poured a second cup for Davin and one for Connie.

"No, you're right, Davin," commented Connie. "But our man has proof that a bomb was being shipped to Europe via a convoy leaving New York in January '43. And," Connie said, pausing to take a sip of coffee, "the *MaryJean* took on a secret cargo with a squad of Marines to guard it just before she set sail, correct?"

"Okay, okay, pretty strong argument. But if there was a bomb, how come there isn't any accounting for it?" Davin continued to play the devil's advocate, seeking answers where there weren't any.

"Oh, but there is, my old friend. It looks like it became a major screwup and the only way to save face was to cover it. And when dealing with wartime secrets, it looks as though a cover-up was very easy," Connie answered as she thumbed through the stack of documents.

At ten o'clock, Davin called St. Mary's Hospital to inquire on Josh. When he finally hung up the phone, he didn't look too happy.

"How is he?" Connie asked sincerely.

"Still in a coma. They have high hopes, but it will be touch-and-go for the next couple of days," Davin replied.

"Not real encouraging," Jack commented.

"He's strong. He'll be okay, Davin," Connie assured him as they left the apartment.

Soon they were back in the car and heading south on Riverside.

"Where to first, Jack?" Connie asked quietly.

"Over to the British Embassy to talk with an Ambassador Rodgers, formally Captain Rodgers of the Royal Air Force. You remember him, Davin?" Jack asked as they headed out.

"No, can't say as I do, Jack," Davin answered as he thought about who Rodgers was.

"Come on, you know, the short guy with the big ears, the one who receives briefcases that have been dragged around the North Atlantic and has all that secret stuff in it," Jack replied, kidding around with Davin.

"Yeah, boy, I must be tired. The same Rodgers that Jorgenson gave the briefcase to after their rescue," Davin said, finally realizing.

"Rodgers agreed to talk to us, unofficially. But maybe he can shed some light on the picture," Jack volunteered while he dodged through the midmorning traffic.

"Davin, you haven't said a word about what went on over in Germany," Connie asked, hoping to hear some good news for a change.

"Sorry, I forgot. You got me so worked up about the bomb and all," Davin said, hoping that she wouldn't ask.

"Yeah, sorry about that," Jack said, smiling.

"You're going to love this: I talked at length with the only living survivor of the U-49. That's the boat that was credited for sinking the *MaryJean*. Well, he told me that their captain made his first and last tactical error by firing on a freighter on January 19, 1943. It seems that the U-49 was supposed to rendezvous with the *MaryJean* at 0600 hours on the twentieth of January. They had been out for a long time, and while running on the surface, they saw a single ship on the horizon. They planned and executed an attack on this single ship, only to have both torpedoes malfunction and not strike the target. With only two torpedoes left, they decided to surface and sink her with their deck gun. But you will like this. Before they were ready to resume the attack, their target exploded. Unsure of what had just happened, they surfaced, only to find the ship bearing down on them in an attempt to ram and firing their deck gun at the U-boat. Acting quickly, the U-49's captain dived for safety and saved his boat. Before he dived, he noticed that the ship trying to ram them was the *MaryJean*."

"Damn!" Connie said. "That's wild."

"It gets better. After diving for the depths, the captain turned his U-boat toward the rendezvous point. Surfacing en route, they made some repairs and took care of their injured. They were not sure what to make of the events of the day before, but they would follow their orders to meet the *MaryJean* and unload the cargo. The next morning, the *MaryJean* arrived. After the cargo was transferred, the plan was for the crew of the *MaryJean* to board lifeboats, but instead, they transferred to an American Gato-class submarine along with two more crates. The U-49 was then supposed to sink her, but as she positioned herself to fire, the *MaryJean* exploded and sank," Davin concluded.

"That is interesting, a Gato-class boat. What was it doing in the North Sea?" Jack questioned as he turned up on Independence Avenue. "They, I believe, were built for Pacific duty,"

"Yes, I believe that's correct, Jack," Davin commented.

"Hey, guys, do you have any idea which submarine the bomb went on?" Connie asked.

"No, but maybe the good Captain Rodgers does."

Washington, DC
British Embassy
April 29, 1996
1325 Hours, EST

The rain had slowed down a little. For April, the weather was classic. First week, it rained. Second week, it rained. And now it was raining again. If it continued, Washington would float away.

The British Embassy looked no different from the rest of the buildings on Massachusetts Avenue, except for the statue of Winston Churchill out front. All of them were built in the early twenties and now were the embassies of many countries. They did have adequate parking, which was a must in this town for any type of government building.

A stately English gentleman who didn't say a word but escorted them to a room that could have been Sherlock Holmes's library greeted Davin, Jack, and Connie. The decor was old English, and the books reached from floor to ceiling. In the middle of the room was a large desk, very old and stately, in mint condition. Connie and Jack sat down in a couple of overstuffed chairs while Davin proceeded to scan a group of books on the south wall.

They didn't have long to wait. A gentleman entered, dressed in a black pin-striped suit, walking with a slight limp and using a cane for support.

"Mr. Malone, I presume?" he said as he approached, speaking with a heavy British accent.

"You presume correct, Ambassador Rodgers," Jack said, extending his hand to the outstretched hand of Rodgers.

"And this must be Ms. Young and Davin Pierce. I've heard about you, sir. Please have a seat." He waved his hand toward a couple of chairs as he himself limped over to the other side of the desk.

"You have, Ambassador? I do hope it's all good," Davin commented as he took a seat across from the ambassador.

"As a matter of fact, no," he said with a little laugh, one that Davin could not hear.

"Oh, well, I guess that's the end of my career."

"No, no, my boy." The ambassador stopped and looked around the room slowly. "I've heard that you had a bit of a ruckus in your hotel room a few nights ago, am I correct?"

"Well, yeah, but how did you know?" Davin questioned.

"Let's just say a little bird told me," Rodgers remarked again with a little smile.

Jack started, "Ambassador, we have come to see you about—"

But he was interrupted by Rodgers. "About the *MaryJean* and the briefcase that Lieutenant Jorgenson was carrying. I've been waiting and wondering when someone would come by about that," Rodgers finished Jack's sentence and picked up the telephone and pushed two numbers.

"What, you knew we were coming about the *MaryJean*?" Connie asked, surprised, looking over at Jack and Davin.

"Yes, my dear, I've known all along that someone would find out about the cover-up and come over to talk to me. I'm just glad that I'm still alive to answer your questions," he said assuredly. Then he held up one finger, indicating that someone had answered the intercom, and he said into the phone, "Maxwell, would you be so kind as to retrieve that old briefcase from the safe marked PRIVATE in the back office? Thank you." Then he hung up the receiver.

"Okay, now that we are here, will you tell us what you know about the *MaryJean*?" Davin asked to press on after waiting for Rodgers to finish his request on the phone.

"Impatient, aren't we?" he said to Davin's question and then proceeded. "It's only been fifty-three years since that ship and her cargo sailed into my life. And I'll be damn glad when all this is over."

"So will we, sir, so will we," Jack said in reply.

"I don't know what happened on board the ship. What I do know is that Lieutenant Jorgenson was dispatched from the American War Department with a briefcase full of documents, or rather plans and diagrams that were supposed to end the war, if implemented.

Along with the briefcase, unknown to Jorgenson, were three crates with the means to end the war."

"The bomb?" Davin said, half a question, half a statement.

"Oh, I see you have figured out what was in two of the crates. Good, very good. Then you must know what was in the briefcase too," Rodgers commented.

"Not exactly, but we have a pretty good idea. Why don't you tell us?" Davin said to his question.

"Well, since I was the receiving officer and had to account for all the contents of that briefcase, I took the case to my office, along with Colonel Schinder of the American Intelligence, and he and I inventoried and read the procedure and orders. After that, we placed the case and contents in a safe and secured it," Rodgers said, looking directly at Davin.

"What did the documents say?" Jack urged, getting impatient.

"Would you care for some tea?" Rodgers asked, avoiding Jack's persistence.

"Yes, please, that sounds great," Connie answered, hoping that the tea would help ease the tension building in the room.

Rodgers turned in his chair and again rang the intercom, asking his aide to bring tea and a snack. Then he returned his attention to Connie.

"Ms. Young, you must come by and visit more often. This old house has many a story and would welcome such a lovely listener." He stopped as the door opened and the butler entered with a tray of tea and snacks and an old black briefcase.

"Your tea, sir, and your briefcase. Shall I pour?"

"No, Maxwell, we can get it. Would you bring the case over here? Thank you. That will be all," Rodgers ordered, holding his hands out for the briefcase.

"As you wish, sir," Maxwell said, bowed slightly at the waist, turned, and left the library.

Davin, Connie, and Jack just sat there, looking at the black case. Was this the same case that Jorgenson carried across the North Atlantic and gave to Rodgers fifty-three years ago?

"Is that what I think it is?" Davin asked after a long silence that had to be broken.

"Yes, it is. As I said earlier, I knew someone would come, and you did. I knew someone would be asking about this case, and you did. Now, most of your questions will be answered. But do you really want to know? Knowing may get you all killed, or worse."

"What's worse than death?" Connie asked unknowingly.

"You don't want to know, my dear. Believe me, you don't want to know."

Ambassador Rodgers sipped on his tea as they just sat there looking at that case. Then after what seemed to be hours, he stood up, closed the curtains, limped over to the door, and locked it.

"What is in that case could get us all killed by people that you would not suspect. So it is better that you not discuss the contents or anything about this ship with anyone outside this room. If it were known that I still had this, I would have been long dead and buried and not with any ceremony that is to my liking. Do you understand?" Rodgers was very serious and almost demanding.

"Yes, Ambassador, but who would care after fifty-three years? This stuff doesn't mean anything except that it was an attempt that failed to end the war," Jack said in response.

"True, Mr. Malone, quite true, but the names on these documents are of people who have attained great wealth and position in your government and wish to never hear about this major cover-up, which cost lives. Many were people very close to them, and some they didn't know but were not their enemy either. What they did was wrong in every sense of the word. They killed people in an attempt to gain upward mobility and fame. Many eventually gained that position they wanted, but not without stepping on a few people."

"How do you know all this?" Davin asked, believing he knew the answer before he asked the question but hoping it wasn't true.

"I know of this because I am one of those that were in on it from the beginning, and I'm here now, as you see, a man who is of some importance, a man of honor," Rodgers answered.

"Rodgers, I don't understand. You said you were in on it from the beginning, the beginning of what?" Jack asked, doing his best to cover up the fact that he, too, was involved. But Rodgers didn't know this, as most members of the organization only knew one, maybe two, other members that were in the hierarchy. Of course, the workers knew one another, but they didn't really know whom they were working for.

"Let me give you a brief history of events. First, a young Army Air Corps captain contacted me, by the name of Frazier. He said he was working with the Eighth Bombardment Group and had a mission planned for a drop over three major German cities and asked if I would like to assist in the logistics of the mission. Before I knew it, I was acting as a liaison between him and my command in a mission that had no right to ever begin. The plan was to bomb Berlin, Munich, and Stuttgart, all at the same time, with one added frill. And that was, the run to Berlin was going to be with one bomb, the A-bomb.

"He had been talking to his brother back in the States about a bomb that was being developed that would destroy a whole city by itself. Well, being the young enterprising soul he was, he planned the whole thing while flying over Germany. They were to steal a prototype and ship it over to England, and he would drop it on Berlin. If he was shot down before reaching his destination, he was to drop it on the nearest city and still get the message across to the Germans. Great idea so far."

"But no one could have pulled that off, Rodgers. Not without some high-ranking help, anyway," Jack said, interrupting, with a puzzled look. Even he did not know the whole story as it was being told to him now.

"Remember, Mr. Malone, there was a war going on, and things didn't require as much red tape as now. Besides, a few dollars here, a few there, and some good forgery of signatures, and things started to fall in place. Orders were cut and men assigned to guard the bomb. The documents in this case, well, some are real, some are forgery. The names of the players are, well, let's say, not as they seem. When you read these, you will see that even in a war, people are corrupt and will do anything to accomplish a mission. Lieutenant Jorgenson was a pawn, and a good one, if I might add. I hear he retired a full colonel and is living nicely in Palm Beach, Florida."

"Yes, he is. Can we see that case now?" Davin asked, standing to walk over to the desk.

"Sure." He turned the case so Davin might reach it. Davin picked it up and placed it on the table in front of Connie and Jack, hesitated a moment, then opened the locks and lifted the lid. Inside were a couple of folders; they looked old and fragile. But upon picking them up, they discovered that they felt brand-new.

"Where did you store this, Rodgers?" Jack asked as he looked over the first page of a document marked "Top Secret: Assembly Procedure Model 001 43 00098, Atomic Bomb, dated 12/13/42."

"Oh, Jack, it's been safe. The embassy has a very secure vault that even an A-bomb couldn't penetrate. Don't let that concern you. Just read them and say nothing," Rodgers stated.

All were silent for the next hour. Rodgers got up and poured himself some more tea and walked around the room, looking up at the mass of books he and the other ambassadors had collected over the years. He paused at a window on the far side of the room and opened the curtains slightly. The sun was on its way down, and the shadows were growing in length with each passing minute. Ambassador Rodgers had been carrying a heavy load for many years, and now he was finally free of the threat, now that the end was near.

"Ambassador, the names of the men who signed the orders, were they just pawns, or were they involved as deep as you?" Davin asked after finishing the last document.

"That is a very good question, son. And to answer, it may incriminate some good men, men that were not so smart in '42. Why don't you ask by name, Mr. Pierce, and we will all know, won't we?"

"It says here that a General Mark Sloan of the War Department ordered the Eighth Army Air Corps to prepare three B-17 bombers to be ready for high-altitude runs over Berlin, Stuttgart, and Munich. The Munich run would be one way. They were to crash or land in Switzerland if they survived the attack. Each aircraft would carry a load of five-hundred-pound bombs, with the exception on the Berlin bird. It had a single bomb, an atomic bomb. Who is Sloan? I don't remember hearing about him," Davin said while reading over a document marked TOP SECRET, EYES ONLY.

"General Sloan was a figment of our imagination. In reality, he was a clerk working in the War Department who was able to provide the proper stationery and stamps needed to validate the orders. He was able to really get the ball rolling, as you might say."

"Who was he?" Jack asked with a tone of anger.

"That doesn't matter now, Mr. Malone. You see, he died in an automobile accident shortly after the mission went off-line."

"You mean he was murdered," Jack insisted.

"Those are pretty harsh words, Mr. Malone. Let's just say he died in an auto accident. And no one can prove otherwise."

"What about this Lieutenant Adam Smith? It looks like he was the liaison between the Atomic Research Group and the military. Was he or wasn't he a player?" Jack asked after he poured himself some more tea and had a few minutes to collect his thoughts. Jack's name would not be in here; he got involved years later, but he still was sweating.

"Now, he was an interesting fellow. He played along with the scenario as if he knew what was really going on, but he was just a pawn, and I understand he now heads up a small security company on the West Coast, Silicon Valley Securities, I believe."

"What exactly did he do for you?" Connie asked as she stood up to get more tea.

"Lieutenant Smith carried the orders over to the Atomic Research Group and convinced them to prepare a bomb to be used in March of 1943. He didn't know exactly when or where. All he was required to do was to see that the bomb was delivered to a Lieutenant Jacobs at the New York pier for loading on a freighter. Jacobs was to get the Marines to guard it from there to its destination. Jacobs didn't even know what he was shipping. Another pawn," he said, bending the truth to cover Jacobs. Rodgers then reached into a handcrafted wooden box and pulled out three expensive Cuban cigars, handing one each to Jack and Davin.

"How many actually knew what was going on?" Davin asked after listening to all this. "Thank you," he said, accepting the cigar.

"Let's see now." Rodgers paused and thought. "I believe, counting myself, seven—no, eight, total. The rest were pawns and did what they were told either by us or by written order. You see, we covered everything, well, almost everything, till now."

"Why tell us all this now? You could have continued the cover-up and maybe nobody would have discovered the secret?" Connie asked, still a bit puzzled.

"I'm getting old, my dear. Too old to be carrying this burden any longer. It's time the world knew of what only a few overzealous warmongers did in the name of peace. Besides, if I don't tell you, someone else would. I just want the story to be correct. You see, my dear, the whole thing is coming apart right in front of our eyes. It's over, and there isn't anything we can do to stop it. Nothing," Rodgers stated sadly, lighting his cigar.

"Rodgers," Davin asked as he leaned back in the overstuffed chair, "you said only eight knew of the bomb. You probably won't disclose the others, but would you tell us if they are alive? And are these the only copies of the contents of the briefcase?"

"Yes and yes. We tried to be complete and cover every possible trail. Nobody knows I even have those." He pointed to the briefcase and the stack of documents.

"Okay, Rodgers, one final question. What do you expect to get out of this confession?" Jack asked point-blank.

"Nothing, my dear boy. I've gotten what I want. I need nothing more. Now, if I may, I have some work to do before nightfall," he said as he stood to escort them out.

"The briefcase?" Jack started to ask but was interrupted.

"No, you may not take it. It's the property of the British government and will not leave this embassy. Good day."

"Before we leave, I have to ask, Do you know where it is?" Connie asked as they reached the door.

"The bomb?" he asked to Connie's question. As she nodded, he continued speaking. "Oh, that old thing. Well, no, I can't say as I do, but if you should find it, please let me know."

"Oh, which submarine did the bomb go on, anyway?" Davin asked as they reached the library door.

"Were there more than one?" Rodgers asked in return.

"Yes, you didn't know. There was a German U-boat picking up cargo from the *MaryJean* also," Davin stated, watching Rodgers closely, seeing only a surprised reaction.

"I only knew of the *Wolverine*. That does complicate things a bit. The bomb was supposed to be transferred to the *Wolverine*. Good day," Rodgers said as he closed the library door behind them.

They were escorted to the front door and back out into the late-afternoon sun. It had stopped raining while they were inside, and the air felt fresh and clean. As they walked to the car, Davin couldn't help but think about the previous two hours. Ambassador Rodgers was hiding something. He didn't know what, but he wasn't telling everything. It was almost five o'clock, and the traffic would start to become a nightmare in a few minutes.

"I'm a little hungry. What do you say about leaving the car here for a short while and walking over to the deli on Dupont Circle for a little chow?" Jack asked before opening his door. "I need to call the office and can do that while we wait for dinner."

"Sounds good to me. Let's go," Davin replied and turned toward the corner. Connie had no objection and followed without a word.

Chapter 16

DOOM'S DAY

General Samula's Office, Lagos, Nigeria
April 30, 1996
1800 Hours, GMT

"Sir, the airplane has departed Fayetteville and is on schedule with its moment in history. We will launch on time," General Samula's new aide reported as he stood at rigid attention in front of the general's desk.

"Thank you, Captain. Anything else to report?" General Samula asked. After getting a no response from the captain, he queried, "Has Colonel Amid's quarters been searched?"

"Yes, sir. A radio transmitter has been located and is being analyzed as we speak, sir. Nothing else of importance, no records or anything relating whom he was in contact with," the captain replied.

"Nothing. Search again. We must know for whom he was working and what he may have told them. That we may never know, but whom was he working for?" General Samula insisted on knowing. He knew that he might never know the answers to his questions, but he needed to try.

Colonel Amid had been a trusted aide for many years, but his actions lately had been very guarded, and General Samula suspected something was wrong. So he had had Amid followed. His suspicions were correct. Amid had been caught in an attempt to cross the border. He was dressed and attempted to pass himself off as a reporter for a Western newspaper. He carried forged documents identifying him as Al Kolbaris, from Egypt. And in a secret compartment in his briefcase were classified documents from the general's safe. The documents would give the buyer the exact location to the nuclear research facility, the airfield, and all the targets planned for destruction.

Amid never made it to a trial. He died attempting an escape, shot in the back as he ran. Better than torture by the general's interrogators.

British Embassy, Washington, DC
April 30, 1996
1930 Hours, EST

After a good sandwich and a couple of cold beers, Davin, Connie, and Jack Malone were ready to head back to the hotel. Jack had made several calls from the deli, one to his office to check in and get some messages.

"Jacobs, Jack Malone," Jack said.

"What is it, Jack?" Jacobs asked.

"I just left the British Embassy. While there, I viewed some very old documents concerning a ship and a mission that failed years ago that you may be interested in."

"Really. That is interesting. You said the British Embassy. I always wondered what happened to those papers. Thank you, Jack. You will be rewarded well for this information."

"No killing, Jacobs. Or I'm out," Jack insisted.

"Don't worry, I'll just have the case picked up and be done with it. Thank you," Jacobs said and hung up without waiting for a reply.

Jack stared at the phone for a moment before he hung up, thinking, *I may have just condemned them to death. I've got to get out.*

He returned to the table where he left Davin and Connie moments later after a brief stop in the bathroom to wash his face. The food had arrived while he was on the phone. Noticing the clock on the wall to be almost eight o'clock in the evening, they decided they better went home. They had talked and drunk for longer than they had planned. The evening had turned a little cool, so the walk back to the car was very refreshing now that the rain had completely stopped.

The blare of sirens and flashing lights caught their immediate attention as they approached the British Embassy, where they'd left their car. The street was full of police cars and people running up and back from the embassy door. An ambulance came to a screeching halt outside the entrance, and two medics carrying a stretcher climbed out and raced up the steps.

As they got closer, Jack and Connie pulled out their identification so they could get past the officers blocking off the area.

"Malone, FBI. He's with us," he told the patrolman, pointing to Davin. The patrolman checked Jack's badge and let them pass. Once past, Jack looked around for the head cop and finally saw him. It was a friend, John Norton, senior agent with the FBI.

"John, what's going on? A murder at the embassy?" Jack asked as they walked up.

"Jack Malone, what the hell are you doing here?" Norton said as he saw the three of them walk up. "State Department guy will be here soon."

"Who's the stiff? And what happened?" Jack asked again. He and Connie looked around as the local police and FBI agents raced in and out of the embassy.

"The stiff is Ambassador Rodgers, and I don't have any details yet," Norton replied. "Do you know him?"

"Dead?" Connie asked, disbelieving what she had just heard.

"Very. All we know is he died by a gunshot wound to the head by a large-caliber pistol, at close range. It's not a pretty sight. Not much left of his face."

"Okay, John, it's your case for now, but can we go up and take a look around? Are you sure it's the ambassador?" Jack asked as Connie stared up the steps at the door that was standing wide open.

"Sure, help yourself. You know the procedure. And we don't have a positive ID. But he fits the description of his driver's license and the embassy security file photo."

Davin, Connie, and Jack turned and started for the steps to the main entrance and went in. The first thing they saw was that the place had been gone over and it was a wreck, really trashed, unlike the place they left just over two hours ago.

"What in holy hell happened here?" Jack exclaimed as they entered the library, looking around the room. Everything was turned over. Not a single piece of furniture was left unscathed. Whoever was here, they surely were thorough. But did they find what they came for?

The medics were just leaving with the body when the three walked over to them.

"May we?" Jack asked as he stopped the medic. Then to Connie, he added, "You don't need to look at this."

Connie turned and walked over to the big desk as Jack and Davin raised the sheet on the body. Without saying a word, they looked at each other, then back to the body under the sheet, almost knowing what the other was thinking. Jack lowered the sheet and let the medics leave.

As the other officers dusted and examined the room, Jack and Davin walked over to the officer at the door.

"Only one body?" he asked the officer.

"Yes. Should there be more?" the officer asked in reply.

"No, no, just wondering, thank you," Jack said and looked seriously at Davin again. They headed over toward Connie.

"Connie, any sign of the briefcase?" Davin asked quietly.

"No. He must have locked it up before this or it's been taken," she replied, biting her lip. "He was such a nice man. Why would anyone want to do this?"

"He isn't, and until we find out what is going on, we need to watch our backs," Davin said, grabbing Connie by the elbow and guiding her toward the door. "Let's get outa here." They never made it out. John, the head cop, was waiting outside on the steps for them. He didn't look happy, not happy at all.

"Okay, Jack, what do you three know about this Rodgers character? I know you were here until about five o'clock. Are you working a case with the British?" Norton asked, sounding a bit aggravated with the whole situation. "If so, I'll turn this whole thing over to you, right now."

"Yes, John, we were here, and yes, we are on a case that concerns the Brits and us. This little scenario doesn't fit. Have you got any clues yet?" Jack answered casually.

"Yeah. It seems that after you left, a couple of men showed up about five thirty and were seen leaving an hour later in rather a hurry. We have a license number of the car along with make and model from the embassy next door. She didn't hear any gunshots or any ruckus, just was sitting in her office, looking out the window, and thought it strange how those guys seemed in such a hurry," Norton replied.

"Did she say if they were carrying anything?" Davin asked almost too quickly.

"Yeah. She said they were carrying a large paper bag, that's all," Norton answered. "Why? Do you know of something missing?"

"John, I'd like to talk to the aide. You did say he was the one who called you, right?" Jack asked, trying to divert the questioning and keep control of the conversation. Agent Norton did not need to know too much, for his own safety.

"He's gone. We can't find him. He wasn't here when we arrived, and the neighbor across the street said she didn't see him leave."

A young patrolman approached from the hallway, looking as if he had just seen a ghost.

"Agent Norton, I think you need to see this," he said and turned back down the hall from which he just came, not waiting for the lieutenant to follow.

Norton turned without saying another word and started down a flight of stairs headed to what looked like a cellar. Davin, Connie, and Jack were close on his heels. Whatever he had found, they wanted to know about. Reaching the bottom of the steps, they all stopped and looked around, unaware of what they were supposed to see.

"Well, what is it, Kowalski?" John Norton asked, directing his gaze at the officer. "This looks like a basement to me."

"Over here, sir." Pointing toward the back wall, he walked around behind the stairs and toward it.

The others followed, but they still didn't see what he had found.

"Here, sir," the officer said, pointing to the floor. "Do you see it, sir? The blood, a couple of fresh drops of blood. If you follow them, they start on the steps and head for this wall and then disappear."

"What do you make of that, Jack?" John asked as he looked around at the floor and then the wall.

"I don't really know. Maybe a secret door in the wall or something. Good work, Kowalski. We'll take it from here." Jack tended to take control in tight situations, and things were getting tight.

"Thanks. Anything else, Kowalski?" Norton asked.

"No, sir. I've looked around but could not locate a button handle to open a door or hatch of any kind," Officer Kowalski replied.

"Good work! Wait for us at the top of the stairs. Don't let anyone else down here," Norton ordered.

Kowalski turned, said "Good day" to Connie, and headed up the stairs.

The four of them started to search for a door of some kind. Remembering that Rodgers had said the place could withstand a direct hit, they were looking for any clue, but it was like looking for a needle in a haystack.

"Okay, I give up," John said after about twenty minutes of looking. "We know there's a door, but where is the opener, the door handle? How do we open it?"

"I don't know," Jack said loudly.

"Maybe a little dynamite will help open it up," John said in disgust.

"I don't think so, Agent. Rodgers told us that this place could withstand a direct hit from an atomic bomb, and I think he was referring to this shelter. What we have to do is find someone who works here daily and have them let us in. And we better do it quickly. There may be someone in there dying."

"Yeah, I'll get right on it," Norton said as he headed up the stairs to get someone to run down some of the administration personnel from the embassy.

"Now that he is gone, Connie, the body upstairs was the aide, and Rodgers is either alive or dead behind this wall. Let's just hope he has that briefcase," Davin told her as they continued to search for the thing that would open the door.

"Look at this," Jack said as he uncovered a hidden panel behind a fake cement block on the connecting wall. "Damn, it's got a lot of buttons. I wonder which one will open the door."

"Hell, that would take forever to decipher," Davin said, looking over the panel.

"Hell, let's try something," Jack said as he pushed a couple of buttons. Nothing happened; he tried again, but nothing. "Well, you know, three strikes, you're out. One more try, then call in the experts." He pushed a couple more buttons, but nothing. They heard a door at the top of the stairs slam, locking in place. The whine of an electric motor caught their attention for a moment; this was closing a metal trapdoor over the stairwell. Thinking nothing of it, they continued to look at the panel, as if staring at it would make it work. Suddenly, the door on the panel slammed shut, almost cutting off Jack's hand. If he hadn't pulled back when he did, his hand, or at least a couple of fingers, would still be inside the control panel.

"I don't think you should have done that, Jack," Connie said as they all heard the low whine of an electric motor.

"Holy shit, Jack, there's water coming in here!" Davin yelled as water started to pour in through vents on the walls. Within a couple of minutes, it was ankle-deep, and rising fast. Two minutes later, it was knee-deep. They ran to the top of the stairs, only to find a metal door between them and the wooden door that had been standing open moments before. It looked like the whole basement was designed as a bomb shelter and this outer area was intended to keep out intruders, or at least it seemed that way.

"Okay, you got us into this. How do we get out?" Davin said to Jack, quickly scanning around the basement for anything to pry open that door.

"Well, I guess we're gonna die, *ole* buddy, unless you have a can opener on you," Jack said with a little laugh. "Surely, they heard the door slam and are working right now to open it, and I only hope real fast. That water is rising pretty quick."

"Hey, stop the kidding, fellas. I can't die yet. My mom hasn't any grandkids yet," Connie said as the water went past her waist. It was filling up a foot a minute, and at that rate, they would be underwater in about six to seven minutes. Not a lot of time for anything.

"Jack, can you get that panel open again?" Davin asked. "Connie, stay on the steps for now."

"I'm trying, but it seems to be locked. I need a screw driver or hammer."

"There's a workbench over in the corner. Maybe," Davin said as he swam over to the bench.

"Yeah, a hammer and screwdriver." Connie swam over to help. "What are you doing here? Get back on the steps."

"I don't want to just sit there," said Connie. "Besides, if I'm going to die, I don't want to go alone. This water is getting colder, guys. Hurry up." Connie picked up a screwdriver.

With a little persuasion and a large hammer, the panel door opened again. The water was chest-high to Davin, and Connie was almost underwater, but she could tread water indefinitely if need be.

"Come on, guys, the fun's over. Let's get outa here," Connie said as she treaded water. "The ceiling is getting closer." But they heard nothing, because Jack and Davin were underwater, trying to get that panel to reverse its decision to drown them.

Gasping for air, Jack and Davin popped up and banged their heads on the ceiling.

"Any luck? Can I help?" Connie yelled. Just then, the lights went out and they were in the dark and treading water. The ceiling was only about a foot away when Connie and Davin dived down to the panel to give it one last try, because at the rate the water was coming in, there would not be any air pocket left after this dive.

It was dark, and Connie and Davin bumped into each other a lot as they tried to get to the panel. Finally, they made it down and discovered the panel had a light. They tried to jam the box to cause the water to withdraw, with no luck. They were running out of air and started back to the surface, only to find the ceiling and no air. At that point in the dark, they almost gave up. Searching for Jack in the dark with no luck, Connie and Davin started a desperate swim toward where they thought the stairs were. The last thing Davin remembered was holding on to Connie and losing consciousness.

Abidjan, Ivory Coast
Headquarters, Eighty-Second Airborne Division
May 1, 1996
0500 Hours, GMT

"General Sellers, this just came in," Sergeant Rosco said as he entered the war room, handing the general a message.

"Wait for a reply, son," General Sellers said, indicating for the Sergeant to take a seat across the room. He unfolded the message and read.

> To: Eighty-Second Airborne Commander
> From: 502 MI BN
> Classification: Top Secret
>
> Operation greetings in place. Waiting for the word to move. Advise of any changes. Please advise on situation of incoming flight. Good day, sir.
>
> End Transmission
> Top Secret

General Sellers looked at the message and smiled the first smile anyone had seen since this had started. The general just drew to an inside straight and got the card he needed.

"Sergeant, did anything come in on the three insurgent teams?" General Sellers asked, still smiling.

"Nothing more than what has already been reported. Team 1 made it to the first checkpoint and has not reported in yet. They are due to report in at 06:00. Team 2 had trouble with their aircraft and are waiting for another, scheduled departure at 05:45. Team 3 has avoided capture, but as of their last report, they had been detected and are attempting to alter their route. Mission is still a go, but not without problems," the sergeant replied.

"Thank you. Dismissed." General Sellers turned his attention to the situation map, indicating all friendly and enemy forces. His senior order of battle specialist was just adding the finishing touches to the latest battle maps. With this information, the overhead photos provided by the latest in American space technology, and all the intelligence that came in from the many other areas under his control, General Sellers had a very good idea of where he stood in this war.

If only Saddam Hussein had known what President Bush had known, he would have never attempted his little war. Now, almost a duplicate of what happened there was happening now. General Samula, like many power-hungry men, tried to take on the world, only to lose more than they bargained for. General Samula did, however, have a few things that Hussein only wished he had. First and foremost, Samula had nuclear weapons, and secondly, Samula studied what Hussein did and did not do. He was not going to make the same mistakes. He wasn't going to threaten and not follow through. His plan was to strike first, strike fast, and with the most destruction he could deliver by detonating five atomic weapons. And third, the Americans had a new, inexperienced president in office. George Bush had not run for another term, and Lawrence Furgerson, a Democrat from Virginia, sat in the White House now. He was running in this year's election but was not favored to win. But if he was able to smooth relations with Nigeria, he might have a chance on Election Day.

Washington, DC
Georgetown Hospital
April 30, 1996
Hours later, EST

"Where am I?" Davin said as he woke up, staring at the stark-white walls of his hospital room. He was dry and in a soft bed. *Is this heaven? If so, where are the angels?* Dazed and in kind of a drunken state, he looked around the room, trying to figure out where he was. The place resembled a hospital, all white and clean. It smelled like a hospital, too, all disinfectant. Davin hated that smell.

"Just lie back down, Mr. Pierce. You've been through a lot in the past couple of hours," an unfamiliar voice from out of nowhere replied.

"Who are you? Where am I? Where are my friends?" Davin asked the voice, still looking for the source, finally looking down to see the owner sitting in a low chair near the head of his bed.

"Your friends are okay. Just lie down and be quiet," she said again. She stood and walked over to Davin, placing her hand on his forehead and reaching for his wrist. Checking for temperature and pulse manually was preferred, even though he was hooked up to several machines that monitored everything about his body.

"Only if you tell me what's going on," Davin demanded.

Just then, the door opened and Agent John Norton entered. He was smiling a little as he walked over to Davin's bed.

"I see that you have come back to earth, Davin Pierce. How do you feel?" Norton asked and then looked at the nurse. "I see you have the best-looking nurse on the floor watching over you. You must be doing just fine."

"I feel terrible, but I guess Miss, ah…," Davin said, waiting for a reply from the nurse.

"Mitchell," she replied softly.

"I guess Nurse Mitchell will make sure I will be okay. Where are Connie and Jack?" Davin asked, diverting his attention to Norton.

The nurse left, and Davin settled back in the bed, trying to gather his thoughts, while Norton filled him in.

"Connie is fine and in the next room. Jack isn't so well. He is in intensive care. They say he may not make it."

"When can I see them?" Davin demanded.

"Let me get the nurse, and we'll see. You stay in bed."

John Norton walked over to the door and called the nurse. Quietly they talked, and then he returned to the side of Davin's bed.

"She says that you are not to get out of bed but that she will bring Connie over to you in a few minutes," Norton said as he returned to the side of the bed.

"What happened? How'd we get out?"

"What happened? I don't know. How you got out is easy. Once the door slammed to the cellar, we figured it was some kind of intruder defense and proceeded to blow the door. The water, well, we didn't expect that, but after looking it over, we discovered that it wasn't meant to be a trap. It took us a little time to get set, and by that time, the chamber was flooded and you guys were unconscious. You were lucky, damn lucky!"

"You said it looked like it wasn't supposed to be a trap. If not a trap, then what?" Davin asked.

"We put our experts on it, and they, well, to make it short, it seems that the water is used as an insulator in case of a nuclear explosion. It is channeled all around a central chamber to act as a barrier to shock and nuclear fallout. After the initial explosion and shock wave, they could drain the chamber and would be able to move about in the cellar without much worry of the fallout or radiation penetrating their temporary home. Neat idea."

"Yeah, neat, but it didn't work right. No people are supposed to be on the outside when it floods, right?" Davin responded.

"Somebody rewired the control panel as a booby trap, in case someone attempted access to the main chamber."

"Well, did you get in the main chamber?" Davin asked.

"No, but we haven't given up," Norton answered.

"Thanks, John. We owe you one." Then looking up as the door opened again, he added, "Connie, you gorgeous lady, how are you feeling?"

"Terrible. I hope I don't look as bad as I feel," she replied as she was wheeled over to the side of the bed.

"Babe, you are the most beautiful sight I've ever seen," Davin said with a small laugh.

"Doc said I can leave in the morning, and if you are up to it, maybe you too. Jack will have to stay a few days."

"Okay, okay, that's enough talking. Let's get you some food and sleep. The rest of you, outa here," a large nurse interrupted as she burst into the room.

"Damn, Sam, who the hell are you?" Davin asked.

"I'm the night nurse, sport, and you are the patient," she said as Connie wheeled herself toward the door. "Hold it, honey. You can stay. The rest of ya, outa here!" she exclaimed, referring to Agent Norton and his partner, who had just arrived.

Once they left, the night nurse wheeled Connie closer to Davin's bed and set the brake on her wheelchair.

"You two almost died together, and it's only right that you spend some quiet time together. Look, honey, if you get tired and want to go back to your room, just call or just crawl into that other bed if you want. I'll keep you posted on your other friend. Dinner was special-ordered for you two. It should be here pretty soon. By the way, I'm Gertrude. Just call me Gerty if you need anything." Then she turned and left the room, smiling.

Jack didn't make it through the night. At 9:00 p.m., Gerty came in and advised them that Jack had died from the accident. They were quiet for a while, with Connie crying, and then they rested.

After dinner, Connie wheeled herself over to the other bed and crawled in. Within a few minutes, she was asleep. Davin was awake for about an hour before sleep finally took over.

Washington, DC
FBI Building, Pennsylvania Avenue
May 1, 1996
0205 Hours, EST

In the late hours of the evening, deep in the fingerprint department of the FBI building, twenty-five technicians were busy trying to complete the hundreds of fingerprint identifications that came in daily. It was a never-ending process. Once they thought they would catch up and complete all they had before the shift ended, but just before the time ran out, a new batch would arrive over the fax machines. Tonight was no different, hundreds of requests, and each one would take up to an hour each, unless they got lucky and hit it quickly. But even with the new, high-speed computers and laser scanners, the process was slow and tedious.

Around midnight, they had received two requests from Tampa, Florida, twenty from Los Angeles, and about fifteen more from various parts of the country. New York requests were so numerous that a separate section handled all of them. They averaged two hundred a night.

John Hamilton was working late tonight. He had the two sets of prints from Tampa on his desk and was working with his computer to get a positive identification on them. One was an unidentified murder victim, white male, five feet, eight inches tall, brown hair, and green eyes. He had been shot and left on the side of I-75 just north of Tampa.

The other Tampa request was for a young man, initially identified as Donald Peterson. He had been beaten and then been in an auto accident. A routine check of fingerprints would make a positive identification.

"John, how much longer on those Tampa requests?" John's supervisor asked as he walked over to John's desk.

"Not much longer, sir. But there is something wrong with the Peterson file. I can't put my finger on it yet, but it looks like some of the dates don't jibe," John responded.

"How so?"

"Well, look here," John said, pointing to the date on the screen. "First, the individual is Donald Peterson of Cedar Creek, Florida. But according to the record, his father is in the Navy serving on board a destroyer, USS *George Washington*. Father's name, Jeffery Peterson, a chief petty officer, born October 14, 1944, to Donald and Helena Peterson in Rockville, Maryland."

"What's wrong with that?" John's supervisor questioned.

"Nothing, except that Donald Peterson Sr. was a Major in the Marines who was reported missing in action in November of 1943," John said, then he continued. "I want to check this out to see if it is a glitch on our part or if he is really missing."

"Keep me posted on that one, but don't spend all night on it either. We have a backlog again, and I would like to eat breakfast with my wife for a change."

"Not a problem, Sherry," John commented and immediately went back to his computer and started a search. He figured he would access the IRS files, Social Security, and military record on Jeff Peterson. Maybe the date was put in the computer incorrectly.

Palm Beach, Florida
St. Mary's Hospital
May 1, 1996
0800 Hours, EST

Josh Randel was sitting up in his hospital bed, eating his breakfast and scanning the morning newspaper. On the fourth page in the front section, he caught a small article about a young man identified as Donald Peterson. The article said Peterson had been beaten and then almost drowned when the car he was in plunged into Tampa Bay. The incident had been listed as attempted murder by the Tampa Police, and any information leading to the arrest and conviction of the people who did this would be helpful.

"Peterson?" Josh said to himself, wondering where he had heard that name before. It would come to him sooner or later.

Outside his door was Matthew Jarvis, a member of the Palm Beach Police Department. The floor that he and two Palm Beach police officers that had been shot recently were on had been closed off to everyone not required to be there.

"Josh, how you feeling?" Captain O'Quinn asked as he entered the room.

"Not too bad. I guess I'm going to be down and out for a while. Doc says this was a close one," Josh answered.

"Glad to see you up and eating real food," O'Quinn commented.

"Well, did you find out who wants me dead?" Josh asked as he folded up the newspaper and laid it on the table beside the bed.

"Yes and no. This guy Harris was hired by some unknown person to finish the job. The original shooter, well, I was hoping you would tell me," O'Quinn stated as he took a seat beside the bed.

Josh related what he knew of the shooting. "That is going to be a tough one. You see, I was down in the lounge, fixing a tall ice tea, when I heard my intruder alarm go off. I have one on deck, to give me a heads-up on any visitors. This guy was quick. Before I could turn around, he was down in the lounge, pointing a very serious magnum at me. His face was covered with a mask, but the eyes were green. Or at least they appeared to be green. We talked for a moment, or rather I talked. He didn't say a word, just pointed that magnum, waving it around to get me to move. After a minute or so, I was leaning on the dining table with my arms crossed, and the next thing I heard and saw was the muzzle flash from that magnum. I guess I'm one very lucky guy."

"You are. The bullet went clean through you and ended up in the head. The repairs should not run more than a hundred or so. You were knocked out by the impact and fell to the deck, where Pierce found you. You are one very lucky man. If he had used a smaller-caliber weapon, we would not be talking right now," O'Quinn commented.

Twenty minutes later, after some small talk, O'Quinn left. Josh picked up the paper again and remembered about Peterson.

Josh picked up the telephone and punched in the number for David Malone at the CIA building. After four rings, it was finally answered.

"Hello, David Malone, can I help you?" David answered.

"Dave, this is Josh Randel. How you doing?" Josh said quietly.

"Real good, sir. When are they going to release you?" David asked.

"Soon, I hope. Look, I need a little help. And since I'm kind of laid up for a while, I wonder if you would do me a favor?" Josh asked.

"Sure, I'll make the time. What do you need?" David responded. He liked Josh a lot and kind of looked up to him for advice and guidance.

"Well, a kid by the name of Donald Peterson was in an accident in Tampa a couple of days ago. See what you can find out about him, who he is, home, background, parents, and especially grandparents. As much as you can find out," Josh directed.

"No problem, Josh. How soon do you need it?" David asked. This was great; if Josh Randel asked for something, then he must be on to something hot.

"Week or so. Can't do much with it here, but see what you can do."

"Okay. Anything else?"

"No, that's it. How's your dad?" Josh asked, not knowing about Jack's death. "Haven't seen him for a while."

"Josh, my dad was killed yesterday," David sadly said.

"I didn't know. He was a good man. Damn." Josh felt really bad. He and Jack had been friends for years.

"No problem. There was no way for you to know," David said. "I'll have this for you real soon, Josh."

"Thanks, again. Sorry about your dad. Bye," Josh said and then hung up the telephone.

"Bye, Josh," David said as he replaced the phone in the cradle.

Chapter 17

SURVIVAL

USS Washington
Off the Coast of Nigeria
April 30, 1996
0600 Hours, GMT

T ime was running out. This was the morning of the third day that they had been working on the submarine *Wolverine*. So far, everything was going as predicted. Power had been partially restored, and life support equipment was operational again. The submarine was in excellent shape for its age.

Captain Grey of the USS *George Washington* didn't like the situation that Nigeria had put him in. They had a war going on, and his position off their coast made him very nervous. The 82nd and 101st Airborne Divisions and many other countries had already dispatched forces to the area, land forces and air forces, but few had their navies in place. Ships took longer to get to where they were going. He had his lookouts on watch twenty-four hours a day, and the ship was in constant red alert.

The HMS *Montgomery* was slowly cruising around the area. The British destroyer had been assigned escort duty to the *Washington* while she was this close to a hostile country. When the communication came in ordering the *Washington* to proceed to Nigerian waters, the *Montgomery* was the closest warship to the area and was asked to assist.

The diving bell was readied and lowered into the water, with Batman, Micky, and Alan on board. They were going down to relieve some of the work crew and send Alan back up for JD and Kelly. Once they were on board, four more crew were to be brought down to help prepare for the first attempt to raise the *Wolverine*. If they could get her to the surface, they would refuel her and sail her to Norfolk Naval Yard in Virginia, with the *Washington* and *Montgomery* escorting.

Batman and JD were double-checking all the systems; the engine room assured them that the engines would run when needed, but for how long wasn't for sure. The *Wolverine* had not been run for at least three to four months, from everything the chief engineer could tell. Also, the last entry in the captain's log was dated less than four months ago. The chief engineer, Scott "Scotty" O'Bryan, ran some fuel samples and discovered that two of the fuel cells were contaminated. There was good fuel in two tanks, but there wasn't enough fuel there to get this boat back to Norfolk, Virginia. After cleaning the filters and igniters, Scotty was satisfied that when she settled here the engine problem had been the bad fuel. Now, with good fuel and fresh air, they would run. The electric motors were running, but only at 60 percent power. Some water had leaked into one of the motors, and he was in the process of repairing it. With the electric motor running, he was then able to recharge the compressed air cylinders.

USS Wolverine
Eighty Feet below the South Atlantic Ocean
May 1, 1996
0915 Hours, GMT

It was a long night, with little sleep for those on the *Wolverine*. Along with JD and Batman, fifteen crewmen from the *Washington* were working around the clock to be ready for what was termed now launch time of 12:00. They had set the clocks on board to reflect a new beginning of noon on May 1. The noon meal was being prepared on the *Washington*, to be served on the deck of the *Wolverine* in celebration of a successful launch, or rather in this case, resurrection.

Their concentration was disturbed on this morning with the sound of the *Washington*'s engines starting and immediately going to full power. The sound of the huge sixteen-foot twin propellers was unmistakable to a submariner. The surface ship was in a hurry to move, and that was what she did best.

"What the hell?" Batman yelled. He and JD looked up, as if they could see through the hull to the surface where the *Washington* was. "The diving bell is still connected to the boat!"

Then the clatter of the cable striking the submarine hull answered Batman's unspoken question of what was going to happen to the bell if the *Washington* moved. Moments later, they heard the first explosion of the battle that had just started on the surface. Helpless, the men and women on the *Wolverine* just stood and listened.

Snapping back into reality, JD and Batman turned and ran toward the torpedo room, where the diving bell was attached. Alan Carpenter was there, securing the internal hatch.

"What's going on, Alan?" JD asked hurriedly. Sweat started to run down his forehead as the temperature started to rise within the boat.

"Got a quick message from above, just before they cut the cables. They said they had MiGs inbound with weapons armed and a radar lock on the ship. They had no choice but to cut and run. Stationary, they would not survive. Depending on what is thrown at them, they may not survive, anyway."

"Let's hope Grey is quick enough to save his butt. Or our butts are also cooked," Batman commented.

"Attention on the boat!" JD said into the intercom box over the torpedo room hatchway. "Everyone can hear what is going on upstairs. Getting this boat off the bottom may be our only hope of survival. And time is running out. All stations report in."

Ten minutes later, JD had the status of his new boat. They had a chance, slim, but workable. It was going to take time, and time they didn't have much of.

USS George Washington
May 1, 1996
0915 Hours, GMT

"Incoming bogeys, sir. Forty miles and closing fast," the radar operator reported.

"Keep me posted, Smitty," Lieutenant Commander Sheppard ordered. Then turning to the intercom, he said, "Attention on deck! Attention on deck! We have bogeys inbound! BATTLE STATIONS! BATTLE STATIONS! ARM ALL WEAPONS! REPEAT, ARM ALL WEAPONS! THIS IS NOT A DRILL. FIRE WHEN YOU HAVE A LOCK!"

"What do we have, Shep?" Captain Grey asked as he rushed into the combat information center, CIC.

"Bogeys inbound," Sheppard answered, pausing to peer at the scope just as a second blip appeared from the bogey. "MISSILE LAUNCHED! WE HAVE INBOUND MISSILE—MAKE THAT FOUR INBOUND! THIRTY MILES AND CLOSING!"

Grey then yelled in the intercom, "CUT THE BELL! FULL SPEED AHEAD, NOW! EVASIVE MANEUVERS, NOW!"

"THREE MORE BOGEYS, MISSILES FIRED!" the radar operator yelled.

"HOW MANY INBOUND?" Grey asked as he issued more orders. "What is the *Montgomery* doing?"

"Eight missiles inbound, six aircraft!" the radar operator yelled in return.

A quick message was transmitted to the *Wolverine* just before the axes cut the large cables, airlines, and communication lines that were supporting the downed submarine.

Immediately, the huge turbines ran up to full power and engaged the props. The destroyer seemed to leap out of the water, racing to full speed.

"Hard right rudder, establish evasive patterns. FIRE WHEN READY!" Grey yelled into the intercom and then quickly ran to the bridge to coordinate the maneuvers. The ship was rapidly accelerating to maximum speed and turning hard to starboard. As Grey reached the bridge, his weapons' crews opened fire on the incoming missiles, hoping to stop them in flight.

"Sheppard, STATUS?" Grey yelled into the intercom as he reached the bridge.

"Four missiles still inbound, five miles, closing fast…make that three, and lock on two more," Sheppard replied. The weapons took out four of the inbound missiles on the *Washington* within seconds of identification. "The *Montgomery* is turning south, engaging four MiGs, trying to draw them away from us."

Grey and Sheppard knew that Exocet missiles were among the deadliest missiles on the market, but he had what was the free world's answer to them. All eight of his Phalanx 76 mm antimissile guns were firing at the incoming missiles. Five had already been taken out by these weapons. Three to go. In addition to the Phalanx guns, rapid-fire chaff dispensers were ready to add another diversion to the incoming missiles, and superhot flares were readied to divert any heat-seeking missiles that were to be launched if the Exocets failed.

"Captain, *all* missiles down—wait!" Sheppard yelled, still on the intercom. "FOUR MORE MISSILES FIRED, RANGE FIFTEEN MILES!" he said, letting his words trail off as he watched the radarscope. The Phalanx guns were temporarily quiet as they were reloaded and their radars locked on the new targets.

"Helm, LEFT FULL RUDDER, maintain full speed, heading one-three-five degrees. Get us out of here!" Grey ordered.

The MiG-23s that were heading for the *Washington* would not give up the attack, and they were equipped to make three passes before running critically low on fuel. There were six of them, each armed with two Exocet missiles, four heat-seeking missiles, and a 120mm cannon. As the first MiG passed over the *Washington*, six .50-caliber machine guns and two 80mm recoilless guns opened up on him. The pilot only saw a flash in his cockpit before his plane disintegrated around him.

The pilot of the second MiG was a little careless after seeing his wingman destroyed and dropped in for a low pass on the ship. Misjudging his speed and altitude, he dipped his left wing into the ocean, causing him to cartwheel toward the ship, cartwheeling to within one hundred yards off the port side. The debris from the exploding jet was sent hurling into the ship, causing major damage and injury to the crew. Two Phalanx guns were temporarily knocked out of commission when jet parts killed the gunners. However, within a minute, they were up and operational again. The fuel and wreckage ignited several fires.

"Damage report?" Grey yelled in the intercom as he scanned the damage to his ship from the bridge. He still had his engines and could maneuver. His helmsman was sweating bullets but performing the difficult task before him with the ease of a seasoned seaman. Steering a ship of this size in sharp evasive turns without capsizing her was a feat.

"Engine Room, minimal damage," came the reply from below. "We still have full power, sir."

"Hard right rudder!" Grey ordered, but too late. One of the Exocet missiles had been missed during the temporary loss of the two Phalanx guns, and it hit just behind the bridge, destroying the forward stack and the entire bridge. Captain Grey and the bridge crew, several sailors on deck around the bridge, and three machine gunners died instantly. It was a lucky hit for the MiG pilot, but he would not live to tell about it.

As the third MiG pilot was surveying his missile strike, he noticed his fuel pressure was almost zero. A quick check of his altimeter, eight hundred feet, and speed, 475 knots, told him that to eject now could mean that his parachute might not have enough time to open or he would die because of the excessive speed he was flying at. Jamming the throttle to max and hitting his afterburners, he pulled back on his control stick, attempting to make a rapid climb to altitude before his fuel ran out. His miscalculation was the death of him. During his rapid climb, he had to apply extra right-rudder pressure. Unknown to him, part of his rudder had been shot off. His fuel was siphoned out rapidly due to a hole in his left-wing fuel cell, along with a malfunction in his fuel control system. His right-wing tank had about forty gallons of fuel left that he could not use. This added weight and the loss of part of his rudder, which required him to apply extra rudder pressure, was a sure means to disaster. His

MiG was still accelerating in steep climb when his engine flamed out, immediately sending the MiG into an inverted spin to the right from an altitude of two thousand feet. Very few high-performance aircraft could recover from an inverted spin. To eject from this spin was not impossible, but the pilot stood a chance of ejecting into the path of the falling aircraft. He could only watch as the ocean came up to meet his aircraft. The impact on the water, and the subsequent explosion from the ordnance left on board, sent a funnel of water three hundred feet into the air.

The *Washington* wasn't through this yet. The fourth MiG was still full of life and wasn't going to leave until the *Washington* was sunk, even if he had to die by crashing his MiG into her. He didn't have enough fuel to return to base, so his plane was a loss now too. Two other MiGs had fired their missiles and immediately returned to base upon seeing the destruction of the first two fighters, so he knew his was the last chance. As he made his approach from out of the sun from a range of three miles, like the classic war movie, he opened fire with everything he had left. He felt his MiG taking hit after hit from the exploding antiaircraft shells and saw three of his missiles explode before reaching the ship. He was determined and pushed his plane to the limits and beyond. Maintaining a straight course, he dived toward the *Washington*; his speed approached Mach 1 in the dive. Sweating and bleeding from several wounds, he pressed on.

Lagos, Nigeria
National Airport
May 1, 1996
1000 Hours, GMT

General Samula stood at the window in the control tower, watching intently as four Boeing 727s and one Boeing 747 aircraft rolled into position to take off. Each had a special mission: deliver one atomic bomb to a preselected target. The pilots knew that their enemy would be looking for any abnormalities in flight plans, but as commercial aircraft, they had a chance.

Each aircraft had been modified with a bomb bay door. The plan had been put into motion earlier when five identical aircraft took off from various airports around the world with destinations of the Ivory Coast and other strategic targets. The first five were decoys, only used to establish a flight plan and clearance to the areas that were to be targeted. At a location outside the limits of coastal radar, the second five aircraft would intercept and change places with the first five.

The only weapons on board the aircraft were the bombs they carried and the standard small arms for personal protection in case they had to abort and crash-land somewhere. No fighter support would be provided, and once they left the ground, they were to maintain total radio silence.

"General, do we have permission to proceed?" the tower operator asked.

"Let it begin," General Samula answered as he watched the huge aircraft taxi into position.

The roar of the departing aircraft could barely be heard in the tower, but the sight of their departure was a dream for which Samula had worked his whole life.

"General, we just received a report from two of our fighters. The American ship is severely damaged and appears to be sinking. The British ship is burning severely and also appears to be sinking. We lost three fighters, and one is still engaging the American ship."

"Very good, Captain. Now, let's get out of here. We have things to do," General Samula said, showing no pity for the downed pilots. "The Americans are like sleeping tigers, and we are kicking sand in their face. We have a lot to do. Let us go and prepare. We have just started World War III."

USS Wolverine
May 1, 1996
1100 Hours, GMT

"What the hell is going on up there?" Kelly asked in near tears. "Are we at war?"

"I don't know, but if we stay here, we will never see the sun again," JD said coldly as they stood in the galley.

"To the control room," Batman said, interrupted by a massive explosion, then another, and another. These explosions were more severe than the earlier ones. Then, as they stood in silence, waiting, trying to figure out what had happened, they heard a sound that JD, Batman, and any submariner who had been in combat had heard before. These were the muffled sounds of bulkheads collapsing and water filling ship's compartments, as well as the faint cries of the men who could not escape and would die at their assigned stations.

"What's that sound, JD?" Micky asked, knowing what it was before she asked but not wanting to believe it.

"That's a sinking ship!" Kelly replied soberly. Then turning to Micky, she said, "We lost."

"Scotty!" JD yelled into the intercom.

"Aye," was the response.

"Can we do it?" JD asked, sensing the urgency to get this boat off the bottom. The survivors, if any, needed assistance now.

"It's now or never, Captain. We are running out of battery power!" Scotty replied. "But I cannot guarantee we will. Give you the best we can. Just give the word!"

"Let's do it!" JD said. Then turning, he ran back to the control room and said in between gasping for his breath, "Let's get this boat off the bottom."

Immediately, he started issuing orders to start the procedure to raise the sub.

"Prepare to blow ballast!" he yelled into the intercom. The Klaxton sounded, warning the entire boat of the impending attempt to raise the boat.

JD turned to Batman, who had followed from the engine room. "You and Carpenter, get your dive gear on. As soon as you are ready, go up and see if there are any survivors. If there are, stay there and help. If not, well, pray for us. Don't come back down. Understand?"

"The bell is still on the escape trunk, sir," Carpenter said, reminding JD.

"Damn! Can we break it off from down here?" JD asked.

"We can get that bell off the boat, but it's damn tricky. If we screw up, we could damage the boat," Carpenter stated, not sounding real worked up about trying to remove the bell. "There is a way, though. Not real popular, but workable. Or we could just seal the hatches and leave it there."

"I don't want to know how. Just do it and do it quick, and as safely as possible," JD ordered, then turned back to what he needed to do to get this boat off the bottom.

"If there are any survivors, get them together as quickly as possible. If we get this sucker off the bottom, then it's a quick load and then un-ass the area pronto. It isn't too friendly here anymore," JD said as Batman and Carpenter started out of the control room. "Be careful!"

"Roger, sir," Carpenter said as he and Batman turned and ran down to the engine room.

Twenty minutes later, Batman and Carpenter were in the escape trunk in scuba gear and closing the hatch to the bell. With the hatch closed, the bell would stay dry inside and maybe someday be retrieved. It took ten minutes to complete the closure and flooding of the trunk. With the trunk flooded and the escape hatch open to the bottom of the bell, Carpenter would add air to the chamber. Then, at a precise moment, Batman would reach up and pull the lever that released the claw-type hooks that held the bell to the deck of the submarine. Also, they had released the switch that controlled the ballast on the bell. With no ballast and a shot of air pushing the bell upward, it should head for the surface as soon as the latch was released. If enough air pressure was used, the bell might reach the surface. If not enough, then the bell would not move at all or rise off the deck, roll over, and fall to the sandy floor below. The only real problem was that if the bell fell to the bottom, she would most likely hit the pressure hull of the submarine, causing severe, if not fatal, damage to the hull. The same principle was used in modern-day ballistic missiles, but never on a World War II Gato-class boat.

Carpenter turned the high-pressure valve, which would normally cause the water in the chamber to be pushed out and back into the ocean. This was the same air that would be used to blow the ballast from the sub, so he had to be very careful and had to ensure that the valve was fully closed before he and Batman headed for the surface. Or else, the *Wolverine* would never surface.

He carefully watched the pressure gauge as it approached the maximum level. Once the indicator reached maximum pressure, he turned the valve off. With the escape trunk full of water and the air pressure building and pushing on the bottom of the bell, the impending release of air should send that bell to the surface.

The time had come. Batman reached up and pushed the lever that held the bell to the deck. It didn't move. Stuck. The air pressure caused the lever to stick.

Each diver looked at the other, then back to the lever. With all their combined years of training, both of them had forgotten about what happens when air pressure is increased in a confined area. If only they had given it some thought. Batman reached down to the deck and picked up a crowbar that he had remembered was lodged under one of the water evacuation pipes. He and Carpenter lodged the crowbar between the lever and the lip of the hatch and pulled. No luck. They pulled and pushed together. A slight movement. Swimming upside down, they both put their feet on the bar, and using their backs against the bulkhead, Batman counted down from three with his left hand. Then with a push and with all the strength between them, the lever started to move slowly. Pushing as hard as they could, they moved the lever to within an inch of opening, then stopped. Each man was sweating in the tight confines of the escape trunk, and neither man was thinking clearly. Their only desire was to get the bell off the deck so they could swim to the surface and help the injured men of the *Washington* and the *Montgomery*. After a moment of rest, Batman and Carpenter reached up and grabbed the handle one more time, this time determined to release the bell. With one powerful push, the lever snapped open, sending the diving bell up toward the surface. In the giant air bubble that forced the bell off the submarine, the two divers were pulled from the escape chamber and toward the surface with the expanding air. They were hurling toward the surface much faster than they wanted to go but could not stop the rapid ascent.

Batman and Carpenter attempted to flare to stop their rate of ascent but were unsuccessful, and they reached the surface right behind the bell. Luckily for the both of them, they had been exhaling great amounts of air on the ascent and did not burst a lung in the journey. Decompression sickness might be another problem, but time would be the determining factor there, because it was too late to decompress now.

South Atlantic Ocean
May 1, 1996
1045 Hours, GMT

Batman and Carpenter broke the surface and, after a couple of minutes, gathered their thoughts and checked to see if they were alive. They looked around, only to see a large oil slick to the west of them and lots of pieces of debris, but no ship. Two life rafts were about thirty yards away, with survivors on board. They looked like they were paddling around, picking up more survivors.

To the south, they could see a ship burning and listing severely. They could not tell which one it was, just that it was in bad shape.

Waving his hand and blowing his whistle, Batman finally got one raft's attention and was soon on board it.

"What the hell happened up here?" Batman asked as the sailor was helping Carpenter on board.

"The best I could tell, sir, was that we were attacked by a couple of Russian MiGs. Lieutenant Commander Sheppard is in the other raft. Maybe he can tell you more. But with all due respect, sir, I need to get the rest of these men on board," the young sailor replied and returned to his work, obviously in shock over this whole episode.

"Carpenter, stay here and help him. I'll go to the other raft and help there," Batman said as he re-entered the water and swam to the other raft, knowing now that the ship on the horizon was the *Montgomery*.

"Jake, what happened?" Batman asked as he removed his equipment and sat down beside Sheppard.

Jake was not in the best of shape. He had been bleeding severely from cuts and lacerations over about 50 percent of his body.

"Batman, *ole* buddy, how'd you get here? Oh, never mind. We gave 'em hell, but that last one just…cough…wouldn't give up," Jake replied painfully, holding a blood-soaked bandage to his side.

"Where's Doc?" Batman asked, scanning around at the destruction and looking for more survivors.

"Don't know. Haven't found him or the captain. Expect Captain Grey is still with the ship, took…cough…a hit behind the…cough…bridge. Got a Mayday off, but don't know when the cavalry will a…cough…arrive."

"Were the helos on board?" Batman asked, seeking assistance from anywhere.

"One. The other took on a MiG, well…cough, Henry…was good, but not good enough…cough…to take on a MiG. Henry got 'em, but…cough…another MiG got him…cough…ran a heat seeker…cough…right up that MiG's ass. Ha! Oh! That…cough…hurts. You okay, Batman?"

"Enough talkin', Jake. You rest for now as we gather the rest of the crew," Batman stated as he helped pull a man out of the sea.

"Hey…cough…Mon. It's just another day in paradise," Jake said just before he passed out from the pain, trying his best Caribbean accent.

"Yeah, that's right, just another day in paradise," Batman repeated quietly to himself. Two hours later, all the survivors they could find were huddled on board a group of five rafts that were now tied together.

Lieutenant Commander Sheppard had awakened several times during the two hours, only to pass out again. He was awake now, talking with Batman about what was happening.

"Jake, the crew down below is attempting to bring up the *Wolverine*. If they do, it will be a miracle, but once on the surface, we load up and get out of here as quick as she will take us." Batman stopped to scan the horizon before continuing. The *Montgomery* was still burning, and he could not tell if there were any survivors. "Carpenter and I dived on the *Washington*. Couldn't locate any more survivors but were able to retrieve three more rafts, so we aren't so crowded. We have a count of fifty-eight alive, in five rafts. The ship is about a hundred yards west, and the *Wolverine* is about two hundred yards east of us," Batman concluded.

"Where's the *Montgomery*?" Jake asked.

"She's about two miles to the south, burning. Not much we can do for her from here," Batman said.

He was starting to show signs of decompression sickness, caused by that rapid ascent and the additional dive to the *Washington*. But in an emergency such as this, he and Carpenter had put their personal safety in check to help save the crew of the *Washington*.

The pain started in his right shoulder and arm, and he began to wonder about Carpenter. Did he get hit also? They should not have gone down again, but they had to. After searching the *Washington*, they had returned to the *Wolverine* to close the hatch. With it open, the boat would not have been able to leave the bottom. The escape trunk was full of water, which could not be discharged with the hatch open.

Decompression sickness could be fatal if not treated, Jake Sheppard thought as he saw the pain on Batman's face. It can be very painful, as nitrogen bubbles form in your joints during rapid ascents. Divers are taught to ascend slowly to prevent the nitrogen bubbles from forming. "You okay, Batman?" Jake asked.

"You noticed," Batman said, then after a short pause, he continued. "A little bit of the *ole* bends, I guess."

"The nearest chamber is now on the bottom of the ocean." Jake grimaced with pain, then shifted his weight, trying to get comfortable.

Batman and Carpenter were going to hurt, and they couldn't do anything about it. "The only treatment is a trip to a decompression chamber, and right now there doesn't seem to be one in the immediate area," Batman stated as he gripped his arm tightly, trying to ease the pain.

Carpenter was starting to hurt also. Not as bad as Batman, but it started to limit his assistance. Chief Austin noticed it first and was able to get Carpenter down and relaxed before he fell down.

Batman described the damage he and Carpenter had found on the *Washington*, saying that most of the superstructure was gone and she had a large hole in her side with the remains of a MiG-23 scattered all over her deck and inside the hull. Oil was leaking from several holes in the hull.

Washington, DC
White House Press Conference
May 1, 1996
0950 Hours, EST
1450 Hours, GMT

"At 09:50, Greenwich Mean Time, approximately two hours ago, the United States destroyer USS *George Washington* and British destroyer HMS *Montgomery* were attacked off the coast of Nigeria. This act is an unprovoked act of war against the United States and will not be tolerated. Rescue operations have been initiated for the survivors. Full details are not known at this time. The carrier *Nimitz* and her escorts are en route and are instructed to take appropriate action for their own safety. As you know, the country of Nigeria is under a state of civil war, and we feel that the presence of the *Washington* and *Montgomery* may have been construed as a threat to their interests. Are there any questions?"

"Sir, NBC. What were the *Washington* and *Montgomery* doing so close to the Nigerian coast?" asked the correspondent from National Broadcasting Corporation.

"Very good question, one that is probably in all your thoughts. First off, the *Washington* is, was, a naval research vessel with minimal weapons. Enough, of course, to defend herself if required, but she had raced to the site in response to a distress signal from a sinking ship, only to arrive and find no survivors. And during the run to save lives, she had sustained damage to herself and was making repairs in the relatively calm waters. I must emphasize that both ships were in international waters at all times. They were attacked approximately thirty miles from the coast in international waters. Yes, you, sir," he said, pointing toward a gray-haired man in a black suit.

"Mr. President, Art Wilson, *Miami Herald*. What type of ship was the *Washington*?" asked Mr. Wilson.

As with all news conferences, some truth was actually spoken. "The *Washington* was a research vessel, and she carried a diving bell and support equipment that would make Jacques Cousteau proud. But she was not just a research vessel. She was originally a destroyer and still carried the weapons of a destroyer. This was for her protection, as she usually traveled by herself. She was also equipped with two helicopters, designed for rescue and long-range recon. Each helo was armed and lethal. And in her defense, she had used everything at her disposal to protect herself. But due to the nature and location of this mission, the HMS *Montgomery* was with her to provide added protection," the president concluded and pointed to another raised hand.

"Mr. President, John Dorrety, *Newsweek*. Was the *Washington* a spy ship and attempting to spy on the Nigerian government or the war that is going on within that country?"

"No, sir, the *Washington* was not a spy ship. As I said before, she was a research vessel for undersea activities, not communications or the like. She was there on a rescue mission and repairs when she was attacked. Thank you. We will keep you and the public advised as we know more. Good day."

"Mr. President! Mr. President!" came the response from several more reporters as the president left the podium and retired to his chambers. His sympathy and concern were clearly visible on his face.

Admiral Jacobs's Office
May 1, 1996
0915 Hours, EST

"Commander, who's supplying weapons to the Nigerians?" Admiral Jacobs asked, knowing full well the answer to that question.

"Sir, as far as the public knows, most of the weapons being used by Samula are Soviet-, Chinese-, and a few US-made M16s and various other small arms," Commander Fred Brenachic answered as he dug through his briefcase for a pencil. "Can we talk freely here?"

Receiving a nod of approval from Jacobs, he continued. "As you know, sales have been good this year, but the war may cause us problems, as you are well aware of."

Commander Brenachic was the head of the Naval Weapons Procurement Office in Washington, with final signature authority to purchase everything from a small handgun to an F-15 TomCat jet fighter. Ships were not his line; he had enough to handle with his small office and the list of items for which he was responsible.

"Fred, how long have you been with the organization?" Jacobs asked candidly.

"About twenty-six years, sir," Fred replied, unsure of what Jacobs was leading up to.

"Twenty-six years, huh? Have we treated you well, you know, pay, benefits, etc.?" Jacobs continued, seemingly in no real direction.

"Yes, sir. What are you driving at, sir?" he answered, still puzzled.

"Well, Fred, we have a problem, a very large problem. You see," Jacobs continued without letting Fred say a word, "the *Washington* was destroyed because she was very close to discovering one of our little secrets."

"But the Nigerians sank her, didn't they?" Fred interrupted.

"Yes and no. You see, we, or I, ordered her sinking. I made a deal with the Nigerian government to supply them with weapons, a small assortment, in exchange for the sinking of the *Washington*. That was hard for me to do, because Captain Grey was an old friend. But that's war." Jacobs stopped, reached for a Cuban cigar, and proceeded to lean back and light it, waiting to see the reaction on Fred's face.

"That's murder and treason! You have sold out to the enemy!" Fred exclaimed, standing up as if to leave.

"Keep your voice down, Fred, or we'll all go to jail. And sit down. Besides, it isn't exactly murder, and it isn't treason yet," Jacobs reassured him.

"Yet! Look, sir, when I joined your little group, I didn't agree to murder or to sell out my country. I just needed some extra cash, but this is going too far. You can count me out from now on. I won't be a part of murder!" Fred said matter-of-factly and remained standing, leaning over Jacobs's desk, palms firmly placed, and staring directly into Jacobs's eyes. He had hatred written all over his face, disgust and hatred. He had not bargained to be part of murder, but now it was too late.

"Sorry, Fred," Jacobs said as he sucked on the cigar. "Really, sorry to hear you say that, because the only way out is on a stretcher. You cannot afford to stop now. You're in too deep, and if we go down, so do you."

"No, sir, I want out. I will not be a part of murder and treason!" he yelled almost too loud. Jacobs tried to quiet him with hand gestures but failed.

"Look, okay, you supply me with the items on this list, and I will see to it that you are out of the program. Now, lower your voice or neither one of us will see the end of this. I guess it's about time to retire, anyway," he said, handing Fred a single page listing twenty items, nothing big, mostly light personnel weapons and missiles.

"Wait a minute, Jacobs. What about that secret the *Washington* was close to? Did that problem get solved with her sinking?" Fred asked, sweating, knowing that the organization was standing on very unsteady ground.

"I sure hope so, I sure hope so," Jacobs replied, letting his voice trail off as he smoked his cigar.

Chapter 18

BOMBS AWAY

Boeing 747
Forty-Three Thousand Feet over Ghana
May 1, 1996
1145 Hours, GMT

"A bidjan Approach Control, this is flight six-zero-three, at flight-level four-three, inbound for landing. Six-zero DME from airport. Please advise." The radio in the Abidjan control room crackled.

"Flight six-zero-three, squawk four-niner-six-two and ident," the approach control operator responded and checked his list for inbound aircraft. If the aircraft was not listed, he was to notify security and divert the aircraft away from the city. After a moment of looking, he located flight 603 on his list. It had departed Fayetteville, North Carolina, about twenty-three hours ago and was right on schedule.

"Six-zero-three, turn left to one-four-zero and start descent when ready. No reported traffic in your sector," the controller radioed back to flight 603.

Two F-15 Air Force fighters were closing at Mach 1.4 on the Boeing 747. This was a precaution that was being used to ensure the aircraft in question were truly what they said they were. A visual identification was the best means to ensure safety.

Maintaining strict radio silence between each F-15, the pilots flew toward the Boeing, approaching from the rear and above, so the pilot of the Boeing could not see them approach. They did not want to spook the passengers or flight crew if they were friendlies and, for sure, did not want to spook them if they were not, causing the non-friendly crew to do something stupid and dangerous.

As the two F-15s approached from each side, both pilots and electronic warfare operators on each aircraft scanned the Boeing for anything that would indicate that she wasn't what she was supposed to be. Seeing nothing out of the ordinary, both pilots gave the other a thumbs-up and pulled back on their control sticks to climb high above the inbound aircraft.

"Approach, Viking 1," the lead F-15 called on a discreet ultra-high frequency (UHF) that was also scrambled so nobody could understand what was being said.

"Viking 1, go," was the short response from Approach Control.

"She looks like the real McCoy to us. She's all yours," Viking 1 stated.

"Roger, Viking 1. Be on the lookout for some bad boys, due in anytime now. Approach, standing by."

"Roger, Viking 1, searching," the pilot of Viking 1 replied, leveled his aircraft at fifty-one thousand feet, and pulled the throttle lever back to a cruise setting to conserve on fuel. From this altitude, they could still watch the Boeing and see a greater distance for any other approaching aircraft.

The first three Boeing 727s had already landed in their assigned target airports, and the pilots and crew of each were heading out of the city as fast as they could. Timers had been set on each to detonate at 1400 hours, giving the crews two hours to get as far away as possible.

The Boeing 747 was supposed to drop his bomb over the city, causing an air burst, which would create more destruction and fall-out. His bomb was scheduled for release at thirty-five thousand feet at 1200 hours.

"Flight six-zero-three, turn right to one-eight-zero, descend to flight level two-zero," Approach Control said into his microphone, asking flight six-zero-three to descend to twenty thousand feet.

"Roger, six-zero-three, starting descent now," the pilot responded. He reached over and pulled the four engine throttle levers back to slow his aircraft. Then to his crew, he said, "Prepare for bombing run. We have only one chance as we pass over the city. Arm the weapon."

There were few clouds in the sky today, so visibility was not a problem. The pilot of the Boeing could easily see the city from his cockpit. Checking his time, he discovered they were right on schedule. As the aircraft slowly descended through forty thousand feet, he thought of his wife and children. They were never to see him again, but to die for a cause was good in the eyes of his countrymen. They were about to make history and die doing so.

"Thirty-eight thousand," the copilot said as he watched the altimeter closely.

"We don't want any mistakes. Open the doors at thirty-six thousand," the pilot said as he adjusted his descent.

"Flight six-zero-three, you need to increase your descent rate or you will never make it to the runway," Approach Control called to the incoming flight.

"Roger. We have a few sick passengers descending, slowing for them," the pilot lied.

Sensing something not quite right with that remark—this flight was supposed to be cargo only, no passengers—the controller switched to his discreet UHF radio and called the F-15 flight leader, Viking 1.

"Viking 1, Approach Control," he called.

"Go, Approach," Viking responded almost immediately.

"Would you go back and check that Boeing 747, flight six-zero-three, again? He is descending very slowly and says he has sick passengers. He is a cargo flight, no passengers listed," Approach Control requested, indicating a lot of concern in his voice.

"Roger, we will call you!" Viking 1 responded, and with a hand gesture to his wingman, they descended to the Boeing once again.

"Flight six-zero-three, turn right to one-niner-five for straight-in approach to runway one-niner. Descend to one-zero-thousand," Approach called to Flight six-zero-three.

"Six-zero-three, roger," the pilot responded, and then to his crew, he said, "Open doors, thirty-six thousand, on course. Bombardier, it's your aircraft." Then he released the controls.

"Doors opened. Weapon armed. Twenty seconds to release," the bombardier said into his intercom.

"Look!" yelled the copilot, pointing out the cockpit window at the F-15 Eagle screaming toward them.

"It's too late. In ten seconds, the bomb will be dropped. Nine... eight...," the pilot responded.

"Missiles, drop the bomb, NOW!" he yelled into the intercom, the last words he would speak on this earth. Feeling the sudden lurch of the aircraft as the weight of the bomb separated from the Boeing and started its fall toward earth, he and his crew knew they had succeeded and did not die for nothing.

A half-second later, the Boeing 747 disintegrated from the impact of two Sidewinder missiles fired from the F-15 Eagle, but too late to stop the release of the bomb.

The remains of the Boeing raced the bomb to the city, the bomb on a controlled descent toward the center of the city and the aircraft spiraling down uncontrolled.

USS Wolverine
Eighty Feet below the Surface
May 1, 1996
1300 Hours, GMT

"Damn, there must be a leak. We don't have enough stored air pressure to blow the ballast," Micky said, perspiration running down her face and into her eyes. She was continually wiping the sweat from her face so she could see what she was doing.

The temperature in the boat had been rising since the diving bell was cut loose. That had been their source for fresh, cool air, and now that it was gone, they had to rely on the internal system. JD had not turned it on to conserve on power, since the batteries were weak and could not handle the extra strain. They needed the batteries to run the pumps to raise the boat. The air was starting to turn bad, carbon monoxide was building, and their time was running out.

"Engine room, is there enough juice in the batteries to run the electric long enough to build up air pressure?" JD asked into the intercom.

"Sir, we'll have to shut down everything else to do so. Including what life support we have on now," was the reply, one that he didn't want to hear. Scotty had been turning life support on and off to help maintain breathable air, but that was a strain on the system too.

"Best estimate on air for life support?" JD asked, hoping for a solid answer. He got his wish, but would it be enough?

"Three hours, sir, unless, of course, we make it to the surface."

"Odds, Scotty," he said, probing for their chances.

"Slim and none, sir. But we have no other choice, do we? The longer we wait, the weaker the batteries get," Scotty said casually.

"Start the electric, Scotty. Let me know when you're ready," JD ordered.

"Aye, sir," Scotty responded.

"You heard it too. Let's get ready," JD said to the control room personnel and then switched the intercom on again. "Attention on deck. We have to get this tub to the surface, and the only way is to start the electric. But to do so, everything else has to be shut down. Prepare your stations for blackout and surfacing. As you may know, if this doesn't work, well, we may have just sealed our fate. We won't be able to use the emergency escape chamber if this doesn't work, because all the high-pressure air will be used to blow ballast. If you are a religious person, now would be a good time to ask for assistance. Prepare your stations. Blackout in five minutes. Surface soon afterward," JD said and switched off the intercom.

Scotty and his crew in the engine room were working as fast as they could to increase their odds, but as each second went by, so did more energy in the batteries. Soon the power to the boat would be turned off, leaving the boat in near darkness except for the emergency lighting, which was very weak because of age. The low light on board and tension mix gave the members of the crew a feeling of near death. Sweat poured off everyone on board. Most had stripped down to the bare minimum in clothing, shorts and T-shirts for the ladies and shorts only for the guys, but even these were now soaked. The only reassurance was the hum of the electric motors running, building up the high-pressure air tanks, which would allow them to reach the surface and life.

"Stay here. I'll be right back," JD said to his control room as he picked up a flashlight and headed toward the engine room.

"Scotty, how much time before we can try?" JD asked when he entered the engine room, scanning around at the electric motors and the gauges.

"I hope, in about thirty-five minutes. We need to leave some power in the batteries to run the pumps, and I don't think we can push them much longer than that. We still won't have enough pressure, but if we run longer, we won't have any power left."

"That's reassuring! Okay, send a runner up to let me know when you're ready."

"No need, sir. When the electric stops, blow the tanks. If we wait, it'll leak out again. Just blow 'em fast," Scotty said bluntly.

"Okay, thirty-four minutes, or less, we go," JD said as he turned to leave. "Thanks, Scotty."

"Just doing my job, sir," Scotty said and returned to work in the near darkness.

"What do you think we'll find up there?" Micky asked when JD returned.

"A lot of friendlies and no bad guys, I hope. Micky, you on the planes, full up angle. Kelly, steering, straight, and true. Anderson, ballast. When you don't hear the motors running, blow them. Don't wait for an order, just blow 'em. Understand?" JD ordered, not telling them about the high-pressure leak that might just prevent them from surfacing. "They should run for about thirty more minutes, but stay alert in case they stop earlier."

All was quiet on deck. Only the whine of the electric motor could be heard throughout the boat. Time seemed to stand still as they waited and waited. Ten minutes passed, then fifteen. Nobody said a word, trying to conserve energy and air. All they could hear were the electric motors turning in the distance.

Suddenly, a crewman stormed into the control room.

"BLOW THE TANKS, BLOW THE TANKS! Scotty says blow 'em *now*! We have blown another high-pressure pipe and are losing pressure fast!" the seaman yelled as he ran and stumbled through the dark narrow passageway, striking his head on the bulkhead. He continued on, with blood dripping down his face and hand as he held a dirty handkerchief over the wound.

Immediately, Anderson started turning valves and pulling levers to blow ballast. The hiss of high-pressure air could be heard throughout the boat as air rushed into the ballast tanks, forcing the water contained within to be blown out, which would lighten the boat enough to surface. With luck, the displacement would release them from the bottom and they would rise to the surface.

The electrics were still running in hopes to keep the pressure from dropping any further. Slowly the boat became lighter and started to creak and groan. The bow started to lift but settled again on the bottom. No one said a word, just silently prayed she would make the trip.

More groans and creaks sounded. Breaking the suction of the bottom would be the most difficult part. Once off the bottom, the sub would have little difficulty reaching the surface.

The lights flickered once, then died. The whine of the electric motor was growing weaker and weaker, as if the strain was too much, but it was really the batteries dying. Scotty was frantically working to sustain the power long enough to break the suction from the bottom. With the motors at full power, he engaged the propeller in hope of pushing the sub off the bottom.

A small explosion ripped through the rear of the boat, and then total silence that was almost too much to bear settled in. The explosion was caused when two batteries overheated and the resulting gas ignited. Luckily, no one was near them when they exploded. The boat was totally dead, but moving very slowly.

In total darkness, the only light visible was from the glow off the fluorescent dials of the numerous gauges on the boat.

"JD, we are moving very slow," Micky finally said as she watched the fading glow of the dials in front of her.

"Yeah, I see that. Maybe we will make it yet. Keep your fingers crossed. Maybe we will just make it," JD said hopefully.

Slowly the stricken submarine lifted off the bottom and started toward the surface, gaining momentum as she rose. The journey for the 307-foot boat, from eighty feet below the surface, took a slow and painful hour and forty minutes. The boat was heavy, and not all the ballast was blown out of the tanks. The slowly expanding air in the tanks was overtaking the water and forcing it out of the tanks, but it was slow. The electric motors had quit; the tanks were leaking, but not any worse than when she was new. The boat wanted to survive, and the crew wanted to see the surface. There was no way to lighten the boat any more. To put things in the torpedo tubes and push them out required compressed air, of which they had none to spare. All they could do was wait and hope she would continue her slow trip to the surface.

Abidjan, Ivory Coast
Headquarters, Eighty-Second Airborne Division
May 1, 1996
1230 Hours, GMT

"Sir, two F-15 Eagles just shot down a Boeing 747 inbound from Fayetteville. It seems that she was carrying a bomb and dropped it over the city. The Eagles were a second late in stopping the drop but destroyed the aircraft. The wreckage landed north of the city in a small village. I'm afraid there was a loss of life. How many, we are not sure about as yet," Sergeant Rosco reported to General Sellers.

"What about the bomb, Rosco?" General Sellers asked.

"Oh, yes, sir. The bomb landed and did not detonate. The bomb disposal team is at the site right now, trying to determine why it didn't blow and what type of bomb it was," Rosco replied. Then he continued, "It landed six blocks from the city center, sir, in the middle of the street. The area has been sealed off, and with luck, they can disarm it."

"If not, then we are dead. Is that what you're saying?" General Sellers asked.

"I guess so, sir," Rosco answered.

"If they got one in, maybe they got more. Have all the airports check each and every aircraft on the ground and restrict any more incoming flights until we can establish a better way to bring in civilian aircraft. In other words, no more civilian aircraft allowed in the airspace, period," General Sellers ordered. "Keep me posted on the casualties and that damn bomb."

"Yes, sir," Rosco said and then turned to leave.

"Rosco, who's the senior intel officer on duty now?" General Sellers said as Rosco opened the door.

"Captain Houston, sir."

"Have him report to me ASAP," General Sellers ordered.

"Yes, sir."

Twenty minutes later, the senior intel officer approached General Sellers, who was busy reading more intelligence reports.

"Sir, Captain Houston, reporting as ordered," the young intelligence officer said as he caught the general's eye.

"Sit down, Captain. We have something to discuss that could change the tides of world opinion of our country," General Sellers said, pointing to a chair on the other side of his table.

Twenty-five minutes later, the discussion was over and Captain Houston stood, saluted, and started for the door. Operation Greetings was going into motion. Captain Houston would oversee its completion.

Site of USS George Washington Sinking
May 1, 1996
1420 Hours GMT

"Skipper, look over there!" yelled a young seaman.

"Looks like they are trying to surface her," Batman said painfully. His decompression sickness was getting worse. Carpenter was unconscious in the other raft. "Keep an eye on that spot, son. You are about to see something spectacular!"

After a long wait and worry, the bow of the *Wolverine* broke the surface in a not-so-spectacular appearance. You could see she struggled to make it to the surface. But soon, the entire boat was sitting quietly on the surface. Minutes later, the hatches started to open and men and women climbed on deck. The fresh air was great, but the site of five orange rafts was not so great; there were no ships in sight. Looking around, they also saw the *Montgomery* on the horizon, still burning.

"Skipper, aircraft inbound!" another seaman yelled from an adjoining raft, pointing toward the horizon northwest of their position.

"Skipper, more aircraft inbound, from the east!" another seaman yelled.

"Holy mother of pearl! What now?" Lieutenant Commander Sheppard exclaimed to Batman.

"Hard to tell who are the good guys from the bad at this distance," Batman stated. "Good, JD has run up the colors to let the good guys know they are on our side," he said, seeing the American flag going up on the stern of the *Wolverine*.

Soon, four F-14 Tomcats from the carrier *Nimitz* were circling the *Wolverine* and the five orange rafts.

"If they are ours, who the hell are they?" a young seaman asked, pointing to the incoming aircraft from the east.

"My guess is we are in for a little show of power, son. Just lean back and watch. This could be real interesting." Sheppard replied, smiling but still in great pain.

"Six-Shooter to Home Plate, you aren't gonna believe what I see," Lieutenant Commander John Markus reported back to the *Nimitz* from the lead F-14.

"Go ahead, Six-Shooter, enlighten us," was the reply from the *Nimitz*.

"Home Plate, we have five orange rafts with about sixty survivors on board and a World War II Gato-class sub alongside starting to take on the survivors. She's gorgeous. I haven't seen one of those in years. And just off to the south is a burning ship, possibly what is left of one of the destroyers. We are checking it out for survivors. Will advise."

"You have a what picking up the survivors? We have helos in the air," *Nimitz* replied.

"A Gato-class submarine and, wait…got to go, Home Plate. We have bad guys at three o'clock low, moving in fast."

"Roger, Six-Shooter, end of transmission from the *Nimitz*."

The four F-14s turned toward the incoming aircraft with intent to engage if required. But when the incoming aircraft saw they had a welcoming committee, they turned and headed northeast as fast as they could.

Abidjan
Headquarters, Eighty-Second Airborne Division
May 1, 1996
1400 Hours, GMT

"Gentleman, war has been declared by Nigeria. We have been sent to stop it, here and now, at whatever cost." General Sellers started to address the room full of commanders. Sellers had been appointed the supreme commander of the multinational forces in the combat zone. Now he had to end the war the politicians had failed to end.

"Less than an hour ago, the Nigerian government made a futile attempt to bomb our installation here with at least three atomic bombs, all of which failed. One was actually dropped from a modified Boeing 747. Two more were located in parked aircraft at two separate airports around the city." This comment started a low rumble of conversation around the room.

"AT EASE! Gentlemen, time is of the essence. We must act now and swiftly! As I was saying, we were very lucky and were able to destroy the aircraft that carried the first bomb and locate two more. But there may be more." General Sellers stopped and looked around the room carefully, as if looking for someone in particular. Upon finding the person he required and receiving the nod he expected, he continued.

"Now, down to business. All naval forces will fall under the command of Admiral Hemsley of the Royal Navy. Admiral Hemsley, your orders are in the envelope in front of you. Please read them carefully and do exactly as directed." After a short pause and a deep breath, General Sellers continued. "At 0200 hours tonight, the first of many flights will take off for Nigeria. We will repeat here what was done in Iraq four years ago and Libya in '94, but with one major exception. General Samula will be rendered helpless. His military equipment will be destroyed totally. No piece of hardware is to be left intact. The exact numbers of aircraft are known by the Air Force commanders and need not be discussed here."

A knock on the door interrupted the general. "Answer that door, Captain," he said, pointing to the last officer nearest the door.

Upon the door's opening, Sergeant Rosco stepped in. "Sir, sorry to interrupt, but I just received this report. Which I think you need to see now," Rosco said with what looked like a tear forming in his eye. He walked over to General Sellers, handed him the message, and then stood back.

The general read it, sat down in the chair beside the map, shook his head, and mumbled a few quiet words to himself. The room grew so quiet you could hear some of the heavy breathing caused by the tension that was building.

"Gentlemen," General Sellers said as he stood and walked to the edge of the stage, "gentlemen, two atomic bombs were detonated at 1400 hours today, one in Yaounde, the capital of Cameroon, and the other in Niamey, the capital of Niger. The destruction and death toll is not fully known as yet, but the initial estimates are that over one hundred thousand died in each city. The man is mad and must be stopped. You have your orders, and unless told directly by this office, do not, I repeat, *do not* act on your own." General Sellers then started out of the conference room. All the members in the room immediately stood to attention as he departed.

USS Wolverine
May 1, 1996
1435 Hours, GMT

"Scotty, can you start those diesels?" JD asked after getting his chance at some fresh air and viewing the sight that lay before him.

"Just give the word, sir," was Scotty's reply.

"You've been watching too much Star Trek, Scotty. Consider it given," JD replied with a small chuckle.

With that, Scotty and his men returned below to start the diesel engines, with hopes of departing the area soon afterward. The batteries were very weak, but Scotty had a few tricks left. He didn't plan on spending much time sitting here, waiting for the bad guys to come back.

With a lot of black smoke and coughing and some tender loving care from Scotty, the engines finally came to life and were roaring like the pride of the jungle. Once the engines were running, they were able to start picking up the survivors from the rafts.

With the fuel system cleaned and the glow plugs replaced, Scotty prayed that they would start on command. His prayers were answered. Now, if they had enough fuel to reach the *Nimitz*, they might just survive.

"Home Plate, Six-Shooter. We have four bad guys running northeast—no, wait…" After a long pause from the flight leader of the F-14s, he said, "The bad guys are turning back, heading directly for us. The four are now six—no, ten. We have ten bad guys inbound. All flight…lock and load. It's party time! Home Plate, send backup now. We're gonna need some help here, fast. Out."

"Boomer, Wolfman, break right. Spiderman, follow me. Let's go get 'em, boys!" Six-Shooter directed his flight.

"Home Plate, we are engaging. Mike will be hot. Stand by." Six-Shooter indicated that the communications between aircraft and the ship would remain on so the ship could hear what was going on.

"Roger, Six-Shooter. Backup is airborne. Be careful," the flight commander of the *Nimitz* acknowledged. "Backup will be on-site in ten minutes."

"Roger, Home Plate. WATCH YOUR TAIL, BOOMER!" Six-Shooter yelled. "Take that, sucker!" He fired a Sidewinder heat-seeking missile up the exhaust of the MiG-23 Flogger, destroying the MiG instantly.

"Good shot, Six-Shooter. Watch this one," Spiderman said confidently, letting off a burst of .50-caliber rounds into the wing of the MiG-29 in front of him. The MiG-29 didn't explode but dived toward the ocean. Spiderman chased, with Six-Shooter covering his tail. At one thousand feet over the ocean, the MiG-29 started to pull up, and Spiderman fired a Sidewinder just ahead of the MiG-29. The pilot of the MiG turned to see the Sidewinder cutting a path directly to his canopy. He saw death coming and could not avoid it. The missile tore into the cockpit and detonated, ripping the MiG apart.

The rest of the air war was short-lived. Minutes later, the backup F-14s arrived. Four of the MiGs were destroyed, two damaged and heading back to the coast with the escort of the remaining four. Losses to the F-14s were two down, one crew dead when their plane exploded after being hit by a missile. The other crew were able to parachute to safety.

"Home Plate, Six-Shooter, inbound for landing, damage to three aircraft. Backup flight will remain on-site. Backup flight lost one aircraft. Lead lost one. Boomer and EW ejected when aircraft severely damaged. Only three chutes deployed. Repeat, only three chutes deployed. Three in water, waiting pickup. Have medics standing by. Several returning with injuries. Out," Six-Shooter reported as he struggled to keep his Tomcat flying. His Tomcat had received several severe hits to the vertical stabilizers, and he was losing fuel from his fuselage tank.

"Six-Shooter, get them on the deck as quick as possible. You know the procedure. Keep this channel open," Home Plate ordered.

Six-Shooter and his flight knew the procedure: the most damaged aircraft would land last. The thinking behind that is that if they crashed on deck, then no aircraft could land until the damaged aircraft was moved from the flight deck. This could cause the rest of the aircraft to be lost.

Spiderman was the most damaged and severely injured but could maintain flight for a while. Six-Shooter was first to land and did so exactly by the book, even with the damage to his fuel system and stabilizers. His engines flamed out just before touchdown.

Digger landed next without any problems. His aircraft was moved immediately off the deck to leave plenty of room for Spiderman to bring in his crippled aircraft.

His approach was a little low, but he recovered in time, dipping his wings from left to right, listening to the controller give him instructions about his approach.

"Spiderman, bring your nose up a little, maintain power, gear down, and locked. Gear down and locked. Spiderman, acknowledge. Gear down and locked...," the controller asked repeatedly.

"Roger, lever down and shows locked," Spiderman responded.

"Gear not down, recycle, recycle your gear, Spiderman."

"Roger, recycle gear," Spiderman acknowledged but with a lot of pain in his voice.

The deck crew watched patiently for the F-14 to drop its gear, but so far, no gear.

"Spiderman, no gear. Can you make another pass?"

"Negative. Fuel low, and I'm not doing so well myself, and my back seat is unconscious. Need to get down now or ditch this rock."

"Roger, Spiderman, we're foaming the deck now, straight in, two miles to touchdown. Easy now, you'll make it. Nose up a little. The foam and nets are ready. The deck is clear. Ease off on the power...dump your remaining fuel and dead-stick the last half-mile. Easy does it. Looking real good, Spiderman, looking good."

Spiderman did the best he could. His aircraft approached the deck at minimal speed, struck the deck hard, and slid into the pair of nets, where he stopped ten feet from the base of the control tower. Emergency crews climbed all over the downed F-14, removing Spiderman from the cockpit as quickly as possible. His injuries would put him out of commission for a while, but not permanently. His electronic warfare operator was removed and rushed to sickbay immediately. He had lost a lot of blood and was barely breathing. He would survive but would never fly again. His lung was punctured and left leg broken in four places.

USS Wolverine Control Room
May 1, 1996
1800 Hours, GMT

"Full steam ahead, two-eight-zero degrees. Try to contact the *Nimitz* or at least one of those F-14s. Let's see if there are any survivors over on the *Montgomery*," JD ordered.

They had to run on the surface to recharge their batteries, but with the F-14s flying cover, JD felt fairly safe for now.

"Skipper, the F-14 flight commander said the *Nimitz* is two-one-zero miles from here and they will fly cover as long as possible, then another flight will come out to escort. He also said that the commander of the *Nimitz* needed a head count of all on board and number of injured and if we needed medical assistance. I passed on the information. There are three helos headed for us and the *Montgomery*."

"Great. Maybe we can get a real doctor here. Did you tell him we had two with the bends?" JD asked the radio operator.

"*Wolverine*, this is Knight Rider, over," the radio blared.

"Roger, Knight Rider. Go ahead."

The conversation between the F-14 pilot and the *Wolverine* was short but important. Another helo was dispatched with a doctor and supplies and would arrive in about an hour. The worst cases would be evacuated to the *Nimitz* on the helos. There were only four survivors from the *Montgomery*, severely burned but alive.

JD reactivated the ship's log with entries pertaining to the rescue, recovery of the sub itself, and her condition. Estimated time to the *Nimitz* would be about twenty hours. With any luck at all, they could even make it to Norfolk. They were given fuel, which had been ferried out from the *Nimitz*. The bad fuel was pumped into the empty fuel drums and transported back to the *Nimitz* for disposal.

Scotty was keeping the diesel running and had repaired the high-pressure leak during the run to the *Nimitz*. Batman and Carpenter were transferred to the *Nimitz* for treatment along with twenty-three injured men and the fourteen bodies found on the

Wolverine when they came on board. The doctor returned with the injured on the last run to the *Nimitz*.

With full fuel and the injured safely on the *Nimitz*, JD and his crew only had to worry about keeping the *Wolverine* afloat and to open the ship's safe.

Chapter 19

OPERATION GREETINGS

Mercy Hospital, Washington, DC
May 1, 1996
0945 Hours, EST

Morning came as expected, but much too early. Davin still felt a little weak after his ordeal in the flooded vault, and his lungs felt very dry and rung out. He didn't know how much water they had pumped out of him; what he did know was that he never ever wanted to go through that again.

The nurse came in with Dr. Burns. He looked like Major Frank Burns in the TV show *M*A*S*H*. Davin couldn't help but think that he was going to die in the hands of an incompetent boob they called Ferret Face, but he was pleasantly surprised to discover differently.

"Mr. Pierce, you are one lucky man. Another pint of water and we would be looking at you down in the basement instead of this comfortable room with a view." Without much of a pause, he looked at Davin's record and continued, "Your lungs will hurt for a few days. That's from the pump drying out the tissue. And I don't want you to overdo it for a few days. No running or heavy breathing like I hear you have been doing to my nurses. Just take it a little slow for a couple of days and you'll be fine," Dr. Burns said. Then he turned to the nurse and quietly gave some additional instructions.

Dr. Burns turned back to Davin. "I'm sorry about your friend. We did all we could, but due to his advanced years and a weak heart… again, I'm terribly sorry." Dr. Burns turned to leave.

"Thanks, Doc. I'm sure you did. Has his son and daughter been notified? One other thing I have to ask," Davin persisted.

"No, my first name isn't Frank, it's Larry. Frank is my older brother. And yes, he is a doctor too. And yes, we are trying to locate Mr. Malone's family," he said as he left.

An hour later, Connie and Davin were chatting quietly. After a few minutes of small talk, she broke down and cried. Jack had been her mentor and friend for years. Both she and Davin were going to miss him. His son and daughter had been notified and would claim the body later that day.

At eleven that morning, Agent John Norton of the Washington, DC, Police Department sent a car over to pick up Connie and Davin and drive them over to the British Embassy, where he was waiting. The officer driving had said something about a little discovery that he wanted to share.

"Great, you're here and breathing," Agent Norton said as they were escorted into the library of the embassy. Around the room were several other officers and some people they had not met. "Come on in and sit down. How are you feeling? Really sorry about Jack. He was a good cop."

"We're fine, thanks. What have you found?" Davin asked as Connie and he took a couple of seats across from him.

"First, this is Reginald Pirkens. He's the embassy's security manager, and he helped us open the vault that almost killed you two," Norton said as he crossed the room to the large desk previously used by Ambassador Rodgers.

"Mr. Pirkens, what kind of trap have you developed down there?" Connie asked, staring at Pirkens coldly.

"I'm terribly sorry about that, ma'am. The device was designed as a buffer in case of a nuclear strike on the city. It seems that it malfunctioned when you were attempting to open the door, or someone may have rewired it to activate if tampered with. It is only supposed to fill when a special code is entered into the computer, which is located inside the vault. And not by the entry control panel. I'm truly sorry and am very relieved that you were not killed. Did I hear that your Mr. Malone wasn't so lucky? Is that true?"

"Yes, and charges may be filed for his death on completion of the investigation," Connie said.

"The embassy will make it up to you. To start with, all your hospital costs have been taken care of, and we will be arranging an extended, all-expense paid vacation for the two of you to help in your recovery. Don't get me wrong, miss, we are not trying to buy you off but only want to help in your recovery. As for Mr. Malone, all his expenses, funeral, etc., will be covered by the embassy. Did he have any relatives?" Pirkens continued.

"Yes, a son and daughter, David and Susan," Davin replied. "They have been notified and are at the hospital now."

"When will you see them, sir?" Pirkens asked.

"Probably later today. Why?" Davin answered.

"Please ask them to stop by at their earliest convenience, sir."

"Thank you, Mr. Pirkens. That's very kind of you." Then he turned back to Agent Norton. "John, what have you uncovered that required our presence?" Davin asked point-blank.

"Do you think you could go back down to the cellar?" Norton asked, looking at them seriously. As they nodded, indicating that they were ready, he said, "Good. Would you come with me?"

Norton led the way, with Davin, Connie, Pirkens, and two uniformed officers bringing up the rear.

Returning to the scene of the crime had always been a means of catching the criminal, but in this case, returning to the scene of where they almost died was unnerving. However, they managed. The cellar was relatively dry now. *Damn, it's cold enough to chill a beer down here,* Davin thought.

Reginald walked over to the control panel and pushed a few buttons. The door, or rather the wall, started to move to the right. It continued to move for about eight feet, and then stopped. They walked over to the opening and saw that the area was dry and had some more blood on the floor. It was a small room, about fifteen by ten feet, with a door on the back wall. The blood led to the door and stopped. There was nothing special about this room; it had a small desk like a receptionist would use and a couple of pictures on the wall, mostly of castles in England.

They walked to the door, and Reginald opened it slightly, and then stopped.

"Agent Norton, I think you better explain to them what is going on before we proceed," Reginald said as he leaned against the doorframe.

"Explain what, Norton?" Connie questioned.

"Reginald, I think they will have the answers once they see what's behind that door. Go ahead and open it," Norton said as he stepped aside so Connie and Davin could go through the door.

"Holy shit!" Connie and Davin said in a whisper. They both looked at Norton and Reginald and back to each other and then to the room in front of them.

"I knew nothing of this until this morning, Mr. Pierce. The ambassador was the only one who could get in here. I just know the system well enough to change the combination to make access available now," Reginald confessed sadly.

"Norton, what do you suppose the ambassador was doing?" Davin asked to see how much he knew.

"We were hoping you could tell us," Norton replied as he looked around the room, which was full of old crates, ones marked US ARMY, MUNITIONS AND WEAPONS. Opening a nearby crate exposed M1 Garand rifles, still in their protective wrappers, never fired, in mint condition. A rifle of this kind would bring a nice price from a collector or in the black market."

"What about the blood, John?" Connie asked, trying to be less formal and get back to a friendlier situation. In light of what had happened, it seemed the right thing to do.

"We found two bodies in here. One was the real ambassador, and the other his personal secretary, both very dead. Shame, too, she didn't look to be more than twenty years old. He must have killed her to keep his secret. And to make it look like a robbery, killed the butler upstairs to help throw us off."

"I don't think so, John. We had talked to him, and he wouldn't kill any more to cover this up. Someone else would, though. I don't know who yet, but I have an idea," Davin said as he and Connie slowly walked around the crates, not looking for anything in particular but everything in general.

"So you do know where this stuff came from?" John Norton asked.

"Yeah, we know where, but not how yet. For now, don't close this case, I can't prove it wasn't murder/suicide yet, but I will," Davin said. "Let's get outa here, Connie. This place gives me the creeps."

"Me too," Connie agreed as they started for the door.

"I'll have one of my men drive you to your hotel," Norton offered.

"Thanks, but I think our car is still in the parking lot. Unless you had it towed," Connie said as we headed up the stairs.

"Keep in touch, will ya? I'd like to solve this before Christmas, okay?" Norton insisted as they went out of sight.

"Sure, John, anything you say," Davin said as they reached the top of the stairs.

Neither one spoke during the short drive back to the hotel, and soon they were walking across the parking lot toward the lobby.

The hotel manager met them as they came through the front door. He had a concerned look on his face, one that Davin didn't care for.

"Mr. Pierce, Ms. Young, I'm so glad you are all right. I was just floored when I heard about the accident on the radio."

"Thank you. We are fine now. Is there anything else? We would like to get upstairs and just rest for a while," Davin insisted as they started to walk across the lobby toward the waiting elevator.

"Mr. Pierce, wait…there have been several callers, most saying it was urgent that you call. Here are the numbers," he said, handing Davin a sheet of paper with the numbers printed on it. "If there is anything you need, call me personally. I'll see to it that it is delivered immediately."

"Thank you," Davin said as they entered the elevator. "There is one thing. Have room service bring up some breakfast. I'm starving."

"I'll see to it myself, sir," he said as the elevator door closed in front of him.

Pushing the button to their floor, Davin and Connie stood in silence as the elevator rose from the lobby.

Admiral Jacobs Office
May 1, 1996
0955 Hours, EST

Admiral Jacobs was reading a message, which he'd recently received from the *Nimitz* battle group. The *Nimitz* was on station, prepared to defend or attack Nigeria as ordered, with a second mission of supplying air cover to the USS *Washington* and HMS *Montgomery*. The *Washington* had been sunk before their arrival, and the *Montgomery* was burning out of control. Upon reaching the site, they discovered a World War II submarine picking up the survivors of the *Washington* and *Montgomery*.

The message described briefly the air attack, the sinking of the two ships, the number of casualties and lost aircraft. The number of downed enemy aircraft was also listed. The line about a World War II submarine picking up survivors hit him like a knife in the heart. He felt that his life was going to end soon, unless that boat never made it to land.

"Damn!" was all the admiral could say. He immediately picked up the secure telephone and started to dial a special number. He did not finish dialing when his secretary interrupted on the intercom.

"Sir, there are two FBI agents here to see you," she said into the intercom.

"Names, Susan?" he asked nervously.

"Agents Lassiter and Crenshaw, sir," she said.

"Tell them to wait. I'll be right with them," Admiral Jacobs said as he continued to dial the secure telephone. After six rings without an answer, he hung up.

"Susan, send in the agents," he said into the intercom.

"Lock the door!" Jacobs demanded as the two agents walked into the office. "Did you get that case?"

"Yes, sir, we have it!" Crenshaw answered as he and Lassiter sat down across from Jacobs.

"After Jack called, we went right over and tore the place apart. Rodgers is dead. His butler and secretary got in the way, and we had to eliminate them too. But somehow, they got away before we were sure they were dead. The local police helped us there. They and an agent named Norton from the FBI discovered a secret vault of some kind in the cellar with two bodies, the ambassador and his secretary. Oh, you know Jack Malone is dead too. Seems there was an accident at the embassy and he and two friends were caught in it. Well, Jack died in the hospital last night."

"Jack wanted out. I guess he got his wish. Too bad. He was an asset," Admiral Jacobs stated. "Where's the case now?"

"Safely tucked away, where no one will ever find it," Lassiter said with confidence.

"Good. Now that we have the case, all we have to worry about is the *Wolverine*," Admiral Jacobs stated, closely watching the expression on their faces.

"The *Wolverine*, what is that?" Crenshaw asked, looking briefly at Lassiter.

"The *Wolverine* is a Gato-class submarine that has been in our organization for more than forty years, and three and a half months ago, she disappeared with some incriminating documents on board, along with my older brother," Admiral Jacobs started.

"So what has that got to do with us?" Lassiter questioned.

"To make it short, she could sink the organization if she were to get into the wrong hands, which right now she is," Jacobs continued.

"What do we do?" Crenshaw asked.

"To start, just keep your eyes and ears open. I'll take care of the sub. Now get out of here," Jacobs ordered. "I've got work to do."

Palm Beach, Florida
St. Mary's Hospital
May 1, 1996
1000 Hours, EST

"Josh, how you doing?" David Malone asked as he entered the hospital room.

"I'll live. What are you doing down here?" Josh answered, surprised to see David.

"I just got in from Tampa, running down that Peterson case you had asked me about. And thought I'd just stop in and see how you were doing," David said as he took a seat across from Josh.

"Really sorry about your dad, Dave. We go back many years. He was a good cop and good friend," Josh said sadly.

"The funeral is day after tomorrow. If they bust you out of here in time, I know Dad would like you to be there but would understand if you were not," David commented. They conversed for a short while about Jack Malone and his career with the FBI and how he and Josh first met.

Twenty minutes later, David got around to discussing what he had found out about young Donald Peterson. David had talked to young Peterson briefly at the hospital and was told a strange story that David had a hard time believing.

"Donald said that he was approached several days ago by two men whom he had described to the police," David said. "They told him that if he did not cooperate, he would be killed. Of course, when receiving a deal such as this, he could not refuse. Donald was only the pawn. What they really wanted was for him to get his father to sabotage the operation he was working on. Donald said his father was assigned to the destroyer USS *George Washington* somewhere in the Atlantic. The beating was just some insurance, they told him. He was on his way to the hospital when he passed out. He lost control of his car and crashed into Tampa Bay. The two men did not put him in the car and attempt to drown him, but they did beat him. As soon as he was able to respond, he was to contact his father and tell him to sabotage the mission. But because of the accident, he has not been able to accomplish what they wanted him to do," David finished.

Neither Josh, David, nor Donald knew of the sinking of the *George Washington*. They would not learn of this till later in the day.

Washington, DC
Twin Bridges Hotel
May 1, 1996
1030 Hours, EST

The elevator stopped before Davin was able to finish reading the list of calls they had. Some were for Connie, asking about her condition, some were from Davin's office, and some unknown. After breakfast and a hot shower, they would start returning calls that seemed to be of any major importance. A person had to set priorities and maintain them as best as he or she could.

Most of the names and numbers were easily recognizable, except one. One was a local call, a number and the name Batman. *What does he want? The last time we saw Batman was in the vaults of the naval classified archives. And it's marked urgent. Well, it's a local call. I'll try him first,* Davin thought. Then he asked, "Connie, what do you suppose *ole* Batman wants with us?"

"Who's to know? He was kinda cute, maybe a date," Connie teased.

"He's not my type."

"Not with you, silly, with me, and maybe I might accept," she said as she scooted off to her room with Davin right behind her.

"With you, not on your life," Davin said as he followed her to her room in a quick little shuffle.

"Oh, no, you don't, big boy. This girl needs a nice, hot bath, as well as some time to herself, and you're not invited. Besides, the doc said no heavy exercise," Connie said, turning him around and pushing him back toward his room.

"Party pooper!" Davin said as the door closed behind him.

"I'm not that kind of girl, and you know that. Now get," she said as she opened the door a crack, still teasing Davin.

"Oh, all right. I guess I have to make some phone calls, anyway," Davin replied as he shuffled reluctantly toward his room.

A knock on the door changed the direction he was heading.

"Yes, just a minute!" he yelled.

"Room service!" yelled a voice from beyond the door.

"Okay, just a minute. I am coming," he called as he opened the door to find the manager and a young man with a cart, obviously full of food and drink.

"Wow, that was quick!"

"Just put it over there, John," the manager indicated to the young man as he wheeled in the cart.

"Why, thank you. This is really unexpected," Davin said as he looked over the cart at all the food and champagne.

"No problem, Mr. Pierce. Please enjoy," he said as he headed back for the door. "We will pick up the cart anytime, if you would just call me when done."

"Connie, are you hungry?" Davin yelled to her after they had left.

"Yeah, I'll be out after my bath!" she yelled back. Forty-five minutes later, Connie appeared, wearing only a white bath robe and a towel around her wet head.

After eating a rather large portion of the food from the cart, she returned to her room to finish dressing, and Davin picked up the message sheet and started to return some of the calls. He started with Batman, but with no luck.

After calling his secretary, Stephanie, to get the information she had, and after relating the problems they had encountered, he attempted Batman again, with no luck. The next call was to Admiral Owen Haynes, retired, in McLean, Virginia.

Admiral Haynes had been the convoy commander in 1943 when the *MaryJean* disappeared from his convoy. He expressed an interest in finding out what had happened to her. He said that he had attempted to research the mystery himself but ended up in too many dead ends. Admiral Haynes had told Davin about the search he conducted and what he had done to locate her. But fearing for the safety of the rest of the convoy, he was unable to do a proper search. He had lost 14 ships out of 102 on that crossing, which was not good, but in a time of war, 14 ships wasn't a lot. But then, on those 14 ships, 3,400 men lost their lives.

One last try to Batman still was unsuccessful; he'd try again later, maybe.

It was nearing two in the afternoon, and they were planning on going over to the Norfolk Naval Yard to see an old friend in the pubs and printing area. He was known to be able to locate things in those old records that no one else could find. They were to meet at three thirty and see how good he was.

Carl Sandberg was a man of his word, but not one that knew how to tell time. Connie and Davin arrived at the Office of Publications and Printing at three thirty but didn't find Carl. Instead, a secretary of the worst kind greeted them. After fifteen minutes of talking with her, they discovered that she had an answer for everything—maybe not the correct answer, but an answer nonetheless.

It was four o'clock when Carl finally arrived, looking rather surprised to see his guests.

"Well, it's about time you two got here. I've been a little worried about you. How ya doing, Davin? And who is this vision of loveliness?" Carl asked as he crossed the room, heading toward Connie.

"Hands off, sport. This is Connie Young, special investigator for the FBI. Connie, this is Carl Sandberg, bullshit artist extraordinaire. Sometimes goes by Mongo the Barbarian," Davin introduced them as Carl eyed Connie from head to toe.

"Pleasure to make your acquaintance, Ms. Young. Or may I call you Connie?"

"Please call me Connie, Mongo," Connie replied, glancing at Davin. "And it is also a pleasure to meet a friend of Davin's. He has told me nothing about you, so you have a lot of ground to cover," she said.

"Come on down to my office and fill me in on what you need and I'll tell you my life story. Shouldn't take very long. Ten or twelve nights alone with you should do," Carl said as he escorted them back through the corridors leading to his office. Connie was gripped under his massive shoulder.

"Davin did tell me you and he played some football," Connie said as they entered his office.

"Yeah, played fullback for Alabama. Until I broke my knee and the doc told me to stop or lose it," Carl stated as he guided Connie toward a chair.

"How did you get into this line of work?" Connie asked as she sat down. "Not exactly what you would expect a jock to be doing."

"That was the easy part. I was a history major in college, and naval history was a hobby. Well, I just convinced the Navy that I was their man to run their new research department, and well, here I am."

"Interesting."

"Okay, Connie, what can I do for you? Just name it. Your every wish is my command," Carl commented as he sat in the large chair behind his desk.

"Oh, Harry, I'll let Davin explain. I really think he has a better handle on the scope of things than I do. Go ahead, Davin," Connie said as she tried to get comfortable in the overstuffed chair across from Carl's big cluttered desk.

Davin took a seat near the door on a hardback chair that looked like it came off the Titanic.

"It's safe, don't worry. You know where I got that chair?"

"Looks like a reject from a rummage sale, Mongo," Davin said jokingly.

"Hell, I picked that up off the destroyer HMS *Valiant*, which sank in 1944 off the coast of Spain. A little cleaning up and it would be as good as new," he said seriously.

"Amazing, simply amazing. How the hell did you ever recover it? After forty years in the water, it should have rotted away, shouldn't it?" Connie asked.

"I can't do it, Davin. She's too easy. Honey, it's true that the chair was on the *Valiant*, but I bought it in a flea market in a London shipyard a couple of years ago," Carl admitted.

"Don't look at me like that, Connie. I didn't do anything," Davin said as she gave him a look that could kill.

"I was believing you, and you were going along with him," she said angrily. "Let's get down to business. We haven't all day, you know."

"Okay, just chill out, little lady. I do get a little outa hand once in a while, so just set me straight and on an even keel and all will be fine."

"Okay, fine," Connie agreed.

"Well, Carl, we have a little problem, and we're hoping that you could do some research on a freighter that disappeared from a convoy in '43."

"Sure. Which one?"

Davin said, "She was known as the *MaryJean*, commanded by—"

"Commanded by Captain Bronsly," Carl interrupted.

"Captain...," Davin said, letting his words fade away as Carl picked up the conversation.

"Carrying munitions, vehicles, and an unknown cargo in three crates in the number 3 hold," Carl continued. "She had a squad of Marines guarding the crates and disappeared without a trace in January 1943 with only nineteen survivors. The ship has never been located and is assumed to be on the bottom of the North Atlantic along with thousands of other ships. Don't know a thing about her," Carl continued where he stopped Davin.

Connie and Davin just stared at each other, then back to Carl for a few seconds. Then they hit him.

"Son of a bitch, what else can you tell us about her?" Davin asked.

"Nothin'!" Carl replied.

"Nothing!" Davin repeated, looking deep into Carl's eyes.

"Well, not really. I guess I could fill you in on some, but let's skip around the crap that you may already know and get to the stuff you don't, which is, that she left the harbor loaded with a cargo of rice and beans and some military hardware. The original cargo sat in a warehouse on dock 3-A for about a year, and then it was transferred to two unknown locations. Captain Bronsly and crew, along with some military types, planned on selling the weapons to make a little working capital for after the war. The unknown cargo…well, this boy hasn't found out yet what it was, but he has a good idea. But you know all this, don't you?"

"We didn't know about the rice and beans, but the rest is known history. What we need to find out is who was involved in the mystery cargo that was put on board."

"Something tells me that you know what was in those crates. It would help a lot if I knew what was in them."

"I really don't think you want to know, Carl. The less you know, the safer you are."

"No joke. Well, if you won't spill the beans, then I guess I'll have to find out on my own," Carl said with a slight tone of disappointment in his voice. "When do you need the information?"

"In a couple of days, or sooner, if possible," Connie finally said.

"Before we go, would it be possible to use your phone?" Davin asked Carl. Then he said to Connie, "Think I'll try Batman again."

"Great. Maybe he came home."

"Hello, Batman, this is Davin Pierce. I hear you've been looking for me. What's up?" Davin asked after the phone had rung only two times.

Listening to Batman, Davin slowly sat down in the chair across from the desk, with a look of disbelief.

"Holy shit! Where can we meet you…we can't. You're where? Okay…yeah…it's almost five here. We should be back at the hotel by six thirty or so. Why don't you have your friends meet us there then? Fine…okay…take care. Bye." Davin held the phone for a few minutes, just staring at it in disbelief.

"Davin, what is it?" Connie asked. "Davin?"

"He thinks they have found the *MaryJean* and wants to meet with us as soon as possible," Davin said, hanging up the phone.

"Do you still need the info, Davin?"

"Yeah. We gotta go, Carl. Thanks for your time. Call me as soon as you have something," Davin said as he got up to leave.

"Davin, are we meeting with Batman tonight or what?" Connie finally asked as they walked across the parking lot.

"No, not just yet."

"Okay, then who are we meeting at six thirty?" Connie demanded. "You're holding out on me. What did Batman tell you?"

"I'm having a hard time believing what I heard, but here it is. Batman had this guy Phillips, a Navy pilot, rig his phone to forward all his calls to him while he is in sick bay," Davin said as they were driving off the base.

"Sick bay—what happened to him? Is he okay?" Connie interrupted.

"He'll be fine. He made a rapid ascent from eighty feet and got the bends. But he'll be fine. The real trick is that he is in sick bay on the *Nimitz*, somewhere in the Atlantic Ocean. He wouldn't say exactly where. This Captain Phillips will give us more details and outline what Batman wants us to do. It seems that the submarine they were researching and the *MaryJean* are related. It is beginning to look like that U-boat and their sub and the *MaryJean* were all involved in this together."

"Wait a minute. Batman is on the *Nimitz* and receiving phone calls that are call-forwarded from his house?"

"That's what he said. Oh, yeah, he is in a hyperbolic chamber for the bends. It seems the *Nimitz* has a very well-equipped sick bay. Boy, isn't technology great?" Davin stated.

"It sure is," Connie replied.

Connie and Davin finished the drive in silence. Davin could see that the excitement was building in her, and hell, they were very close. Just how close, they didn't know. And what did Batman and JD stumble across that linked the two ships together? Was it the other submarine that Von Hofner and his crew saw back in 1943 with the *MaryJean*?

Operation Jungle Storm
Ivory Coast, Nigeria, and Surrounding Countries
May 1, 1996
1900 Hours, GMT

"Sir!" Captain Houston said as he entered the war room. "A word with you, sir."

"In my office, Captain," General Sellers said, pointing toward his temporary office in the rear of the war room.

Both men headed immediately toward the office. Once they arrived, Captain Houston closed the door and waited until the general had taken his place behind his desk.

"Sir, we just received a report that our insurgent team 3 had reached its objective and is now heading for their pickup point. Mission accomplished, total destruction of both targets," Captain Houston reported.

Team 3 was supposed to destroy two chemical manufacturing plants deep in Nigeria. Each plant was producing nerve agents, to be used against allied forces. The plant and stockpiles were destroyed during the mission.

"Anything else, Captain?" General Sellers asked, looking for a report on Operation Greetings.

"Yes, sir. Operation Greetings is in motion. We expect results before nightfall tomorrow. I'll keep you posted," Houston said with a big smile.

"Let's not get too excited, son. If this works, this could be one of the shortest wars in history, shorter than Operation Desert Storm. I just hope this is the right move, Captain. Is our man ready to assume his duties?"

"Yes, sir. He is more than ready and, once placed, will do what is necessary to ensure peace," Captain Houston assured the general.

"Good, real good. Has relief been sent to those cities that were bombed?" General Sellers asked.

"An update on those explosions. It seems that they have been reported incorrectly. The atomic warheads did not detonate, just the detonator that should have caused the reaction. Our bomb disposal team on-site has discovered that the force of the explosion was equal to about a two-thousand-pound bomb. There was extensive damage, and death, but not to the numbers first reported. Less than seven to ten thousand were killed, and only because the location of the bombs was very near a heavily populated part of the city that was on the edge of the airport. The bomb was a dud as far as an atomic capability is concerned."

"That is a relief in itself, but still many people died for no reason, civilians who have no interest in this war. See that everything possible is done to help those people," General Sellers ordered.

"The president has been notified, and relief is on its way," Houston said.

"Thank you, Captain," General Sellers said, then stood and started for the door. Captain Houston followed closely behind.

Chapter 20

JOINING FORCES

Washington, DC
Twin Bridges Hotel
May 1, 1996
1600 Hours, EST

P hillips and a young female officer, Sonja MacGuire, were waiting in the lobby as Davin and Connie walked in. Sonja had temporarily replaced Rhonda, his regular copilot, while she was on leave. They looked tired and well tanned, like they had just returned from a vacation on the beach somewhere in the tropics. After a few minutes of introductions and pleasantries, they headed up to the suite to continue their discussion.

"Okay, Phillips, how did you find her, and where is she?" Davin asked impatiently.

"Well, Davin, they haven't exactly found her yet, but we do know about where she should be. The main thing is, we have a connection between your ship and our submarine. And the how we know about her is a little classified at the moment. We will be showing you tomorrow if you want, but I can't tell you here."

"Classified? How so? No, don't answer that," Davin started but decided it could wait.

"Tomorrow the puzzle will come together," Phillips said without expanding any further.

"Did your sub and our ship meet somewhere in the North Atlantic and then continue together to somewhere for some unknown reason?"

"Yeah, you could say that, but not exactly," Ensign McGuire said as Phillips poured a drink at the bar. This was her first assignment with Phillips, and she was enjoying it. She had been assigned to fly with Phillips when Rhonda put in for leave.

"Okay, damn, is it possible that your sub was an unknown escort to the *MaryJean* and her secret cargo and she was to make sure that the *MaryJean* made it to an undisclosed meeting?" Davin continued to probe.

"Yes, that's possible, but let's wait until you get the rest of the story instead of grabbing at straws. Once we put together what you know and what Batman and JD know, we feel we will have a pretty strong case," Phillips commented as he sipped his drink.

"I'm hungry. What about you guys?" Connie asked, trying to break up Davin's puzzle solving.

"Me too," Sonya said. "I haven't eaten all day."

"Okay, let's get something to eat and I'll tell you what is on the agenda. If, of course, you are interested in finding out the rest of the story, that is," Phillips teased.

"Lead on, Phillips, lead on. We were running out of trails to chase down, anyway," Davin said as they headed out the door.

Dinner was at a fine little restaurant about a block from the hotel. During dinner, Phillips outlined the plans he and Sonya had laid for tomorrow. They finished and returned to the hotel. Phillips and Sonya had secured rooms down the hall so they could get an early start in the morning.

Admiral Jacobs's Office
May 1, 1996
1615 Hours, EST

"Come in and sit down, please," Jacobs said to the three civilians as they entered his office.

"Admiral, we are required by law and naval doctrine to inform your office and the president of our findings concerning the incident with Commander Henderson's submarine on the morning of March 21 of this year," the tallest gentleman stated after introductions.

He was Chief Inspector David Carlson from the Defense Investigative Agency. Tall, dark, the perfect look of a spy, but without the coldness.

"Well, get on with it, Carlson. I haven't all day," Jacobs demanded.

"Right, sir. An official inquiry will convene on May 30 of this year to present our final report to the Navy. This incident was first believed to be an accident of the shipping line, but now we have substantial proof that a Nigerian terrorist group had planned and executed the explosion that sank Commander Henderson's submarine and killed over 70 percent of his crew. The freighter was heavily loaded with high explosives, with a remote control detonator that was operated from shore. The vessel was also believed to be void of any human life, as the ship was also controlled remotely. It is believed that the intention of the explosion was merely to block the harbor, but Commander Henderson's untimely return to port put him and his crew at risk, unknown to him at that time. His actions were in proper order, and no charges of negligence will be brought to bear," David Carlson told Jacobs of the preliminary findings on the explosion that destroyed JD Henderson's brand-new nuclear submarine.

"And you have proof of what you say?" Jacobs asked.

"Yes, sir. A full report will be on your desk in two weeks, outlining all the details, and the final outcome will be determined by May 30," Carlson answered.

"Thank you for your report, Carlson. Good day," Jacobs said as he stood to see his three visitors out.

"Good day, sir," Carlson said as they left.

Ten minutes after his guest left, Jacobs placed a call to Norfolk Naval Yard precisely to the office of Commander Malcolm DeForrest, chief of Naval Special Security Branch and Combat Operations in the South Atlantic area. Commander DeForrest would have all the information on the sinking of the *Washington* and *Montgomery*, the recovery of the *Wolverine*, and the naval loses during the conflict.

"Commander DeForrest, this is Admiral Jacobs. Good morning," Jacobs started.

"Good morning, sir. What can I do for you?" DeForrest replied. He knew who Jacobs was and didn't like him one bit. He knew that Jacobs bought his rank and that somehow Jacobs was corrupt. He just didn't know in what way, nor could he prove it.

"Need a bit of information concerning the outcome of the USS *George Washington* incident," Jacobs stated, hoping he could convince DeForrest that he had a need to know.

"Sir, I cannot discuss that over the telephone, but if you have your security officer contact mine, I will see that you receive the whole report via secure fax," DeForrest answered, buying some time. Jacobs wasn't responsible for this area and didn't have the need to know this information. What was his angle? Why the interest in an old submarine?

"That will be just fine, Commander. Thank you." Jacobs hung up without waiting for a reply. Leaning back in his chair, Jacobs lit a Cuban cigar and turned to face the window, deep in thought. As much as it hurt, he could not let that submarine return to Norfolk, ever. She must be destroyed.

Nigerian Air Space
May 2, 1996
0430 Hours, GMT

The air was full of aircraft, all heading toward Nigeria. The air war had begun. This was the largest concentration of bomber and fighter aircraft since the formations of World War II. Even the flights over Iraq were smaller than this.

A communication had been sent to General Samula to surrender his forces or the destruction of his country would be on his hands.

There was no reply from General Samula.

The flight to Nigeria would take about one and a half hours. The plan was to start the attack at 06:00 on tactical and strategic targets. The flight could only be stopped with the transmission of one word from Command Headquarters.

"General Samula, the Americans and allies have launched their air war. The force is massive. We do not stand a chance against stopping them. I suggest you surrender now before it is too late," General Samula's new aide, Captain Mohammed, said. The clock on the wall indicated it was four thirty in the morning.

"Captain, it isn't over until I say so!" General Samula roared to the young captain.

"But it is over, General!" Captain Mohammed said, looking into the general's eyes. "This first wave will be overhead by 0600 hours."

"What did you say, Captain?" General Samula asked, returning the stare. "Who the hell do you think you are, talking back to me? I'll have you shot!"

The general did not see the Glock 17 9mm pistol with silencer pointing at his chest as the two men stared at each other. He was too content on staring this arrogant young Captain down and convincing him that he was the supreme power and nobody could defeat him.

"General, you will pick up that phone and dial this number and tell the man on the other end that you have surrendered to me," the arrogant young captain said.

"I will do no such thing!" General Samula responded before he saw the weapon pointed at his chest.

"Don't think about pushing that button on the edge of your desk. I disconnected it days ago. Now, make the call while you still have the chance," Captain Mohammed ordered.

Captain Mohammed was a deep operative for the CIA, real name John Sabastian Roberts, who had been living and working in Nigeria for the past ten years. He joined the Nigerian Army to get to the position that he was at now, aide to General Samula. The information he provided the United States over the past years had been minimal, but now his position put him in a place that could change the entire war.

"I will make no such call. You may as well kill me, and then die yourself, my friend," Samula threatened.

"General Sellers and the president of the United States send their personal greetings, and now it's time to say goodbye, General." Roberts fired three shots at Samula. The first two struck the general in the chest and the third penetrated deep in his head as he fell backward into his chair. General Hector Samula died instantly. The sound from the silenced 9-mm Glock 17 wasn't heard beyond the walls of the office. General Samula had had his office soundproofed the year before for his own personal assassinations so even his secretary could not hear the shots.

Immediately Roberts reached into his coat pocket and removed a small cellular telephone and punched in a special code.

"Sellers," General Sellers answered on the secure line after the first ring.

"Operation Greetings, mission accomplished. The problem is no problem anymore," Roberts said into the telephone.

"Thank you, son. Now get to safety. I'll stop the raid," General Sellers said and then hung up. He immediately dialed another number to cancel the mission.

Of the nearly fifteen hundred aircraft inbound to Nigeria, all but two hundred made a slow turn to return to their own airfields. The bombing mission had been called off. Members of the 82nd and 101st Airborne Divisions were on the transport aircraft that continued on toward Nigeria. They had fighter cover for the entire flight, to ensure their safety.

A new mission had unfolded from within the original bombing mission. The entire mission was supposed to be a complete strike: first, bomb the targets, then bomb them again, then bomb them one more time. Once all the bombing was complete, the 82nd and 101st Airborne, along with forces from six other nations, were to parachute outside the major cities and attack. Tanks and light Bradley Fighting Vehicles were to be air-dropped into the area for support. By proceeding this way, it was felt that there would be minimal ground fighting. The forces would become occupation forces and would start in the rebuilding of the occupied country.

When the combined forces landed, they were greeted with open arms, not weapons. The forces were surrendering as the parachutists were landing. They found very little resistance from the Nigerian military forces. They, like the troops in Iraq, were tired of fighting someone else's war. They just wanted peace and to be with their families.

By noon of that day, a new president had stepped in to pick up the pieces that Samula had tried to destroy.

Andrews Air Force Base
Washington, DC
May 2, 1996
0600 Hours, EST

The Navy Gulfstream was waiting on the ramp at 06:00 for the arrival of Davin Pierce and Connie Young. Phillips had said it would take most of the day to get to their final destination, but first they had a stop to make in Norfolk, Virginia.

Captain Phillips had advised them to pack light and bring swimming attire. Once they were airborne, he told them they had to make a brief stop in Norfolk to meet with a friend of his, Commander Malcolm DeForrest. Once finished, they would then proceed to Andros Island and wait for further instructions from either Batman on the *Nimitz* or Commander Henderson on board the *Wolverine*. He explained what had happened without revealing anything classified and expanded on what he knew of the developing scenario. The wait on Andros Island might be from a few hours to several days.

The flight to Norfolk, Virginia, was uneventful. Phillips was in the back with Davin and Connie most of the flight, while Sonja flew the aircraft down the coast toward Norfolk. The flight only lasted forty minutes.

"Davin, Commander DeForrest is responsible for what goes on in the Atlantic, and he has the latest information on the USS *George Washington*, HMS *Montgomery*, and the *Wolverine*. DeForrest has also dug up some interesting information about our buddy Admiral Jacobs," Phillips commented.

"This Jacobs, is he a big shot in Washington?" Davin asked, sipping on a Coke.

"You could say that. He heads up one section of the Naval Security Group. Getting so you can't trust anyone," Phillips replied.

"What about your new copilot?" Connie inquired, curious about the sudden switch in crew. "Is she trustworthy?"

"Don't know much about her. She's on temporary duty in Washington, working on some special project in the Pentagon in the logistics area. When Rhonda had to take an emergency leave, Sonja volunteered to sit in until Rhonda returned. She was at Andrews, checking on getting some flight time to remain current while on temporary duty. The dispatcher told her that I needed a copilot, and after checking her credentials, I said why not. She is qualified, and I needed a copilot," Phillips explained about how Sonja had joined in.

"Rather coincidental that she is here, working in the Pentagon, and just happens to be at Andrews Flight Ops the same time you need a copilot, and able to get off that project to fly with you," Connie said, still not convinced that Sonja was telling all she knew.

"Look, if it makes you feel better, I'll keep her in the dark about what we are doing," Phillips assured Connie.

"That may be easier said than done. She has to know where we are going to help you fly us there. Now, the whys, she does not need to know," Connie insisted.

"Okay, she stays in the dark about why and as much as we can about what we are doing," Phillips agreed. "Buckle up. We should be almost there."

Phillips got up and returned to the cockpit to assist in the landing of the Gulfstream at Norfolk Naval Air Station on the coast of Virginia.

After an hour's delay at Norfolk, they headed for Andros Island in the Bahamas. Flight time was about four hours, just long enough to read the information that Phillips had received from Commander DeForrest and also to catch a couple hours of sleep.

USS Wolverine
One Hundred Miles Southeast of the Nimitz
May 2, 1996
1800 Hours, GMT

"Skipper, just got word from the *Nimitz* that Carpenter and Batman will be fine. They are coming out of the chamber in about an hour and should be ready for duty by tomorrow morning," the radio operator told JD.

"Great. Maybe they can catch a helo back to us. We could use the help," JD replied.

"Sir, your wish is their command. The message also said they would be transported back to us at 2000 hours tonight."

"Helmsperson, course and speed?" JD asked Micky, who was still at the helm, steering the vintage submarine toward the *Nimitz*. "Ask them how Lieutenant Commander Sheppard is doing."

"Two-niner-zero true, eight knots, sir," came the reply from Micky, who, for the first time since the attack, was having some real fun.

"Sir, Lieutenant Commander Sheppard is doing fine. The doc says he is pretty torn up but will mend in time. He should be up and around in a couple of months. Says he has four broken ribs, two of which had punched holes in his lungs, a broken wrist, broken ankle, and numerous cuts, bruises, and some internal bleeding. All are under control, and if no infections set in, he will be standing on the dock when we get there," the radio operator relayed to JD and the crew. "Half of other injured have already been released from sick bay and are enjoying the luxury of an aircraft carrier. The rest are still being treated."

With the information provided by Micky, JD leaned over the chart table and checked the course to the *Nimitz*. They were still approximately ninety miles from her, but closing.

Scotty entered the bridge with a smile on his face so large that you would think he had just gotten away with a major crime and was very proud of it. In fact, he was proud, and the item he carried under his arm was proof.

"Skipper, here is what you have been waiting for," Scotty said as he handed JD the personal logbook of the previous captain of the *Wolverine*, Lieutenant Commander Jacobs, which had been sealed in his personal safe. The book looked undamaged, no burns, cuts, or abuse other than from normal use. Along with that, he had two envelopes, one that looked like a personal letter, the other a large manila envelope.

"Scotty, how did you...no, don't tell me, but thanks. Let's see what we have here," JD said, laying the book on the chart table.

"Before you read that, sir, you may want to open this," Scotty said as he handed him an old manila envelope marked TOP SECRET: CAPTAIN'S EYES ONLY.

USS Nimitz, Flight Deck
South Atlantic Ocean
May 2, 1996
1945 hours, GMT

Two helos lifted off from the deck of the *Nimitz* en route to the *Wolverine*. One carried Carpenter, Batman, and about two hundred pounds of food. The other was a fuel tanker, which was carrying two thousand gallons of diesel fuel.

The weather report indicated that a storm was brewing, and a meeting of the two warships might prove to be hazardous. Along with Batman were new charts and a suggested change in course to avoid the storm. The *Nimitz* would join them at another point in the trip.

USS Wolverine
Same Day
2015 Hours, GMT

Thirty minutes later, the fuel, passengers, and cargo were being trans-ferred to the small submarine. The seas were starting to grow rough, and the transfer had to be done quickly to keep from losing any material or men. By 2115 hours, all the cargo and passengers were transferred and the helos were on their way back to the *Nimitz* with a complete list of the survivors from the sinking of the two ships.

"Helmsperson, heading two-five-zero, speed eight knots," JD ordered after looking over the new chart and weather report. "Welcome back, Batman, Carp. How're you feeling?"

"Oh, about 80 percent, I'd say." Batman and Carpenter glanced at each other in agreement.

"Good. It's going to be a rough ride. Stations," JD ordered.

"Aye, sir," came the response. They turned and started out of the control room.

"Get back here, Batman. Where are you going?" JD demanded, seeing them attempting to leave.

"To sick bay, Capt'n," Batman said, turning slightly to face JD.

"Sick bay! Before you go, you may want to read this," JD said, indicating the envelope and captain's personal log. "They are going to be best sellers."

USS Nimitz
2110 Hours, GMT

"Sir, this message just came in, on an open channel to all ships at sea." The *Nimitz* radio operator handed the commander a folded single sheet of paper.

"Wait, sailor," the commander ordered. "Would you reconfirm this message for me, immediately?"

"Aye, sir." The operator turned and ran back to the radio control room.

USS Wolverine
Eighty Nautical Miles Southeast of the Nimitz
Same Time

"Skipper, I have just received the strangest message, something about a renegade World War II submarine loose in the South Atlantic, and all ships should be on the lookout for her. The sub is considered dangerous and should be avoided at all costs. Any naval ship seeing the sub should destroy it on sight!" the radio operator quoted. "They don't mean us, do they?"

"That was sent clear?" Batman asked, looking cold at JD.

"Yes, sir, sent to all ships at sea, on an open marine channel. I just got lucky and picked it up on this rig."

"Helm, alter course to two-three-zero," JD ordered Micky. "Maintain present speed." Then to radio, he said, "Contact the *Nimitz* and ask for the commander. I need some confirmation on that message!"

"Batman, read through the log as quickly as possible. Carpenter, take over as navigator and lay out a course to the Bahamas. When you read the papers in that envelope, you'll know where and why. The boat is now on yellow alert. Lookouts, to your posts," JD ordered, then switched on the intercom to communicate with the engine room. "Scotty, can we dive this tub and return if we have to?"

"Aye, sir. We have repaired almost everything we can get our hands on. We should be able to, sir. But a few more hours to charge the batteries would be very helpful," Scotty replied over the intercom.

"We may not have that luxury," JD responded.

"Aye, Captain. Just give the word. We will do the best we can," Scotty replied.

Batman and Carpenter took the log and other documents and, sitting down in the galley with a cup of coffee, started to read each page carefully.

Washington, DC
CIA Building
May 2, 1996
2100 Hours, EST

David Malone sat alone in his office. It was late, and what he was seeing didn't make sense. After gathering information from Donald Peterson, the FBI file on his father, naval and Marine records on Jeffery and Donald Senior, he sat there confused. Josh Randel had told him where to look and what to be especially watchful for. Now he had it.

Major Donald Peterson had been assigned to guard a special delivery to England. This special delivery was supposed to be on the ship *MaryJean* that departed New York early in 1943. The orders were not specific as to how the delivery was to take place, only that he and his men were to be on the *MaryJean* and guard the three crates. The records showed that Major Peterson was one of the survivors of the U-boat attack on the *MaryJean* but was reported missing in action in November 1943 somewhere in France. Yet his son was born in Rockville, Maryland, October 12, 1944. Something was not right with the dates, or Major Donald Peterson was not missing in action, as reported.

Chapter 21

REVENGE

USS Wolverine
May 2, 1996
2200 Hours, GMT

"Captain, I have the *Nimitz*. Standby, they are switching to the bridge for the admiral." The radio operator leaned out of the cramped radio room and called to JD.

"Commander Henderson, this is Admiral Feldings of the USS *Nimitz*. How are things going over there?" Admiral Feldings asked when he picked up the microphone on the bridge of the *Nimitz*.

"Sir, Henderson here. The boat is in pretty good shape for being as old as she is. We had a few scares at first but seem to have her under control now," JD answered, as if they were talking over a telephone.

"If you need anything, you had better let me know now. There is a hell of a storm brewing between us," Feldings said.

"I think we have what we need, except for one thing, sir. That is, we just intercepted a message about a renegade sub. Are they referring to us? And if so, can you help us?" JD asked.

"Yes, I believe they are talking about you. I don't know what is going on, but the way I see it, someone doesn't want you to return with that boat," the admiral stated.

"Who signed our death warrant, sir?" JD asked.

"The order was signed by an Admiral Jacobs from the Naval Security Group in the Pentagon," Admiral Feldings stated, then continued. "The classified version describes what that sub was supposed to have done and the parameters of what we can and cannot do if we find you."

"Damn! What does it say?" JD could not resist asking.

"In a nutshell, Commander, it says that your sub has been hijacking ships up and down the coast for years, killing the crews and stealing the cargo. Once the cargo is unloaded, you would sink the ship. We know now that that is true, but with the old crew, not you. But the world doesn't know who is driving that boat." Feldings paused and then continued. "I never did trust Jacobs, always thought he wasn't shooting straight. If he is behind this, then, well, you are in a tough spot, Commander."

"Sir, they are trying everything possible to keep us from arriving at a safe port. And they are using the Navy to do their dirty work, sir. Will you run interference for us until we can get this cleared up?" JD added. "Sir, we have enough evidence on board to tie in a lot of very important people to this organization, to include Admiral Jacobs."

"I'll do the best I can, Commander. But what I see is that we are fighting an enemy who has a lot of power and is holding all the cards. Look, with that storm brewing between us, we can't reach you for at least another day. Can you maneuver enough to avoid the storm and remain hidden until we get to you?" Admiral Feldings suggested.

"Yes, sir. Will you divert the search to the north for a day or two to give us enough time to make land and try to resolve this problem?" JD asked. He paused for a moment to think about what to do.

JD didn't like what was brewing but was glad to know that at least one high-ranking member of the Navy was on their side.

"Good luck. I'll do my best to divert the Navy off your tail," Admiral Feldings assured JD. "One more thing, before you go, I have a report on those bodies you found on board that boat."

"Yes, sir. Go ahead. What did the good doctor discover?" JD asked, hoping they did not die from some strange disease that would wipe out this entire crew too.

"Well, Doc did an autopsy on one of them and did not like what he found, so he dug a little deeper, so to speak. It seems they didn't die of old age. In fact, most of them were between twenty and forty years old. Two were very old—Doc thinks somewhere between seventy and eighty years old—but they all died of poison, taken orally, either in food or water. It was a slow, painless death. Most died in their sleep. It'll be hard to tell if it was murder or suicide," Admiral Feldings continued. "I hope you got rid of all the food and water on board her."

"We did, sir. And thanks to you and your crew, we have fresh food and plenty of fresh water. According to the captain's log, they spent their final days in Port Harcourt, Nigeria, delivering some cargo to a Mr. Corning at the US Embassy. And they took on some provisions also. Maybe it was poisoned!" JD said as he read over the log again. He thought, *Why would someone want to kill the crew of this boat? Maybe they wanted to cover up any trace of what they were doing.*

"You dumped all the food and water?" Admiral Feldings asked again.

"Yes, sir. No way now to be sure if it was the food they got in Nigeria or not," JD answered, thinking that maybe somewhere on the boat there might be something to link the deaths with the provisions they got in Nigeria.

"I'll check in with Mr. Corning about those crates and the provisions, now that the war is over, and we are occupying the country," Feldings said.

"Did you say the war is over?" JD asked, just to be sure of what he had heard.

"Yes, it ended before it really got started, around 0700. General Samula is dead, and occupation forces are in the capital, cleaning up the corrupt government as we speak. A new president has taken over and is working closely with NATO to make the transition," Feldings stated over the radio.

"Thank you, sir. Out here," JD said and then handed the microphone back to his operator.

"Engine Room, how are things going back there?" JD said into the intercom from the radio room.

"Just fine, sir. We should be able to hold this speed a bit longer, if the seas don't get any rougher," was the reply from Scotty in the engine room.

"Thanks, Scotty." After flipping a switch to the forward torpedo room, he called. "Fire Control, what's the status of our armament?"

"We have six torpedoes and lots of small-arms ammunition. The three-inch deck gun is in fair shape, maybe usable. The fifty is almost new, but remember the age of some of this stuff. The 20mm Oerlikons is old, but looks serviceable. In the weapons locker, we have ten new M16A2s, an even dozen .45 automatics, and four brand-new 9-millimeter Berettas."

"Understand. What about the aft torpedo room?" JD asked.

"Four fish there and three more M16A2s, and a couple more .45s in the locker," was the reply.

"Thanks. Send a couple of men up to test-fire the three-inch, the 50, and the Oerlikons." JD switched the intercom to off after receiving an acknowledgment from Scotty. He turned and walked out of the radio room and over to the chart table in the control room. He wanted to see what Carpenter had come up with after reading the top secret document. Batman walked over with the captain's personal log, shaking his head.

"I just can't believe it—fifty years of running this boat up and down the Bermuda Triangle, hijacking ships of all sizes. If these guys were not dead, the courts would have a field day with them," Batman said finally, shaking his head, still in disbelief.

"Yeah, they had a policy of no survivors, a ghost ship. The list of members looks like an invitation to the White House. You see the part about the cave and dry dock in the Bahamas? Well, guess where we are going?" JD said as he scanned over Carpenter's shoulder at the track he had plotted.

"The top secret document had put this boat into a special operation, covert type, during the war, starting with the ship *MaryJean*. If some of the people on that list are for real involved in this, then they are people in the right places to cause us to be the target of every nation in the world. With that radio message, it would seem that it has already begun," Carpenter said with a little nervousness in his voice. "Someone with a lot of money and power had to be backing these pirates. This boat is in too good condition, and with new, state-of-the-art computers marked US Navy issue," he said, pointing toward the identification plate on the side of a new IBM computer terminal. "Which means that list of names may just be true. Hard to believe, though."

"That's right. What we have to do is make it to a safe port and expose the guilty parties, before they find us," JD commented as Kelly walked over. "It isn't going to be a cakewalk, either. They were able to hide this boat and the whole mess for over fifty years. We may have a hard time convincing the right people that we are not involved."

"JD, if all the Navy is looking for us, using all that expensive spy stuff, what chance do we have?" Kelly asked, trying to make eye contact with everyone in the group.

"That is a good point, and they are probably tracking us right now. But we have to stay on the surface long enough to recharge the batteries. However, once we dive and change course, we will be a little more difficult to track. These old diesel boats are easier to hide than some of our newer nukes," JD added, pointing to a spot not far from a small island on the eastern side of the Bahamas. "Besides, if Admiral Feldings has some influence, then he may be able to divert the Navy long enough for us to make it to hiding."

"According to the log, there is a cave entrance at 225 feet that is large enough for this boat. Once inside, about two hundred yards, we can surface to what is written as a mammoth cavern and dry dock. From there, we can get to civilization and expose the guilty. This outlines the complete procedure to enter and surface safely," Batman said with hesitation in his voice.

"Easier said than done. We have a lot of ocean between us and that cave, and the US Navy is in hot pursuit," Carpenter volunteered.

"Quite true, but this storm and cover of darkness may be our saving grace," JD responded.

"Let's say we make it to the cave and there is a cavern and we don't die trying to enter the cave. Let's say we make it in the cave. What happens if our bad admiral has a welcoming committee waiting for us? Just what if?" Micky piped up from across the control room.

"We will have to plan for that as we get closer. Right now, let's just get there," JD came back with the only answer possible.

USS Nimitz
May 2, 1996
2200 Hours, GMT

"Admiral, the weather is closing in. We are unable to launch any aircraft, helos, or fighters. We were just able to recover the last flight, with that F-14 flat on the flight deck," reported the deck commander to Admiral Feldings.

"What is the status of that wrecked F-14, Commander?" Admiral Feldings asked his watch commander.

"As soon as the weather breaks, we will get her up on wheels and moved to the hangar deck. Her damage is not severe enough to scrap her. No structural damage, just shot up pretty bad, hydraulic lines and cables cut. It is amazing he was able to land. He had no stabilizer and very little aileron control. Damn good pilot, sir," the watch commander stated.

"Yes, he is," Admiral Feldings agreed, thinking of Lieutenant Martin James, also known as Spiderman. He always gave 110 percent, no matter the job. He'd taken in shrapnel on the entire left side of his body—ripped him up pretty bad.

"One hell of a pilot to be able to bring in that plane in his condition," the watch commander commented.

"He's a Navy pilot, right?" After getting a nod, Admiral Feldings continued. "He was trained to survive. I'll put him in for the Distinguished Flying Cross. He does deserve at least that, maybe more." He hated to see young men die, especially for the wrong reason. Spiderman was lucky to be alive. He would never fly again, but at least he was alive. Paralyzed from the waist down from a piece of metal cutting his spinal cord, he would recover, and maybe with the help of modern medical technology, he might walk again.

"Aye, sir," the watch commander replied, turned, and departed.

"Keep me posted on the weather," the admiral ordered. "That sub may not be able to maneuver very well and may need our help." Admiral Feldings stood on the bridge, looking out over the vast ocean, and thought, *Why does old Admiral Jacobs want that sub destroyed? What secrets does she hold that would cause him to put out an order to destroy on sight? I hope Henderson and his crew survive long enough to find out.*

"Admiral, this is the latest on the weather," the watch officer said, handing him a single sheet of paper.

"What is our estimated time of arrival in Fort Lauderdale?" Admiral Feldings asked.

"Three days, sir, at cruise speed."

"Change course to Fort Lauderdale," Admiral Feldings ordered.

"Aye, sir," the watch officer responded and then turned to issue the order.

Admiral Jacobs's Office
May 2, 1996
1700 Hours, EST

"Admiral, what have you done to ensure our safety?" asked the voice on the phone.

"The whole Navy is out searching for them with orders to destroy on sight. They should not last through the night," Jacobs answered somberly, recognizing the voice instantly. Even with the secure voice scrambler on, his voice was not difficult to recognize.

"Very good, Admiral. We cannot afford to be implicated in this, and I hope for your sake that they are destroyed. Goodbye, Admiral." The voice hung up, without waiting for a reply.

Admiral Jacobs wasn't worried. He had been in this game too long to let this set him back. The Navy would locate them, and that would be the end of it. He reached over and opened a hand-carved cigar box that was sitting on the edge of his desk. He pulled out a new, fresh Cuban cigar, one of the most expensive cigars in the world. But he got them free, through his personal trade agreement with the Cuban government. His boat would stop once a month to pick up the cigars and other contraband in exchange for products that could not be found in Cuba. The arrangement had been made in the early sixties, and Jacobs never found a reason to stop trading with his friends.

A recent message from Sonja MacGuire indicated that she and Phillips had picked up Mr. Pierce and Connie Young. They flew to Norfolk, delayed for an hour, and then continued on to Andros Island, where they were enjoying a restful vacation at the Holiday Inn Resort Complex on the beach. She didn't know anything else. She sensed that they did not trust her yet and would not bring her into the conversations about what they were doing on Andros.

USS Wolverine
May 2, 1996
2230 Hours, GMT

"Prepare to dive!" JD finally ordered after several hours of running on the surface. At the sound of the Klaxton, the crew members that were enjoying the fresh air while the diesels were running immediately started down the hatches to the confines of the boat.

"Aye, Captain," came the reply from around the control room.

"Clear the bridge! Dive! Dive!" Batman yelled into the interphone.

Within ten minutes, they were one hundred feet below the Atlantic surface and cruising at five knots.

"Estimated time of arrival at the island, Carpenter?" Batman asked, anticipating what JD wanted to know.

"Current speed, sixty-two hours, sir," Carpenter replied, with a tone of confidence in his voice.

The routines used to submerge a submarine need to be practiced continuously to be sure that when it is an emergency, everyone on board knows what his or her job is. This dive was only a drill. JD wanted to test his new crew, to see if they could actually go through the proper procedures required to take a boat underwater safely. They had succeeded this time.

"Scotty," JD said into the intercom.

"Engine Room, Scotty," the reply came after a few moments.

"Scotty, status of boat?" JD asked, hoping to get a positive answer.

"Cap, she's holding together. The pressure leaks seem to be doing just fine. We have some problems with the recirculation system but are working on it. I just need more time, sir," Scotty answered, almost pleading.

"You got it, Scotty. Prepare to surface. We have almost seven hours till sunlight," JD ordered. After getting the proper response from the control room, he stood back and watched.

Within minutes of the command to prepare to surface, the boat was set and ready.

"Batman, take us up!" JD ordered, again studying the control room crew. Watching their every move, he was proud of them. They had done the near impossible and were now operating as a well-trained crew, in a very tight situation. How long would they be able to do it? They had a long way to go before reaching the Bahamas, and the entire world was looking for them to destroy them on sight.

"Captain, about to break surface!" Carpenter bellowed from his station in front of the depth and ballast controls.

"Thanks. Lookouts to your posts! Batman, I'll take first watch, you get some sleep. You are on at three. Carp, Micky, and Kelly, get some sleep also. You're on at four. James, Harry, and Matt, you'll be relieved at four, for four hours," JD said, looking at his watch. Then he turned the intercom switch to all sections. "Attention on the boat! All personnel not required to run the boat will stand down now for the next four hours. Sections will relieve one another every four hours, unless all hands are required for the safety of the boat. We will rotate for as long as we can. If you want to get some fresh air, come up to the control room and up to the sail, no more than two at a time. It will be a little rough going, but we need to run the diesels. And thank you, you have done one hell of a job for getting us this far."

The lookouts were standing at the foot of the ladder, which would allow them access to the sail, waiting for the word to proceed up to open the hatch and exit.

"We are up!" Carpenter announced when the boat broke the surface again and was level.

"Okay, open the hatch," JD ordered, looking at the two sailors standing there in wet-weather gear.

"Aye, sir," one said and proceeded up the ladder. He unlatched the hatch and then proceeded up to the bridge, with the second close behind. Once on the bridge, they positioned themselves where they would get the best view of the horizon. All was clear in all directions.

Andros Island, Bahamas
Holiday Inn Resort and Conference Center
May 2, 1996
2230 Hours, EST

"Connie, I booked us on the morning boat. Are you two lovely ladies up to a little diving on some of the most beautiful reefs in the world?" Davin asked as he sat down beside Sonya and Connie in the hotel lobby bar.

"Sure. With an offer like that, a girl just can't refuse. All of us going?" Connie asked.

"Yeah. I booked four spaces on the dive boat, and they supply all the gear. It looks like we are going to be sitting here for a couple of days. We might as well enjoy it," Davin said, looking over at Sonya, wondering what she was really like behind that imitation front she put up.

"What time?" Sonya asked.

"Oh, eight o'clock on the dock," Davin answered. Then he added, "Just bring a towel, suntan lotion, and bathing suits are optional."

"Sounds like fun. Is everyone diving naked?" Sonja teased.

"Sure. If you are, then we are," Davin came back.

"In that case, see you guys in the morning." Sonya stood up to leave. "I need to get all the rest I can, to keep away from you dirty old men."

"That goes for me too. Good night," Connie said as she stood and left.

"Who's old?" Davin threw back.

"Nobody here," Connie answered as they left the lounge.

"I guess it's just you and me, Phillips," Davin said, then turned toward the bar and ordered another round for the two of them.

"Davin, why don't you call me Max instead? I hear Phillips all the time while on duty. Okay?" Max Phillips asked, sipping on a cold beer.

"Sure, Max. I just didn't know your first name. Sorry," Davin apologized.

"No harm done. What do you think is going on with the *Wolverine*?" Max Phillips asked after taking another sip from his beer.

"I don't really know, but with that recent news broadcast about a renegade submarine, I am beginning to wonder whom we are dealing with. It is really looking like someone in Washington has dirty fingers and doesn't want anyone to find out."

"Yeah, well, it's late and I have to go over to flight operations in the morning and see that the bird is serviced. So it's good night, Davin," Max said after glancing at his watch and seeing it was almost eleven o'clock.

"You're not going diving with us?" Davin asked, getting up and putting a twenty on the table to cover the drinks.

"No, I can't, but I know you will have enough fun for both of us. Besides, if that plane isn't fueled and ready to leave at a moment's notice, then we may not be able to make contact with Henderson."

"Right, well, we will have fun anyway."

Washington, DC
CIA Headquarters
May 3, 1996
0830 Hours, EST

"Hey, Dave. You may want to read this," the director of the CIA said as he stood in the doorway to David Malone's office after handing Dave a single sheet of paper. "By the way, sorry to hear about your dad.

"Damn," was all Dave said as he scanned the paper that was handed to him. It was a list of dead and survivors of the USS *George Washington*'s sinking.

"Dave, does that have an impact on your case?" the director asked.

"Yes and no. Peterson. Young Donald Peterson is laid up in a Tampa hospital, beaten and almost killed by some men who wanted him to convince his father to sabotage the operation he was working on," Dave said.

"So?" the director said, confused.

"So! Jeffery Peterson was a chief on the USS *George Washington*. He is presumed dead. No body was recovered after the attack. The kid is going to take this real bad. I understand they were real close," Dave said, ignoring his own pain of losing his father just days before. He knew how this kid was going to feel.

"Yeah. What now, Dave?" he asked.

"Why did that mad man attack the *Washington*? What did it prove?" Dave was getting angry—too much death for no reason.

"Dave, he was ordered to," he commented.

"Ordered to! By whom? That wimpy president? No way!" Dave said, his anger building.

"No, by someone else. A person I don't know by name yet. But I have a feeling the order came from somewhere in our government," he said with confidence. Then he stepped inside Dave's office and closed the door.

"No way! Why would someone in our government want to destroy one of our ships?" Dave asked, disbelieving.

"That is what I want to know. Now listen, what I'm about to say is very sensitive. We don't know whom we can trust. There are too many people involved in this thing that are not on our side. And I don't have a complete list yet of all the players," Sam Harrison, director of the CIA, said. "Look, I've been working with an undercover agent that has just recently given me some information that confirms my belief that a large black market ring is being run from within our government. Many of the players are high officials, or high-ranking members of our armed forces. It's hard to believe, but I have the evidence, locked in a safe place. Dave, I know who some of the players are, but I need more proof. I need some help, and I think the submarine that is connected with the *Washington* sinking has that information."

"Damn!" Dave said, shaking his head in disbelief. "How long have you and this agent been working the case?"

"I've been on it about a year. The undercover guy has been deep for about five years now, working his way up through the organization, but it has only been recently that he could supply me with enough information to make a convincing case. But now, he has gone deeper, and I'm unable to make contact without compromising his cover," he stated. "Dave, the case that got your dad killed may also be linked to this."

"How so?" Dave asked.

"Okay, listen carefully," the director said and then went on to explain what he knew of the organization, information that he had pieced together over the past years and what had been recently supplied to him by his deep agent. "See what I mean?"

"Yeah. I just find it hard to believe. Where do I fit in?" Dave asked.

"Okay, first, you go to Tampa and talk to that kid again. And you may want to tell him about his father and why he was killed. Then when you get done, get with me as soon as you are back. By then, I should have some more information and a plan of action outlined," he concluded.

Andros Air Force Base, Bahamas
Flight Operations
May 3, 1996
0830 Hours, EST

"Captain Phillips, yes, sir, your aircraft has been pulled in the hangar for repair. It should be done in about a week."

"Repair, I didn't authorize any repair work!" Max stated.

"Sorry, sir. Someone dropped off your logbook last night with a lot of redlines in it, with your signature. With one big redline about sucking up a bird in your right engine and requiring immediate tear-down and inspection," the airman behind the counter said.

"I need that aircraft ready to fly at a moment's notice. I didn't redline anything in the log. That plane just came out of a major overhaul three weeks ago. Who was on duty last night?"

"Ensign Smith, but he was only doing what he was directed by you and your log."

"Maybe they haven't started?"

"Sorry, sir, they tore into it last night and your engine is all over the hangar by now. Could be ready by day after tomorrow, if they hustle and don't need any parts that have to be brought over from the States."

"I guess there are no aircraft available for me to use, if I'm called to fly out of here?" Max Phillips asked, becoming slightly irate.

"No, sir, there is only the admiral's King Air. But the only way you will get that is with his permission, or steal it. And figuring the odds of that, it stays in the hangar until he wants it. So walking in and taking it would not be an easy task either. I guess you're stuck, sir. Sorry. You could try the flying club in hangar 1403. They may have a rental, not quite what you are used to, but flyable," the young airman said, trying not to be too sarcastic. He was talking to a captain in the Navy, and he was only a little airman in the Air Force. Proper respect is supposed to cross between the services. The Navy and Air Force did share this airfield and the services it provided, and it was not uncommon to have Navy F-14 Tomcats sitting right next to the Air Forces F-15 Eagles. Even in the lounges, you might see the two rival forces sitting and having a drink together as if there were no differences or rivalries. Down in the islands, one tended to forget those old college days with the Navy against the Air Force. Down in the islands, all they knew was it was another day in paradise.

"I guess speaking to your commander won't change a thing, will it?" Phillips questioned, getting angrier as time passed.

"No, sir. He will be in around noon, if you want to talk to him. But your bird is in pieces, the repair was at your request, and there isn't much we can do about that now. I'm sorry about the screwup, but it happens sometimes. We will get her back together as fast as we can, sir. But keep in mind, if they find anything wrong that requires parts that we do not have on hand, well, that might delay the process, sir," the airman said, trying to calm down this commander. He realized he had been a little too flippant with him and decided to straighten his act out before he really got him angry.

"Right!" Max said as he turned and left flight operations. On his way to his rental car, he stopped at the hangar to check on his jet. The airman was right; the engine was off and was in the process of being torn down.

Holiday Inn Resort Hotel
May 3, 1996
1230 Hours, EST

"We have a small problem, Davin. Someone ordered our airplane to be repaired, and it's going to take three, maybe four, days to do it," Max said as he met Davin in the lobby of the hotel.

"Damn, how did they know we were here?" Davin said, not expecting an answer. "Can we get another plane?"

"Nothing military, maybe the flying club on base. I'll check after lunch," Max answered as he and Davin entered the coffee shop to meet the girls for a late lunch. "By the way, how was the diving this morning?"

"Great! The visibility was hundred plus, and the reefs were super. Critters galore, nurse sharks, barracuda, sergeant majors, saw a couple large morays!" Connie said without hesitation, obviously excited about the morning dives.

"Yeah, wish you could have seen it," Sonya replied between sips on her ice tea. "I haven't seen that many fish in a long time."

"Well, ladies, we have a small problem," Max broke in and then went on to explain about the aircraft being overhauled.

"What happens if JD tries to reach us and we are stuck?" Connie asked, forgetting that she wasn't supposed to say anything around Sonja about why they were in the Bahamas.

"We just sit and wait and hope the plane is ready when we need it," Davin said.

"Who is JD?" Sonja asked.

"JD, oh, he's a friend that asked us to come down here to join him in a little party on his private island. The only trouble is, he just said to wait here at the Holiday Inn until he called. Something about a scavenger hunt and he would give us the clue we needed if we waited here," Davin said, telling an obvious lie.

"Do you really expect me to believe that lame story?" Sonja asked. "What do you take me for, a dumb blonde?" she continued, showing not just a little but a lot of anger.

"No, but for right now, that is the only story you need to know," Davin said in a very serious tone, looking straight at her. "Sorry, we cannot tell you what is going on, but I hope you understand. It is for your own safety."

"No, I don't understand," Sonja replied, getting angry.

"Davin, that wasn't very nice!" Connie said, defending Sonja.

"The world isn't a nice place, and sometimes we have to set a few ground rules, the first being not to tell the world your business. The second, be kind to dumb animals," Davin said and then continued. "Sonja, keeping you in the dark is for your own safety. We are up against some very nasty people. Just hang in there. Soon we will tell you the whole story."

"Okay, I will hold you to that," Sonja replied, cooling down a little.

"I hope so," Davin said and then took a big gulp from his drink.

It was quiet for about twenty minutes while everyone thought about what was happening and ate some lunch.

"Davin, what's the next move?" Connie asked to break the silence.

"We wait and see what happens," Davin answered as he carefully looked at Max Phillips and Sonja MacGuire. He knew Max was okay but still wasn't sure about Sonja. Time would tell.

USS Wolverine
May 3, 1996
1030 Hours, EST

"Captain, did the *Nimitz* say if they had any warships in this area?" asked the sonar operator.

"No. Why?" JD asked with a little concern.

"Well, if I am not mistaken, we have a surface contact bearing two-eight-niner degrees, and he has his active sonar on and is searching for something, possibly us."

"Range?" JD asked, hoping they were not the target but sure they were. "I thought we lost that one."

"About sixty thousand yards, sir, and closing fast," was the reply. "Can't tell if it is the same guy."

"Helm, left to one-niner-zero, speed five knots, rig for silent running," JD ordered and then quickly scanned the control room for any problems. Seeing none, except for the concerned faces, he turned his attention to sonar again.

"Left to one-niner-zero, speed five knots, aye, sir," Micky replied, controlling the boat like she had been doing it for years.

"Sonar, keep me posted on our friend," JD said. He then turned and walked over to the chart table.

"What do you think, friend or foe?" Batman asked as they both looked over the charts for places to hide.

"At this point, they are all bad guys, but we will not fire on any ship unless we are damn positive it's the only way to survive."

"That doesn't need to be said, but we need to get to that cave and fast," Carpenter said, acting a little scared.

"Doesn't Patrick Air Force Base in Florida have the new P3 Orion?" Micky asked to no one in particular.

"Yes, they do, and they are probably already in the air and looking for us. And this boat should be easy to identify because of the signature she puts out, unlike the newer boats, which have all been ID'd already. If we move, they may be able to track us. I'm surprised the Navy doesn't already have a signature on her and did something about it years ago. Unless, maybe they had orders to leave her alone,"

JD speculated, still looking at the chart for hiding places along their route.

"Damn, you're not saying that the Navy sanctioned this pirate ship?" Batman questioned, looking hard at JD.

"Maybe someone, some of the someones listed on that document, may have been supplying this boat for years, right under the Navy's nose. And maybe even using unsuspecting Navy personnel to do their dirty work," JD continued to speculate. "You pointed out that most of the gear on this boat has US Navy ID tags on them."

"This is getting too hard to swallow, guys. Who has enough power to pull that off, and for fifty years no less?" Micky questioned, glancing back over her shoulder at JD and Batman.

"We know who, from the previous captain's confession. That list he has provided us has enough power on it to alter history," Batman commented.

"All the more reason to get to that cave and then back to Washington to expose them," JD said.

"They have us, sir!" yelled Sonar.

"Scotty, how deep can we take her?" JD asked over the intercom to the engine room.

"I wouldn't push more than three hundred feet, sir," was Scotty's reply.

"Right, take her to three hundred and level. That's still not out of range, but maybe we can fool them," JD ordered.

"Aye, sir, just passing one-niner-zero feet!" Batman yelled as the boat dived toward three hundred feet and the unknown. They were not real sure if this old boat could handle the pressure at three hundred feet or more anymore. They could be diving their last dive. Even if the pressure did not crush the boat, could Scotty get her back to the surface?

"Range?" JD yelled at the Sonar operator.

"Forty thousand yards, sir, closing," Sonar replied without lifting his head from the scope.

"Right, two-six-zero degrees, all stop," JD ordered. "Find us a thermocline, Batman."

"Right, two-six-zero, all stop. Aye," Micky echoed.

"Depth?"

"Level three hundred feet, sir," Batman answered, almost whispering, just loud enough for JD to hear and not so his voice would travel through the hull and be picked up by the supersensitive electronic sonar on board the surface ship. "Thermo at two hundred feet. We are below it now."

Once the boat went to silent running, that also meant to speak in whispers, or not speak at all. No noise was to be generated by anyone on board. Dead quiet or dead *dead*.

"How much below us?" JD asked quietly.

"Plenty of room, two thousand feet, sir," Batman replied, barely above a whisper.

"Sonar, target?" JD asked as he walked over to the sonar control station.

"Zigzaggin', sir, wait…turning to two-eight-zero, fifteen knots and accelerating…seventeen…nineteen…twenty-one knots and holding, sir, heading now two-niner-five. He may have lost us," Sonar replied in a whisper, sweats pouring off his brow, dripping on the sonar scope. He continually had to wipe it off to be able to read it.

"We stay put until he is out of range, then head one-niner-zero, seven knots, level two-five-oh," JD ordered as he turned and headed back to the chart table.

"Aye, sir, just give the word," Micky responded, not taking her eyes off her collection of gauges.

"Turning, sir, target heading two-four-five. Looks like he's starting another search pattern," Sonar said in a whisper.

"Damn, persistent SOB," Batman said, shaking his head. "Maybe here!" He pointed to a spot on the chart. "No, here, in this deep trench. The bottom comes up to five hundred feet, then drops in the trench. We could hide just above it. Should have a nice thermocline to cover us for a while, anyway."

"Maintain position," JD replied. "That is a possibility. Keep it in mind. We may need it."

Three hours later, the surface ship finally gave up and turned to a new heading of 0-5-5 z-f-fidegrees and proceeded out of the area.

JD held his position for an additional hour before he ordered his boat to turn and take the new heading and depth. He ordered dead slow. The surface ship was just out of range of the sonar on board the *Wolverine* but had left a trail of sonar buoys to alert him if any activity should start in the search area.

"Captain, we have a surface contact bearing three-four-five and closing, twenty three knots. I don't think he left. Must have left a few of his markers!" Sonar yelled. Considering the noise the boat was making, his yell would not travel far.

"Damn, he must have left some sonar buoys and we just fell into his trap," JD cursed. "Batman, heading for that trench?"

Looking around the control room, JD decided to take a calculated risk with this old boat and his new crew. He really didn't have a lot of choice if they were to survive.

"One-eight-zero," Batman responded immediately, his voice cracking weakly.

"Take her down to three-five-zero feet, heading one-eight-zero, flank speed," JD ordered. "Scotty, keep a sharp eye on our condition. We may have to push her to the limit!" he yelled into the intercom to the engine room. "Let's get way under that thermo."

Then he turned to Batman, seeing him gripping the chart table as hard as he could, trying to maintain balance.

"You okay, Batman?" JD asked as he put a hand on Batman's shoulder to steady him.

"Not really," Batman replied as his knees gave out and he slumped down to the deck.

"Get the medic up here on the double!" JD yelled.

He eased Batman down to the deck as Kelly called over the intercom for the medic. Then she rushed over to him.

Minutes later, the medic was at his side.

"Help me get him to the showers. He's suffering from heat exhaustion. Get some water—he needs fluids!" the medic ordered.

Ten minutes later, Batman was sitting in the shower, partially dressed, with cold water pouring over him. He had consumed a gallon of water and was right now working on his fourth large bucket of cool water.

"Damn! What happened, Doc?" Batman finally asked after taking a big drink.

"The heat in this tub got to you. It's about 106 in here, and on top of what has already happened to you, I'm not surprised," the medic said.

"What about Carp?" Batman asked.

"He's in the next stall, cooling down. He isn't as bad as you, my friend," the medic replied.

Chapter 22

WHEN TROUBLE COMES KNOCKING

Holiday Inn Resort
Andros Island
May 3, 1996
1300 Hours, EST

"Excuse me, are you Captain Max Phillips and Ensign Sonya McGuire?" the two shore patrolmen asked as they entered the coffee shop.

"Yes, we are. Can we help you?" Phillips responded without looking up from his coffee.

"We have to ask you to come with us, sir," the largest of the two responded. He was an ensign wearing a pistol on his hip and looked like he could handle almost any situation without ever using his pistol. His partner was also wearing a pistol and carried a large nightstick, like the ones you see in the movies, used for hitting people over the head and getting someone's attention real fast.

"May I ask why and where you are planning on taking us?" Phillips asked, obviously showing displeasure in being rudely disturbed.

"Sir, I have orders to escort the two of you to Commander Garrett's office. I do not know why, sir," the young ensign replied, sounding a bit nervous at addressing a senior officer in the manner in which he was ordered to do.

"Who is Commander Garrett?" Davin asked, directing his question at the young ensign.

"Sir, Commander Garrett is head of base security, sir," was the reply. "Sir, I'm just following orders. Commander Garrett would like to speak to you, and he said it was urgent and ordered me to find you and escort you to him."

"Ensign, I understand your position. Now, understand mine. You can tell Commander Garrett that I got his message and will call him later today to set an appointment to see him," Phillips said, becoming a little irate. "Tell him that using force is not my idea of a request and I will respond to his request at my earliest convenience. Got the message?"

"Yes, sir," the ensign replied.

"Now, before you go, did he tell you to use force if I resisted?" Phillips asked.

"But, sir, you don't understand, he said to bring you with me now. And yes, he said to use force if we had to," the young ensign said, becoming a little flushed. He did not want to use force on a senior officer, but orders were orders.

"Ensign, tell your commander that I decline his rude invitation and will call him later, unless you are arresting us."

"I will relate your response, sir," the young ensign replied and turned to leave. He stopped in the doorway and turned back to face Captain Phillips.

"Sir, I was ordered to bring you in, but I don't have any charges to arrest you on. So can we compromise here before I leave?" The ensign, being an intelligent young man and not wanting to kill his career before it really got started, decided to talk to Phillips and work a deal.

"What do you have on your mind?" Phillips asked, impressed with the young ensign not backing down so easily.

"Well, sir, I got off on the wrong foot when we came in here. I would like to apologize for my rudeness and wish to make amends of this whole affair," he continued, looking Phillips in the eye.

"Go on, you have my attention. And I accept your apology," Phillips said, thinking he'd also been young and foolish many years ago.

"Sir, if I call Commander Garrett right now, when would be the best time that you and he could meet and discuss whatever is so important that caused him to send me down here to interrupt your lunch?" The young ensign was good, and this impressed Phillips.

"Tell him I'll be at his office at 1400 hours, sharp, today, Ensign," Phillips said.

"Thank you, sir. And have a good day, sir," the ensign said, saluted, and left.

After the young ensign and his gorilla left, Davin looked over at Sonya and, without really saying anything, got a very scared look in return.

"What do you think ole Garrett wants?" Max Phillips asked to no one in particular but looking at Sonya also.

"Why is everyone looking at me?" Sonya demanded, turning red as she attempted to hide her embarrassment.

"Oh, nothing, except you looked like you were going to have a chicken right there when those two came in," Davin said with a little laugh.

"How did you expect me to look when threatened to be escorted to the head of base security for some unknown reason?" Sonja replied in her defense.

"About the way you looked. Let's get out of here," Davin said as he stood up to leave.

"Right," Max replied, standing and picking up the check and walking over to the cashier.

USS Wolverine
May 3, 1996
1900 Hours, EST

"Range?" JD asked as they cruised, hopefully away from the enemy above.

"Fifty thousand yards, heading two-zero-five, intercept course. They are good," the sonar operator answered.

"Damn. Depth, heading?"

"Three hundred fifty feet, heading one-eight-four, sir," Kelly replied and noticed they were deeper than Scotty recommended, yet still alive.

The tension was high. This was the second time in two days that they had been in a cat-and-mouse game that wasn't a game. Were the warships above playing for real with all the intentions in the world to track down and destroy the *Wolverine*, or were they just playing?

"Where's that thermocline? We need it now," JD ordered, then looked over at Micky and lost track of his thoughts for a moment.

"Aye, sir," Carpenter and Batman said together as they re-entered the control room. Soaking wet and dripping on the deck, each carried a large container of liquid, which they sipped on constantly. Both had a wet cloth tied around their foreheads and didn't look good but were functioning extremely well.

Batman turned to his panel, which had been updated with the newest gauges, temperature probes, and everything a well-equipped nuclear submarine had. He was surprised to discover the state-of-the-art equipment on a fifty-year-old boat. But with all the other surprises they had been confronted with, this was just a little benefit. If all of it just worked as designed.

"Forty thousand yards, heading two-zero-zero, speed fifteen knots, closing!" the sonar operator yelled. The sonar he was operating was also state-of-the-art, built by Honeywell in 1989, color display, better sensitivity, and longer range. Even with this new, state-of-the-art equipment, he had not been able to accurately identify their friends above yet.

"Distance to the island?" JD asked.

"Four hundred sixty miles," Carpenter replied, measuring the distance again on the chart.

"We need a thermocline," JD said to himself.

"Right, forty degrees. Got a weak indication of a temperature difference," Batman finally said.

"Go, Micky, right, forty degrees," JD ordered.

Turning rapidly, they headed for the suspected thermocline, with hopes of outsmarting their unwanted visitor.

"What's it look like, Batman?" JD asked again.

"Real good so far. Take her down fifty feet," Batman started, then paused. Thinking they were already at 350 feet, this would really be pushing her, maybe too far. "Ignore that last order."

Three minutes passed before another word was said by anyone. The tension was growing.

"Target, twenty-five thousand yards and turning to...he's starting to zigzag...wait...a...minute. Maybe...," Carpenter reported. "Target Identification, two US-made destroyers. Definitely US! Not the same as yesterday's. These guys are teaming up on us, and they are damn good!"

"All stop!" JD ordered and then looked back at sonar.

The boat came to a stop, and all was silent for the next fifteen minutes. Level at 350 feet, they sat and waited. The thermocline was just above them, masking their position. Hopefully, the two ships would not be able to see through to find them.

"What's he doing?" JD asked quietly.

"Still zigging. I think they lost us. Yeah, they are turning north and turning on the steam," Carpenter answered quietly.

"All right! Heading two-one-zero, dead slow, as soon as he is off the scope," JD ordered, standing in a pool of sweat. The air-conditioning had been turned off since it generated a lot of noise that would travel great distances underwater.

"Aye, aye, sir, just give the word, Carp," Micky answered, just barely above a whisper. The heat and tension for the past ten hours was showing on everyone.

"Engine Room, this is Bridge. How are we doing back there?" JD asked over the intercom.

"Engine Room. A few leaks, but we're holding together for now. Just don't take us into any rough water or combat," Scotty replied.

"Right!" JD said, then turned to the bridge crew. "We are not out of the woods yet. Keep on your toes. Target status?"

"Just now leaving the scope," Carpenter replied, leaning over the sonar operator's shoulder to watch the targets. He took a big drink, then turned back to walk over to the chart table, still a little shaky on his feet.

"The thermocline is running about 250 feet. If we can stay under it, then just maybe, we can beat those sonar buoys he dropped," Batman commented. "And can we get that air back on? It is getting a bit warm down here," he said, looking at the temperature gauge, showing 115 degrees Fahrenheit. No wonder he had collapsed; this heat could take almost anyone down.

"Okay, change heading to two-zero-zero, maintain three-five-zero feet, and dead slow. I don't want to take any chances," JD ordered, looking around at his crew. They'd been through a lot in the past couple of days and came through it well. He would put everyone in for a Bronze Star when they got home, if they survived the trip.

The next four hours were not as hard on the crew. They didn't go very far, but they also did not have the unwanted surface ship show up again. After the first four hours, JD ordered the boat to five knots but maintained depth and heading, hoping to remain under the thermocline as long as possible. The change in water density due to the change in temperature would deflect the sonar pulses from the surface ship. Unless it had variable-depth sonar to avoid this problem, they would not be able to track the submarine effectively. At the end of four hours, JD felt reasonably sure they were safe and had the air turned on. By now the air was very stale, and the temperature had reached 122 degrees inside.

Washington, DC
May 3, 1996
1730 Hours, EST

"Admiral Jacobs, we had a report from Soviet Embassy that one of their destroyers en route to the *Nimitz* carrier group had encountered an unidentified submarine heading southwest away from the *Nimitz*," the admiral's aide reported.

"Heading away from the *Nimitz*? What did the Soviet destroyer do?" Jacobs asked.

"According to the message, and I quote, 'While en route to join the *Nimitz* battle group for support of Operation Jungle Storm, the destroyer came across an unidentified submarine on the surface. Turning to investigate, the submarine immediately submerged and an eight-hour cat-and-mouse game followed. The destroyer thought the sub was part of some special operations, as it did not display a signature known to his sonar operator, so they played along until notified by the *Nimitz* that the sub was not to be messed with. The sub was an American problem, the *Nimitz* said, and they would handle it as soon as the storm broke that blocked his ship's direct passage to her. And he should break off his pursuit and proceed to the battle group as ordered," the aide finished as the admiral lit another Cuban cigar.

"The *Nimitz* knows that the sub is to be destroyed, yet he ordered the Soviets to back off," Admiral Jacobs commented.

"He did say that the sub is a United States problem, and if the Soviets sank her, that might cause an international incident," the aide replied.

"Yeah, maybe you're right. What's the *Nimitz* doing now?" asked the admiral, taking a long pull on his cigar.

"At last contact, she had an aircraft crashed on the deck, and severe weather prevented them from clearing the deck and launching search aircraft. The storm is between them and the sub. The Soviet destroyer is making a wide turn around the storm also."

"Damn, we may lose them!" the admiral cursed, knowing there is no way they could. He did not know that Admiral Feldings had two destroyers shadowing them.

"Patrick Air Force Base and Homestead Air Force Base have launched P3 Orions to search the area, but no luck yet. The storm is east of them but growing into what may be an early summer hurricane. Satellite coverage is limited due to the storm, and if they should submerge, well, it is difficult at best."

"Keep me posted of all traffic on that sub," Jacobs ordered.

"Aye, aye, sir," the aide said as he turned and left the admiral's office.

"Get me the latest satellite photos as soon as you can," Jacobs ordered.

"The next pass is in two hours, sir. I'll have them to you within fifteen minutes of our receipt. Will there be anything else, sir?"

"No, that's all. Dismissed," Jacobs said and turned his attention to a stack of messages on his desk.

Chapter 23

RETURN TO THE NEST

Admiral Jacobs' Office
May 4, 1991
1035 Hours, EST

"Listen, Senator, we have not stopped them yet. I've alerted the island to be on the lookout in case they found the captain's log and are heading there. They are to move what they can and destroy the rest if they get too close. This operation is coming very close to closing time. If my damn brother hadn't...well," Jacobs was saying when interrupted, not knowing his brother did not go against the organization until death was at hand.

"Yeah, if your brother hadn't decided to do some freelancing and taken our boat, we wouldn't be in this fix now, would we?" the senator said coldly.

"Okay, so it's my brother's fault. But now that it's started, we have to stop it, right?" Jacobs asked and then continued without waiting for a reply. "Okay, Nigeria is quiet now, and the *Nimitz* group has a major storm between them and the last-known location of that damn sub. The Coast Guard is on alert, and so is the entire East Coast. If they surface anywhere, we will be waiting for them and send them to the bottom with all the evidence they have."

"No survivors, right?" the senator demanded.

"Right! No survivors!" Jacobs agreed.

"What about that Phillips and Pierce group on Andros?" the senator asked.

"No problem. They have been delayed and are just about to have some more problems. Phillips is going to be ordered back to Washington," Jacobs stated.

"For what?" the senator asked.

"It seems our good commander has become AWOL, absent without leave," Jacobs said. "I had Phillips's leave request canceled and some false orders typed up, ordering him to duty in Seattle, Washington, for a special survival course. Of course, he did not know about these orders, and now he is AWOL from the course."

"Real good. Maybe that might just put a real damper on his plans," the senator said, thinking about what was going on with the organization. "Is your information reliable, Admiral?"

"The best! I have planted one of my own pilots with Captain Phillips. His regular copilot had to take emergency leave, so I was able to slip in another. Without him suspecting a thing, he took her on."

"Her? Did you say *her*?" the senator bellowed.

"Yes, Senator, I said *her*. She doesn't know a thing about the organization. I instructed her to call me at least every other day, but daily if she could," Jacobs replied.

"A woman. Can we trust her?" the senator asked, still not quite sure about the admiral's informant. He did not believe in equality among women.

"Yes, Senator. We can trust her. As I said, she doesn't know about the organization. She thinks she is helping me help them."

"Good. The fewer people that know about the organization, the better," the senator commented.

"Yes, Senator," Jacobs replied. Jacobs did not like the senator; he just tolerated him. The man was a glory hound, and it showed in everything he did.

"Is Jack Malone's death going to cause problems?" the senator asked.

"No. His assignment with the FBI has been trash-canned as a nonrecoverable. All suspects are dead, and his link with us died with him. Too bad too. He was a good man," Jacobs said.

"Okay, one last thing. We had a report from a P3 Orion that she had contact with the sub but was near the end of her flight time and could not stay on to track her. Her course indicated she was heading straight for our nest. We do have satellite tracking, but that is slow once it gets back to earth, too much paperwork to keep up with," Jacobs commented as he lit a fresh Cuban cigar.

"Just sink her and do it fast. It's not just our lives that are at stake now, Jacobs. We have a lot of power on the payroll, and you have the power and the resources to finish the job. Don't fail now, or we all fail." The senator was firm. "And quit screwing around with diversions. Eliminate Phillips as soon as he arrives in Washington." He hung up his phone without letting Jacobs say another word.

Jacobs hung up and switched off the secure encryption device located under the telephone. Once he was satisfied the device was off, he closed and locked the cabinet door. Jacobs used the system to help him run his part of the organization. Whatever it was, if he needed it for the organization, he took it and used it, whether it was equipment, such as the secure telephone system, men and women of the armed forces, or a Navy destroyer. He had ordered the entire United States Navy to search for and destroy the USS *Wolverine*. The senator was very concerned. His whole career, lifestyle, and very life depended on Jacobs doing his job.

After ten minutes, Admiral Jacobs stood and walked over to a file cabinet in the corner of his office. With the key he removed from his pocket, he unlocked the cabinet and retrieved a bottle of expensive brandy from the top drawer. He didn't like to drink alone, but today was an exception. His life and the lifestyle he had become accustomed to was coming to an end. He had to ensure their safety by sinking that submarine before she reached land. He had warned their island in the Bahamas, but he knew that might not be enough. The fortifications there were not designed to stop a major attack, and there were not enough men on the island to defend it.

After pouring himself a drink, Admiral Jacobs returned the bottle to the top drawer and locked the cabinet. He walked over to his desk and sat, chewing on his cigar and thinking, thinking of some way to stop that sub and its crew. He tried not to think of what had happened in Nigeria, a war that he and his organization were part of. It was over, but a lot of innocent people died because of him, and a lot more might die real soon.

USS Wolverine
May 4, 1991
1345 Hours
One Day from Marsh Harbor, Bahamas

"Air contact, sir, bearing one-three-zero degrees and closing!" the radar operator yelled.

"Clear the bridge, prepare to dive, RANGE!" JD yelled.

"Sixty miles, sir, and closing fast. Altitude two hundred feet. They have us on their scope!"

"DIVE, DIVE! RIG FOR SILENT RUNNING, TAKE HER TO 350 FEET!" JD ordered.

Normally during a crash dive, each member of the crew had a specific job to do, and if it was not done properly, it could cost the lives of everyone on board. Each submarine crew was trained and ran drill after drill to ensure there was not a hatch left open, a watertight door not sealed, or a valve left open when it was supposed to be closed or closed if it was supposed to be opened. Each man on board knew his job and would perform it without a problem, cross-checking everyone else's job for safety.

On this fifty-year-old boat, the crew was made of many types of sailors, mostly from surface ships; some of them didn't know anything about how a submarine operated until a very few days ago. Only six ever served on a submarine, and those six had served only on new nuclear-powered boats, not a diesel boat that was built before anyone of them was born.

Tension was at the boiling point. This was the third time they had been forced to dive to evade an enemy. The interior temperature of the boat was still over one hundred degrees. Even running on the surface and pumping in fresh air, the boat had remained hot. The air conditioner had worked, but not well, and the midday sun had borne down with the heat of a million candles. JD had done what he could by allowing the crew to come up on deck to get some fresh air. It had been dangerous to run on the surface during the day, but they had had to charge the batteries; otherwise, they might not be able to surface when they wanted to. As it was, they were running on half of the required batteries for this size boat. Some were not recharging as they should, and others had been damaged when two exploded several days earlier.

Diving again was risky; every time they dived, something else went wrong. Scotty was doing his best, but time was catching up to the *Wolverine* and even Scotty couldn't second-guess the effects of time.

"Level three-five-zero, sir," Micky finally said as the boat leveled off at the assigned depth. Sweat poured in her eyes and dripped down on her already-soaked T-shirt. Sweaty hands made it difficult to hold the steering console. The temperature was not climbing as they dived, but the humidity was climbing. The air on board had turned stale within minutes of diving.

"All stop!" JD ordered while scanning the control room for potential problems.

"All stop!" was the reply, and then there was silence throughout the entire boat.

He wiped the sweat from his forehead and prayed for some cloud cover. They could make better time on the surface. Running submerged forced them to run at no more than six knots, pushing the boat to the limit. On the surface, they could cruise at least eleven, seas permitting.

It would be hours before the sun would set and the opportunity to surface again. They had gambled on a surface run and lost; now they were back underwater and waiting. After sitting silently for about two hours, JD ordered the boat to a new heading and sped toward Marsh Harbor.

They had not moved more than four hundred yards when a massive explosion rocked the boat. Crew members were thrown to the deck. Several were seriously injured. Lights flickered, pipes broke, gauges cracked. The boat dived out of control. Water was rushing in from cracked pipes. Confusion was the order on deck.

"Scotty, what the hell happened?" JD yelled into the intercom as soon as he picked himself off the deck. Before Scotty could reply, another explosion rocked the boat. JD knew then what was happening. They were under attack from the air. Depth charges were being dropped, accurately.

"Take her deep! Level four hundred!" JD ordered. "Shut down all systems, NOW! Make us silent!" Blood was running down his check from the cut over his left eye, but he didn't notice.

Micky was unconscious on the deck. Carpenter managed to get to the dive console and put the boat into a steep controlled dive.

The engine room crew fought to maintain power and stop the leaks at the same time. In the forward torpedo room, one seaman was killed when a pressure valve exploded beside his head. The ship was severely damaged and heading down.

"All stop!" Carpenter yelled over the confusion.

Silence, no more explosions. Maybe they had left or at least thought they had a victory.

On board the US Navy patrol bomber, the crew was watching the growing oil slick near the spot where the two depth charges exploded. They were sure the *Wolverine* was destroyed but waited to see if she would surface or just sink to the bottom.

Twenty-five minutes later, seeing some wreckage, wooden deck planks, and more oil in the ever-growing slick, they turned and headed home.

"Skipper, Engine Room!" Scotty yelled into the intercom.

"Go!" JD responded immediately.

"We have some major damage. We need to surface real soon," Scotty said. "Losing oil pressure in the hydraulics. We're hurt bad, sir."

"Damn, okay. Prepare to surface!" JD ordered. "Medic to the Control Room."

"Skipper, the medic is dead," the intercom crackled.

"Take us up, Carp," JD said quietly as he scanned the control room. "Damage report, all sections."

Minutes later, each section reported in. They had three dead, a dozen injured, cuts, bruises, no broken bones, and two still unconscious. The boat had survived but was leaking hydraulic fluid, which meant if they did not stop it, they would lose all control of the rudder and dive planes.

Surfacing meant they might die at the hands of the aircraft that injured them, which might still be flying overhead. But staying submerged meant certain death.

Thirty minutes later, the *Wolverine* was on the surface and all members of the crew that were not directly involved in repairing the boat were sitting on deck. The *Wolverine* was dead in the water. Only a small generator was running to provide lights for repairs and to operate the radar.

They were lucky the aircraft that had attacked had left, thinking he was victorious. Good, let them think they were successful; maybe the hunt would be called off.

Two hours before sunset and the cover of darkness, Scotty and his teams worked as fast as they could. Micky and the other unconscious crew recovered shortly after sundown with severe headaches, but otherwise, no damage.

During the night, JD had sent a message over the amateur radio bands to a ham operator in the States with instructions to call Davin Pierce's office and relay the message to Davin in the Bahamas. If successful, Davin and group would be waiting in the Hilltop Restaurant and Bar when the *Wolverine* arrived.

It was estimated that cruising at four knots would enable the *Wolverine* to make Marsh Harbor by early evening the next day. Once they arrived at the island, the plan was to surface and launch a small rubber raft, which they would paddle to shore, since there was not an outboard motor for the raft. The *Wolverine* would then sail out about two miles, staying out of the shipping lanes. She would sit and wait on the surface till 2300 hours. At that time, she would return to the spot where she let the raft go and pick up her passengers at midnight.

As the hours dragged on, while waiting for the repairs to be completed, each member of the crew was given time to sleep and refresh in the shower. Fresh water was limited on a submarine, so the showers were short but refreshing. There was no hot water on board. All showers were cold, which ensured they would be short. Fresh clothes were also limited to what the previous crew had left. These items were passed around to those who wanted to change.

After their break and showers, Kelly and Micky returned to the control room, wearing very baggy shorts cut from long slacks, and short-sleeve button shirts that were tied at the waist. Each had a handkerchief tied around their necks and one on their foreheads.

In the early hours of the morning, Scotty and his crew completed the repairs and the boat was moving again.

USS Normandy and Reagan
May 4, 1996
1400 Hours, EST

"Message coming in, sir, from ComNavPac, Washington. It's encrypted, sir. I'll have it deciphered in a moment!" the radio operator informed the captain of the *Reagan*. The USS *Ronald Reagan* was the newest destroyer in the fleet, named after former president Ronald Reagan. It was felt that naming a destroyer after Reagan was appropriate, because a destroyer was fast and didn't take any crap from anyone. She was equipped with the latest in electronic warfare equipment, sonar, and weapons that would put a World War II battleship to shame.

Moments later, the radio operator handed Captain MacIntyre the message that informed him of the last known position and heading of the *Wolverine*. Then it added that the possible destination was Treasure Island down at the lower end of the Bahamas. An update would follow soon.

"New heading of two-zero-zero degrees, full speed ahead!" Captain MacIntyre ordered, figuring that he would just meet the sub at the other end instead of trying to follow. Along with satellite imagery provided by some of the latest in high technology, when the clouds allowed the satellites to see, the *Reagan* did not need to follow. Besides, Captain MacIntyre did not want to sink the *Wolverine*. He was there to assist in her efforts to discover the source of the corruption.

"Aye, aye, sir, heading two-zero-zero, full!" the helmsman replied.

"Radio, signal the *Normandy* of our new course and destination," Captain MacIntyre said to the radio operator. He reached over and retrieved a pair of binoculars to scan the horizon. Then he turned to look at the *Normandy* cruising two hundred yards west of them. The sea was calm and sky clear; it was a beautiful day to be at sea.

"Aye, sir," responded the helmsman.

Something strange about this mission, MacIntyre thought. *A rogue World War II Gato-class submarine that was supposed to be a pirate ship and commanded by my old buddy JD Henderson. Feldings ordered us to follow and assist in whatever or wherever the sub went. But going against an order from the Pentagon. Damn, I hope Feldings knows what he is doing. That explanation we got is still a bit weak. It just seems strange to ignore an order.*

"Sir, this message just came in." The seaman handed him the folded paper.

Captain MacIntyre read quietly.

"Did the *Normandy* get this?" MacIntyre asked.

"No, sir."

"Retrans to them. Also tell them we will continue to Treasure Island, their possible destination. I don't believe she is destroyed. Henderson is too good to lose that easily."

"Aye, sir," the young seaman responded, then turned and departed.

Andros Island
Office of Commander Garrett
May 4, 1996
1400 Hours, EST

"Sorry about my overzealous ensign, Captain Phillips, but we had been looking all over the island for the two of you," Commander Garrett said after Phillips and Sonya reported in that afternoon. "He was following orders, though. I wish you had come with him, Captain."

"Excuse me, Commander, but let's cut out the niceties and get right to the point of this meeting," Phillips demanded, still a bit irritated over the whole affair.

"Easy does it, Captain. This was not meant to be a hostile meeting, but we needed to locate you immediately. It seems someone high up in the chain wants the two of you to report back to Washington ASAP. Some screwup about you being AWOL from a survival course in Seattle. They wanted me to arrest you, but after a lengthy talk with some friends of mine in the security group at the Pentagon, they said to have you and MacGuire fly back to Washington immediately and they would handle the problem. My connection said it looked like an oversight and you never received your orders. We unfortunately do not have transportation for you, and I understand your Gulfstream is down for maintenance. Am I correct on that count?" He received a nod acknowledging the affirmative. "That does pose a problem, getting you out of here quickly," he continued and then leaned back to take a better position to think.

"Who requires us to return?" Phillips asked, looking at Garrett's face to see if he lied. Lack of eye contact might indicate an untrue statement.

Garrett started, "An Admiral Jacobs, head of—"

But he was unable to finish his sentence as Phillips interrupted, maintaining eye contact.

"Jacobs, yeah, we know who he is, but what is his concern in this matter?" Pausing briefly, Phillips turned to Sonja and asked,

"Do you have any idea why Jacobs might want us to rush back to Washington?"

"No, I've only met him once. He seems pretty nice," Sonja answered, wondering herself why Jacobs would want Phillips to return to Washington. She thought he was helping them, not trying to stop Phillips and Davin.

"Garrett, what do you know about what Jacobs is up to?" Phillips asked.

"Nothing, except what he, or rather, they, said in the message. Just that I was to arrest you and escort you back to Washington," Garrett said, shuffling papers on his desk in an attempt to locate the message.

"Will somebody tell me what is going on?" Sonja asked, very confused about Phillips and Jacobs and the conflicting information she had been receiving.

"I'll explain later," Phillips said and then turned his attention back to Commander Garrett. "Commander, how much pull do you have with aircraft maintenance?"

"Some. Why?" he said, questioning the sudden change in Phillips's attitude.

"Can you get my bird back together by noon tomorrow?" he asked.

"I'll give it a try, Phillips. Standby one and we shall see." Garrett picked up the phone and asked his secretary to call the hangar where the Gulfstream was parked.

After a couple of very silent minutes, the phone rang. Garrett picked up the receiver and spoke quickly and quietly, so Phillips was unable to hear all of the conversation.

"Okay, Chief, sounds great. Phillips will be by at 1100 hours to check out the work and sign for his aircraft. Thanks, Chief," Garrett said and hung up. "The chief said no problem. She should be ready by morning, but don't get there before 11:00, to give him time to clean her up and do his final checks."

"Great. One other thing, Commander. Would you send a message to Washington to confirm receipt of orders and let them know our estimated departure of 1400 hours tomorrow?" Phillips asked and then looked over at Sonya. "Let's go. We have a lot to do before we leave tomorrow." Then he turned to Commander Garrett. "Thank you for your help, and tell your young ensign to keep up the good attitude. See you, Commander."

Holiday Inn Resort
May 5, 1996
1045 Hours, EST

"Mr. Pierce, sorry to interrupt you while you're relaxing, but you have a telephone call from the States. The individual said it was urgent," the hotel manager said when he approached Davin and Connie on the terrace. They were enjoying the view, catching some sun, and watching the afternoon activities in the harbor when the manager approached.

"Where can I take the call?" Davin asked, starting to stand. But with a quick flick of his wrist and snap of his fingers, the manager had a young waiter bring a cordless telephone to the table. Davin sat down again and took the telephone from the waiter.

"Thank you, sir," Davin said.

"Just push 7 to retrieve your call, sir," the young waiter said as he and the manager departed.

"Hello, this is Davin Pierce," Davin said into the receiver after pressing the number 7 as told.

"Good. Mr. Pierce, you don't know me, and that doesn't really matter anyway. I was trying to reach you or Captain Phillips to forward an urgent message. I'm a ham radio operator in South Carolina and just recently received a strange message from a JD Henderson. He would not disclose his location, but he asked me to call your office to relay this message, which I did," the voice started out rapidly.

"Slow down a bit. I hear you just fine. Whom am I speaking with?" Davin asked when he was able to break in.

"Oh, sorry, Mr. Pierce. I'm Mike Butler, of Hilton Head, but as I was saying, I called your office and your secretary told me where you were, only after my insistence that I relay the message personally. She still didn't want to let me know, since she knew that you really didn't want to be disturbed while on vacation. By the way, I hope you're having a good time," Butler went on to say, quite a bit slower now.

"We're having a great time, Mr. Butler. The weather is perfect and the company is excellent." Davin was referring to Connie lying on her stomach on the chaise lounge beside him. The top of her bikini was unhooked, exposing a perfectly shaped back, so she could get a near-perfect tan without tan lines. "Now, you said you had a message from JD. What did the old boy have to say?"

"He said, and I will read this just as he said it. 'Tell Pierce and Phillips to meet us at Treasure Island on Friday at 1800 hours at the Hilltop Restaurant and Bar. Hope to see you there. JD. End of message.' That's all he said. Is there any reply, Mr. Pierce?" Mike asked, hoping for the chance to take a larger role in this mystery.

Mike was a retired Air Force colonel, and amateur radio operation was his only hobby. He relished the opportunity to assist in any type of emergency, mystery, or anything else as long as it involved amateur radio. Mike could not do anything else, as he'd been paralyzed from the waist down when his F-4 was shot down over Vietnam. He remained a prisoner of war for two years and then was transferred back to the States, where he spent the best part of four years in therapy and in the operating room. He was not discouraged because of his disability; in fact, he had grown from it. Teaching others to help themselves, to learn, to go to school, he was a guiding light for many war veterans and others that had come to him. But age was catching up to him, and amateur radio and his wife of thirty-eight years were all he had left.

"No reply, Mike. Thanks for the information. This really sounds like it's going to be a great party," Davin said.

"It's a strange way to send a party invite but does make it interesting," Mike replied. "Drink a cold one for me, Mr. Pierce."

"Thanks for your time, Mike. Goodbye," Davin said as he stared over at Connie.

"Goodbye, Mr. Pierce. Have a nice vacation," Mike said and hung up.

"What was all that about?" Connie asked as she hooked the clasp on her bikini top and adjusted the front so Davin and the world would not get a free show. Then she rolled over and sat up facing Davin.

"It's our invite to the hottest party in the islands tomorrow at 1800 on Treasure Island," Davin said as he looked at Connie sitting in her hot-pink string bikini. The scar from her wound was still visible, but other than that, her body was perfect. With the small size of her string bikini, Davin was able to enjoy most of her beautiful, soft skin. Desires of spending the night with this woman were growing within Davin. Over the past two weeks, they had become very close, but both were doing their best to keep this relationship in check, at least until this mission was over.

Chapter 24

B MOVIES

USS Wolverine
May 5, 1996
2130 Hours, EST

"Captain, surface contact, two ships, possibly the same destroyers we had earlier. The signature sounds familiar. Unable to confirm yet, heading southwest at twenty-four knots!" Kelly yelled across the control room to JD as he was studying his charts. They had been on the surface since the attack, charging the batteries that provided power to the boat and doing some major repair work.

"Do we have visual?" he yelled up to the tower.

"Aye, sir, just on the horizon," came the response from the tower.

"Scotty, can we dive?" JD asked reluctantly.

"Closing fast, sir," Kelly interrupted.

"Aye, Captain. But not too deep or too long. We are being held together with bailing wire and a prayer," Scotty said as he wiped the grease from his hands.

"Prepare to dive. Rig for silent running!" JD ordered. "Take her to one hundred feet, level." *Damn,* he thought, *this is getting to be like an old B movie. Up and down! At least on a nuclear boat we dived and stayed there.*

They didn't surface much during the course of a mission since the nuclear boats did not need to surface to recharge their batteries or to get fresh air. Their systems were all self-contained and could stay under for months at a time.

"Ready, sir!" Batman said after he had secured the tower hatch and quickly scanned the bridge, double-checking the safety lights that were displayed on a panel above the dive control station. Each light corresponded to a hatch, which, if left open, would flood the boat. All lights showed green and safe.

"Take her down," JD said calmly, smiling at the efficiency of his crew. "Damn, they're good," he added quietly.

Ten minutes later, they were running quietly at one hundred feet, waiting for the two destroyers to pass by. The waiting was the worst part for the crew of the World War II boats. They did not have all the comforts the newer boats had. The air-conditioning had failed again, and the temperature and humidity were rising fast since the hatches were closed. The computers on board were cooled internally, but even with that, some of them failed to operate at full capacity or at all.

USS Normandy
South Atlantic Ocean
May 5, 1996
2126 Hours, EST

"Captain, we have a surface contact, forty thousand yards, bearing one-two-zero degrees, speed five knots, heading…wait one, sir. He's turning. Okay, heading is two-one-zero," the sonar operator reported to the deck officer.

"Thank you, Radar. That must be our boy," Captain Jones commented to his executive office when he received the report from his deck officer. "JD Henderson is good, considering he is working with an untrained crew in a boat older than he is. He is doing an excellent job. I knew they didn't get him. Radio to the *Reagan* and tell MacIntyre he was right. The *Wolverine* lives."

"What now, sir?" His executive officer asked.

"Did you know Henderson is the youngest officer in the Navy to secure the command of a nuke boat?" Jones commented, not expecting an answer and ignoring the question his exec had asked.

"No, sir. He must be good," his executive officer remarked.

"He is, and we are going to do just as Admiral Feldings has directed us, assist them as best as we can. And the best way right now is to get out of his sonar and meet them at Treasure Island," Captain Jones said, looking at his executive officer. The exec was young, and this was his first assignment after graduating from the academy last year. He liked Captain Jones a lot and only wanted to learn so he could command someday.

"Are you sure that is where they are headed?" his exec asked.

"Not exactly, but we can track him, using our satellites, and not get in his way. So turn this boat toward Treasure Island and give him a very wide berth. Just like the *Reagan* instructed. We will play this game until the end. Something is up, and I want to find out first-hand. Do you like a good mystery, Sam?" Jones asked. "I do. Well, according to Admiral Feldings, we are right in a mystery that started over forty years ago, one that may just be solved in the next few days. And we have a part in it."

"Kind of exciting, sir. Is that why we are tracking one of our own submarines?" Sam asked.

"Yeah, but that isn't an ordinary sub. She was commissioned in 1943, and well, she disappeared near the end of the war, and now she is sailing again. This time toward the Bahamas, to end a life. Her own."

"Interesting," Sam replied.

"Helmsman, new heading, one-four-zero, flank speed. Follow the *Reagan* out of the area."

USS Wolverine
May 5, 1996
2200 Hours, EST

"Sir, those two destroyers, they ventured to within thirty-eight thousand yards, then turned southwest, about one-four-zero degrees, and steamed off my scope at twenty-two knots. Kind of strange, sir," Kelly said as she watched the scope. It was her turn in sonar. Due to the limited number of trained crew, they rotated four on and four off, each member taking turns on sonar. And when they could, each member took four hours of sleep between shifts.

"Keep an eye on that scope. They may be just out of range," JD responded.

JD and Carpenter were trying to figure out where that cave entrance might be in relation to the islands in the area. They wanted to locate the correct island and put a landing party onshore as back up in case they didn't locate the entrance or didn't survive entering it.

Three hours after submerging, they surfaced to find a cloudless night and millions of stars. JD ordered all crew to take a trip up on deck for fresh air and to view the heavens. No ships were in sight, and radar did not show any aircraft. They felt safe for the time being and would proceed on the surface till morning. The only ones looking at them were the satellites, and they were no threat right now. By the time an aircraft or ship could get within range to cause them trouble, they would be safely underwater and moving to a new location.

USS Normandy
South Atlantic Ocean
May 6, 1991
0130 Hours, EST

They were cruising at twenty-two knots, just out of range of the *Wolverine's* passive sonar. The *Reagan* and *Normandy* had a direct link to a Navstar 5 satellite and could track a sub, nuclear or otherwise, from anywhere in the world. And the sub could be as deep as ten thousand feet, far deeper than any submarine could possibly go, and stay in one piece. With the new Navstar, Navy commanders could track their enemies with greater accuracy and also avoid being a target themselves. There were few places to hide in the oceans anymore with the technology that had been developed since Vietnam.

"What's their location, Radar?" Captain Jones of the *Normandy* asked.

"Sir, the Navstar has them on the surface, running at eight knots, heading two-zero-zero degrees true. In a minute, we will have a nice picture of them. Without a cloud cover, they are taking a real risk running as they are," Radar replied.

"Yes, they are. But that commander knows what he is doing. He knows we are following, and he wants us to be there when he arrives. He's no fool," Captain Jones commented. "As soon as you get that photo, send it up to the bridge."

"Aye, sir," Radar said, then went back to his scope.

"Ensign Bell, meet me on the bridge in ten minutes," Captain Jones ordered his deck officer.

Ten minutes later, Ensign Bell, with photo in hand, reported to the bridge. Handing Captain Jones the photo, he then walked over the chart table, with Jones behind him.

"Sir, when that photo was taken, the *Wolverine* was right here," Locke said, pointing to a spot on the chart.

"Mark that. Now, where are we?" Jones asked.

"Here, sir." Again he pointed to a spot on the chart that Jones marked in with a pencil.

"Time and distance to the nearest island along his track, and time and distance to his possible destination?" Jones requested.

"One moment, sir," Locke said and then started to do some calculations and measuring on the chart. "Approximately ten hours to the nearest island and sixteen to Treasure Island, present course and speed. That is, of course, if he doesn't have any delays or interruptions from unfriendly ships or planes."

"Right. Plot a course for us to be just out of their radar and sonar range. I want to be there at least four hours ahead of them. The *Reagan* has given us the lead. She has developed a problem with her number 1 turbine and will have to slow down for repairs," Jones said. "She will catch up later, but we need to be on station early."

Andros Island
May 6, 1996
1045 Hours, EST

The sun was already up, and it looked like the beginning of another beautiful day in paradise. It was a shame to waste a day like this by working. But if you had to work, then this was the best place in the world to do it.

Phillips approached his aircraft on the ramp in front of the hangar, expecting to find his aircraft still in pieces but was pleasantly surprised.

"Good morning, sir." The airman snapped to attention as Phillips approached. "Your aircraft is almost ready. Just need to do the final run-up and sign-off."

"Great. Where's the chief?" Phillips asked, returning the salute, and started looking over his aircraft.

"In his office, sir. Over in the corner of the hangar," he said as he started to secure the cowling on the left engine. Several panels were still off, but everything looked like it would be together soon.

"Thank you," he said and headed over to the office, pausing to admire the F-14 Tomcat jet fighter in the hangar for a few minutes, remembering when he had his. Being stationed on the *Independence* and flying the Tomcat was the best time in his life. Now, due to mandatory removal from fighters because of age, he could only dream and remember the thrill of the most powerful combat weapon in the US Navy arsenal. Well, that was his opinion of this machine. *I wonder why this one is here,* he thought to himself and then went into the chief's office.

"Good morning, sir. Beautiful day, isn't it?" the chief said as Phillips entered the office. The chief was checking an aircraft logbook and making notes on a separate yellow legal pad. "I'll be right with you. Help yourself to some coffee and have a seat."

"Thank you, Chief," Phillips replied as he turned to the coffeepot and poured himself a cup, taking it black, without any sugar or cream. Slowly he turned, sipping his coffee, and took a seat near the window, admiring the F-14 and thinking.

A couple of minutes later, the chief stood up, shaking his head, and proceeded to pour himself a cup of coffee.

"Damn paperwork! I tell you what, sir. It takes almost as long to fill out the paperwork as it does to fix these birds. I show a full sheet, a full sheet of yellow legal pad of paper of discrepancies on that F-14 Tomcat in the hangar. Damn, it's going to be down for a long time," the chief said, as if he had to do all the work.

"What's wrong with her?" Phillips asked, expecting an expression from the chief indicating that he didn't really want to know.

"Well, we have this young hotshot lieutenant from the Kennedy who flew her in, saying he was having trouble with the heads-up display, which was just an excuse to spend a few days on the beach with his girl. Damn fine girl too. Well, in checking out the bird, we did find a few problems in the cockpit. Some kind of liquid was spilled on the comm pack and fried the radio. The bird does need some TLC to get it in top shape, but nothing that would ground her. In a few days, she will be flying again. No rush. He wants at least two days on the beach, anyway. We try to help when we can. Besides, it's my daughter he's here to see. Really fine pilot, just a little cocky. Know what I mean, sir?"

"Yeah, guess I do. I used to fly an F-14 a few years back. They grow on you, kinda. Well, thanks for getting my bird back together. She isn't much, but she's all I got now."

"Yeah, I know what you mean, sir. Age kinda sneaks up on ya and takes a lot of the fun out of living. How much fuel you want?" the chief asked.

"To the tabs on all tanks," Phillips said, then changed his mind. "No, you better top everything off. I'm heading back to Washington today."

Two hours later, Davin, Connie, and Sonya arrived and loaded the Gulfstream and were waiting for Phillips to give the final word on departure. He had gone over to check weather and file a flight plan. At 1325 hours, he approached his companions and gave a thumbs-up. Twenty minutes later, they were airborne, heading for Treasure Island.

Treasure Island
Hilltop Restaurant and Bar
May 6, 1996
1820 Hours, EST

Waiting was something few people can get used to, but here Davin and Connie were making it easier, sipping margaritas. Phillips passed on the drink since he was flying out as soon as possible. It was twenty minutes past the hour, and JD was late, which wasn't normal for him.

"Mr. Pierce, is there a Mr. Pierce in the lounge?" the waitress asked to no one in particular. "Mr. Pierce?"

"Over here," Davin said as he raised his hand and waved at the waitress.

"Oh, okay. You have a phone call, sir. You can take it in the lobby," she said, pointing toward the lobby.

"Thank you," Davin replied. As he got up, he said to the group, "Hope that's JD and he is going to tell us where he is."

Davin got up and walked out to the lobby. Seeing the courtesy phone in the corner, he walked over and picked it up.

"Hello, this is Davin Pierce," he said.

"One moment, please. I'll connect you to your party," the operator said.

"Hello, Davin," the voice finally said after a couple of seconds. The voice was weak and raspy.

"Yes, this is Davin Pierce," he said, not recognizing the voice. "It's your nickel. What can I do for you?"

"No, it's what I can do for you, Davin. This is Jack Malone. I know what you are going to say, but I'm not dead. I cannot explain everything right now, but I had to fake my death or be dead for sure. You and my children are the only ones that know, and we need to keep it that way. Now, listen, and listen close." Jack Malone then briefed Davin about the organization and about the island fortress they were headed for. "Okay, that's all for now. I'll contact you in a few weeks to fill you in on the whole story, but right now, a package will be at the lobby desk with a complete set of drawings of the island

and other information you will need to bring in the rest of the ring. Good luck, Davin."

Ten minutes later, Davin returned, not smiling.

"What's wrong, fella? Look like you've seen a ghost," Phillips said jokingly.

"I didn't see one, just talked to one," Davin said as he sat down in sort of a daze.

"Well, what's going on?" Connie asked impatiently.

"Hey, why the sad faces? Ole Batman is here!" Batman yelled as he and JD approached the table, distracting Connie away from Davin's condition.

"Hi! Pull up a couple of chairs," Phillips greeted the two. Then he directed his attention to the lovely little waitress. "Miss, we need another round of drinks, please, and…wait." He turned back to Batman and JD. "What'll you have?" Phillips commented.

"Beer, ice-cold beer, please, two *each*," Batman said to the waitress.

"What's wrong with Davin?" JD asked.

"Oh, nothing. A friend of mine was able to get some information we needed," Davin commented casually.

"The island?" Connie asked, sensing that Davin was covering up something.

"Yeah, it doesn't sound easy, guys," Davin said.

"What did your friend say?" JD asked quietly as he sipped on his drink.

"A lot. He gave me details about the fortress we are about to overrun, and a map will be at the front desk of this hotel addressed to me at 2200 hours tonight." Davin stopped and was thinking to himself, *How did he know we were here? And how did he know what our intentions are?*

"Can this guy be trusted?" JD asked.

"Yes, you can trust him. He was working as a mole in the black market organization that owns the island we are about to visit. And they have a real interest in that boat of yours, JD," Davin commented, hiding the fact that he knew now that Jack was inside the organization only to destroy it.

"All we know is that you got a call from someone and that it may or may not be leading us into a trap," Phillips commented.

"Yeah, I guess you are right too," Davin said. "But I don't think so. I can't go into details, but I trust him."

"Well, be careful. Now, let's stop all this speculating and get down to business. I have a plane to catch," Phillips stated matter-of-factly.

"Okay," said JD. "Phillips, take this envelope to the vice president, or rather to a man named John Horton of the CIA, not the president. It seems that our voted-into-office president is a crook too. There is enough evidence in that envelope to bring down the president, at least three aides, four congressmen, and countless military personnel ranging from Admiral Jacobs to some senior enlisted in several branches."

"Damn, where did you get that stuff?" Davin asked before the others had a chance to open their mouths. "The envelope that is being left for us has information and lists of people involved in the market also."

"It seems the crew of the *Wolverine* and these people have had a long run of extortion, murder, piracy, and grand theft, to name a few. From what it looks like, the crew was putting together a means to extort more, or maybe a means to buy their way out of jail. They just ran out of time, and while returning from a delivery, they died or were sabotaged by a customer. They had a lot of evidence on board to put a lot of big shots behind bars. And this is only part of it. The rest is still on the boat and on that island," JD said coldly.

"Who's this Horton fella?" Phillips asked.

"He's my brother-in-law, married to my younger sister. He can be trusted, not real high in the chain, but high enough to know what to do with that stuff," JD said.

"What's next?" Davin asked as Connie sat back and took all the planning in. She was on her third drink and starting to loosen up.

"We move back out to the boat and head south to the island. At dawn tomorrow, we take the island," Batman said positively.

"Look, I've got to get to Washington and back as quick as I can, so Sonja and I better be off," Phillips said.

"Right. Guard that with your life, and be careful," JD said as they got up to leave.

"We need to leave also, before it gets too late," Batman commented.

"I guess you're right. Let's go," JD said.

"What time is it?" Davin asked.

"Twenty-two ten hours, Davin," Batman replied. "Why?"

"It must be true that a naval officer's memory is as long as his, well, his gun. I have to pick up that envelope at the front desk. Let's go," Davin said as he got up to leave. Connie stood, a little shaky, so Davin put his arm around her, wishing they had the time to spend together alone.

Sonja and Phillips departed the lounge. Sonja stopped as they crossed the lobby, saying she had to go to the powder room.

While there, she placed a call to Admiral Jacobs. She told him they were leaving for Washington. She decided not to say anything about the raid on the island or the information they already had. Her instinct told her that Jacobs was up to something, and she wanted to check it out a little more before telling him any more than what he needed to know, which in this case was very little.

Chapter 25

PARADISE LOST

Washington, DC
Andrews Air Force Base
May 7, 1996
0130 Hours, EST

"Andrews Tower, this is Gulfstream four-niner-seven, with you, at ten thousand, heading two-niner-zero," Phillips said into the microphone. Sonja was asleep in the back, stretched out on one of the larger sofas. Phillips flew a lot of VIPs around, and his Gulfstream III was set up for comfort, complete with a wet bar, two sofas, and several overstuffed chairs.

"Gulfstream four-niner-seven, cleared to land runway niner right, winds zero-eight-zero at four. Your driver is waiting in the lounge. I'll wake him just before you land," the tower operator responded to Phillips's call. At this hour, the tower operator took over as the approach and departure control as well since there were very few flights landing or departing after 2200 hours daily.

"What driver? I don't have a driver," Phillips said to the controller. There was something suspicious here.

"Don't you have code 6 on board?" Tower asked. A *code 6* is a general officer or other VIP.

"Negative. Standby, tower," Phillips said as he turned to yell for Sonja to wake up. "Hey, honey, we are almost home. Wake up back there!"

At first, he didn't get a response or hear any sounds from the passenger compartment. He yelled again, thinking he would have to set the autopilot and go back to wake her up, but soon he heard a noise as she slowly awoke and stretched.

She adjusted her clothes, which she had loosened and partly removed so she could sleep more comfortably. Her blouse was still unbuttoned to her waist. She stood and walked to the cockpit, rubbing the sleep from her eyes.

"Did you yell? Are we almost home? I'm hungry," Sonja said as she stretched again and yawned. Stepping into the cockpit, she wiggled into the copilot's seat and started to look for the safety belt. Finding only one end, she held it up as if the other end would surface if it knew it was being looked for.

"Do you know anything about a driver waiting for a code 6 at Andrews?" he asked, sounding a bit angry. Looking over at her, he saw her blouse open but did not say anything. She had obviously removed her bra.

"What driver? No…ah…yeah, maybe. Oh, I guess that might be the admiral's driver. He may have sent his driver over to pick us up since it is so late," she replied, then started to button her blouse.

"Admiral? Which admiral? Who did you call in the States before we left?" Phillips demanded, raising his voice and looking at her with a cold stare.

"Admiral Jacobs, Admiral Harold Jacobs. Yes, I did. I'm supposed to report in every day," Sonja admitted, stopping to rub her eyes again, still trying to wake up.

"Report in? REPORT IN! Damn it, you're working for Admiral Jacobs? Don't you know he's one of the bad guys?" Phillips yelled.

"No, not him. He's too sweet," Sonja said, still trying to get the sleep out of her head. "What time is it, anyway?"

"Too sweet. DAMN IT, SONJA! YOU HAVE BEEN USED, BIG-TIME, little lady! He's had good men killed. Damn it, Sonja, how could you…" Phillips was yelling when the tower interrupted him.

"Gulfstream niner-seven, what are your intentions?" the Andrews Tower operator asked.

"Vector to Fort Meade Tipton and tell that driver we crashed."

"What?" the tower operator requested. "Would you repeat last transmission?"

"I can't explain now, but we didn't call for a driver. Just tell him we landed at Norfolk for fuel and will not arrive until noon. I'll land at Fort Meade Tipton," Phillips said to the controller, then looked hard at Sonja. She was smart but was working for the wrong side and probably didn't know it. Could he trust her, or should he dump her as soon as they landed?

"Roger, four-niner-seven, turn to zero-two-zero descend to five thousand," the operator requested. "Squawk zero-three-four-two."

"Roger, descending and turning to zero-two-zero," Phillips replied, controlling his aircraft like the fighter pilot he once was, hard and fast. Almost too hard for the type of aircraft they were in, but he knew his jet, what she could take and what she couldn't. Max Phillips was considered an ace during his younger years, and just because of age, they took him out of fighters, but not out of jets. His Gulfstream was a medium-size corporate-type jet, not as fast as a fighter, but he was happy flying her. It beat flying a desk, anyway.

Then he turned to Sonja, who was as mad as a hen for being deceived so easily.

"I'm sorry I yelled, but you have been telling Jacobs where we are and what we are doing," Max Phillips said quietly. He tried to calm her down and to continue to fly his aircraft.

"But I thought he was on our side and was doing things to help us," Sonja admitted. She didn't know who or what he was. She was following orders from a superior officer.

"Wrong. He has had people killed, and I don't know how, but he probably had a hand in sinking the *Washington* too," Max commented as he scanned his instrument. Then his eyes looked outside the cockpit as he thought of what to say next.

"Gulfstream niner-seven, Fort Meade Tipton is closed, but the runway lights are on and the wind is light to variable. Good luck, sir,"

Tower called. "I told the driver what you said, and he just left. Said he had to report the delay to an admiral."

"Thank you, Tower. You may have saved our lives," Phillips replied, then looked again at Sonja, who was still boiling mad.

"I didn't know. I was ordered to work with you and assist wherever I could but also to report to him everything we did and where we were. I didn't know…" Sonja was fuming.

"Okay, you didn't know. But now you do. Can I trust you not to call him again?" Max asked as he reached over to lower his flaps for the approach into Fort Meade Tipton. Then he called the Andrews Air Force Base control tower. "Andrews Tower, Gulfstream niner-seven, we have Tipton in sight."

"Roger, four-niner-seven. Remain on this frequency if you need anything. Good night," the operator said, then went silent.

"Thank you, Andrews. Good night," Phillips said, then turned his attention to Sonja.

"Yes, I hope you can. I will not call him or even my office again," Sonja said. "I have a confession to make, Max."

"What now?" Max asked as he turned on his landing lights and lowered the flaps another notch. Pulling back on the throttles, he eased the Gulfstream toward the ground. Pulling out his checklist, he handed it to her. "Read this."

She started to read the checklist out loud so he could perform each step required to land his aircraft. Most of which he had done from memory as he approached the airport. Unlike less-safety-conscious pilots, he used his checklist on every flight for takeoff, for landing, and while cruising. This time he was also using it to help calm Sonja down and to ease his tension.

"Gear," Sonja said as the plane approached the airfield.

"Gear coming down. We have three green," Phillips said as he put the landing gear lever in the down position. Then he reported gear safe in the down position with the three green gear indicator lights.

"Confirm," Sonja said as she looked down at the handle and the three green lights. She had calmed down and was concentrating on doing the job of a copilot.

"Flaps," Sonja continued.

"Check, down thirty degrees," Phillips acknowledged.

They continued until they were almost to the ground.

"Max, well, maybe I better not. Damn. Here goes," Sonja said. "Max, have you ever heard of Operation Aquarius?"

"No, but that doesn't mean a thing. I just fly airplanes and don't get involved with any operations anymore. Well, except this one with the sub," he stated, pulling lightly back on the control column to establish a better rate of descent. The Gulfstream was descending toward the runway at 150 knots indicated airspeed. A little fast, but the extra speed meant a smoother landing.

"Well, I know you hold a top secret security clearance with departmental access. I will not tell you everything yet, but well, here goes," Sonja started as the wheels of the jet touched the runway as smooth as a newborn baby's rear end. Then he pulled back on the throttle levers beyond the indent to engage the reverse thrusters, slowing the aircraft to a safe taxiing speed of three to four knots per hour.

"Hold that thought till we stop," Max said as he maneuvered his aircraft toward the terminal building.

Minutes later, the Gulfstream was rolling to a stop in front of the terminal building. After shutting down the engines and securing the aircraft, they figured they had to wait about twenty more minutes before Phillips's sister would arrive. He had used the air phone to call her. She lived about fifteen miles from the airport.

Phillips took the checklist and read it silently as he switched off the systems on his aircraft in the order as prescribed on the checklist. Within minutes of landing, he had the aircraft ready for the night and just operating with the interior lights on, and the APU, to give the aircraft lights and ground power.

"Okay, Sonja, we aren't out of the woods yet, but at least we have a chance. No more calls to Jacobs, right? Now, what did you start to tell me before we landed?"

"Right!" Sonja said, still mad at being deceived; her eyes were red, but she was in control again. "Max, Operation Aquarius is a deep-cover operation to uncover some bad apples in our government. Very few people know about it. The president doesn't even know. The CIA, in conjunction with the FBI and Naval Security Group, set it up. Only about twenty people know of the operation."

"What has this got to do with us?" Max asked as he continued to tie down his aircraft. "Is what Pierce was saying about the CIA and FBI for real?"

"Yes. I work for Navy Security Group, as a deep-cover operative. I was assigned to a logistical group in the Pentagon to watch several individuals. My supervisor was asked by Admiral Jacobs to assign someone from her department to work with you on this case. With my aviation background, I became the lucky choice," Sonja continued.

"Why are you telling me all this?" Max asked, looking at this young female in a totally different light.

"Max, don't you see? I was assigned to spy on members of the Pentagon because of suspected crooked dealings and then reassigned to the very admiral who is the leader, or one of the leaders, in a black market organization," Sonja said, hoping he would understand.

"Okay, now I see. You are in a tight spot too. If Jacobs finds out you were sent to spy on his operation, well, I don't want to think about what he would do to you," Phillips said as he continued to tie down his aircraft.

"Me neither. When is your sister going to get here? I'm getting cold," Sonja said as she attempted to snuggle up under Max's arm to keep warm, after he had finished tying the jet down and was walking around the wing.

"Soon, Sonja, too soon. Go back on board. It will be warmer there," was all that Max said, feeling that young body pressing up against his. He shouldn't be, but he wanted to take her back inside the Gulfstream and get real close to Sonja. But he knew he was too old for her; still, age shouldn't hold anyone back. But here and now were not the time and/or the place.

Forty minutes later, Max Phillips's sister Susan arrived and drove them back to her house. The drive over was quiet. Max's sister knew not to ask a lot of questions about things that did not concern her.

After arriving at his sister's house, Max had Sonja report to her headquarters, not to Jacobs. After several more calls, Max discovered the source of the AWOL charge and that it was bogus. Jacobs just wanted to get Max away from Pierce and Connie. Intentions were unknown, but he suspected that the guy at National Airport was a hit man.

"Hi, Colonel Alex Gardener, please. Thank you, I'll hold," Max said into the telephone. "Colonel Gardener is the flight commander of the 475th Aggressor Division at Boca Chica Naval Air Station in Key West," he told Sonja and Susan as he waited for the colonel to pick up the receiver.

"Colonel Gardener, may I help you?" the response finally came.

"Alex, this is Captain Max Phillips. How you doing?"

"Just great, Max. How's the Navy treating you?" Alex answered.

"Can't complain too much. Hey, Alex, I need a favor," Max said, then continued to ask for four F-14 Tomcats or F-15 Eagles, whichever Alex had available this week. Alex Gardener's division trained air combat tactics to the Air Force and Navy. They had at their disposal a variety of aircraft from F-14s to French Mirages. Most recently receiving a MiG-23 Flogger from Cuba, courtesy of a defecting Cuba pilot.

Max outlined that he needed the aircraft to buzz an island in the Bahamas at 0700 hours. Alex agreed and said he would lead the simulated attack himself. Good training mission for his men.

"Thanks, Alex. I owe you one," Max concluded.

"And you will pay, Max. Next time you are down here. Out here," Alex said, hanging up.

"Bye!" Max hung up.

USS Wolverine
Off the Coast of Treasure Island
May 6, 1996
2100 Hours, EST

The *Wolverine* had been cruising submerged during the day to avoid being seen, but as soon as the sun went down, they came up to get fresh air and recharge their batteries. All was going well, so far. Maybe Admiral Feldings was successful in diverting the Navy off their trail.

"Okay, then it's agreed. The landing party will be dropped off here," JD said, pointing toward the far side of the island. "The rest of us will make an attempt to penetrate their forces from the inside, by going in through the cave with the boat. Those diagrams from Davin's friend are great. That may give us the edge we need."

JD paused to get agreements from everyone in the control room as to the situation and plans.

"Time set at 04:00 for the landing party to hit the shore. At 07:00, we take the boat into the cave and surface at 07:30. At the same time, you, Batman, with your band of Indians, are taking the house and cave entrance. With any luck, they won't know we are here until it's too late."

Davin and Connie were in complete amazement as to the condition and lack of space in this old boat. They were full of questions as to where and how she operated. After a short nickel tour by Carpenter and a question-and-answer session, Davin and Connie just wandered around, looking.

"JD, you said this was a World War II boat?" Davin asked as he looked around the control room.

"Yeah, but she has been in service for Jacobs and crew for forty-plus years, and in that time, she has had some refits. Such as the color radar and advanced tactical control center over there," JD replied, pointing toward the new panels.

"Looks like Jacobs was running his own private Navy," Connie commented.

"Yeah, which brings up a very important question," Davin started.

"And that is?" Batman interrupted.

"Well, if he had this one boat, maybe he had others...," Davin said, letting his words trail off.

"That's right. Does he have more in the fleet, or is this it?" Batman returned the thought. "Nothing was mentioned in the documents we found on board."

"What if he does?" Connie asked, looking at the others around the room.

"Well, if he does, then we may have to defend ourselves against two enemies that have more firepower than us," JD said as a matter of fact.

"Okay, so the element of surprise must be ours, or we may not live to talk about it," Davin concluded.

"Plan for another boat and hope to hell that she is moored in the cave without a crew," JD said, then went on. "Look, its 2130 hours. We have a long ways to go and a good possibility of a fight when we show our faces. You had best get some sleep. Davin and Connie, take my quarters. I'll wake you at 06:00, just before we start the penetration of the cave. Now, get out of here."

USS Wolverine, Captain's Quarters
May 6, 1996
2120 Hours, EST

Davin and Connie entered the captain's quarters. The room wasn't much larger than a closet but had a small desk, with chair, a wash-basin, mirror, a single bunk, and a private shower stall in the corner.

"Damn, don't they air-condition these boats?" Connie asked as she scanned the small room.

"Look, this is pretty tight. I'll go find a bunk in the crew area," Davin said as he, too, looked around.

"No, don't go. I don't want to be alone," Connie insisted.

"Well, I don't know. It is pretty tight in here," Davin said again.

"Look here, Davin Pierce. I want you to stay. We both need a shower, and well, I want you here. Now stop complaining about it being small in here. I kind of like the closeness," she said and then kissed him hard on the lips.

Slowly she started to unbutton Davin's shirt and then pulled it back over his shoulders. She stepped back and started to unbutton her blouse. Davin reached back to lock the door with his right hand, then slipped out of his shirt.

Connie slowly teased Davin. Once she had her blouse unbuttoned, she turned her back toward him and let it fall. She wore no bra. Davin walked up behind her and put his arms around her. She turned in his arms and they kissed again.

As they helped each other out off the remainder of their clothes, she took his hand and guided him into the shower.

Jacobs Island, Bahamas
Living Room Overlooking the Ocean
May 7, 1996
0630 Hours, EST

"Jacobs radioed last night that we may have visitors, of the unfriendly kind. Get your men into place and activate the defense systems. Put six men in the cave with orders to load everything they can on the *Excalibur*, just in case we can't handle a bunch of renegade sailors. Nothing can fall into their hands. Nothing! If we can't load it, we destroy it," the headman said to two of his subordinates. "Now move. We don't have much time."

The *Excalibur* was the USS *706*, the second of the three modified Gato-class submarines built for special missions during the war. Built exactly like the *Wolverine*, it was modified more once the war ended. She was never completed according to Navy records, as was their other sister ship.

The two men departed and started preparation for an invasion from an unknown force.

They had thought of everything; the outer perimeter had sensors to detect if an intruder was within five hundred yards of the main house. There were land mines at three hundred yards that were remotely activated, and claymore mines at intervals between one and two hundred yards. If anyone survived all the explosives, there were automatic machine guns and 40mm cannons mounted in block houses at five points around the house. This wasn't a house, but a fortress that didn't want to be overrun. The house itself sat high on a hill overlooking the ocean and all vantage points except one.

Because an attack would only likely come from the landside of the house, the rear cliff area was not as heavily fortified. The cliff wasn't high, only fifty feet to the crest, with a sandy beach at the bottom and a set of stairs ascending to the top. The cliff itself was rocky but otherwise sheer from top to bottom. One man armed with an M60 machine gun and a 9mm automatic pistol guarded the stairs. The stairs also had motion detectors placed at the bottom and again at twenty feet from the top, aimed down the stairs. So anyone approaching up the stairs would immediately set off the silent alarm, alerting the guard that he had visitors. Additionally, he was relieved every two hours by one of his buddies so he was able to stretch and get a little exercise instead of just sitting there, watching the ocean and reading his book.

Sitting in a pair of shorts and Ray-Bans, catching the early morning sun, was about all the excitement the guard ever got, until today. With one eye on the stairs and the other in a good book, he passed his time on duty. The installed trip wires and motion detectors on the stairs were checked when he came on duty at 06:00, so no one could get up without his knowing it.

No one but Seaman Jerry Grant, Cherokee Indian and SEAL, was able to sneak up on a cobra without detection. Seaman Grant let the guard remain seated but very much unconscious as he disconnected the wires that would set off the alarm in the house. The guard never saw or heard Grant approach from behind and expertly put him to sleep with a quick chop to the neck, a trick taught only by his martial arts instructor. But to ensure the guard would sleep, he injected him with a little sleep-inducing drug that was liberated from the boat's medical cabinet.

Grant traced the trip wires and sensor cables to a central control box and, with a little pair of wire clips, disabled them. Quickly he ran back to the top of the stairs and signaled to Batman and the rest of his force to come on up.

Five minutes later, Batman and six more men were at the top of the stairs, hiding behind the concrete wall surrounding the pool area. Nobody spoke. So far, so good. Batman signaled to three of his men to proceed to his right around the wall and take positions as close to the house as possible without being seen. He then sent Grant and two men the other way to take up a crossfire position. Batman and the last man sat back and waited. It was 07:15. The attack was set for 07:30, unless they had to defend themselves. They were armed with light weapons, two M1 carbines, one Thompson .45-caliber machine gun, four M16s, and an assortment of sidearms, mostly .45-caliber automatic pistols, your basic military issue. Add to that one almost-new M60 machine gun complete with a case of ammunition and a brand-new 9mm Beretta automatic pistol, both just liberated from the very sleepy guard.

Grant heard it first but couldn't be sure. Then he was. Looking up toward the north, he saw four F-14 Tomcats flying overhead. Damn, they were beautiful. Sometimes he wished he had studied harder and tried to fly for the Navy. Then he thought, *No way, man, being a SEAL was the way to go. Pilots are drivers, but SEALs can do it all.*

Suddenly, the first F-14 Tomcat turned and banked into a dive with the other three in close pursuit. Each one made a low pass over the house, so low, in fact, that the exhaust of the first jet blew off some of the roof tiles. The sound was deafening. They were so close to the house Batman and his team immediately dropped down to a prone position and hugged the ground. Glancing over his shoulder, Batman could swear he could count the rivets on the wings of the last F-14 that buzzed the house.

Immediately, four men, with automatic weapons in hand, came running out of the house to investigate. Their timing could not have been more perfect. Without firing a shot at the aircraft, they just stood there and watched as the four Tomcats climbed vertically out of sight.

Cursing and yelling at the Tomcats, the four stood unsuspecting that Batman and his merry men were about to change their luck for the day.

"Who the hell do they think they are?" yelled one of the four men. "Look at me. It looks like I pissed my pants. They knocked my beer off the table and onto my lap."

"Yeah, sure, Johnny. Sure. They just scared the piss out of you. Admit it. Come on, Johnny," another one of the four kidded with Johnny.

It was now or never, Batman thought and took the cue. As he stood up with his weapon pointed at the four men, his men followed his lead, standing and aiming at the four armed men.

"DROP YOUR WEAPONS AND PUT YOUR HANDS ON YOUR HEADS, NOW!" Batman yelled across the pool. The men looked dumbfounded but did as they were told when they saw they were outnumbered and outgunned.

Immediately, three of Batman's men jumped over the wall and removed the weapons from the easy reach of the four men and ordered them to the ground.

"Face on the ground, move it, move it! Now, hands behind the head, and no heroics. I'd hate to blow your heads off," Grant ordered.

"Grant, tie them up. Baker, Max, Wyman, check the house for more personnel. Be careful," Batman ordered.

"Okay, how many more on this island, sport?" Batman asked one of the prisoners.

"Eat shit and die, asshole!" was his reply, feeling pretty stupid for what just happened. Batman just stuck the barrel of the M60 on the cheek of the smart-ass and asked again, but not as politely as before.

Three shots were heard from inside the house before he could get an answer from the prisoner. Batman turned toward the door just as Baker exited, bleeding from his left shoulder.

"What the hell happened?" Batman yelled, then turned quickly to two of his men. "Watch them!"

"Hey, we're okay. Some creep thought he could outgun us and tried. Well, he's not going to give us any more trouble. Max and Wyman are checking out the rest of the house," Baker replied as he sat down in a chaise lounge. "Damn, this hurts!"

"Grant, see what you can do for him. I'll be right back," Batman ordered and headed into the house.

"Aye, sir, be careful," Grant answered, starting to take care of Baker's wound. Seaman Mark Russell had retrieved the other guard and had all five prisoners sitting with their backs against the wall and their hands and feet tied together, with the Thompson machine gun pointed at them.

"Hey, Grant, what we gonna do with these clowns?" Russell asked as Grant was patching up Baker's arm.

"I don't know. Maybe cut them a little and then feed them to the sharks. Or maybe just shoot them. We will have to wait and see," Grant answered without even looking up from patching Baker's shoulder.

Chapter 26

INSTRUCTIONS

USS Wolverine
250 Feet below the Surface
May 7, 1996
0700 Hours, EST

"Okay, we're here," JD said, looking at the chart. He knew he and Carpenter were correct, but they were not real sure of what they were putting this boat and its crew into. "Wherever here is!"

"Sir, the procedure says to tune the radio direction finder to one-eighty-six-point-niner and steer for the null." Carpenter read the document marked CAVE ENTRANCE PROCEDURE, dated June 8, 1955. "Okay, Micky, it says to turn on the bow camera using the switch marked Alpha 1 on the tactical control panel and switch on the monitor above the console by depressing the power switch on the monitor. And set the signal switch marked Alpha 6 to the *monitor* position."

Micky threw switches and watched as the monitor came to life, but the picture was very dark, not at all usable.

"We can't operate with that quality of picture!" she yelled at Carpenter. "What about some lights?"

"Wait, we also need to turn on switch Lima 4 and Lima 5 on the tactical panel. Try that and see what happens," Carpenter said confidently as he read more of the instruction manual. "As they say, when in doubt, read the instructions."

As soon as she flipped up those two switches, the once-dull, almost-unviewable picture literally jumped into living color, showing a beautiful wall at 250 feet below the surface. The wall was about 175 yards dead ahead, but no cave entrance was visible.

"Damn, that sure made a difference. What next?" Micky exclaimed.

"Isn't that beautiful? Wish I could dive here someday, wait... what the hell is that?" Connie said as she viewed the screen.

"Looks like a whale shark...yeah, it is. Damn, he must be nearly fifty feet long. Enough of that. You got a tone on that radio yet?" JD asked the direction finding (DF) operator. "I hope they didn't turn off the signal."

"Aye, sir, very weak, but readable," the DF operator answered. "Can we stop and try to find the null, sir? The signal is there, but well, we need to proceed very slow, sir."

"All stop. It's your boat, Chuck," JD ordered Ensign Chuck Harrelson, from the late USS *George Washington*. Ensign Harrelson was the fire control officer on the *Washington*; he had been in the combat control center (CIC) during the attack. He and four others in the CIC survived and were rescued by the *Wolverine*.

Harrelson looked at the monitor again. "Whoever built this system is a genius. At least I hope he thought of everything. And remembered to write it down in that instruction book."

"All stop," Scotty in the engine room replied.

"Turn left ten degrees...ten more...ahead slow...ten degrees left. Hold. Heading zero-six-two degrees," the DF operator ordered, looking for the null. The *null* is a radio signal where the two side bands overlap and cancel each other out, creating a void in the signal, called a null. Finding the null in a signal while flying helps pilots follow a radio wave to different locations around the country. "Okay, the cave is either right in front of us or directly behind us. My guess is, the wall will expose its mouth real soon."

To locate the null, the boat, while at full stop, would pivot on its center axis by putting one engine in forward and the other in reverse, with the rudder turned to the new heading. This would keep the boat relatively stationary yet turning to locate the null in the weak radio transmission. Sound travels much faster underwater, making a normal signal distorted and unreadable, but by using microwaves, the signal is more defined and can be used for navigation.

"There it is. Damn, he's good. He found the wall, but where is the cave entrance, Chuck?" Micky looked intently at the monitor.

"Carp, anything else in that document about this cave entrance? Maybe we aren't deep enough, maybe too deep. Look it over again, will ya?" JD said with much concern as he glanced at the monitor, then to his watch. It was 07:24. Batman would be starting his advance any moment now.

"Range from wall?" Carpenter asked, scanning the manual as fast and accurately as he could. He had read it at least six times as they traveled across the Atlantic to get here. He should know it by heart, but he kept looking, hoping he had not missed something.

"One hundred fifty-five yards and holding," Micky replied.

"Ahead dead slow, sir. Bring us within fifty yards of the wall," Carpenter suggested, biting his lower lip as they moved closer to the wall.

"You heard the man, dead slow," JD ordered. "You get that, Scotty?"

"Aye, sir, dead slow," Scotty replied, sweating heavily in the engine room. No matter how much air-conditioning these old boats had, it was never enough for the engine room. Temperatures consistently ran between ninety-five and over a hundred degrees. You had to be real dedicated to work the engine room on these boats.

"Depth?" JD asked without looking away from the monitor.

"Right on 250 feet, sir," Micky replied as she glanced up at the monitor.

"Hey, what's that?" Davin said, pointing toward the monitor picture on the wall, speaking for the first time since they had arrived at the wall. He and Connie were in a state of shock at the condition and sophistication of this old submarine. They were guests on a history-making trip. They, like everyone else, hoped they would survive to tell the story. "On the left of the monitor."

"I don't know, but it looks like a door cut into the side of the wall to me," JD said as he looked closely at the monitor. "All stop!"

"Damn, it doesn't say how to open the door!" Carpenter said as he reread the document.

"Okay, who has the garage door opener?" Micky jokingly questioned.

"That's it. All we need to do is transmit the correct frequency and the door should open," Davin suggested. "This place is a fortress, with the latest technology. Maybe all we need to do is push the right button."

"Chuck, start with the microwave frequency that got us here and start transmitting until that door opens. And let's hope it isn't booby-trapped," JD ordered, thinking it sounded crazy, but what the hell! They were sitting in front of a very large garage door, 250 feet below the surface. Maybe just a push of a button would open that door. Or maybe not.

Time passed and nothing happened. Batman might have started his assault and was waiting for the cavalry to arrive. And here they sat without a garage door opener.

Suddenly, the door started to move, exposing a dark hole in the side of the wall. As the doors opened, the cave was immediately awash with lights, two rows on the cave floor like runway lights and about twenty, marking the exterior of the entrance, and more on the ceiling to mark the top of the cave, running the entire length of the cave.

"I'll be damned!" Kelly said from across the control room, completely amazed by what was going on.

"Okay, we're in. I hope," JD said, swallowing hard. "Dead slow!"

"Doesn't look big enough for this boat!" Carpenter said, then turned back to the document in hand. "Okay, it says here to follow the null to the entrance, then with all masts down as tight as they will go, we are to descend to the bottom of the cave entrance with our bow inside the entrance—damn, sounds tricky—using the runway lights as a guide to position the boat straight down the middle. It says the track will split about two hundred yards in to allow for more than one boat in the docking area."

"Read on. We are getting too close to stop now. We are going in!" JD said as he gripped the handrail around the periscope stand.

"Right, okay…once our bow is in the entrance, we are to descend until the bow rests on the bottom of the cave entrance. Once on the bottom, activate switch Romeo Six 6, then Romeo 5. With the engines at dead slow, we will creep into the cave entrance. Once we are in, we will approach an arrow indicating which dock to ascend to. It will point to the empty dock. We proceed in the proper direction to the end of the cave, about ten minutes, when we reach the stop sign—huh, that's what it says. At the stop sign, we go to all stop and surface slowly, remaining level. We'll reach the surface inside the cave at a depth of seventy-five feet. That's all, except to exit, we must reverse the sequence."

"I hope this is the right house!" Micky said quietly.

"Me too! Hope the neighbors are friendly." Carpenter nodded in agreement, watching the monitor closely.

"Let's do it," JD ordered, then kept his eyes on the monitor until they were resting in the entrance of the cave. Only then did he take the time to wipe the sweat from his forehead.

"It still looks like a single-car garage to me," Micky finally said to break the silence.

"Yeah, okay. No wonder nobody ever found this place. It's not easy to park a boat this big in a single-car garage," Carpenter remarked, almost cheerfully.

Creeping along on an underwater railroad track was a little unnerving at first, but once they realized what was happening, they settled down for the ride. The track took several turns inside the cavern, which was growing larger as they got deeper in. Then they noticed the track split, as it said in the document. They proceeded on the right-hand track for another hundred yards.

"JD, we are slowly going up on these tracks. Depth now, 200—no, 175 feet," Micky remarked as she intently watched the gauges and the monitor.

"Great idea, this railroad track. You sure couldn't maneuver down here, just too tight," JD commented. "We should be reaching the end of the line in a couple of minutes." He paused, then continued, "ATTENTION, ATTENTION! We are able to surface. Prepare to man your surface battle stations. We don't know the kind of reception we are going to get. Be ready. Thank you."

"We're there, sir. Ready to blow ballast!" Micky exclaimed.

"Do it!" JD ordered.

Three sailors were standing by on the bridge with automatic weapons, ready to head up the ladder to the tower in defense of the boat. The rest of the boat was also ready. Several men were ready to handle the three-inch gun on the main deck, others the .50-caliber machine gun located on the sail in a watertight locker that could be opened and readied in a matter of seconds. The boat was as ready as she was going to get, expecting almost anything.

"Attention on deck. We are about to break surface. On my command, break the hatches and go. One hundred...ninety...eighty... NOW! NOW!" JD yelled into the intercom, watching the monitor closely. It showed that they had surfaced and he was looking at the inside of a large cavern with men running across a small bridge. They were taking positions to fire on the boat.

Before the hatches were opened, they could hear the pinging of small-arms fire hitting the hull. Within a few seconds, fifteen men had climbed on deck, taken up their positions, and started to return fire. Two men were immediately hit and went down. A third, handling the .50-caliber machine gun, was hit in the shoulder but continued to pour heavy fire into the cavern. The return fire started to diminish when several heavy rounds slammed into an area of heavy fire. The heavy .50-caliber rounds were able to penetrate the wooden boxes that two of the would-be defenders were hiding behind. They would not be telling any stories today.

On the surface, Batman and his Indians had secured the house and were heading toward the cave entrance. Grant was heading down a path that was marked on the map they had been supplied. Stopping suddenly, he signaled with a raised hand for the group to stop and take cover. He had heard something up ahead and needed to investigate before moving the group forward.

Batman quickly joined him at point to see what was going on. Once there, he and Grant slowly moved forward toward the sound.

Stopping at the base of a small rise, they dropped to their knees and crawled to the top of it, staying in the thick brush to avoid being seen. In a small clearing on the other side, and about twenty yards ahead, they saw a group of men sitting comfortably. Several of their men were on guard duty, but not close enough to see Grant and Batman. The men were wearing Navy camouflage uniforms and carried a variety of high-tech weapons. The kind Navy SEALs would use. *Are these guys on our side or on the other side?*

Batman and Grant slid back down the rise to talk about their next move. Once at the bottom, they rolled over on their backs to stand up but were greeted with the muzzles of two automatic weapons, known as SAWS, short for squad automatic weapons system.

"Damn!" Grant and Batman said in unison, looking at each other, hoping the other would have a plan.

"Lieutenant Commander Batuman, I presume?" the tallest of the two asked.

"Yes. Are you good guys or bad?" Batman asked.

"Depends on whose side you are on. But for this mission, we are the good guys. Lieutenant Grims, US Navy SEALs. We came to help secure the island, but it seems you guys have it mostly in hand," Grims said, extending his hand to help Batman stand and lowering his weapon at the same time.

Batman and Grant laughed lightly. With all this help, this war would be over before it really started.

"Grant, go up and bring the guys down," Batman ordered. "Where did you come from?"

"You remember a few days ago, you had an encounter with a couple of destroyers? Well, they were sent here to help you by Admiral Feldings. We are off the USS *Normandy*, which is sitting just over the horizon, waiting for me to call in. I have twenty of the guys with me, and we are ready to support you in any way you wish, sir," Lieutenant Grims said as he pulled a small radio from his breast pocket.

"Damn, I knew Feldings was straight. Call your ship. Tell them you have linked up with us and that the *Wolverine* is now attempting to enter the cave from offshore. There is a rear entrance below the surface that will put them inside the cave before, hopefully, the bad guys know we are here."

"Just a minute. That one is hard to believe, but this whole thing seems way out in left field. I better call Captain Jones. Standby," Grims said before he turned his attention to his radio. Minutes later, he returned his attention to Batman and his men, who had just arrived in their little encampment.

"What's your plan?" Grims asked, first sending his man to let the rest of his group know they would be coming into camp with friends.

"Well, the cave is about five hundred yards over there," Batman started, pointing toward the cave. "To tell you the truth, I don't know. Any suggestions?"

"Yeah, let me take the lead and your men fall in with mine. We have a bit of training that should make this pretty easy," Grims said.

Ten minutes later, the SEALs and Batman's group were approaching the cave entrance, experiencing no resistance at all. They moved cautiously toward the entrance, disabling several trip wires as they were encountered. Fifty yards from the entrance, a machine gun opened fire on them, taking down the point man. Only one machine gun position was noted, and within two minutes, Grims had his men in position and took out the machine gun without losing another man.

With the machine gun silenced, they moved forward once again. At the entrance, they could hear gunfire deep down within the cave. This could only mean one thing: the *Wolverine* had made it in and had surfaced. Cautiously, Grims and his men led the way, disarming several more booby traps as they progressed. It was slow, but soon they could see and hear the fighting below. Taking position, Grims ordered the group to open fire.

After what seemed like hours but what were really only minutes, the defenders' return fire moved up toward the entrance of the cavern and not at the boat. This didn't last more than a minute when they realized they were in a crossfire and threw out their weapons.

"Hold your fire! Hold your fire! They are giving up!" yelled Carpenter, seeing the group of men heading in from the entrance of the cavern. It looked like Batman, his band of merry men, and a group of Navy SEALs had found the way in and quickly brought down the opposition. "I'm glad that's over, sir!" one of the machine gunners replied, wiping the sweat from his forehead.

"Me too," Carpenter said. Then he yelled down the hatch, "Get a medic up here! We have wounded."

"We woulda had more, sir. I only have about twenty rounds left!" the gunner said to Carpenter.

"Don't let the bad guys know that," Carpenter said quietly.

"Roger that, sir," he said as he started to laugh. But his laugh was cut short with an amazed expression as he pointed toward the other side of the cave and exclaimed, "Holy cow, sir. Look!"

There sat the *Excalibur*, the sister ship to the *Wolverine*. She looked like she had just come out of dry dock.

"Damn!" Carpenter exclaimed as he stood and looked at the other boat. "She's beautiful."

"Must be the sister ship that was also supposed to be MIA," JD commented.

Washington, DC
Office of Admiral Jacobs
May 20, 1996
1330 Hours, EST

"Admiral Jacobs, I'm Special Agent Baxter, and this is my assistant, Special Agent Maxwell. We have a warrant for your arrest. Would you please come with us, sir?" Agent Baxter said as he entered Jacobs's office, bypassing his secretary, who insisted that the admiral was not in his office.

"May I ask the charges, sir?" Jacobs asked without moving from his desk. He reached over and retrieved a Cuban cigar from the hand-carved box on his desk. He proceeded to light it, blowing smoke up toward the agent, who attempted to wave it away from his face.

"You may, sir. I'll start with the most severe. That is, you are charged with treason, piracy, murder, grand theft of government equipment and materials, misappropriation of funds, and using the

US Navy personnel and equipment for personal gains. To name a few of the more important charges, sir. Now, if you would be so kind as to come with us," Agent Baxter insisted. "I must inform you of your rights." He read the admiral his rights from a small card he had pulled from his pocket.

"Okay, let's go." Admiral Jacobs stood, straightened his uniform, and went with the two agents, knowing that if he resisted, they would get rough. Or they might have help out in the outer office. He figured it was over and going with them was not as bad as dying by his own hands.

"I may not be back for a while. Call Admiral Barker and tell him I've been arrested by the FBI," Admiral Jacobs said, stopping at his secretary's desk for a moment.

His secretary called Admiral Barker as instructed, turned off the lights, and left for home. She did not know what was going on, only that she would be answering a lot of questions soon. They would suspect her but had no evidence to connect her with anything the admiral had done.

Once in the hall, Admiral Jacobs was greeted by several other members of the FBI and two other members of his organization who were also under arrest and being escorted out of the building.

Admiral Jacobs was escorted out to a waiting sedan and then transported to the FBI building a few blocks from his Nebraska Avenue office.

Lieutenant Commander Sally Morrison and several members of the Pentagon staff were never seen at the Pentagon again after they left the Pentagon parking lot. They were last seen leaving in three black Fords, destination FBI building, for questioning.

Office of the President of the United States
Oval Office
1445 Hours, Same Day

Vice President Carol Jefferson and the White House Chief of Staff had a meeting with the president at 1500 hours in the Oval Office to discuss the situation in Nigeria. As they approached the office, they heard a single gunshot. Racing to the door of the Oval Office, they found it locked. Within seconds, they forced it open and found the president slumped over his desk in a pool of blood with an Army-issue Colt .45 pistol in his left hand, the president's favorite weapon. He had carried a similar one during his military tour in Vietnam.

A note was in the president's right hand. The vice president picked it up and read:

> Mr. President,
>
> We have evidence to prove that you are involved in a black market ring and have used government personnel and equipment in your pursuit of this illegal venture.
>
> We will give you a chance to turn yourself in without creating a scandal. If you don't, we will be forced to produce the evidence and create a world-class scandal that the American people do not need at this time.
>
> Signed,
> A friend

There was an additional letter written and signed by the president that admitted to his guilt and listed other members of the organization.

"This is Dan Rather at the White House. We have just been informed by the White House press secretary that the president has died from a massive coronary at two forty-five this afternoon. The White House Chief of Staff will be speaking in a moment. I repeat, the president of the United States is dead, today, at two forty-five. Wait. Now, we are going live into the White House press room for comments by the Chief of Staff." The camera faded out and went to the conference room and the face of the Chief of Staff.

"The president was pronounced dead at two forty-five in the afternoon," he read. "His death was caused by a massive stroke and heart failure while he was going over some reports in the Oval Office. My staff will report further findings as we have them. Thank you," he concluded and then left the room.

The vice president and chief of security quickly disposed of all traces of the gunshot wound and information about the organization for the White House. Nothing would be mentioned about his involvement with the black market.

At 1530 hours (3:30 p.m.), in a formal swearing-in by the chief justice, Vice President Carol Jefferson assumed the duties of the president of the United States, on the lawn of the White House. Thus, she became the first female to reach the highest government office in the United States.

EPILOGUE

And Then?

Davin Pierce's Office, Palm Beach
May 21, 1996
1000 Hours, EST

Connie and Davin were waiting for a call from JD Henderson as to the final outcome of the operation. The newspapers had picked up on a story about two World War II Gato-class submarines but missed the story of murder, black market dealings, and piracy on the high seas.

The American public never heard about the dealings of many of the government's top people, including the president. The CIA and FBI worked closely in rounding up the suspects. Many were never seen again. Admiral Jacobs and two senators turned state's evidence in a trade for lesser sentences but still received sixty years in a federal prison. Two other Pentagon staff members were also found guilty and sentenced in different states to fifty years each. Each trial was handled separately in closed sessions and in different states, so the public would not associate the crimes and produce the scandal that would destroy the rest of the government.

Few people knew the whole story. Some of the ones that did were sitting in Davin's office.

"You know it says here that the president was the ringleader and Admiral Jacobs was his right-hand man. The list of members has about a hundred names on it, ranging from admirals to senior enlisted military personnel and numerous FBI agents and various other people. Damn, that ring was large," Davin said as he scanned one of the documents that implicated many of the guilty. This document was among the ones provided to him by the not-so-dead Jack Malone. He wondered where Jack was right now. Maybe on some tropical island, soaking up the sun, with a gorgeous lady at his side. It never failed; every time Davin ran into Jack, he had a great lady with him. He gave up one when he faked his death. Connie and Davin were working closer than ever now.

"Yeah, and what started as a covert operation in the war grew to murder and dealings in the black market. Power was bought and sold at the drop of a hat," Davin commented.

"I guess the taste of power was too much and it got out of control and they just wanted more," Connie noted. "But the president—he was the most powerful man in the government, and yet he wanted more."

"Power has nailed many a man, and woman, as far as that goes," Davin said as he glanced at his watch.

"What do we do now, Davin? The war is over, the bomb located in Nigerian hands. What next, big guy?" Connie questioned, smiling at Davin, hoping they could slip away to some enchanted little island and relax for a while, just the two of them.

"That, my dear, is a good question, and the only answer is to go for the gold. We know where it is. Let's go get it. We have the logbook from the *MaryJean*. We could go find her. You need to read that. It is pretty darn interesting. Bronsly documented everything, his crooked dealings, the meeting with the Germans, all of it," Davin said as the phone rang. "That should be JD and crew."

"What gold?" Connie asked as the phone rang.

"Hi, Jane. I've been trying to reach you…okay, see you in fifteen minutes," Davin said as he hung up. "Jane is on her way over here with some very interesting information about the *MaryJean*."

"What gold were you talking about before Jane called?" Connie asked again.

"The third crate on the *MaryJean* was full of gold, destination Germany. It appears that there were two missions, one to destroy Germany and the other to help the German underground overthrow their own government and use the gold to rebuild. As history has shown us, neither plan succeeded," Davin said.

"When did you find this out?" Connie asked.

"My visit to Germany put me with the only living survivor of the U-49, Josef Von Hofner, the executive officer. He told me about the gold and where it may be. On the condition that we salvage it and he gets half and we get the rest, I agreed."

"So when do we go get it?"

"It's not that simple—"

The phone interrupted Davin. He picked it up, only to hear a voice from the past, one that sounded strong and cheerful, like he once knew.

"Josh, where are you? I checked the hospital when we got into town, and they told me you checked out. Your boat was gone. Where are you?" Davin asked his old friend.

"Davin, you and the little lady need to fly down here. I have plenty of room for the two of you. Hell, bring your beautiful secretary, Stephanie too," Josh Randel said over his cellular phone.

"Where is *there*?" Davin asked again.

"Oh, Rose and I are in Bimini. The diving is great and the fishing is great, and all I need is more of my friends," Josh insisted. "And there are some friends of mine over here that are dying to meet you."

"Who?" Davin questioned.

"The crew of the *Ghostfinder II*," Josh said. "They are the guys who located the *Wolverine*."

"Yeah, I'd like to talk to them. I'll get Bud to prep the plane so we can fly over this afternoon. Meet you at the Red Lion Pub at eight o'clock," Davin agreed, then said goodbye and hung up. Turning back to his desk, he buzzed Stephanie to come into the office.

"Ladies, we are going to Bimini. How soon can you be ready?" Davin asked as Stephanie entered the office.

"Two hours! Great, but we have to pack," Connie insisted. She really had hoped they could just get off together, but what the hell, a trip to Bimini was better as a group anyway.

"Okay. Stephanie, call Bud and ask him to get the plane ready. We leave in two hours. Then you go home and pack. Connie and I will pick you up in an hour and a half," Davin said as he smiled.

"What about the gold?" Connie asked, wanting to know more.

"It's waited over fifty years. A couple more weeks won't hurt," he said, smiling at two of the most beautiful women he knew. The gold would wait. Only Von Hofner knew the exact location, but Davin had made a deal with him and he was going to fulfill his end of the bargain. But not until after they returned from Bimini.

"Hey, what's all the commotion?" Jane said as she entered the office. She was carrying a large box. "Can someone help me with this?"

"Sure," Davin said, jumping up to help. "What the hell is it?"

"The answer to all our research," Jane said as she opened the box, exposing a ship's bell.

"Where did this come from?" Davin asked as he bent down to examine it. "Is this what I think it is?"

"Sure is," Jane replied.

"Where? How?" Connie asked.

"The *where* is simple. A small dive shop in Key Largo had it. They retrieved it from a wreck they discovered diving in the Azores— to be more accurate, in 110 feet of water about six hundred yards off the coast of Ponta Delgada. They have had dive trips to her for years. Says it is a neat wreck. And it is the *MaryJean*. They even have videos and photos, some of which are right here," Jane said and then handed Davin another small box. "I have to return the bell in a few weeks."

"That's great, Jane. We are going to the Bahamas in a couple of hours. Want to join us?" Connie asked. Davin was still examining the bell and the photos.

"Sure, sounds great. I need a break," Jane answered.

Only the beginning…

To Be Continued…

ABOUT THE AUTHOR

David McIntosh spent over twenty-five years with Army Military Intelligence, working in electronic warfare and communications, retiring in 1996 as a master sergeant (E-8). His career dealt with ground and airborne electronic warfare equipment and operation. He was head trainer on several airborne electronic warfare aircraft and ground operation equipment. Some of his more interesting assignments were in locations such as Japan, Hawaii, Panama, and Saudi Arabia (Desert Storm), to name a few. He has been working in the telecommunications and military intelligence collection field for over thirty years. His career spans many areas of information protection, information acquisition, systems security, government security planning and implementation. As a civilian, he taught graduate school classes in network and systems security for Webster University.

He holds an MBA, BS in business, and AS in aerospace technology. He is a pilot, scuba instructor, writer, semiprofessional photographer, and father of four, who have produced eleven grandchildren for him.

Hobbies include writing, flying, traveling, photography, sports cars, sailing, woodworking, and camping.

Presently, he is traveling around the country in his motor home with his wife and German shepherd, enjoying our great country and writing novels.

Other Novels by D.A.McIntosh (Dave)

Retribution, Book 2

T Minus 36, Book 3

Final Report, Book 4

Wounded Eagle, Book 5

Schutzstaffel Rising, Book 6

The Island, Book 7

Target, Book 8

Vengeance, Book 9

Survival, Book 10

And coming in 2021

Sisters, Book 11

www.ingramcontent.com/pod-product-compliance
Lightning Source LLC
Chambersburg PA
CBHW051545250626
47157CB00001B/186